UNITY

UNITY

BOOK 3 IN THE UN SERIES

KAILEY BRIGHT

And who knows whether you have not come to the kingdom for such a time as this? (Esther 4:14, ESV)

Unity

Book 3 in the UN Series

Content warning: Abusive relationship and emotional abuse

ISBN

979-8-9882306-2-5 *Paperback*

979-8-9882306-3-2 *Ebook*

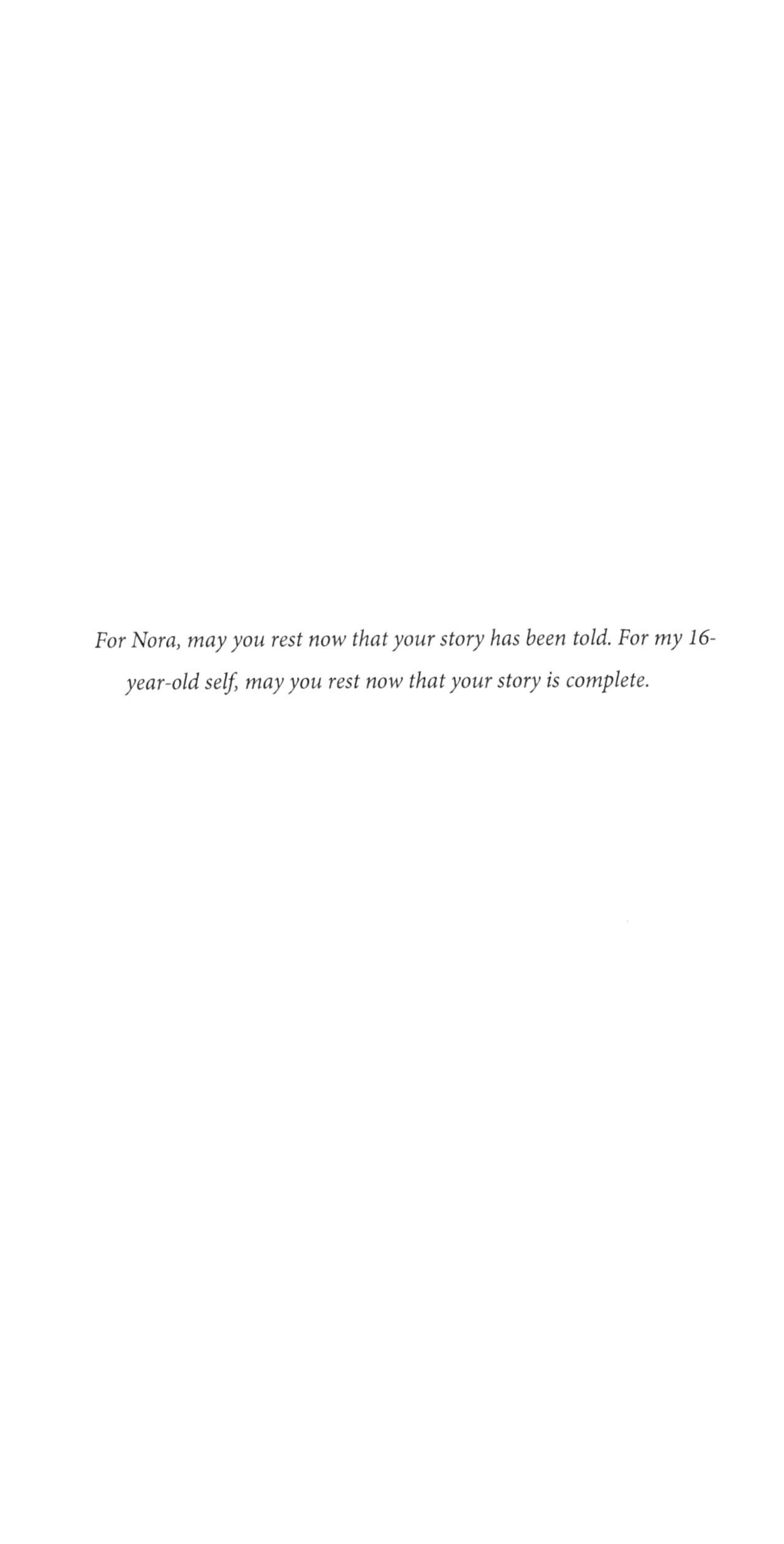

For Nora, may you rest now that your story has been told. For my 16-year-old self, may you rest now that your story is complete.

Contents

Author's Note

Dear Reader,

Here we are. The final book in this trilogy. Go on ahead; I won't keep you. I'm so happy you're here.

From one Unfortunate to another,

Kailey Bright

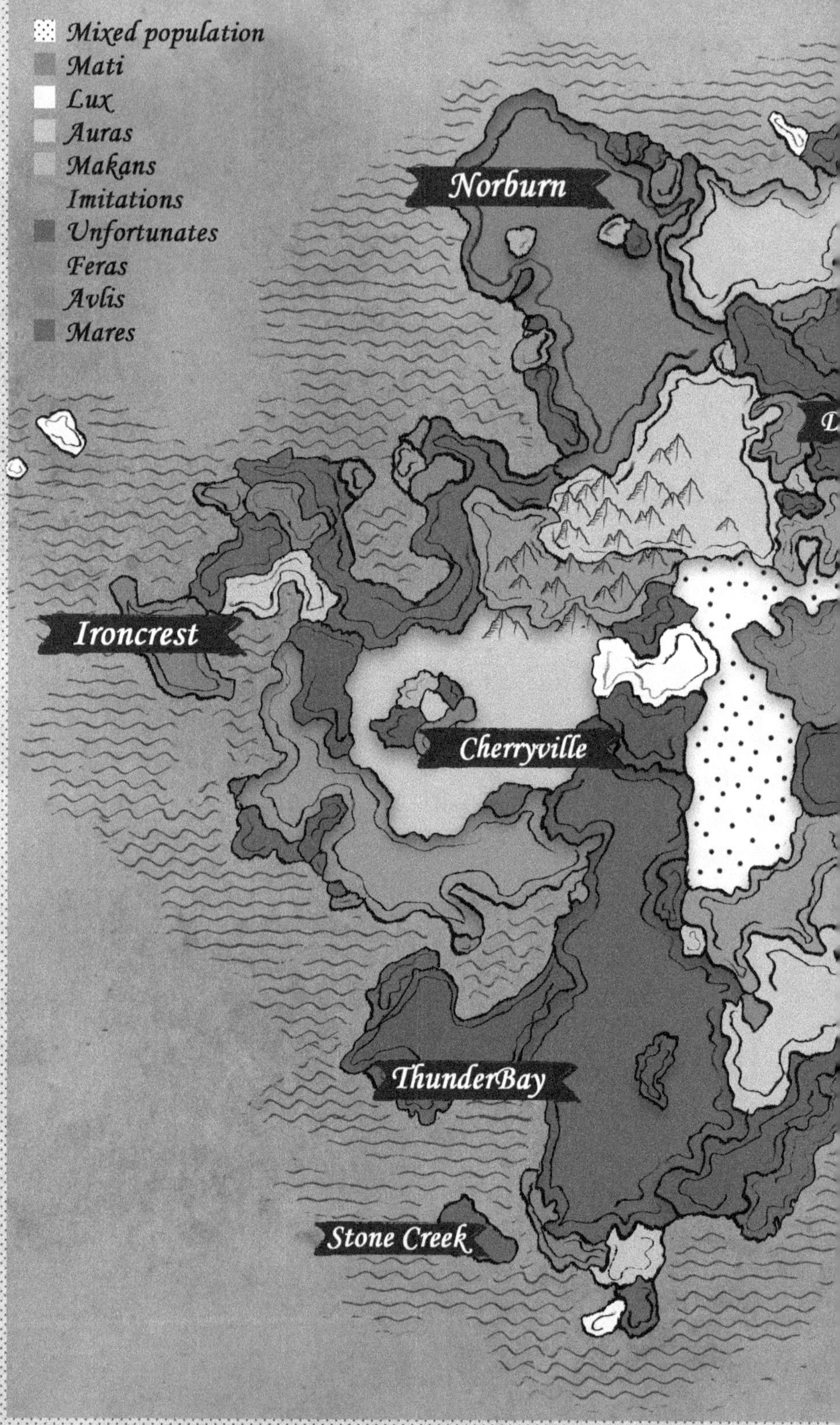

Mixed population
Mati
Lux
Auras
Makans
Imitations
Unfortunates
Feras
Avlis
Mares
Norburn
Ironcrest
Cherryville
ThunderBay
Stone Creek

Caliel
Bellhaven
Osthall
ldor
Northbrook
water

Iridion C
Simulation
lab #2
Simulat
lab #
Training field
#4 with track
Information
Square
Storage
Training
field #1
Training
field #2
Training
field #3
Infir

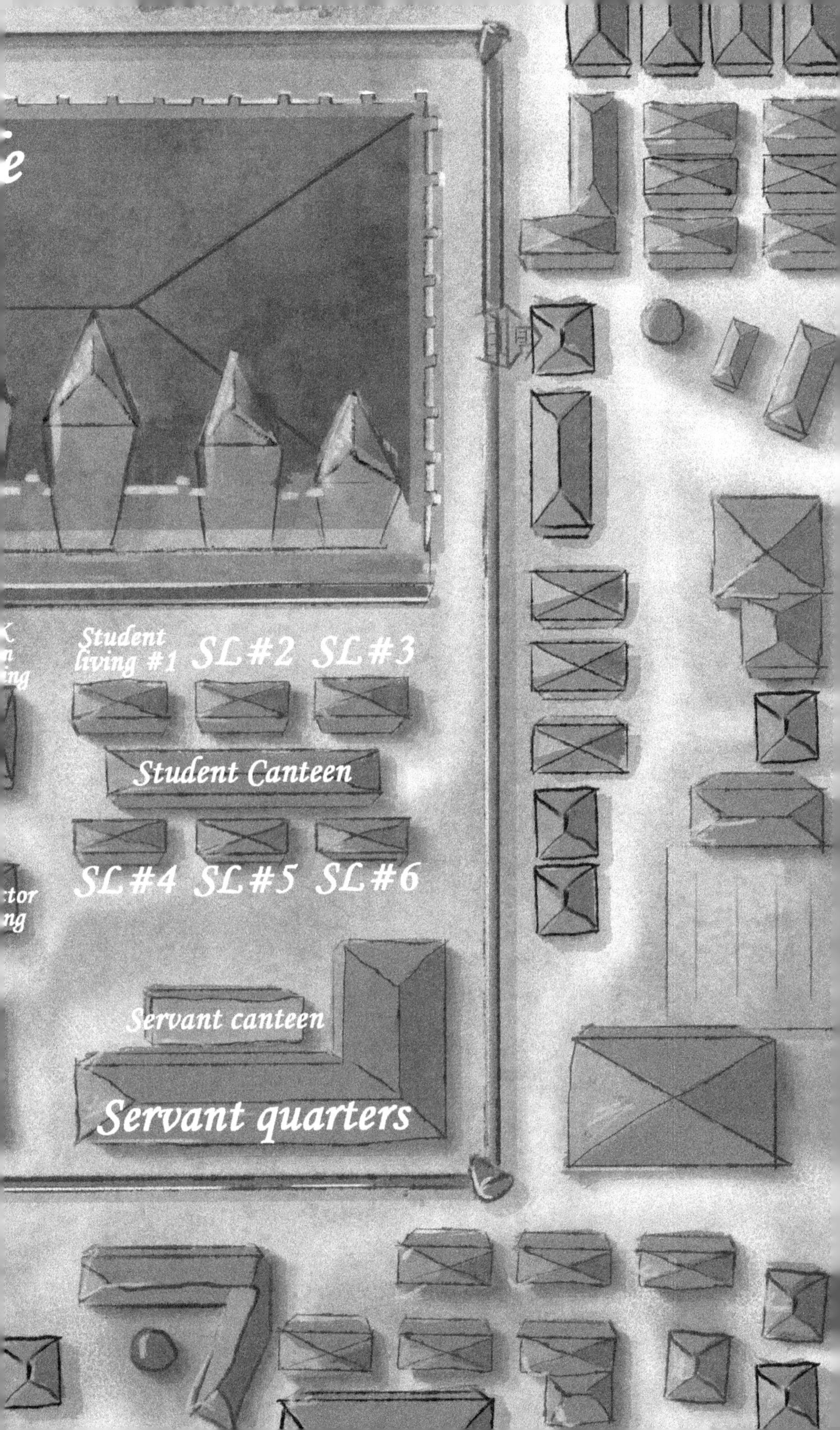

Student living #1
SL #2
SL #3
Student Canteen
SL #4
SL #5
SL #6
Servant canteen
Servant quarters

CHAPTER ONE

Property of Iridion
NORA

Rain splattered against the Iridion Castle. Each drop the same as the last—no different from ten years prior. No different from the Determination two years prior. No different from the day Mr. Harris arrived at the Montgomery House.

Now, rain marked the third day after Cassius seized the throne and anointed himself as both king and messiah.

I stared out the window in an intentional torment.

Paralyzed and sunken, I replayed each misstep that brought me here. Memories came in rolling waves—taking their time to build, fully develop, and collide with my misery. My "what-ifs" became my "should-haves."

I should have seen through Maya. I should have stopped her before she gave the throne to him. I should have held her hand right before her coronation when she was still a Nox. Contradict her belief before Cassius used them for his own gain. I should have never trusted him. Never trained with him. I should have refused Mr. Harris's proposition to enroll as a student, and I should have never made Gifted friends at Galdor Academy. I should have never made my promise to you, Valerie.

That last should-have I couldn't hold onto for long—even as I replayed the discovery of her death. Paled and limp. Blue like the rain. In stark contrast to the light in her step and the cheer in her voice when we made our promise.

"Promise me you'll escape at any chance you get. No matter what happens. Whatever it costs."

I would have honored her in any opportunity. I had. And it cost me everything. What could you give *after* everything?

Droplets sank down the window pane. My eyes followed ones navigating the paths created by past droplets. So determined to push further than their predecessors. I watched as, eventually, each stopped, absorbed into others, and lost their shape. Giving up just as much as I had.

The door swung open but I didn't turn.

Cassius locked me in a room designated for esteemed guests like regional ministers or passerby high-profile Gifteds. If he kept me under the castle where prisoners ought to be, I would at least be spared from the rain. Even though I sat on cushion and not concrete, regret still reminded me of when I was locked there by Minister Gabriel and freed by none other than Cassius himself. That night I didn't regret killing the minister. But I did regret my hesitation and my inability to stop Maya from continuing her ball anyway and falling into his hands. I was so conflicted then. Now, thoughts washed away as quickly as they came, filling and draining my mind in a numbing sensation. Nothing I did mattered.

"You know, brooding is not a good look on you."

Poppy, the Anti-Gifted soldier I fought at the Flower Festival, was by my side before I could fully turn away from the rain. She joined me in my nook and looked out with a relaxed expression. Her nose wrinkled, "Damn, you have a shitty view."

My sigh brought her focus toward me. She shrugged, "I guess it's better in the sunshine."

I blinked from her to the blue coloring of the world. I could see myself clearly in its emptiness. In Norburn. Entering a warehouse. Watching its consequences. I should have never gone behind Mr. Harris's back. Where was he in this overrun city? Did my friends reach him? Did both flee in opposite directions? The questions, eventually, stopped, absorbed into others, and lost their urgency.

Poppy filled the silence. "Look at you, completely distorted by the rain. Man, I wouldn't get anything done if I had a Choosing Ceremony."

If? My face tried to squint, but my muscles remained neutral.

"It's more than that now," I corrected her, voice dry and cracked.

She nodded like she understood and changed the subject. "Good news, the king has called for you."

I decided any "good news" from Poppy was not good

news. "I don't want to see him."

"*Yeah*," she stretched the word out, "you know you don't have a choice."

When I didn't move, she reached for my forearm.

I slapped her hand away with an audible snap. "Don't touch me."

She recoiled, mouth curled in a snarl, but didn't say anything.

I stood, crossing my arms; I only loosened them to my sides once Poppy led the way.

Two Unfortunates dressed in red stiffened and saluted to Poppy as we entered the hallway. She nodded in acknowledgement, and they assumed their positions flanking me. My fingers brushed along the skirt of my dress for a blade that was no longer at my side.

Servants were defenseless. I never waved as much as a butter knife if the action appeared threatening. We stuck to the shadows until the exact moment we were commanded to make our presence known. We communicated in whispers or in silent gestures lest Gifteds thought we were gossiping or conspiring. We kept our heads down, followed the Unfortunate Laws of Servitude, and did as we were told. If a situation did arise, our only defense was our very bodies. We accepted every punishment deemed necessary under the 4th Unfortunate Law of Servitude. And like Valerie coming into contact with Molly's fangs, we also shielded each other from that punishment and accepted it for ourselves.

I didn't have anyone to shield me from the onslaught of Anti-Gifted soldiers. Their glares prickled at my skin. Their hands slowly motioned to their hips, burning my nerves. I intertwined my fingers and rested my hands in front of myself. I tilted my face downward. All my servant training hadn't left me.

We arrived at a familiar door. The plaque on the wall hadn't been removed yet, so it still read that this was the 1st Senior Royal Crest Knight office. Mr. Harris's office.

Poppy knocked in a quick sequence, waited for acknowledgement, and swung the door wide.

Cassius sat behind the desk and stood once I was through the threshold. The two guards remained outside and Poppy along the doorframe.

"Nora is here as requested, Your Majesty." Poppy bowed, her hand still holding the knob. Her relaxed, carefree demeanor vanished in place of her appointed role.

"Thank you, General." He kept his eyes on me but I kept mine down. "That will be all for now."

Poppy bowed again and closed the door behind her, effectively bolting me inside. Mr. Harris's office was an enclosed room, but I could still hear the rain tap, tap, tapping a floor or two above us.

"I was hoping we could spend time in the courtyard today," Cassius noted. "Give you some time outside."

Even without using his power to read my thoughts, he was one of the few people who knew what the rain meant to me. He must have informed Poppy of my situation, hence her own comment.

When I didn't respond, he stepped out from the desk and closer to me. My breath hitched and my body flinched despite my best efforts, and I snapped my head up to look at him the way a frightened creature would look upon its attacker.

He halted, his arm struggling between reaching out and retracting back.

He retreated back. "Would you please join me, Miss

Nora?"

I looked at the desk decorated as a table. A porcelain white tea set and pastel treats laid out a modest spread. Before I could ask him what this was, he answered me.

"I don't wish to treat you as a prisoner." His voice reminded me of the courteous prince I once met. "I hope that in time, your light will return and we shall be enemies no longer."

My light. What he really wanted was his brightest Unfortunate. Neither of us truly knew what that meant; if he did, he hadn't shared. His priorities shifted; it was important for him that my light return. If a light could return at all once diminished.

The last time Cassius and I saw each other was after my friends got away from the siege. Their safety was all that mattered to me, and the uncertainty of their getaway was all that still mattered to me. All moments in my life came easier than those back in the throne room. Ebony Nique shed her disguise and tore me from my friends. Poppy relieved her of watching over me. Maya grabbed my hand as a downcast Unfortunate. Isaac Winters was held in place by Cassius's Animus Gift and taken away. Then Cassius was shaking me, demanding where my "light" was. I remembered the heaviness of my body, and my mind must have been heavy too.

I sat down across from him.

Cassius poured from the kettle himself, filling each cup in front of us. I looked blankly at my tea, keeping my hands rested on my lap.

"Would you like cream or sugar?"

"I prefer it as is."

He squinted, reading through my lie. Reaching for the

creamer lined with gold, he tilted it over the cup on my side. I watched what Valerie called "the galaxy" erupt into life when the milk arose back to the surface and the contrasting colors folded over each other and swirled. You would probably find joy staring into a teacup at all angles if we could sit still long enough, Fern.

Cassius's fist slammed onto the desk, startling both me and the silverware out of our stillness.

"My, you're mesmerized." A smile crossed his face like he found me amusing. His fist remained clenched between us.

I grabbed the small spoon and mixed until my tea was all one color again, now a few shades lighter. I grabbed the cup and drank quickly, hoping the new movement would occupy my thoughts. The tea didn't burn my lips. He must have brewed ahead of time or I really was staring down for that long.

His fist loosened, and he brought his hands to his chin. "I'm going to make a promise to you."

I paused and managed to keep eye contact with him. He knew what promises meant to me, too.

He continued, "I'll never use my Animus Gift for mind control against you. Anything you do, you will do with your own free will. I hope that can be a way for your light to return sooner."

My cup suddenly weighed like stone. I put it down with both hands so it would remain quiet. Cassius passed the plate of macarons like this was a normal conversation.

My words brimmed to the surface, a harsh whisper. "How can you say that when I'm *here* against my will?"

"I don't wish to treat you like a prisoner, Nora."

"But I am!"

Cassius's face twitched in irritation, but his voice

remained steady. "You're free to roam the Grounds and everywhere else with supervision. All except the east wing of the castle."

The east wing? That was where his parents sectioned off Maya's dwelling so she wouldn't be in constant contact with others. Intrigue tried to push through my neutral features.

"What are you doing there?" I asked.

"Nothing that concerns you."

"Then why tell me at all?"

"Because I don't want to treat you like a prisoner. You'll follow the same rules that apply to my soldiers."

I pushed a little further, "Does that mean I get to leave?"

"Not without my permission."

So many strings. I pulled one more. "Would you permit me into the east wing?"

"*Nora.*"

His glare was enough to quiet my voice and fold my hands over my lap. I kept my eyes down as he spoke, sharp and definitive. "You'll receive the same punishment applied to my soldiers, too. The east wing will be used for those individuals. *Stay away.*"

The rain returned in our silence. We fiddled with the tea and sweets for a minute or two.

"May I see Qu—" I stumbled on my words. "May I see Maya?"

"You may."

I hoped he placed her in the infirmary and not the dungeon. She survived becoming an Unfortunate, but the recovery wasn't guaranteed.

"She's in the infirmary," Cassius confirmed my thoughts. He hadn't promised to stop using his Animus Gift for mind reading.

He absolutely loathed his sister. He would have no motivation to keep her alive if it wasn't for me. Or maybe because she did survive downcastment, in some weird way, she was *meant* to stay alive, and Cassius had to endure what was meant to be. He'd find purpose for her somehow as he was hoping to find purpose for me. I would do my best for him to gain neither.

"Thank you," I muttered.

We sat in silence again until old inquisitive habits poured out of my mouth. "You're king now," I started, my eyes focused on the table.

A bright smile lightened Cassius's face. I ignored it.

"What's next then?" I asked, stopping myself short from adding, *Now that you have exactly what you want.*

He caught it anyway. "Unfortunately, I don't have *exactly* what I want."

I glanced up for a heartbeat and caught his gaze before looking away.

"But besides that," he continued with great eagerness. We locked eyes again. "I must conquer the rest of Iridion."

CHAPTER TWO

Those Awaiting Judgment
NORA

———

We'll stop you.

That was what I should have said in response, but any hope of that conviction left me when I was torn from my friends. *We'll stop you. We'll stop you.* The words stirred but never formed on my tongue. *We'll stop…*

I slumped against the wall, staring out the window in isolation again. I hated the despondence in my heart, returning to the scared servant I was before. Fern promised me they'd escape. I had to hold onto that promise, but by Divine, I kept imagining her in the courtyard. A bright streak against the greyed sky. Vines would burst through the glass— our escape would be anything but subtle—and we'd race out of Galdor before Cassius could comprehend what just happened.

The courtyard remained vacant with each passing heartbeat. It was a silly thought. Straight out of the books my younger brother read. Even if we remained separated and I didn't see our promise fulfilled, I could at least find ways to help see our promise through.

The east wing continued to pull at my thoughts. A mystery. A purpose. A destination. He said I'd be treated equal to his soldiers. If causing trouble led to the east wing, then causing trouble was exactly what I needed to do.

Cautiously, I exited my bedroom. No guards stood facing me, and as I peeked out, the hallway remained empty. My body pressed against the wall, my hand brushing along the marble.

He granted me freedom to move around with supervision, but I couldn't get caught *before* causing trouble. A shiver ran down my spine with each precarious sound—footsteps, the hum of electricity, doors swinging open and closed. Anti-Gifted soldiers now roamed these halls instead of Galdor students.

I made my choice becoming Iridion's first Unfortunate soldier. Now we were all soldiers instead of servants. I just wished we were on the same side.

Along my path, I hid in storage closets and behind pillars until the coast was clear. Finally, I reached the descending staircase that led to the dungeon.

Just as Cassius reigned judgment over those at his sister's ball, the residents of Galdor were commanded into the castle for their own judgment. It was difficult hiding the continuous trail of Gifteds entering in double-file rows through the gated entrance, but I didn't think Cassius meant to hide them at all. Deciding who would keep their Gift and who would perish was his ultimate power. He would not let the world soon forget that he held a Divine power. The touch of his fingertips, and a person's Gift fell into his hands.

I'd only seen them as they waited their turn to enter, but I guessed that he couldn't judge that many people at once nor would Cassius risk too many Gifteds together without firmly pledging their allegiance to him. They had to be locked away below the castle and filed out in smaller groups to the throne room. Even if I was wrong, this expedition to the dungeon would just be a waste of time. And I had plenty of time to waste eroding away or wreaking havoc inside these castle walls.

Four AGM guards stood in front of the dungeon's entryway. I retreated into the adjacent hallway before they could spot me peeking. Reaching to my waist, the emptiness there reminded me that I was without my sword. I made a mental note to raid the training room the next chance I had.

I peered out again. Two men and two women. If there were only two soldiers, I could confidently use my body as a weapon. Three and I had a fighting chance. But four was too many to take on alone.

As I mulled over what to do next, a hard grip wrapped around the fabric at the nape of my neck and dragged me forward with them into the open hall. The sudden shadow crept fear down my spine, and I instinctually clawed the air in an attempt to squirm out of capture. The guards shifted into their own fighting stances, bracing for my escape.

Poppy threw me forward before I could successfully lock onto her arm. "You are not allowed to wander the castle without supervision," she noted with stern authority.

I fell onto the floor, my sprawled position tempting me into sleep for an eternity. Caught before I could even begin. How useless. With tremendous effort, I lifted onto my palms and turned to look at the general.

She half-smiled, the lightness in her tone returning. "I'm

glad to see you away from your window." She looked up to her fellow soldiers, "Let her through."

Confusion crossed over our faces, but I recovered first, clamoring to my feet. Cassius's general couldn't be so stupid as to let me free a bunch of Gifteds inside his stronghold, but I couldn't pass up this bizarre invitation. If I walked away right now, any purpose I was clinging onto would fade away.

I imitated a commanding pose, however fragile, raising my nose as I sauntered past the startled guards and down the steps into the dungeon.

To my dismay, Poppy followed, clipping at my heels with a confidence that shattered any illusion of control. I deflated. We were about to enter a den of anxious, terrified Gifteds. If I could convince even one of them to use their power against the general keeping them in captivity, surely it didn't matter that she came with me.

The silence sent goosebumps along my arms as I made my way down, remembering how thunderous everything sounded when I chased after Minister Gabriel. I shouldn't have fed into my anger. I shouldn't have stood by Cassius in those moments, and I especially shouldn't have let him get away. Even though I stayed by my friends' side, I still let them down that night.

Allow me to rectify my mistake. I thought of them somewhere past the wall. Safe and alive.

Landing at the bottom of the stairs, I paused and listened for signs of life. Still, only silence greeted us. Maybe Poppy let me quench my curiosity with full knowledge that no one was here. But there wouldn't be so many soldiers concentrated around an empty prison, would there?

Mustering an ounce of courage, I began walking down the hallway, my feet squeaking on the damp floor. Murmurs drifted behind cell doors. I inhaled a small gasp, halting in my tracks. None of the torches were lit, so it took a few heartbeats for my eyes to adjust and see the shadows as living, breathing silhouettes.

People crammed in their confined space, some so closely packed together I couldn't discern their features. They were so silent before; I couldn't believe how many I was seeing now. They must have been holding their breath, mistaking me for the king who would take their Gift away.

I twirled around, gaping in horror at their appalling confinement. Catching sight of a little girl who couldn't be more than ten years old, I stepped toward the lock on her cell. The other Gifteds stepped back, adding as much distance as they could from me.

"I'm going to get you out of here," I declared, hoping that would alleviate some of their fear.

Poppy breezed a laugh, leaning all the way down so she could see the child eye-to-eye. "Go ahead. Free yourself and seal your consequence."

"No!" A Gifted clawed forward and pulled the child away from the bars. Her declaration rang so violently, I stumbled back. Poppy simply straightened to her full height, smiling into the darkness.

My anger flared, whirling onto the general. "How can you say that?"

"Oh please," Poppy rolled her eyes. "If that little one was an Unfortunate, she'd be in a pretty pink dress right now getting chosen by a Gifted family."

I blanched, though I hoped Poppy couldn't see my reaction in the dark. Pink was a popular color for Choosing Ceremonies, but her retort sounded too similar to my experience. Either Cassius told her more than he ought or she struck a nerve by chance.

I recovered. "That's not the point."

"Isn't it?"

"No."

Poppy turned to look at me and huffed. "Are you satisfied with your little exploration?"

I fell silent at the change of subject. We were surrounded by Gifteds, and she sounded bored like they were nothing more than an exhibit at the zoo. Which did make me wonder why they hadn't escaped yet. If Fern was locked up under the castle, vines and greenery would already be lining the walls. The scent of florals would be the only thing remaining in her wake. I imagined Kai would somehow carve a key out of water if Persephone didn't have a lockpick in her hair. Skylar could have blown the cell door off its hinges or Leo could have melted the metal down. Even Molly could have spent the first few hours patting the wall down for weak points.

The Gifteds slunk back as she twisted around to find any sign of resistance. They held each other for dear life. Like servants. Like Unfortunates.

"Why aren't any of you using your Gift?" I whispered, spinning faster and faster on my heels in search of someone who wasn't terrified.

The Gifted woman answered me with a dejected voice, her hand still held protectively over the child. "We must pledge our loyalty to the new king. To keep our Gifts and survive."

I stopped spinning and stared at her.

Poppy smacked her lips, "Ah, music to my ears. Well done." She peeked into the bars again with a wiry smile. "I'll make sure to remind His Majesty of your declaration. For you and your little one."

The Gifted woman did not respond.

My blood began to boil and sear my skin. "Why do you even have power if you're going to waste it? Didn't your precious Divine give this to you? Isn't that why it's called a Gift in the first place?"

Shouting now, I swallowed hard. We glared at each other, and then she turned away. Gifted eyes lowered all around me, and their entire bodies fell silent once more.

Despair etched along my face. I came down here hoping to do something right by the people of Iridion. To break them out of bondage. To disrupt Cassius's plans. Instead, they were just as defeated as I was, and I had no right to judge them.

Poppy found my arm and tugged. "Come now. You're disturbing our future subjects."

Future subjects. Bile threatened to rise in my throat. I ripped away from her hold with a snap. "I said don't touch me."

Poppy's eyes narrowed. She waved her arms out to either side and spoke loudly for all to hear. "If you do not leave this instant, all here will be downcast because of your stubbornness."

My defiance immediately crumbled. She wasn't the king, but she was his general. I couldn't discern if she had enough sway to fulfill her threat, but I couldn't risk it and find out. Not this way.

When she outstretched her hand again, I complied.

As we marched out of the dungeon, the guards stood ready, but we passed them without incident.

"Just us returning to the surface," Poppy assured, keeping her fingers in a death grip with mine.

I let her lead me back to my room in a frustrated, defeated silence. I couldn't save these Gifteds from falling into Cassius's hand, and now I feared come judgment, all would.

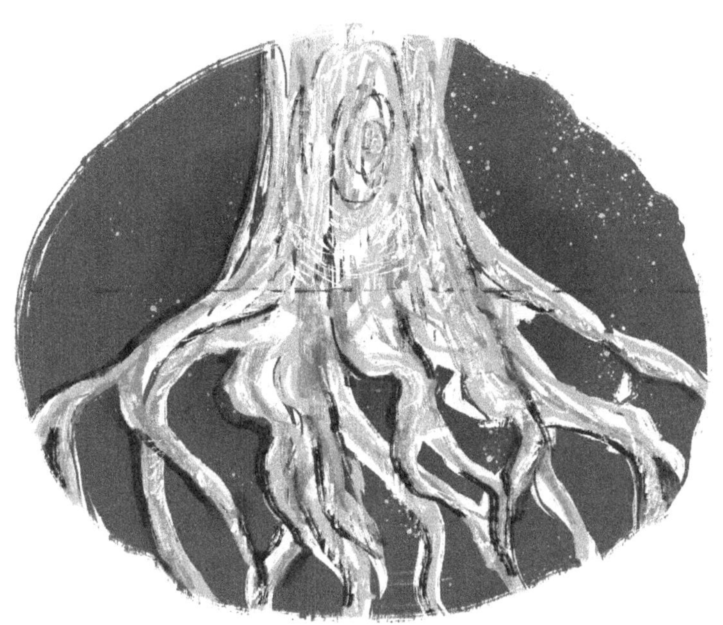

CHAPTER THREE

It Starts Underground

FERN

Steps thudded above us, signaling Anti-Gifted soldiers unaware of our hiding place below the earth.

Everyone kept peering upward, but I stared at the map of Iridion in front of us.

I carved its likeness into the wall, thinking its form and pushing dirt forward with the curl of my fingers. The last thing Nora said to me was a promise: protect each other and protect all I could. Gifteds and Unfortunates. It was a promise she could trust with me, but it was also a promise I couldn't possibly do all on my own.

I tried to decorate the continent with cities. I wanted to denote them with a star shape but my fatigue prevented any more detail than a circle. Galdor stared back at me. An uncomfortable ache absorbed into my chest. Nora was at the center of the world, and I was not there with her. All of my strength, and she was still separated from me.

Before I could convince myself to charge right back into that castle, Kai stopped examining the slice in Persephone's arm and came up to the board. He pointed to the west of Galdor.

"Cherryville is more here."

I stepped back from the map, not remembering when I leaned forward and pressed my forehead against the wall. Nodding a weak "thank you," my left index finger flicked and my right jolted; Cherryville's original circle filled and moved further inland.

Once we were satisfied, we stared at the locations important to us: Stone Creek on the far bottom left below the continent, Norburn to the far top right, Cherryville in between and west of Galdor, Caliel on the far top left, Northbrook on the lower left, and where we were now—a few paces north of the Iridion castle, mere hours after Cassius seized it from his sister.

Skylar stopped clawing her fingers in the dirt to demand, "Why are we wasting our time making maps?"

"We need to reach our loved ones before the AGM do." I pivoted to look at her. "They won't stop here."

"There's no point in going to Norburn," Persephone noted and glanced at her brother, who had successfully taken the baby prince from her arm. "It's just us."

"Or Cherryville," Molly added. "Melanie is safer with her parents than she is with me."

My stare lingered on Molly, but Persephone nudged her in a gesture of support.

I looked back to Skylar who was looking at me with a face that said, *I dare you to ask me right now.* I held firm but chose my words carefully.

"Skylar, is there anyone we should retrieve from Caliel?"

Her mouth tightened like she was about to go off on me, but she decided differently and declared a solid, "No."

It was down to me and Kai. We looked at each other with thin lips like we didn't want to be selfish by naming our own hometown. He had his mom; I had mine and little sister. In our quest to flee Galdor, Stone Creek and Northbrook were in opposite directions. We didn't need to say it.

"Will your mom be home by the time we get there?" I finally asked.

"She's supposed to return from her fishermen post in two days." Kai didn't need to explicitly say *yes* for it to resound in his voice.

My attention deviated away from him as I tried to think out our options.

"Stone Creek isn't attached to the continent, though," Kai added in the silence. "The AGM should focus on the cities to their immediate perimeter. My mom could be safe for some time before she even knows what's happened."

"But she doesn't have military experience like mine does," I replied.

"Which doesn't make her as much as a target as yours, either."

Dread trickled down my shoulders. My mom was a *target.* If the Diviner got his hands on her or Delilah...I shook the thought away as quickly as I could. One worry at a time was enough to fill my mind.

"If Stone Creek is not a top priority, then going there can give us time before the AGM invades," Leo joined in. The *thump, thump, thump* of heavy running from above prickled at our necks.

"I second that," Skylar said through gritted teeth. "*Now can we get out of here?*"

"We will soon," I encouraged.

Kai and I faced each other again. "What are your thoughts?" I asked plainly.

He hesitated but finally straightened, rattling the facts with his arms crossed behind his back. "If we get to Stone Creek, we'll get there right before my mom returns which gives us the best chance to catch her before she goes on another job. I can get Dr. Hansen to come with us, too. We could use a medic besides myself. The AGM might focus on the continental Iridion which gives us time to regroup in Stone Creek."

He waved his hand across the map from his hometown to mine, "We could commandeer a boat and head to Northbrook that way, avoiding the AGM entirely, and then wherever else."

I inhaled. "And if we get my family first?"

"If we get to Northbrook, we can get your mother and sister. The Diviner wouldn't want an Avlis of her background out of his control, and he might even want your sister for her Makan Gift. But I can't see how we'd leave Northbrook once we got there. The AGM have attacked numerous cities on the east side of Iridion in the past, so it's easy to imagine that it's already under his control with what's happened."

Looking down, I tapped my foot lightly against the

ground. The earth shifted as if warning me of my actions, and I stopped. We didn't have time to think every little detail here. Galdor now belonged to Cassius, and we needed to flee as soon as possible.

"Let's go to Stone Creek," I declared.

Kai didn't have to ask whether I was sure. He smiled, a wave of relief washing over his body. Sometimes I pictured he should have glasses (because of his smarts), and in this moment, he would push them back to his face.

"Oh," he blurted, fumbling at his pockets and pulling out a folded piece of paper. "I still have Mr. Harris's address. I think we should try and get out of Galdor with him."

Did we really receive our teacher's address only two weeks prior?

I instinctually bit my lip, thinking about how close Nora was and how we'd soon be further away. *Protect all you can.* Her voice floated through my mind, calling out to me again and again. I couldn't keep our promise and stay underground forever.

Kai's cursive handwriting was so doctor-like I couldn't read it. I looked from the note to the Mare. "How close is he?"

***

The earth parted as I tunneled out like a cautious mole rat; my path jutted out from where my colony resided. There was dirt and then surface tension and then the open air. I peered out, temporarily blind and blinking. Sharp lines of light exposed the night from unseen rooftops, and far-off yelling drowned out the usual bedtime silence.

We were within the commercial ring just outside the castle walls. Two red flags draped over a bank directly in front of me that denoted the Anti-Gifteds Movement. I didn't focus on its detail, receding back into my little tunnel and closing the hole above.

Scurrying back to our central hiding place, I carefully squeezed myself through. Leo's flame dimmed significantly from when he first sparked its existence. There wasn't a moment to lose. Silhouettes faced me expectantly.

"We'll have to leave underground one at a time," I started. If I tore the ground apart at this magnitude, the disturbance alone would be enough to bring the AGM near. "There's a bank right across from us. I can stand there and open the tunnel when its safe. You run toward me and hide behind the pillars."

"I can't believe we're hiding from Unfortunates," commented Skylar.

"What if we get caught?" Leo's voice ricocheted off Skylar's.

"Run toward the side building," I said. "I don't mind occupying their time for everyone else to get away."

Silence threatened to suffocate us.

"Okay," I tried breaking the tension. "I'm going first. Who is taking Prince Henry?"

If you were here, it wouldn't be a question.

"I can," Persephone volunteered.

I paused. That didn't feel right.

"No offense Persy, but I don't think you or Leo should," I said. "We need to move through Galdor with incredible stealth, and that's your forte."

I hesitated to choose another. How would Nora delegate responsibility?

Molly's outline lifted a hand. "I can try."

"Are you sure?" Her voice didn't convince me, but our

other option was Skylar, who probably never interacted with a baby in her entire life.

Molly must have thought the same thing and gave a heavy, "Yeah."

The baby exchanged hands. In doing so, he cried out so sharply I swore he was taking in the last moments of air. Molly held onto him in whichever way she could as he wriggled and writhed like a cat wanting nothing to do with its owner.

He shrieked, and something like radio static pierced my ears. All of their voices—Skylar and Molly's repeated "*Shut up,*" Persy's immediate "*G*ive *him back*", Leo's frustrated "*Come on,*" and Kai's frantic "*I can't think,*"—mixed together with my own thoughts of: *You're being too loud!*

Prince Henry inhaled and then maintained a fit of sniffles. What *was* that? No one moved their mouths, but I heard them like they had.

We tried regaining ourselves, but the Avlis Gift within me charged with each rapid heartbeat. My muscles flinched involuntarily from the fear that we would be found any moment. I combed my fingers through my hair as a way to release my apprehension. If I touched a plant right now, it would sprout ten times its size.

"All right." Now I was the one who didn't sound convincing. "I'm going first. I'll close it behind me and reopen the tunnel when it's safe for *one* person"—I made my index finger known—"to come out and run over to me. We'll do that until everyone is out. Is that understood?"

Their silhouettes nodded.

I traveled through my little tunnel again and peered out into the night once more. Clear.

Pulling myself out, my eyes glanced at every inch of my

surroundings. My knees stayed bent as I planted my feet above ground, trying to minimalize how tall I was in case that brought unnecessary attention. Curving my hands downward, the tunnel entrance closed behind me.

I half-ran, half-walked over to the bank, its presence imposing but dormant. I even spied through the windows to make sure it wasn't some secret Anti-Gifteds base. Only an empty lobby greeted me.

Facing the street again, I waited for anything to tip me off. Beams continued to dance from skylines. I observed their pattern, waiting for the moment one highlighted the misshapen circle of dirt. When none did for a solid two minutes, I knew we were in a good spot. Shouting and the occasional snap of a blow could be heard behind me and to my right. I prayed Kai would take us toward the left.

A clock somewhere close chimed three times, allowing me time to steady myself, taking in three large breaths.

Curling my fingers inward and facing my hands downward, I repelled my connecting index and thumb fingers from each other. The tunnel opened: Skylar jumped out and spread her arms out like she needed to catch a fall. She whirled her head back and forth before half-charging, half-gliding to my side. How her Auran Gift helped her look graceful against her personality, I'd never know.

The tunnel closed. Silence. Opened.

Leo came out next, using both arms to swing himself out. Seeing that the coast was clear, he rolled the rest of his body out and ran toward us. He abruptly stopped and sat down next to Skylar, his back pressed against the wall he almost slammed into.

Closed. Unified stomping caught my attention. We waited, listening to it come close and then away. Opened.

Persephone did a maneuver similar to her brother's, tilting to one side so she wouldn't place any pressure on her wound, and joined us in the new darkness.

Closed. Silence. Opened.

Kai wasted no time propelling himself up and out. He crouched even though he was already short and began running in our direction. The beams above suddenly deviated course and waved closer than they had in the past. Kai halted as light stripped to his left and then to his back.

My fingers clenched, the tunnel closing with a firm shut. He was completely vulnerable. Reading my behavior as usual, Kai didn't try to turn back. Instead, his leg outstretched into a tiptoe as the light continued to sway. Any sudden movement and they were bound to notice.

Each step landed with the utmost precision.

Half-way.

Quarter-way.

Right at the steps.

We were staring at each other with stone-cold faces. If the light beamed on him now, we would all be caught. My muscles tensed with a silent fury in case that reality came to pass.

Kai collapsed at Persephone's side. The light darted in our direction, illuminating the steps of the bank. We pressed into each other and against the wall, scrunched up and wheezing from fright, but the banister shielded us from view. The beam could not shine on us as expected.

After a few shaky breaths, the light moved away and surveyed the ground, now absent of our team. It gave up entirely after a few minutes, returning closer to its usual pattern away from us.

I kept the dirt above the tunnel wound tight until the

silence was unbearable. Opened.

Nothing came out. We all stared, our breathing uneven. I stared harder like I was an Animus and could compel Molly to show herself. It was now or never. Just because their light couldn't reach us didn't mean that we were safe. A troop of soldiers could come by any second as they had been for the past hour. Or a team could have been sent out for suspicious activity.

Prince Henry was revealed to his new world as arms poked out and gingerly placed him above ground. Molly wrestled out of her confinements and landed on her belly, partially exposed. Her fingers found Prince Henry again and looked around, side to side. Once she determined it was safe, the rest of her body followed and she was on her knees. Lifting the baby back to her torso, she sprinted toward us.

All together again. We made it. I closed the tunnel one last time for good measure and collapsed the dirt entirely so no one, not even a turncoat Avlis, could ever know we hid there.

I looked to Kai and Persephone and chose the quietest volume I could, "Lead the way."

CHAPTER FOUR

Escaping Galdor
FERN

We started our journey behind the bank. Avoiding main roads and crisscrossing alleyways, we padded time and distance between ourselves and the Iridion Castle.

I didn't typically sneak around as a child in Northbrook. It was easy to lose myself among the tall trees or follow a little brook until it puddled, but the rumble of life, even humming, always brought me back to center. I think even people who came to Northbrook to purposely separate themselves from the world finally realized they were embracing it more fully than ever.

Leo and Persephone knew how to sneak around. The sister Mati paved the way alongside Kai, who I was surprised could keep up with her stride. The brother Mati resided in the middle alongside Skylar and Molly, running up and giving Persephone silent taps and gestures as a second pair of eyes.

I maintained the back of our formation. Cities methodically placed trees and shrubbery on sidewalks to liven up the dead pavement. If anyone tried to attack us, I was ready to block, cover, or distract at all times.

We reached a midrise apartment complex, its exterior unassuming and worn down. The twins swung up the fire escape two steps—sometimes an entire flight—at a time. Years of practice, I assumed.

Persephone examined Kai's note and compared its information with what floor she was on.

"If we go into the wrong house, we can always check through the lobby after breaking and entering," Leo reminded her with a nonchalant shrug.

Her chuckle matched his. "We'll try this one."

We made it to the fifth floor. Persephone reached into her hair and retrieved a pin. I scanned the ground and skyline. If the AGM tried to run up these stairs, it would be difficult for me to bend the metal and keep the structure's stability. I didn't know much about either, but if it came down to it, I would do my best.

The city stood eerily quiet here. Only a few blocks away, soldiers dressed in crimson shouted orders and pushed people out of their homes. A stream of Gifteds made their way to the castle, its structure more imposing than ever against the night sky. The AGM were corralling the city's citizens, most likely for the Diviner to do what he did best.

Persephone's lockpicking created a metallic clanking sound, amplified by the surrounding silence and noting our location. A wind picked up and drifted the sound to a less suspicious whistle; from the way hair didn't get into Skylar's face, I knew she was the one directing it.

We waited in agonized silence as Persephone took a little

longer, her arm throbbing from its injury.

The latch loosened, and the window opened.

Our attention deviated to the apartment. Its inside was darker than the bank's, and its own silence quieted our breaths.

Leo crawled in first. We watched his form as he took a step forward and glanced about. He inhaled, probably to call out to Mr. Harris, when he gasped instead and rolled out of the way. Something heavy swung through the air, and the rest of us launched forward to help.

Persephone got through first and ignited a flame so bright it burned my eyes. I stumbled in after her and backed away to the left, avoiding the heat. Kai found the light switch and turned it on, forcing Persy to close her fist and distinguish her flame.

The scene halted as followed: Leo propped up against the loveseat and sat on the carpet with his hands up, Persephone stood to the right of the open window in a fighting stance, Kai still held the light switch next to me on the left, Molly and Skylar peered in from outside, and Mr. Harris hovered over Leo with one clenched fist around a baseball bat.

"Oh." All of Mr. Harris's energy left with his voice. His weapon hit the carpet with a muffled thud, and his arms hung from his body with a dead weight. I hadn't considered Mr. Harris an old man until this very moment. Worn and tired.

"Come in." He gestured to the window and then waved at Kai. "Turn that off. We'll use candles to see each other."

We did as we were told, filing in as Mr. Harris left momentarily down the short corridor.

Before plunging back into darkness, I glanced around his place. Necessary features decorated the living room: a couch, a loveseat, a carpet. All neutral in grey tones like he picked the first three that matched. I didn't think he had much of a choice. Silently, I decided that after we succeeded, I'd hire an interior decorator to add color to his space.

But what did "after we succeeded" mean? We failed to stop the Anti-Gifteds Movement from ransacking the capital of Iridion. We failed to stop the Diviner from overtaking the throne. Simply overthrowing *his* overthrowing wouldn't solve anything.

Those closest to seating sat down. Kai and I found ourselves on the carpet. Mr. Harris came back with three candles, and Leo lit each one as our teacher put them down. When they finished, Mr. Harris paused and glanced at our harrowing faces.

"Where is Nora?" he asked.

Our eyes looked to the floor. I found my voice, slow and sincere. "She sacrificed herself so we could escape. Ebony Nique"—a shaking bubbled in my throat, and I rose an octave—"was pretending to be Queen Maya's servant this entire time."

Mr. Harris processed my words. "Is she...?"

"I don't know," I said quickly. I refused to let him even say the word. "Ebony just pulled her away from me, and then she told me to let go, and she was still alive at that point."

Mr. Harris continued to process what I was saying, leaning against the couch's arm for support. "Then Cassius truly has everything he wanted."

When no one responded to that, he added, "Bring me up to speed with everything you know."

We explained what happened earlier that night: how we were assigned during the ball, how Nora and Ebony (disguised as Mercy) were put on the dance floor, how the Diviner revealed himself and his turncoat Gifteds, how

Queen Maya willingly gave up her throne and his Animus Gift against us, how we escaped with Prince Henry, my final moments with Nora, how we planned to head to Stone Creek, and how we got here.

"The AGM should already have control of the trains in and out of Galdor," said Mr. Harris.

"It's still our fastest option. If any trains are leaving the station, we have to take it," Kai insisted.

Mr. Harris huffed, "It's still incredibly dangerous."

"With all due respect sir, everything we do from here on out will be incredibly dangerous."

A thunderous knock commanded our attention. "The king's guard!" A male voice shouted behind our only barrier. "Open up!"

I held myself as the hairs along my arm stood up and the temperature in the air plummeted. The *king's* guard. There was no way in hell I was calling him by that title.

A scream from across the hallway ricocheted through our ears. I stepped forward, but Mr. Harris blocked my path.

Kai moved over to the window. "The AGM are here," he confirmed. "We need to move, *now*."

Another knock, somehow more violent than the last, froze me in place. "The king's guard! *Open now* or we'll force our way through!"

Leo cursed, and Mr. Harris scrambled to the coat closet. The sudden noise and confirmation that someone was indeed home made me jolt.

"*What are you doing?*" Molly hissed as she hid the baby prince from view.

Coats draped over Mr. Harris's arm. Some fell onto the floor in his haste as he rushed to the door. "Put these on over your uniforms and hide at the fire escape."

"What will you do?" I demanded.

He waved his hand fiercely at the jackets in response. We fumbled but obeyed, collecting the coats without thought and hurrying out the window. From the pounding in my ears, I couldn't tell if we were quiet or not. Hopefully, the sound of rumbling feet and slamming doors drowned out our own escape.

Leo and Persy expertly blended into the shadows on the third floor. Skylar took the baby from Molly with a few strained words and ascended so high up, they disappeared into the clouds. I created vines to hold onto the apartment's outer wall and to dangle Kai and Molly a little lower than my own position.

I peeked back into Mr. Harris's apartment as he opened the door. Light streamed in from the hallway, and three Anti-Gifted soldiers casted a long shadow.

The one on the right pushed Mr. Harris aside for them to enter. The center soldier was the only one in an all-red uniform while the other two displayed visible armbands. The center one spoke, "Why didn't you open when we asked?"

Mr. Harris stuttered, "I'm scared. What's going on?"

The center one made a *tsk* sound as the other two began rummaging through the apartment. "All Gifteds are required to report to the palace and be accessed for their allegiance to King Cassius Iridion."

"I am not a Gifted," Mr. Harris said quickly, revealing his brand.

The center one signaled a nod, and the left soldier examined Mr. Harris's hand. "It's real," the left one confirmed.

The leader pondered and nodded again; his comrade walked back toward the TV. The leader continued, suspicion slowing his words, "My apologizes for the mistake. *This* is not where Unfortunates typically live."

"I'm more fortunate than most of my status."

"I see." The leader turned away, and his eyes fixated on the window. I lowered myself out of view, eyes wide.

"You live alone?" The soldier's voice reverberated through the walls, his steps becoming louder.

"I do."

Panic swept through my veins. My Gift reacted—stems began to flower, blossom, and expand. Kai tried to ask what was wrong, but a vine overlapped with his mouth like duct tape. I shifted us right below the window where a small wired box resided. The greenery shifted too and began intertwining with its new home. I encouraged the plants into growth until we were completely hidden from view.

I halted and held my breath as the glass slid open. The wind rustled; the flowers swayed. My head stayed down as I counted out each second in my head.

"You have a lovely garden," noted the AGM soldier.

"You think so?" Weariness cracked Mr. Harris's response. "I, I think it's rather messy. Needs a feminine touch."

"Hm."

I could practically *feel* the soldier linger for a breath longer before retreating back into the apartment. The glass slid back into place with an audible click. I didn't let myself exhale for another three seconds just in case this was a false sense of security.

The leader spoke again, "We will be going. Sorry for the intrusion, Mr...?"

"Pilgrim."

"*Pilgrim*," the AGM soldier repeated. "I suggest you join in the liberation. From one Unfortunate to another."

Mr. Harris didn't respond, or if he did, it was too muffled for me to hear. There was shuffling, a descent, and then more silence.

AGM soldiers continued to shout below our feet, somewhere at the front of the building. It would only be a matter of time before someone checked in the alleyway and looked for stragglers. When the window opened and closed again, Mr. Harris came into view as he exited onto the fire escape.

"Made me a garden, huh?" He was trying to make light of the situation, and I appreciated it.

I scoffed, swinging the three of us off the building and properly to our feet on the stairwell. "You could liven the place up."

Blonde hair and billowing fabric caught my attention. Skylar landed next to us and handed the bundle back to Molly, the prince's entire face swaddled in blanket. Leo and Persephone's shadows shifted.

"We should go before he wakes up," suggested Skylar.

***

We waited, hiding among the trees bordering the station. Dense Anti-Gifted troops lined up and down the tracks and occasionally weaved in and out of empty trains halted there.

Mr. Harris knew the schedule well as both a Galdor resident and as the 1st Senior Royal Crest Knight. On cue, one large light illuminated the scene in stark white, and the familiar blare of a train's arriving horn trembled the ground. We ducked closer into the overgrown foliage, and I was careful not to overgrow it even more in case the movement caught anyone's eye.

Collective shouting tried to match the train as it shrieked to a stop. Anti-Gifted soldiers waved their arms and poured into the compartments. One AGM soldier had a hat, her silhouette distinct among the rest. She headed a siege for the conductor and demanded answers to questions we couldn't hear.

This was a train that cycled through the lower west side of Iridion, stopping into Galdor to deliver food to restaurants and grocery stores. This train also held livestock and this train would take us to Stone Creek on its fourth stop. *Would* was the big word. This could be its last stop for a while.

We watched and we waited.

The soldiers examining the compartments came back out and converged with the ones interrogating the conductor. They shouted, waved their arms, and nodded at each other before separating again.

The distinct silhouette pulled her hat over her face as she entered the driver's cab with the conductor shoved along. The engine whirled.

It's moving! All of our thoughts shouted with a snap of static.

I winced. Mr. Harris whirled his head toward the bundle hiding Prince Henry in Molly's arms, but he kept his mouth shut.

Six pairs of eyes looked in my direction. I nodded, hoping the gesture would communicate, *Let's do this*, and shifted the ground beneath our feet.

We receded further into the darkness, our movement muted over the powering machine.

I turned my wrists over and over again as a warm-up exercise. Then, my hands flew back and my knees bent in a low-bearing pose. The train pushed forward, and I commanded the dirt beneath our feet to do the same.

We glided alongside the tracks, weaving through the still trees. The train accelerated; I tensed and gritted my teeth to follow pace.

Once we were far enough from the Anti-Gifted stronghold, Kai said, "Now!"

I swung both arms up to the moon, extending my legs and lifting the earth underneath our toes. The ground arched like a bridge and flung our bodies on top of the train. I released control, and the makeshift bridge fell back into a heap of loose dirt.

We used all of our Gifts to remain there against the quickening wind. For Kai (who didn't have any nearby water) and Mr. Harris, my vines tied them to rivets leading to a ladder. Leo and Persephone used palms of fire to direct their fall near Skylar, who held Molly close and caught herself easily.

The Aura held her arms out in a blocking position over her chest. She pushed her right hand out and then up, high above her head. As her right hand returned in front of her chest and completed one circular motion, she repeated the action with her left hand.

The air redirected and she and Molly looked like they were in an invisible sphere, barricaded from the outside turbulence. Molly stood upright and stayed close, pressing Prince Henry to her chest. Skylar repeated the hand motion as they walked over to Leo and Persephone, brought them into the barrier, and did the same for Mr. Harris and Kai. Lastly, she drew closer to me, and Kai reached for my hand.

Squeezing into the sphere, the violent whistle of the wind ceased, and I frantically pushed my hair out of my face so I could see properly again. Skylar remained concentrated, the most concentrated I'd seen her since the Determination, spiraling her hands in a fast, methodical rhythm.

We treaded over to the closed hatch at the center of the car. Even though we weren't affected by the wind, the train still rattled from its speed.

Mr. Harris leaned down, opened the hatch, and peered into the darkness. He encouraged us forward.

Climbing in one at a time, we fell into hay, soft and stringy. Skylar floated in last, the wind's whistle returning before she shut the hatch above us.

Our eyes adjusted to the new darkness. If this is how we needed to proceed, then I'd become a maidenhair fern, the kind of plant that thrived in low-lighting.

Someone could finally speak as we caught a collective breath. It was Mr. Harris. "You all should take this time to sleep. Everything we do moving forward will be restless."

CHAPTER FIVE

The Disgraced Monarch
NORA

———

Each time I opened the door again that day, Poppy stood across from me with her arms folded and held an unblinking stare. Ten minutes. Twenty. Thirty. An hour.

I threw the door open again at three hours, my patience worn thin from so much time now slipping through my fingers.

When I didn't slam the door back into her face, she pushed herself into a straightened position. "I can't babysit you like this all the time. I'm a general you know."

"Then get someone else to supervise me, *General.*" I elongated her title in mockery. *General.* The AGM had their own system of rank; I gathered that she was essentially the equivalent of a Senior Royal Crest Knight, though she would never call herself that.

"And have you fight or even kill them? No." Poppy shook her head, "But I like your new fire. It's good to see you this way, even if it's a little inconvenient for me."

I slumped against the doorframe. "Then may we go see Maya?"

Poppy scoffed, "If you ask me, she should be publicly executed."

"I wasn't asking you that." But there was still plenty I wanted to ask the disgraced princess. Even confirmation that she was alive and recovering in the infirmary would mean Cassius wasn't lying earlier.

I stepped into the hallway and glared as I passed.

Poppy halted and then relaxed as I continued walking down the corridor. She followed me in silence.

Outside, the late afternoon sun brightened the Grounds and rested warmly on my skin.

I chose my route in hopes of keeping away from attention, but soldiers seemed to spread themselves out evenly across the space in a mismatch of uniforms and red civilian clothing. Cassius filled the drawers of my new room with red clothes. Mostly jumpers, which was the favored article of clothing among the Ground's expanse. I favored the red dresses.

To my right, Unfortunates sat on the track field where I tried fighting Mr. Harris for a spot on the Diviner taskforce, eating meals and chatting together. The other training fields laid dormant of their usual trampling, too. The storage warehouse was guarded by Unfortunates flashing their weapons, and two other soldiers yelled at each other in front of a pillar at the Information Square. A cascade of IDs fell from one of their hands as they tried shifting through them. I didn't want to know how they obtained all of those obscured Gifted faces, but I *did* want to know what they were learning or trying to learn from their cards.

I drew closer to the infirmary where I'd see Queen Maya. Or Maya now. A heaviness weighed my footsteps. She walked out of her responsibility to her people. All of my encouragement, doubt, and rationalizations fell on deaf ears. She planned the ballroom for a selfish cause, and her coercion with Cassius was the reason why I was separated from the people I cared about most.

Protect all you can. My eyes remained downward at the thought of Fern. I had to let her go because of Maya's stunt.

I sighed again. Even so, a small part of me, a microscopic inkling, could not completely reject Maya from my thoughts. A chasm was left in our wake, but I could still see her in the distance. Sad, desperate, wanting more. Couldn't say I wasn't like that once.

"Hey, sympathizer!" A yell rang out so hostile I flinched.

An aluminum can flew through the air and whizzed past my knee. I turned to the third training field next to the infirmary. An Unfortunate girl in a red uniform stood at the perimeter line, her dinner sitting on the ground next to her. She scooped up small rocks and hurled them at me.

My body didn't react as I wanted to. When I should have dodged, I shielded instead. The stones grazed off my exposed forearm, leaving my flesh red and bruised.

She already strolled toward me by the time I put my hands down to peak out. Making contact with my chest, she pushed me back so hard my heels left an imprint in the grass. I managed to stay standing at least.

The Anti-Gifted soldier crossed her arms. "I can't stand you," she said through a grimace. "Loitering around. Being friends with Gifteds. You're so disgusting. The king should kill you after everything you've put us through."

I remained quiet, staring and blinking. It was all I could

muster.

"Aren't you going to say anything?" she demanded.

No, I wasn't. Looking away from her, I started walking toward the infirmary again. She made a frustrated sound through gritted teeth, but Poppy blocked her with a firm arm.

"That's enough Bree."

Bree stammered, but I didn't turn to face them.

Poppy lowered her voice in a harsh whisper. "She remains unharmed for as long as the king permits. Now get out of here!"

I winced. Cassius was my ultimate protection here, even as his captured prisoner. I reached for my sword for comfort and remembered it still wasn't there.

Bree huffed but obeyed.

Poppy ran back to me. "*You're* popular."

"I don't need your protection," I said quickly, the words not flying out fast enough.

"Uh huh, *sure.*"

We continued walking. Poppy grabbed my shoulder. "You can at least say thank you."

Grabbing her wrist with my opposite hand, I swung her forward. She stumbled from the force, and I continued on my way, my side hurting a little from the over rotation.

A grin formed on her face. "You over rotated!" she teased, spinning for emphasis.

I frowned, and she opened the infirmary door for me with unnecessary enthusiasm. With the exaggerated wave of her hand, I remembered that she used to belong to the Fairaway House. Did she earn any of her flair for the dramatic from Fern? Did Fern like her when she was a servant?

We maneuvered through the infirmary without discussion and found Maya in a hospital bed surrounded by curtains on all sides. Whether this was done to give her privacy or to hide her from the rest of the facility, I wasn't sure. Cassius could have at least given her a private room.

An IV connected to her veins. After the Determination, the princess recovered in her own room, surrounded by the remnants of her court, wishing Cassius had taken her Gift away in the chaos. Now, metal and plastic touched her skin, and everything remained intact. She got what she wanted, and now it was just us. Poppy lingered behind me, her arms folded but more rigid than before as if cold or uncomfortable.

"Nora," Maya mused my name. "I'm so glad you've come to see me."

"Considering you wouldn't let me see Mr. Harris while he recovered, I almost didn't." Bitterness resounded clearly through my voice.

Her smile dropped, and I tried again. "How are you doing?"

"I just need more rest." She ruffled the top of her blanket. "I've been thinking about all the things I can do once I get out. I can sleep in the grass. Brush past someone when I'm not paying attention. Oh, what else? What do Unfortunates do outside of work?"

She glanced from me to Poppy like she was part of this conversation. No one responded in time as Maya gasped, a new idea lighting her face. "I can finally hold my baby brother! Oh my Divine, can you imagine how soft he is?"

She was trying to avoid talking about what happened, but I refused to do the same. "Prince Henry escaped with the rest of my team. You won't get to hug him any time soon."

Maya's stare lingered and then she looked down. "You're still angry with me."

"Do you expect me to be any less? You gave your kingdom

away to a tyrant, and all you can still think about is yourself. I didn't know you to be so selfish."

"What's done is done," she said finally. "There's no going back, and this is what needed to happen."

"But—"

She raised a hand and I halted.

"I'm sorry you're not with Miss Fairaway or Lancer or any of the others, but this kingdom was already spoken for once Cassius became the Diviner. Can you really say you wanted me to remain in power? Could you really see this going any other way?"

Poppy chuffed, and I shot her a warning look.

"Cassius is going to either kill or turn every Gifted into an Unfortunate over this kingdom, you know that right?" I demanded.

Maya picked at her fingers. "I always hoped he would realize he doesn't need to be the deadliest Gifted in this world to gain respect, but that is where he has found it. I can't do anything about it now. I tried so hard, Nora, to be a ruler of peace, but it only left my people suffering. And now all of them, Gifteds and Unfortunates, hate me."

"A ruler of peace," I repeated with vicious annoyance. "You were not ruling under peaceful times, and a peaceful ruler—" I strained to find the words as my temper heated. "A peaceful ruler does not mean you do *nothing*."

A silence enveloped the room, enough time for my temper to simmer down. "And for the record, I *didn't* hate you." My thoughts trailed out of my mouth. "Not until the end, anyway."

A half-smile softened Maya's face as she placed a hand on her cheek. "I can't believe my first touch was a slap to the face. You hit me so hard." A small laugh escaped her lips, the recollection behind her eyes humorous now.

Her laugh surprised me. I found my expression softening too. Maybe one day I could forgive her as she had forgiven me but not until everything was set right. Whatever "set right" actually meant.

"Why did you do it, Maya?" I half-whispered, my shoulders drooping. My hand traced the edge of her cot in order to keep my attention away from her. In the days since her abdication, I replayed what she said in the throne room. Trying to piece together how she could ever believe that handing Cassius the throne would bring anything but destruction.

Maya sighed, reaching for my hand. I withdrew, and we both held our breath.

"Cas reached into my mind."

I looked at her, startled by the new information, and she held my gaze with despondence. "Every chance he had, he told me that I was a failure and how he could do better. He could see how frightened I was, and he was right. Promised to take my Gift and to not harm my subjects so long as I gave him the throne."

"And you believed him."

"I believed him." Maya deflated. "But this really is better. If I stayed queen, he would have just destroyed more and more of Iridion until he got what he wanted anyway."

"Wise decision," Poppy agreed, clicking her tongue in amusement.

I bristled but kept my focus on Maya. "There was still a chance, if you were willing to be a little braver."

"It's too late for that," Maya mused. She paused and then added, "But maybe you will be a little braver in my place."

I recoiled as if physically stricken by her comment. I was

in no condition to be brave. I didn't have the heart to share how I couldn't convince Gifteds to free themselves from under the castle.

Another thought came to mind. "What was your old room like? In the east wing?"

Maya blinked as if caught off guard by my question, but before she could answer, Poppy was pulling at my sleeve.

"Okay that's enough, visit over."

"Just let me—"

Poppy yanked harder, raising her eyebrow to remind me of what she declared earlier. She could use Gifted lives against me, and I hated her for it. I followed her pull instead of fighting her off.

I glanced from the Anti-Gifted general to the Nox-turned-Unfortunate. "Would it be okay if I came back while you're still here?"

Maya nodded, earnest. "Yes, I'd like that."

CHAPTER SIX

Thunder Bay

FERN

———

Awakening, slices of morning light shone through the ceiling and illuminated the train car.

Leo and Persephone huddled in the center of our space like a hearth of fire, their natural warmth the reason why we could sleep so well. Purple blankets bundled Prince Henry between the siblings, Skylar laid on Leo's side to the left, and Molly laid on Persy's side to the right. Kai faced the wall on the third side furthest from me, his head closest to Persephone because Leo would undoubtfully kick him in his sleep.

I couldn't help but smile. Their closeness was unheard of when we first met each other at Galdor Academy. Skylar would claim one corner, Molly would claim another, and the rest of us would have to deal with their unnecessary comments. Maybe if Cal was still with us, he'd be pleasantly surprised to see Skylar now, vulnerable with eyes closed and swaying closer to the center.

Mr. Harris let us sleep longer than he should have. He occupied the corner at a respectful distance. We looked at each other, heads heavy but awake.

"Morning, Mr. Pilgrim," I teased.

He scoffed, "How are you holding up?"

"As well as I can be."

As I yawned with exaggeration, he stared at me. It was the same look he gave when he used his Animus Gift, unknown to us at first. He was an Unfortunate now though, so nothing came of it.

"Is that not enough information?" I asked.

"My apologies." He looked at the straw below us. "I just want to know what happened that night. You've told me, but I'm just so used to replaying it from others' memories. Gives me a full, clear picture."

The train's horn blared. Everyone else stirred awake, some more at the ready than others. Skylar didn't linger in her position, sitting up and opening the hatch. More sunlight beamed into the car; Leo grunted at the sharp change and buried his face in straw.

"Where are we?" Skylar asked, more to herself, as she levitated up to poke her head out.

I could already smell the sea air.

"We're in Thunder Bay," answered Mr. Harris, but he didn't shout for her to hear him over the wind.

"Thunder Bay?" I stood up as far as I could hunch, stepping over to the hatch alongside Skylar while stuffing my hair into my shirt. "Like Nora's hometown?"

My voice disappeared into the open air. White puffy clouds hovered over the coastal village, and the sun glistened over the calm water. We were still a ways away, but I could make out a plethora of short buildings with metal roofs reflective and sparkling as we moved. This is where Nora was from, and we were going without her.

Out in the distance, the massive floating city sailed closer to the docks. *Stone Creek.* Kai's hometown. Begrudgingly, that was what we needed to focus on.

We lowered our heads back down into the train car. "It's not docked yet," I noted.

"That gives us time to get there," Kai perked up hopefully.

We waited until we were closer to jump off the train. Skylar used her Gift to keep us upright, and I commanded branches to bend and help us swing off.

Mr. Harris fell into familiar habits as we moved toward Thunder Bay. "This is an Unfortunate town. Keep to yourself, and do *not* use your Gift under any circumstance." He pointed at Prince Henry in his arms, "And that includes you, Your Highness."

We all exchanged confused looks.

"I don't think the baby understands you yet," Leo said.

"I thought you would be more observant," Mr. Harris retorted, more worried than mean. "You heard each other's thoughts in Galdor. That's because of him."

"*And I thought,*" Skylar clearly took his words as offensive, "Animus could just read thoughts and move things with their mind."

"There's so much you can do with a Gift of the mind," Mr. Harris replied grimly. "You've seen glimpses with the Diviner, so you know that not all powers form at the same time or at all. Like Mares. Kai can't create ice the same way Isaac Winters can."

I caught up with him at the lead. "Wait, wait," I pulled him to stop. "What are you dancing around? We need to know everything before something goes wrong."

We were just outside the city limits, the ugly backs of buildings facing us.

Mr. Harris kept his attention on the prince, who successfully held our teacher's finger with his entire baby fist. "There's no guarantees with an Animus's limits. That's why we're crowned kings. It could be because he's a baby and has little to no control over his power. Regardless, I recognize my Gift anywhere. We heard each other because Prince Henry connected our thoughts together. If he connects us with outsiders, that can spell trouble, so stay focused, keep to yourself, and we can get through this."

Meaning don't think about Nora, I thought. But what was supposed to be my inside thought caused everyone to look in my direction as though I said something out loud.

"Case in point, Fern. Don't think about Cassius or about the Anti-Gifteds Movement or where we're going either. As much as possible."

We nodded, but I still hesitated as we entered Thunder Bay. How was I supposed to ignore thinking about her here of all places? Oh my Divine, I was already failing. Could Prince Henry hear me now? *Let's not worry about it. Flowers.* I concentrated on dandelions springing through the pavement.

Red already adorned the government buildings, and Unfortunates in fresh red uniforms patrolled the same way city guards did. We fanned out, traveling in a disjointed group separated between other passers and at different paces. The twins were bold enough to walk on the opposing sidewalk.

Weaving through the bazaar, I focused on the purple cloth in Mr. Harris's arms until he condensed forward and swept himself in the crowd. Crap. I glanced around, pulling my hair over my shoulders so it framed my face and would hopefully hide my gaze. There wasn't much use. I looked too much like an Avlis—too tall, too pale, and too brightly featured. A beacon rather than another grain of sand.

Don't panic, I thought hastily. My movements staggered and brought me to the bazaar outskirts. I stopped, searching around for a familiar face.

"Are you lost?" Smaller hands touched mine, and I froze.

Looking down, I connected with a young boy with brown curls that hung loosely over his forehead. He came up to my stomach, his age leaning toward the early teens. Brave enough to talk to a stranger at least.

A U branded the back of his hand, but he wasn't wearing a red uniform or armband, and his small frame and patient stare reminded me of Kai. I made sure to stuff my free hand in my pocket and look in his eyes without leering at him.

"Yes." The weariness in my voice seemed natural in this situation. "Can you point me to the docks?"

"Sure." He turned and tugged me forward. "This way, ma'am. I'm on my way myself."

"Oh that's not—" I started, but we were already striding down the street. At least if we drew attention, his pull emulated that of an eager, younger brother.

I'd lose him when we got to the docks. I'd meet back up with Mr. Harris and the others at the docks. I repeated the word *docks* in my mind, unsure of the prince's whereabouts.

The breeze strengthened closer to the water, lifting the salt and sand to our limbs. I hardly visited the ocean on the east coast of Iridion, so I lingered on the view.

The boy, likely accustomed to the sea, continued to lead me down the boardwalk. Steady boats and eager fishermen with branded U's worked here. Stone Creek floated closer. Glancing around the crowd for my friends, I didn't bother to take in where we stopped.

I turned to say a quick "thank you," ready to sprint off, when the words clogged in my throat.

"Who's your friend, Neo?" A muscular older man stepped out onto the dock from his boat, twisting his wrist absentmindedly. Another man, the second evolution between the young boy who helped me and the older man talking to me now, had his hands busy securing the boat to the dock but glanced my way.

This was too much attention.

"She was lost in the bazaar," Neo shrugged like this was something he did often. He hugged who I gathered was his father.

There was a pause, and I knew I needed to speak. Here was my chance. "Thank you for your help." I waved my hand with a pleasant smile, turning.

"Hold up." The second man, the one I gathered as the older brother, had a dark voice that made a person stop in their tracks. I did, my smile straining to remain pleasant.

He stepped onto the wood planks, revealing himself taller than the other two and meeting my eyes. He wore work clothes, but a distinct red armband wrapped around his ankle. His glare sliced through me, and my heart quickened in dread.

"What is your business here?" he asked.

My smile was gone now, replaced by a muted surprise. Hopefully it read as startled. Could I tell them Stone Creek? Would that be too suspicious? What would an Unfortunate need to do in Stone Creek? If it was a Sunday, I could pass as an Unfortunate on her day off, but I didn't actually know the day. Time ticked past. I needed to say something, now!

"Noah," the father scowled, "that's rude to ask of a lady. Go on, girl."

The older man waved me off, but Noah persisted. "Look at her pa! She's an Avlis and should be in a holding cell."

I flinched back at his words. Were they putting Gifteds in holding cells? Held for what? The Diviner? I almost cursed out loud at myself. *Drain him from your mind like water out of your ear*, I thought. But what else was there to focus on? The docks didn't present any flowers for me.

The father grumbled, looking at me with a deeper look. I needed to find an excuse and one so ridiculous that they couldn't deny it.

"That's ridiculous," I half-laughed as a start, playing with my hair for comfort. "I know I look weird. My House...they *are* an Avlis family, and they want us to look just like them. Some sick fantasy."

I held myself now, feigning embarrassment and shame.

"See." The father nudged Noah as if to say, *I told you so*. "Now you've gone and insulted the poor girl."

Past him and further down the boardwalk, I noticed Mr. Harris's peppered hair, purple cloth, Kai's examining figure.

"Be on your way now," the father addressed me. "He doesn't have his sister to belittle."

Nora's image flashed in my mind, sharp and cunning. Slamming the door shut in my face. Noah and I winced, but I tried passing mine off as an itch along my temple.

Noah growled, probably more irritated by the sudden remembrance and the lingering static. "Stop calling her that!" He shouted at his father before going quieter, bitter. "Nora is no longer my sister."

"Nora?" I found myself spilling out in confusion before it

dawned on me. Was this...did I just... Prince Henry was nearby, and I—oh Divine—I stumbled into Nora's blood relatives.

They looked at me, each one displaying either hostility, curiosity, or surprise.

"Do you know her?" her father asked.

"No!" My voice raised an octave. I tried lowering it back down. I was rambling now. "I mean, who hasn't heard of the first Unfortunate soldier? I just can't believe the odds. Okay, I gotta go! Thank you so much for your help."

"Not so fast!" Noah gripped my arm.

Twisting around, I halted and focused on *not* reaching for my Gift. To shrink back and remain still.

"What's the problem?" I managed.

He flipped my arm over with a stone-cold expression. "Your brand isn't here. Show me your other hand."

I pulled gently to no avail. "What?" I asked meekly.

When I didn't retract my wrist from my pocket, he pulled me into him with incredible force and wrapped around my other arm.

"Noah!" his father scowled.

We struggled against each other. He wanted a scene? I'd give him a scene. "*Robber!*" I screamed at the top of my lungs. "Help! I'm being robbed!"

Noah pushed himself away immediately, the bombardment of eyes enough to make him retreat a few more paces. I gave him the nastiest face I could muster before saying, "If I was your sister, I'd leave too. Family is supposed to be loving."

His father grabbed the back of his shirt before he could retaliate. His younger brother giggled but tried to muffle it with his hands. I stormed back into the crowd and made my way further down the dockside, leaning down without being too suspicious in order to make myself smaller.

Finding Kai, I covered him in a half-hug.

"Where were you?" Molly whispered in a raspy, almost snake-like tone.

"Absolutely nowhere," I lied, and it sounded like a lie.

"Are we in danger?" asked Leo.

I shook my head a little too violently, but I couldn't be sure.

We waited for Stone Creek to draw nearer. Those at the bazaar shifted over to the boardwalk, their eyes toward the large floating city coming our way. I scanned for Noah and his family, but I couldn't see them anymore. Either they were successfully obscured from view or they left the docks to flag the authorities. I held firm to the former.

Finally, the city stopped, so massive it expanded the entire width of the shoreline. Its concrete buildings, elevated out of the water, casted a shadow on us standing at the docks. A tropical ecosystem of palmed leaves and wiry bushes invited me. Facing us, the shrubbery lessened into a sandy entrance where merchants with branded U's and Mares, adorned in deep blues and embroidered sea life, hauled their cargo off Stone Creek and onto the docks of Thunder Bay.

I wondered how Kai would look with dolphins swimming along his sleeves, his back telling an epic tale about a special pink dolphin who saved his family from a ruthless hammerhead shark. Mares were known for their folklore, spinning tales just as fast as they could spin thread. I found them fascinating for this, wondering what story they'd tell for an Avlis girl. I was sure Nora would have found them fascinating, too, doing Unfortunate work while maintaining their pride.

I turned to nudge Kai, to point at some Mares and guess what their clothes were saying, but he kept a rigid stance, his eyes searching the port.

Anti-Gifted guards pushed the crowd back to make way for the Stone Creek merchants. They didn't arrest or assault or even confront the Mares as I expected. The Gifteds walked by freely, without hesitation and without disdain on their faces.

"What's going on?" I leaned closer to Kai so he could hear me.

Kai waved his arms like he'd catch an explanation in the air. "They're all tradesmen. Could not be worth the effort."

"*Or*," Skylar tilted herself into the conversation, "they've already pledged themselves to the Diviner."

She would know firsthand. Her father was first in line to do just that.

"An Unfortunate told me that there are Gifteds in a holding cell," I said. "Could be those who haven't pledged their allegiance to the Diviner."

The new information settled into all their ears.

"When were you talking to an Unfortunate?" pried Skylar.

Kai let out a frustrated, smacking sound with his mouth. "We don't have time to speculate right now," he strained. "We need to get onto Stone Creek without being suspicious."

A pause. "Let's steal some crates," said Persephone. "Pretend to be merchants ourselves."

We could walk right through! Everyone looked at each other, waiting for anyone to object. No one did.

We shuffled our way over to the central part of the dockside where planks connected the Stone Creek entrance to Thunder Bay. Guards watched but absently.

Boxes were marked, carried, lifted, put down, and

clustered.

We found the abandoned boxes, the ones unattended as a merchant walked across the bridge to collect more. We separated again so we wouldn't be taking from the same place.

I chose a large crate before I even got to it, fixating my eyes with purpose. Wooden, ordinary; I would make up stories if I got caught. I didn't want to sell this box anymore. My mom told me to put it back. Didn't *you* get the recall notice? Maybe I'd make up something so wild, a Mare would spend three days making it into a dress. If I got caught by an Unfortunate though, there was little I could do to hide my unbranded hands while carrying something this heavy.

Lifting with my legs, I concentrated so I wouldn't accidentally use any vegetation or earth for guidance. The crate was heavy, as expected, but not terrible.

I saw him when I gained my bearings. Noah was talking to an AGM soldier.

I used the crate's size to hide my face as best I could as I walked down the dock, up the plank, and into Stone Creek.

The sand warmed my feet. I looked around, trying to find an inconspicuous place to put the crate down in case anyone was watching and knew I was doing something wrong. If we were caught, it was game over.

Where was the logo on this thing?

Turning the box on its side, I cursed in my mind and hoped Prince Henry didn't hear. A deep red circle and the outline letters, AGM, stared back at me. Fighting the urge to just throw the box and run, I forced my reflexes to remain rigidly calm. My heart betrayed me, but only the nearby palm trees swayed with the knowledge.

Quickly, I glanced around and found a large collection of

other boxes with the same dark red stain. I walked over, my pace more confident than anything else in my body, and I bent down slowly to add it to the top of one of the piles.

The hairs along my neck prickled at the possible glances now that my face was exposed.

A woman in a red uniform looked at me—I know she did—but I refused to acknowledge her and walked away with my back turned like this was normal and not at all a threatening situation. *Remain casual.*

Someone found my hand. My heart sank; the Gift in me swirled. I snapped back, my hand ready to spring the nearby shrubbery into action if Noah had found me again.

Molly inclined her body so it pressed closer into me.

"What are you—?" I started.

"Keep walking."

I did, realizing now that she was pointing her branded hand out as if to signal to someone—the AGM soldier—that I was someone to be trusted around Unfortunates. I silently wished that a different Unfortunate had this task, to feel her skin against mine, but I appreciated Molly for her boldness, her quick thinking. She never would have so willingly flared her new status before Nora helped her.

"Thank you," I whispered back as we walked further up the Stone Creek beach.

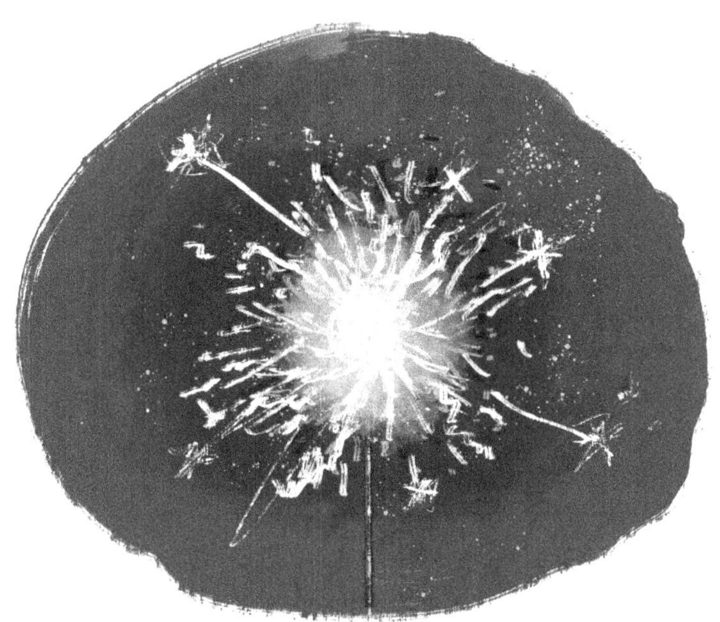

CHAPTER SEVEN

A Spark of Light
NORA

Poppy escorted me to Cassius's office with three guards this time, so I was surrounded on all sides. Soldiers passed by with quick acknowledgments to their general and greeted me with upturned snarls. Didn't they know they were acting just like Gifteds? The people they claimed to despise? They had to know how frightening it was to have so much attention, but maybe they didn't care as much when it was them in control instead of their House masters.

At least I had some closure with Maya. Not the closure that would fill the chasm between us, no. I knew she was alright. I didn't know if my friends were alright. *Fern promised me*, I reminded myself. That had to count for something.

A manic laugh announced Ebony Nique before she turned the corner with a sheepish Unfortunate girl in a red uniform. Her sight fixated on me, and a wide grin darkened her face.

"We meet again." Ebony spread her arms out like I was a grand prize. "Where's your fire, little one?"

I ignored her clear desire for conflict. She mirrored my appearance and mimicked a despondent expression as we walked down the hall.

"Leave her alone, Ebony," Poppy lightly advised.

"General!" The Mute cheered in her direction but continued to match my gait. "I have great news to share with His Majesty."

"You came all the way from Caliel, right?"

Ebony stared at me, "The very same place Ms. Douglas headed an attack."

I side-glanced back at the mention of Sylvia Douglas. She was the first Anti-Gifted Unfortunate I met in Thunder Bay when the movement was small and unorganized. She called me a Gifted sympathizer while in interrogation with Mr. Harris, and she came to my dorm room hoping to finally recruit me in her escape from the Grounds. Then Cassius killed her—placed her right on the flagpole that now waved an AGM symbol. Ebony's sly smile baited me.

"Did you see Mr. Stanton there?" I asked, hoping to gain control of the conversation.

"Oh that pure Aura?" Ebony tasted the air. "We let him keep his servants and stationed soldiers around his estate. He *so* misses his daughter, though. It's a shame we couldn't give her to him. The Divine already claimed his wife, you know."

At the mention of Skylar, the Mute transformed into her likeness. My heart sank as she flipped her blonde hair back, those black eyes reminiscent of a shark training on its prey. Her last comment though was what made my eyes go wide. The last time we saw Mrs. Stanton, she was struggling to recover from downcastment. Ebony used the word "Divine" instead of "Diviner", which meant Skylar's mother was dead.

One of the guards stiffened a laugh as Ebony pranced around with her right hand poised and her left hand on her swaying hips.

"You tried killing Skylar at the Determination." My voice cut through the mockery. "I can't imagine you'd do anything different if she was in your grasp now."

Skylar's frown lines deepened, and she rolled her eyes. "I guess you're right."

Ebony morphed again, growing taller with thicker thighs, an olive skin tone, and red strands. Emerald eyes—Fern's eyes—gleamed in the light with a pleading look.

I halted, my nerves on fire. Ebony smirked, an unnatural expression on Fern's face. "What was the last thing you said to me?" Her voice cooed without the heart behind it. She leaned down like I was a child. "Don't be shy now. Tell me."

My throat tightened, my anger boiling. *Stop it.*

"When I held you on the ledge, what did you say?"

Stop it. Stop it. Stop it.

"Don't tell me you've forgotten already." She grabbed my forearms, replicating our final moment together and I still didn't know if you were alive.

"Stop it!" I screamed, breaking her hold on me.

Ebony's disguise faltered; her wiry black hairs coiled with

red strands and her skin mix-matched. She fully transformed back into herself, her shoulders hunched and teeth clamped shut.

At this point, everyone in the hall paused to a standstill, their heads turned in our direction.

The Mute broke open her mouth to laugh. "There you are!"

"Transform again, and I'll kill you."

She snickered, "You think you can kill me?"

Poppy turned on her heels, her arms out to both sides. "That's enough."

But as Poppy came within a close distance, Ebony grabbed my fingers and twisted hard. Pain flared; I winced back, holding my fist steady with the other hand.

Ebony pushed closer into my face. "I kill Gifteds for a living. Do you really think I'm afraid of *you?*" Her threatening behavior reminded me of Molly when she was still an Imitation. I could do this. I could keep my head up. I wouldn't look away or back down.

I repeated with resolve, "Transform into her again, and I'll kill you."

She laughed, deep in her throat. Her eyes flashed a green hue, and that was enough.

My fist made contact with her cheek, and I clocked her so hard her upper body swayed to my left.

She remained frozen for several heartbeats. Poppy straightened, and the other Unfortunate soldiers stood guard too.

"Ebony," Poppy warned with a much more serious tone than before, "leave her alone. Do not engage."

The Mute tilted her head and lunged at me. Her hand found my neck, pinning me to the wall. She squeezed; my breathing strained. My arms reached out, and my index finger found her eyes. Her face scrunched, and her hold loosened. I threw myself forward, pressing my thumbs deeper into her pupils.

Her elbow connected with my wrists as she screeched, and I faltered. We thrashed and tumbled.

Poppy shouted, but neither of us yielded.

Ebony morphed where she could: cutting down her hair when I pulled, elongating her nails as we clawed at each other, growing smaller when I had the upper-hand and growing larger when she did.

She now had the upper hand. My arms shook more violently than before, my legs kicking with less momentum.

Ebony huffed, unexpectedly standing. Still towering over me, she forced me upright by the collar of my shirt. We met face to face. Her sly grin returned as she freed one hand to twist a doorknob behind me. The door swung open, and I was thrown in.

Falling on my back, I laid there panting, most of my body too sore to do anything else but shake.

Cassius's voice thundered above me. "*What is the meaning of this?*"

Craning my neck, I turned in time to see him step between us. Static rose in the air, and Ebony sank against the wall opposite of me, her hands over her ears and her muffled voice pleading forgiveness.

He continued to pierce through her, the lights flickering above. Poppy held her hands behind her back, regaining a stoic demeanor. Her weak voice betrayed her posture.

"Your Majesty, the altercation is my fault."

"*It's not.*"

The static muted; Ebony huffed even heavier than before,

resigning herself to the wall.

Cassius turned to Poppy. Her flanking guards jumped, but she remained still. "I won't tolerate anyone in my court doing Nora harm. Bring me the soldier who confronted her earlier."

"Sir—"

"And inform the others in your battalion as well as the other generals," he finished.

Poppy's mouth twitched like she wanted to speak her mind. "Yes, sir."

The king didn't look at Ebony as he addressed her. "Come back later with your full report, Ms. Nique. You're dismissed."

She stumbled to her feet, nodded, and left. How could he know about my attack from earlier? Ebony could have replayed her purpose in her mind, but I was too focused on my current fight.

Can you look through memories now? I asked him.

Cassius turned to me, a glare still sharpening his features. "I've been practicing," he answered. "Now let me help you."

I swiped away his outstretched hand. I hated how much everyone was touching me lately, and I especially hated how much he reached out to me. Gifts, tied together in a bracelet, sloshed in their confinement as his wrist flung back.

"Stop doing that!" I made sure my words were biting.

They all watched me try and fail to lift off the ground. My teeth gritted harder. I couldn't be this powerless! I needed...I needed to get back to my friends, wherever they were.

Cassius lingered with a curious stare. *You're sparking,* his voice weaved through my mind.

But it wasn't enough. The burn in my heart dimmed.

"I wonder," he said out loud.

An invisible weight lifted from my neck, followed swiftly by my legs. A new warmth encased half of my body, and I tilted to understand what was happening. He was...he was carrying me.

I inhaled a shriek, "Let me go!"

"Once we get you to your room," he said, calm and almost cheerful. Despite my thrashing, he kept me steady without using his Gift to force me in place. For once, I wanted that icy feeling up my spine so he could break his promise.

Cassius stepped past Poppy who couldn't hide her shocked expression. "Come along, General. I want you to stay with her so she rests. I think she's had enough excitement for one afternoon."

She nodded and mouthed something, but I shouted louder like a child not getting her way. "Put me down this instant!"

"Hey," he placed his hand gently on my chest, and I ceased moving with a surprised embarrassment. "You're a little brighter."

***

I stared out the window, disintegrating into the cushion there. A glimpse of my reflection showed patches of purpled and swollen skin, sinking me further into loathing. *Sparking*, he said. Just when I was beginning to feel a little more like myself again, he was already using it against me. I wouldn't give it to him.

Poppy teetered around my room until she finally joined me. This was becoming routine, us looking out at Iridion. What did she think of when she saw the Galdor skyline? If we had a view of Galdor Square, would she be reminiscing of the massacre there? Or her station during the Determination? My hidden questions drifted off in our silence.

"You know, you're not what I expected," Poppy said with sincerity.

If I didn't already want to throw myself out this window, I would have been more offended. "What were you expecting?"

"I'm not sure." Poppy thought more of her statement. "You want to *see* a disgraced princess. You want to *be* with Gifteds, but you *don't* want to be around our salvation."

"He is not *salvation*." Even speaking the word aloud sent a shiver down my spine.

We finally looked at each other. Poppy crossed her arms, tilted her face, and raised her eyebrows. "He's the *Diviner*. He's been anointed a great power by the Divine, and he uses it to cast punishment on Gifteds and lead a revolution of Unfortunates to their freedom. What would you call that?"

I didn't respond, turning back to the window.

Poppy shot up from her seat, charged over to the small bookshelf across the room, and came back.

"Look," she ordered.

I did; the Great Book stared back at me in the same bold capitalized letters as the Unfortunate Laws of Servitude.

I gasped, throwing my hands at its cover. The book toppled onto the ground with a defiant thud. "What the hell? Why are you bringing *that* over?"

Poppy huffed, bending down and retrieving it. She pressed the book against her chest so I wouldn't have a second chance to toss it.

"Can you read?" she asked, coarse.

"I can read the title!"

"No, I mean can you read in general? Did anyone teach you?"

"Valerie did."

"Who?"

"A fellow servant," I corrected, "when we worked for the Montgomerys. Queen Maya taught me more."

Her stare lingered but she didn't press. "Well, every Anti-Gifted soldier is taught to read with the Great Book, and I can prove to you that our king is our messiah."

I sneered, "This is the same book Minister Gabriel used to justify our status as servants and less than Gifteds."

"That's right." Poppy smirked as she skimmed through the pages like Leo when he intentionally withheld information.

My eyes narrowed, grabbing the book from her hands.

"Hey!" She was tall enough to get it back if she wanted to, but she didn't engage further than a yell.

I played with the white pages as a new plan formed in my mind. I smirked back, "Fine. If you're so confident, then you won't mind if I read along, and *I'll* prove that Cassius isn't what *you* say he is."

If I could convince her, I felt confident that the rest of the AGM would be swayed too.

She matched my smile and extended her hand. "Deal."

CHAPTER EIGHT

Stone Creek
FERN

We regrouped further into the isle, so far away from the entrance I couldn't see it anymore. Even though the sun was setting west now, it still blared down on us. Sweat from heat and tension dampened our clothes.

Buildings remained vacant of the Anti-Gifted Movement's signature red banner and only a few spare people adorned themselves with a red mark. Kai's original theory regarding the Stone Creek residents as free merchants held true as he led us through his hometown without fanfare.

Racing down narrow streets and meticulously spaced buildings, we finally came to a quiet neighborhood and then a cul-de-sac and then a small house. He rummaged through a flowerpot, found a key, and unlocked the door.

The evening light couldn't enter through the closed blinds, so we filed into darkness once more.

"Stay here," Kai pointed to the carpet and started busying

himself around the house, navigating the turns and couch corners without any assisting light. Water began bubbling somewhere in the kitchen.

We obeyed. I sat down on the carpet in the living room, figuring I'd get in his way otherwise.

Finally away from danger, I could breathe again. The others did the same, even lounging like we had just come back from a marathon.

Time passed, and I didn't realize I fell asleep until Kai startled me awake.

"Dinner time," he said.

He stirred the others, either in their own sleep or stupor. Persephone's arm was properly bandaged now, no doubt Kai's work. I sat up, rubbing the drowsiness from my eyes. The scent of fish, lemon, and herbs filled my senses. My stomach rumbled, and I followed the smell to a dining table in an alcove attached to the living room.

We sat down and grumbled a collective thank you before eating in silence. I didn't typically like eating in silence. I enjoyed the jesting between my mom and my sister and the clanking of forks and knives as we laughed so hard we had to exert our energy on nearby objects. Utensils silently cut into fish and slathered butter onto bread instead. We didn't have the same energy here.

Thinking of Delilah and my mom now, a dread threatened to rise and make me throw up. We chose Stone Creek because we could get to Northbrook from the sea faster than land. I prayed they would be safe in the meantime.

I looked out to the dining table: Kai, Leo, Persephone, Molly, Skylar, Mr. Harris, and Prince Henry in a makeshift highchair. Nora was missing from this picture. I prayed that she was safe in the meantime too.

***

We took turns taking showers after dinner. Right now, it was Mr. Harris's turn, insisting he be the last one despite the sleep clearly catching up with him.

Leo, more and more capable of using his Gift through one arm, lit the fireplace with Skylar at the ready to redirect his flame and Persephone to snuff it out. He succeeded, and we huddled near it.

I sat with my hair facing the fire in hopes of drying it faster. Kai offered us new clothes to dress in, clean from sweat and dirt and terror, while Leo took it upon himself to scavenge and critique the Mare's wardrobe. The house was built like a square with all doors leading back to the living room, so we could hear them playfully rummaging through hangers in his small bedroom.

I chose a grey colored t-shirt that Kai might have used for pajamas since it was oversized for him but long enough to cover my torso. A pair of dark sport shorts tied loosely over my hips.

Prince Henry laid on his purple blanket, still wearing his original matching jumper. He wiggled around happily, staring up at me and Persephone with rounded blue eyes like his siblings. The genes were strong in that family.

"Are you a happy baby? A happy baby?" With each repeat of Persy's use of the word *happy*, Prince Henry would jerk his entire body with an open and toothless smile.

We giggled along with each sharp angle of his little dance, and he'd look back and forth as we sounded off. He shrieked in laughter; a photo frame threw itself off the end table with a clattering crash. We halted as he continued to writhe with joy.

Persephone gently allowed the prince to gum her finger as I slowly stood and lifted the frame from the floor. Turning it over, I breathed a sigh of relief at the absence of any crack in the glass. A portrait of four-year-old Kai smiled back at me, his exact age noted by the large "4" block sitting among stuffed animals and a baby blue background.

The sudden whispers between Leo and Kai made our heads turn toward the bedroom door. I placed the photo back onto the end table.

"*Leo,*" Kai whined.

"You look great!"

A sudden silence followed. Kai pulled through the door frame, Leo shoving from behind.

"Look at what I found!" the Mati said, triumphant.

A deep blue robe draped over Kai's entire body, even covering his feet. Embroidered with rainbow fish, the garment sparkled in the fire's light despite Kai's stillness. A deep red creeped up his neck and flushed his freckled cheeks. He partially obscured his face with his hand, the sleeves long enough to completely cover his arms.

"It's for special occasions," Kai explained.

"You look very handsome," I encouraged, and Persephone nodded.

"May I see?" asked Skylar instead of her usual, *I bet that's because you can only afford one* comments. She stood up and started examining his sleeves as Kai nodded weakly.

"What occasions?" Molly piped up from the couch.

Leo started imitating Skylar's concentrated stare as Kai responded, trying to look Molly in the eyes while two people touched his clothes. "Oh just, sometimes the community will gather around a fire and share stories. Or if we're going over to someone else's for a holiday dinner. During Choosing Ceremonies too, but obviously we don't go to those."

Molly began to rub her scar, almost absentmindedly at the reminder of a Choosing Ceremony. Her mouth pouted as she looked down like she was trying to think what it would be like to attend one and be chosen by a House. She owned Nora for almost her entire life. The words came out of my mouth before I could weigh the consequences,

"Did you pick Nora at her Choosing Ceremony?"

Molly went rigid and the air stilled.

"I did," she finally answered, her face hardening. "I shoved her on the ground, and she fell over without any resistance."

There was a finality to her words, the kind when someone knew they did something wrong but retelling the events wouldn't change anything.

"That doesn't sound like our Nora at all," I finally replied. The lightness in my voice brought the fire back to its original warmth, and Molly relaxed, giving a small chuff.

I hope so at least, I wanted to add but I kept that to myself.

"I must get a Mare to add this to my wardrobe," Skylar declared, releasing Kai and stepping back to admire the work as a whole.

"May I suggest starfish, heiress?" Leo teased. "Purple ones though. Not orange. It'll match better with your hair."

"Not if you singe it!" Skylar shoved him away as he twirled blonde strands, but she laughed as she did it.

"I'm going to go change," Kai announced, but his voice was low and hardly audible over Skylar and Leo as they pushed and pulled each other, now connected by intertwined hands. A play fight was brewing, and Skylar's laughter drowned out all other sounds.

They moved closer to the living room and invaded our space.

"Careful," Persephone playfully warned, picking up Prince Henry before someone accidentally stepped on him.

We all watched, curious and attentive. I don't think any of us heard Skylar's genuine laugh before, and she was in a complete fit, uncontrollable and giddy. It must have fueled Leo because he was grinning like an idiot and refused to let go. Just then, the front door opened wide, and the dim moonlight exposed us with a fearful cold. Skylar's voice ceased as we froze in place and stared at the shadowed figure in the doorway. Kai walked back into the living room wearing regular clothes. He looked from our frightful bodies to the door and blinked.

"Hey, Mom."

Even though he was casual, no one else moved for several more moments. Kai gestured in our direction, "These are my classmates, and our teacher is currently in the shower."

Ms. Lancer stepped through and closed the door behind herself, still not speaking. Now illuminated by the fireplace, I could make out her features better. She had both of her legs (unlike my mom who didn't), sturdy arms, and an oval-shaped head. Her lips turned onto their side as she looked at us with bewilderment.

"Hello Ms. Lancer," I greeted for us. Leo and Skylar let go of each other at the same time. The Aura put her hands behind her back as if to show that she was less violent than her first impression suggested.

"What's going on here?" Instead of sounding like an interrogation mixed with anger, her question came out confused and delicate. She looked to her son for an answer.

Kai gave a matter-of-fact explanation. "We're hiding from

the Anti-Gifteds Movement. They took over Galdor, Mom. Has word reached you yet?"

She glided over and gave him a big hug. "You're the first person I've seen since I got off work."

He received her hug warmly.

"Are you hurt?" She examined his face, rubbing her thumb along his cheek, and then his hands.

"No, Mom. We made it out alright."

She frowned, worried, and looked over to the rest of us. "Have you eaten?"

"We have, and I made you a plate, Mom. Please sit down." Kai answered again, walking off into the kitchen.

The microwave hummed as Ms. Lancer slowly made her way over to the reclining chair and sank into it. We stared at her, unsure how to start a conversation. Sorry for coming uninvited? It's nice to meet you? Nothing felt right.

She twirled her ankles one at a time, switching after they snapped.

"Is he yours?" She pointed to the baby in Persephone's arms.

I looked at Prince Henry like he just appeared out of nowhere.

"Oh no," Persephone corrected kindly.

"He's actually Prince Henry," I blurted, "Third Born of the Third Auran Reign." There was no reason to add his full title but hardly anyone knew about the prince's birth. He was kept secret by the royal court and revealed unknowingly to the Diviner and the AGM.

"Really?" Ms. Lancer raised her eyebrows, wrinkling her forehead. She glanced at the other students eyeing her. "That's different."

Kai came back in, carrying a plate of steaming leftovers

and a glass of lemon water.

"He's an Animus, too. Isn't that cool?" He folded out the TV tray and put the food and water down.

"An Animus," Ms. Lancer repeated with wonderment. "Thank you, Kai." She acknowledged the dinner brought to her.

But before she could begin, Prince Henry started to stir and cry.

As he writhed, the TV tray began to tremble as though it alone was experiencing an earthquake. Ms. Lancer steadied herself up from comfort as small ornament objects began to clatter and shift on their wooden surfaces.

"Give him over," she prompted. Persy did, and Kai's mom gently laid the baby down on the carpet.

She didn't bother with modesty, releasing the baby from his jumper with quick, easy movements.

Kai tried protesting over the baby's cry, "Mom, you should rest."

"Kai, would you please get a bedsheet? Dark in color and one you don't like. Scissors and a pin too."

He paused only long enough for a pottery figurine to topple off the mantle before listening. He strode over to a narrow door that held a collection of folded laundry and then into his own room. Coming back with black fabric, scissors, and a small safety pin, he handed them to his mother and helped her lay the sheet out flat.

Ms. Lancer got started right away cutting the sheet into thick strips while the rest of us tried caroling the most breakable-looking decorations. I held a glass bowl filled with loose letters and notices when she calmly requested, "Water and washable cloth please."

Kai fetched those things too.

She chose the fabric closest to her, and Kai collected the remaining strips before they lifted into the air as though influenced by an Auran Gift. She cleaned the baby from his mess, using her Gift to move the water to and from the bowl. As she wrapped the black fabric around Prince Henry and pinned it in place at his hip, she gave him reassuring smiles and sounds that softened his wail. I didn't realize how loud the living room became until everything settled and became quiet.

Ms. Lancer lifted the baby up by his armpits, checking her work even though she made it with a precision that came with lots of practice. "He's almost as much trouble as you were when you were a baby, Kai."

"You can share all the embarrassing stories you want while you eat," Kai nudged.

Ms. Lancer laughed at the retort, rising from the ground and handing Prince Henry back to Persephone. "He busted almost all the pipes in this house. All that rushing water called to him at once." She cackled as though we were all recalling the same memory and walked back to the recliner, dragging her feet more this time. "Can't be blamed for it though. Not until you become self-aware and conscious of your Gift."

Kai sighed in relief as she sat down and picked up her utensils. Mr. Harris suddenly entered through the bathroom door—I didn't catch the water turning off—and the two adult figures made eye contact. Ms. Lancer eyed him, and he tried his best to appear professional with his own clothes slightly dampened, and a towel across his shoulders.

He bowed his head to her, and water droplets fell on the floor. "Ms. Lancer, please pardon our intrusion."

She paused a moment the way her son did, possibly

gathering her thoughts. "My son knows my house is always open," she said, her voice now tired and drained of worry or urgency. "Though, he usually gives me forewarning. Your students say the kingdom is no longer in your control. I'm going to need to know more."

CHAPTER NINE

The Great Book
NORA

———

I immediately regretted calling Poppy's bluff. We spent the morning on my bed, her droning on about creation: man and then woman, people populating the earth, and the first Gift granted after earnest prayer. The Makan Gift was the first Gift granted by the Divine—not to hide as we decided today but to protect from harm and danger. Poppy made that distinction clear. She finished with the first Unfortunate, a Gifted woman downcast. The reason why Unfortunate woman were forced into servitude as both punishment and redemption.

In return, I tried rebuking her at every turn.

"There it is. Clear as day," I proclaimed, hovering my hand over the passage. "How can you follow something that so plainly explains why we're forced into servitude?"

Poppy lit up, unexpectedly smiling. "But you see—her downcastment was never meant to happen. She received the consequence of going against the Divine, yes, but read that line again. He takes no pleasure in giving her punishment. It's just what must be done."

My eyes squinted. "That sounds like a poor excuse. If the Divine has omniscient power, he can spare her. Is that not what supposedly happens throughout the rest of this book?"

"He can, but she makes no attempt to take responsibility or ask for forgiveness. You'll see what I mean *way* down the line." Poppy spoke like we would breeze through the pages. Maybe I needed to in order to counterargue, dreading the thought.

I scanned the chapter we were currently on.

"But..." I murmured.

"Oh! Oh!" She could hardly get the words out in time with her excitement. "Did you also notice that the Divine doesn't single out Unfortunates here? Gifteds are still responsible for their actions and following the Divine's will, so we're all called to mend the bond between Him and us again. Isn't that fascinating?"

She circled the paragraph describing what she said as proof.

My head spun. I tried again. "The first Gift was a Makan. Isn't it just coincidence that Cassius was born one?"

Poppy tsked. "You can't expect coincidences in this book. We're going to make a *lot* of connections. I still find new things, so I'm excited to hear your connections too when you find them."

"Sure," I said, doubtful.

The clouds shifted, and sunlight streamed in through the window. Poppy giggled, childish, and jumped up from the bed. "Let's take a break. What would you like to do?"

I'd like to go to the east wing, I thought but I didn't dare say out loud.

I shrugged, quiet.

She tilted back and forth in her sitting position. "I want to learn more about you. Who's Valerie?"

I feigned interest. "I want to learn more about you too. Why didn't *you* have a Choosing Ceremony?"

"Woah." Poppy raised her hands up in false surrender. "Okay, I won't press."

There was a pause before she added, "I'm a general to the king now. There's no reason to dwell on past things."

"General." The word made me grimace as I tried to pronounce it. The disdain I thought before finally came out. "The AGM chose a strange hierarchy system."

"It's *way* easier to remember than separating *Senior* Royal Crest Knight from Royal Crest Knight," defended Poppy.

"That's because they're palace guards."

"Sure, and there's city guards for, you know, guarding the city. Very creative."

I challenged her smirk. "From where I'm sitting, you look like a glorified servant instead of a general, ordered to follow me around."

She stopped swinging with an abrupt force, her body jolting forward with its momentum. She stood in a sharp and swift motion, challenging me back with a playful menace.

"We'll need to change that then."

*****

Poppy led me to one of the Simulation Labs. Its dark interior greeted me in remembrance, and we walked from the vacant control room to the interior where the simulation would commence. Instead of running a scenario, only the lights glared above like we were on stage and the Anti-Gifted soldiers were players.

The Unfortunates nodded their heads in respect to their commander. One of them was Bree, the soldier who attacked me the day before. Cassius ordered Poppy to bring her to him. She didn't look scarred or beaten for her actions, but she did go out of her way to avoid eye contact.

"Ladies," Poppy greeted. "Take your places. Nora, you can sit on the sidelines for now."

I hesitated at her last words, but I sat anyway, near the far wall where a bench resided like a slab of stone. Now it was my turn to observe as Poppy ordered her battalion the same way Mr. Harris did, demonstrating their warmups and drilling them against each other.

They fought similarly to the combat exam, I realized. One student would oppose another, and the victor would remain until defeated and replaced by a new successor. There were only three of them though, so they continued to rotate out different combinations as they lost and won. I watched them use blunt instruments and shields. Critiquing one girl who fumbled with a wooden sword, I itched for my real one.

They clapped after each fight and sometimes cheered for their favored friends. I missed my team dearly. How Fern defeated Kai in under a minute and jumped high in the air with joy. How my fight with Molly left me more determined than ever to prove myself. How I tried to save Skylar's life in our first simulation and had a building fall on top of me. How Leo and Persephone treated me to snacks in a secret hideout afterward. We could have that again, couldn't we?

Something tapped my shoulder. I looked up and found Poppy standing over me, poking me with a wooden sword.

"Your turn, Nora," she strained, possibly repeating

herself.

"I will not fight you," I said dully.

"Oh, come on," she encouraged. "It'll be our first civil fight since Cherryville."

Where they kidnapped Melanie. Where two Unfortunate soldiers died because they decided it was better than being captured by my Gifted friends, the ones I longed for. Where Poppy took a twisted photo of me so everyone with a red armband could know me as the one still on the opposing side. The sympathizer.

It was still hard to believe that the same woman stood facing me now, teaching me the Great Book and poking me in hopes of another fight. Those past experiences didn't lather her words in venom, and her body language conveyed intrigue instead of revenge.

When a prolonged silence weighed between us, Poppy dropped the wooden sword at my feet and brought out her still, comically large mallet from behind her back. I hadn't even noticed it, which surprised me. I jolted, and then I rolled out of the way as she slashed her weapon in my direction.

The glorified stick fit loosely in my hands. I stood upright, facing my uncompromising opponent. She smiled and lunged; her movements similar to our first battle in Northbrook. When she prevented me from reaching Maya in time; when the princess's entire faith in herself crumbled.

I charged, and we collided, the wood snapping with a lightning crack. Taller than me, she used her height to her advantage and I did the same. She leaned too far forward, and I rounded my back as it hit the floor. My legs connected with her stomach, and she flipped over my head. I stood up quickly, sword whirling in hand. Surprise and shock plastered Poppy's face as she labored back up to her feet and retrieved her weapon.

We continued to strike blows, blocking and parrying when one of us got too close or clever. A laugh bubbled and burned in my throat as we spared, equally matched.

It became a betrayal, that laugh, when we parted from each other, panting.

Poppy smiled and raised her mallet. "Ambush!"

I turned in time to see her three soldiers charge at me, fast on their heels. Steadying my wooden sword, I charged back, sliding and twisting my way through the narrow empty space between their bodies. My weapon swung across their chests and legs in a mock slash, and I whirled to a stop opposing them.

So used to sparring with Gifteds, a new excitement bubbled in my chest at the thought of sparring with Unfortunates. I muted my smile, reminding myself that they were still my enemies.

Poppy gleamed at me while crossing her arms. I couldn't tell if she was pleased by my performance or displeased by her battalion's.

"Excellent training, everyone." Her voice boomed through the large space. "Time to break for lunch."

CHAPTER TEN

Out to Sea

FERN

We caught Ms. Lancer up on the events that happened three days ago, where we needed to go, and how. She listened with vigilant silence and would occasionally eye Mr. Harris with that disappointed I-expected-better-of-you mom face. Even when she noticed his Unfortunate brand, she still didn't hold back that face. Kai interjected every so often when he wasn't speaking to give her explicit context, and she nodded along.

Long after Kai took away her plate and we sat in silence, Ms. Lancer nodded slowly. "If we're going to effectively be on the run, we should take another day to rest, eat, and pack."

"And you're okay with that? Putting yourself and Kai in danger?" Mr. Harris pressed.

I hadn't considered Ms. Lancer's disapproval until now. My mom used to be in the Iridion military and constantly put me and my sister in a controlled state of danger. My Gift honed in by her influence. I attended Galdor Academy to follow in her footsteps.

Kai's mom carried a "go with the flow" energy I expected of a Mare but not of an Avlis. She welcomed us into her home even when she didn't anticipate our arrival, but that didn't mean she'd let us stay or even abandon her home entirely to become an outlaw.

Ms. Lancer sighed deeply, her chest rising and falling with the weight of that question. "I reckon the king will be looking for you, and the AGM might start knocking on doors as you've encountered. If my son will be in danger, I'd rather be with him."

"Thank you, Mom," Kai said, sitting by her side.

She rubbed his hand and gave him a soft smile.

A knock bristled at our backs as though on cue. The AGM could be closer than we anticipated. We collectively turned to the front door; Leo turned off the lamp illuminating us in the living room.

Ms. Lancer patted her son's hand before standing. Mr. Harris gestured for us to hide, our bodies already moving to the nearest door on either side of the central space. I crouched right at the doorway to Kai's room, my form obscured by an armchair.

A switch flicked, and a knob rattled.

"Oh, Ms. Lancer!" a cheery middle-aged voice rang out. "I'm glad to see you're home."

"Just got in tonight, Debra." Ms. Lancer spoke kindly but gave no room for conversation.

"I wanted to check just in case. Did you see the news?"

"No," I could practically feel Ms. Lancer shake her head in alarm, "What's on the news?"

"Turn to channel 7. The world is turning upside down!" Debra's voice drifted away like she was running away as she said her final words. Perhaps to the next house to share the same message.

Ms. Lancer closed the door and switched off the light.

We poked our heads out.

"Kai, will you—?"

Before she could finish her request, the television on the mantle came to life. He turned the channel to 7. Cheers filled the living room, a hollow sound amid our silent terror.

A king's crown of gold and purple adorned the Diviner's head. A smile crossed the monster's face as he bowed to the camera, to his new kingdom. Text on the bottom of the screen read, "King Cassius Iridion, First Makan Reign. Iridion welcomes rightful royal's ascension to throne."

I heard the AGM soldiers distinctly say "the king's orders" when tossing Gifteds out of their home, but to actually see him *crowned*—if I didn't have respect for Ms. Lancer's floors I'd actively vomit. The world was indeed upside down.

Three days. Three measly days ago, we were in that exact ballroom. I kept my attention on the dais, imagining how fun it would be if we were free to dance with the others. When Nora descended hand in hand with Mercy, a disgusting feeling formed in the pit of my stomach and refused to waver. And when the Diviner revealed himself—I should have taken charge the instant their hands touched.

I played with my hair, remembering the torture he inflicted on each of us then. My skull felt like it was splitting in two halves, on the verge of snapping apart. That man was now our king, but I would never swear allegiance to him.

He began speaking, his voice as soothing as a knife. "Citizens of Iridion—"

"Turn him off," I snapped quietly, already hugging myself from the chill.

Kai muted him immediately, but the television remained on.

I turned away, braiding my hair on one side. Nora wasn't there with him. She wasn't by his side or displayed as a prisoner. That was something, even if a despondent voice tried to add a third option. *You're not dead*, I pushed back. *You can't be dead.*

Someone turned on captions, and I sank onto the couch. Reaching for the largest pillow I could find, I held it close to my chest and forced myself to drift off to sleep—to better situations. To her safe and sound on the couch with me.

***

We embraced one final day in Stone Creek. I tried raiding the pantry while Kai was busy stirring our dinner, but he caught me with a sleeve of storebought cookies. He didn't appear fazed. "You can pack them for the trip. I'm sure the twins would like them, too."

I beamed and gleefully added them to a small and worn backpack Kai kept from his childhood. The shrink-wrap crinkled, so I stuffed clothes on either side to muffle any noise.

The day stretched as we prepared ourselves, and the night beckoned us out of Ms. Lancer's home.

Kai walked casually down the street to get Dr. Hansen, his mentor and our potential medic, at her house while the rest of us followed Ms. Lancer among shadows and backyards. Skylar was the only one who used her Gift, gliding from rooftop to rooftop a little further ahead as a scout. She could have been mistaken for an Anti-Gifted soldier, the night too dark to make out her clothes, and her movements subtle to even the trained eye. She kept her toes on roof surfaces like gravity affected her, and when she jumped back and forth, she used the wind as a push but it looked like she was just really skilled at leaping.

I flexed my fingers, ready to use my Gift if we needed to hide or evade.

We made it to the right-most side of Stone Creek. Lapping waves licked the concrete barrier as the city drifted in the water. An empty section where the sand met the sea sloped and then plunged into a drop-off.

Leo stood from his crouching position to move toward the giant locked warehouse, but Persephone caught his arm. He shrank back down into our hiding place among the foliage.

A flashlight came into view and then several people grouped together in a patrol. It was hard to make out their details, but they moved too quietly to be a band of bored friends and too precise to be on a casual stroll. Could the AGM know we were here? Even a neighborhood or city-wide watch would put us in a bind. The nerves along my spine danced in a fearful prickling.

They shuffled along the shoreline, shining their beams at the water and at the trees. Light glided past our heads and even shone slowly, directly along our torso. We stayed still, and the dense shrubbery maintained a fortified shield. They moved on, down the path, close to a point where a turning head might see us straight on. We crept back and rotated to avoid detection, the sand silent beneath our hands and feet.

The lights disappeared out of view, and then the people did too. We waited several more breaths until Leo stood up again. His sister and Ms. Lancer followed, stopping at the locked warehouse where the boats were stored. Skylar and I remained on lookout—sky and earth.

Metal slid over metal as the lock unlatched. Ms. Lancer went inside while the twins widened the entrance.

I glanced back and forth in case the patrol returned. The sea continued to brush against concrete, and the palm trees swayed with the clouds.

Ms. Lancer came back out and called to the sky in a harsh whisper, "Skylar!"

The Aura appeared on top of the warehouse and descended onto the ground in a twirling motion. The two disappeared inside, their figures obscured by darkness. So much for the sky advantage.

Leaves crunched behind us, and I twisted around, my hands arched like claws.

Kai cautiously came into view. I rotated my wrists like that would soothe the tension in every muscle.

"Sorry," I breathed.

He shrugged with an expression that read he understood my guard. Another form revealed herself: a lifted bun, pointed nose, and apple-shaped body. There wasn't time for introductions, but I lightly waved at Dr. Hansen anyway since we made eye-contact. *Welcome to the team*, I gestured.

I motioned to Mr. Harris and Molly hiding well behind the bushes with Prince Henry. Kai nodded, and they did the same. His mentor mouthed something, but I couldn't hear her.

My attention focused on the boat slowly emerging from the warehouse entrance, lifting off the ground as if carried by an invisible force. Though I couldn't see her, this could only be Skylar's doing.

I started to bend the branches of nearby trees to help her when Ms. Lancer squeezed through the exit and put her hand out to hold me off. I hesitated but lowered my arms.

Kai noticed his mother heading toward the bay and shot up, following her lead. They stood on top of the barrier's edge and looked into the depths. Together, the Mares urged the ocean to their command, rounding their arms in a repetitive motion. Water bubbled up from their collective effort, reaching a tall height.

The Mares had their arms stretched up to the moon. As they breathed out, their arms lowered and stopped parallel to their hearts. There was a pause followed by a deep inhale, arms flowing in the boat's direction. The water obeyed and moved inland, catching the bottom of the boat like a giant, supporting hand. Skylar finally appeared, the boat almost fully out of the warehouse now. Veins protruded out of her thin fingers; a clenched jaw permanently set on her face as she continued to circulate wind beneath the ship to keep it lifted off the ground.

But once the water connected with the bow, the front of the boat tilted and relieved Skylar of the entire weight. The Aura and the Mares worked together until our escape gently sat in the water. Ms. Lancer jumped inside and gestured for us to pile in as Kai started on the sails. I didn't know much about vessels, but Kai's mom did. She chose a moderately sized one, not as big as the ones in battle stories but not a raft either. We all piled onto the boat, the deck wide enough for ample movement. There was a door that led below deck, too.

Despite our closeness to freedom, we were still very much exposed out here. I turned back to Stone Creek, my hands clenched onto the boat side to steady myself.

There was nothing. And then there was light and shouting. I cursed (they would make a sailor out of me) and tried to reach any nearby vegetation. My Gift wasn't quick enough to reach an abundance of leaves and bushes and branches further away. The assailants charged forward.

"Molly! Take the baby under the deck!" Mr. Harris pushed his student behind himself, but I didn't look to see if she listened. Instead, I stepped out of the boat alongside our teacher, calling onto my Gift with more urgency for assistance.

He punched the closest silhouette, his impact enough to drive that person into the sand. I halted, amazed at the newfound energy in him. He confronted another, and I snapped back into action. Grass snaked around ankles and tripped the men nearing Mr. Harris. He made contact with another target with little resistance. Leo jumped off the boat next, beelining to the open warehouse.

"Leo!" shouted Skylar, colliding with the boat's side but not jumping overboard.

Fire ignited and caught quickly, illuminating the building and its burning boats inside. Persephone leaped onto the beach, but I put my arm out. We collided, the force of our impact threatening to tilt me off balance. Leo's fire was an intentional one; not something to snuff out.

She must have read my expression because she stayed at my side. The patrol deviated from their priorities as Leo raced back outside, the heat rising and the night sky darkening with smoke. Though I appreciated the distraction, I tried to ignore the crackle of wood turning to ash.

"Get back in the boat!" Ms. Lancer shouted.

We did, the sails catching a huge gust of wind thanks to Skylar's Gift. The Mares—Kai, his mother, and his mentor— directed the water's surface, rolling us out into open water within several breaths.

"Send word to the king!"

I swerved my entire body to the sound, ready to call on

absolutely everything I could command and halt the AGM in their tracks. But Stone Creek was already a large form at a distance, the flames a bright orange in contrast to its nightly greens and blues.

The king. Her capturer. We escaped, but he would know our last known location soon enough.

CHAPTER ELEVEN

Lieutenant

NORA

———

The student canteen looked the same as it had before, except now it was crawling with Anti-Gifted soldiers instead of Galdor Academy students. No one stood at the entrance to watch us scan our IDs because we didn't have any, and the line for food was self-serve. We were trusted to eat our fill without being greedy.

Poppy dragged me to a round table with the rest of the group. Her AGM soldiers condensed on one side and I on the other.

"You should be introduced to your sparrers," said Poppy. She gestured to her left, "Meet the best of my battalion. Bree, Ellie, and Holly. I believe you might recognize Bree's throwing arm."

Her comment was probably meant to bring our grievance out in the open to alleviate tension, but the two girls who weren't present when Bree attacked me quickly concentrated on cutting into their chicken.

I stared at them, fully taking in their features. Bree's hair was dyed a purple hue wrapped in a half-up, half-down bun, and her grey eyes remained perpetually narrowed. Even sitting down, she was the taller of the three and of equal standing to Poppy.

Ellie sat with her legs crisscrossed in the chair, bringing food to her mouth with cautious precision. Dark brown strands frayed from the braid along her back, and her almond-shaped eyes shared the same color as her hair. Of the four, she was the only one who was wearing makeup. Orange painted her eyelids and lips, applied expertly to her dark skin.

Holly couldn't have been any taller than five feet, and I was secretly thankful I wasn't the shortest person in the room anymore. A bright smile lit her face when her name was called, and she waved to me in greeting just as Mr. Harris had when we first met. I liked Holly immediately for this fact. A notepad resided next to her tray, her left hand jotting down words I couldn't see as she ate with her right. Her blonde hair puffed out at her sides, and her rounded hazel eyes added to a child-like appearance.

All looked to be around academy age, seventeen or eighteen, with Bree possibly in her early twenties. None of them reminded me of my friends, which meant I didn't have to feel tortured in their presence. I wondered though, why these young women were Poppy's best soldiers.

"You're very skilled with a sword," Holly chirped.

In my head, I recalled how she fumbled with the wooden one during their training. I realized then, if I couldn't get through Poppy...maybe if I convinced her best soldiers, that would convince her too.

"Thank you," I said, matching her politeness. "How long have you been practicing?"

"Oh, not long." She waved the pen in her hand.

"Holly is first and foremost a writer," Poppy noted in between sips of water. "I recruited her straight from the Divine Observer."

Holly beamed, her pale face turning a shade of bright pink.

An excellent tool used to ruin public opinion for Queen Maya, the Divine Observer was the Anti-Gifted Movement's newspaper. Always calling Unfortunates into action and Gifteds into surrender. I wouldn't openly admit how impressive it all was to be written by Unfortunates. Servants were only taught to read and write until they were chosen, and since I was chosen at ten, I only regained the skill recently. An Unfortunate writer was an odd but fascinating title.

"You must be very skilled with a pen," I said. "How long have you been writing?"

"All my life." Holly brushed her hair behind her ear with a shy smile. "I was chosen at sixteen, but I kept writing stories like I was still in school."

"Did you ever get caught?" The words fell out of my mouth; terror gripped at my ribs at the memory of when Valerie and I practiced copying recipes and burned the evidence.

Holly nodded. "I did. Got ratted out by my head servant, if you believe it."

"She was probably worried about getting punished herself," chimed Bree, but she didn't outright start a debate.

"Well, she had nothing to worry about," replied Holly, her voice rising in excitement. She looked back at me. "I went a day without food, but my House liked my handwriting so much, they started making me scribe their letters and correspondence. The Mrs. had terrible penmanship, but she would always feign it was because the task was 'beneath her.'"

My hands held my mouth in astonishment, but I quickly forced them back down into my lap. What was wrong with me? Was I this starved for Unfortunate company that this one conversation would bring a flutter to my stomach? Could I lean forward any further in my seat?

I pushed my back into alignment with the chair, withdrawing my intrigue as best I could manage. These were people I could relate to most. No wonder the AGM recruited Unfortunates with an incredible surge. We shared a history without ever crossing paths.

"That's amazing," I muttered, and then against my better judgment, I pressed. "And what about you two?" I gestured to Bree and Ellie with my fork. "What made Poppy choose you for her battalion?"

I had to know now instead of simply wondering.

Ellie went first, shrugging. "I'm an archer, though I hope you noticed."

I had. Though no one used their weapon during the makeshift combat exam, there was a good half-hour spent in different stations. Holly sparred against Poppy, which probably gave the general the idea to fight me when her soldier underperformed.

Bree focused on brute strength and boxed with a punching bag. Ellie had targets either set up or programmed all around the Simulation Lab, and she timed herself on how quickly she could hit each circle, going again and again with varying accuracy.

I nodded, and she continued. "I wasn't chosen, but I needed to find work, so I requested to become a servant. My House hired me because I could paint their son's portrait."

I've heard of skilled servants, but I never met one properly before. They were so rare and highly favored among Gifted families. No one in the royal court dared to introduce me to their skilled servants, though I saw them along the wall at Queen Maya's coronation and ball.

The Montgomerys tried to humiliate me for not knowing anything in the realm of arts, but I soon discovered the real reason after Valerie was hired, lacking in the same talents. My chosen House was relatively poor. They had the estate and the land and their House name, but all of that was inherited, not earned. Mr. Montgomery's injury, both his limp and his pride, meant they lived on his benefits as a retired Royal Crest Knight.

"Tell her about the forbidden romance," Holly teased, clasping her hands together and leaning her neck to one side.

Bree snorted, and Ellie looked away, crossing her arms. "That's not what happened!" she refuted, a little too loudly. "Their son and I—never. Never."

"It makes for a good story." Holly continued writing on her notepad as Ellie tried to dissuade any doubt from our faces.

Poppy laughed, amused as she watched her soldier fluster. "Speaking of forbidden romances..." My heart sank as the general's eyes trained on me.

"Yes!" Holly exclaimed, slamming her pen down and staring at me with wide eyes. A jolt ran through my body, but I forced myself to remain pleasant and welcoming. "Oh, you have to tell us about the king's personal life!"

"*Holly,*" Bree strained, gesturing for her to lower her voice.

Ellie snickered, probably grateful that the attention wasn't on her anymore. Poppy smiled, encouraging her soldiers and punishing me all at once.

"Sorry," Holly whispered. "Won't you though? Every move the AGM made had you in mind, even if he didn't explicitly say it." Her hands clasped together in a pleading gesture.

I stared at the four women, desperate to hide and get out of this conversation. From what they were suggesting, I didn't want to feed into the ideas they already had of me and Cassius. We might have been forbidden lovers once but no longer.

"Every move he made wasn't for love," I corrected. "How about I share how we fought? Good vs evil?" I tried to play into the tropes my younger brother would tell me about, hoping that would appease Holly's request. At the mention of fighting instead of swooning, Bree looked up from her meal.

"Isn't that how great love stories start?" asked Holly.

Hopefully not, but I didn't share my thoughts.

Instead, I started with his betrayal, hoping they'd see him as a liar and manipulator. I recalled every word we breathed to each other after he declared a Determination against his sister. How he promised there was nothing to fear for tomorrow. How we kissed at the arena and the bracelet full of stolen Gifts always hidden on his wrist. How my heart wrenched when he revealed himself as the Diviner. How I broke free from his Animus Gift, and how he couldn't possibly care about his Unfortunate followers. He only wanted power. He always wanted power.

They listened, enraptured, though I wasn't sure if my emphasis was getting through to them. I continued, hoping that their interest would persist.

"What did he say when you defied him?" Ellie asked.

"*When he caught your wrist!*" Holly practically screeched.

I stammered, the memory too clear in my mind. "I forced my gaze toward him," I explained, "He held the same expression when we spoke freely to each other. He was vulnerable, and he said..."

Ellie and Holly leaned in.

"I want you by my side." His voice rasped so close to my ear, I almost sprang out of my seat.

The four soldiers did jump to their feet, their expressions a mixture of shock and embarrassment.

The fabric of his clothes brushed along my neck, and my body flashed hot and then cold in alarm. I didn't dare look up. I didn't dare move in case we touched again. He shifted to my side, his fingers trailing my chair.

His soldiers bowed or curtsied to him in quick greeting. "Your Majesty."

My jaw tightened, knowing that his keen gaze was on my form. I still refused to look up at him. I didn't know how my light appeared now. Could I be sparking just from quickened heartbeats? Flickering like a Makan growing into their Gift? I wished I could control this hidden light. To be myself again without giving Cassius any satisfaction from it.

"You are an excellent instructor, General," Cassius said, kind with a hint of conniving. "And an excellent sparer."

I looked at him then. Had he seen our fight? We locked eyes, and his smile deepened. "I'm glad to see your strength returning."

I didn't respond, turning away again and looking at the table.

He addressed Poppy, unbothered. "I've come to tell you to pack what you need. You and your battalion are going to help me take Northbrook."

At the mention of Fern's hometown, I bristled but refused

to give him another satisfying glance. Poppy clasped her hands together, brimming with excitement.

"Yes, sir! When do we depart?"

"Tomorrow," he confirmed, inhaling the murmur of anticipation that swept the other three soldiers. "And you shall be taking Nora with you, too."

Cassius relished in the surprise that brought my attention back to him. My mouth went dry.

"Sir?" Poppy asked.

"Nora will accompany you as your new lieutenant effective immediately."

"The hell I will," I cursed, standing now and throwing my chair back to add distance between us.

"Sir," Poppy repeated, her voice now careful and light. "I trust your judgment, but may I ask why you're assigning Nora as my second in command?"

"I will not go," I intervened.

The three other soldiers glanced at each other in silent shock at my blatant defiance.

Sensing that I was undermining him, the king turned his feet and positioned himself directly in front of me. A fingertips length away. The closest he'd been since he consoled me for killing the minister.

"You will," he declared, confident.

My eyes narrowed, "And what makes you say that?"

I waited for him to use his Gift against me. To lose control of my limbs and watch the world burn with him as I had at the Determination. No matter what, I didn't belong to him. I had to hold true to that sentiment.

"Because," he said simply, forming his palm to my cheek, "this is a chance for you to see your new world. My general will do well to show you our point of view, and if you step out of line or if your light doesn't improve"—he held me with both hands now, and I struggled as he pulled me closer until our noses brushed and all I could see was his blue eyes bearing into my soul—"you'll return as a permanent prisoner of war."

War. Cassius was the first to profess it. We were at war, the first of its kind since Iridion became a unified country under our first king. The only people we had to fight were ourselves, and Cassius wanted to unify us again under his rule. The word startled me so much, he managed to keep me in his hold for several heartbeats longer. Whispers floated back up again, feeding into the king's reputation and their assumptions about us.

I snapped to my senses, using both of my hands to pry his fingers and step several paces back. Poppy shifted, unsettled. She cleared her throat, and her company halted their speech.

"You both have the rest of today to prepare," Cassius reminded, and then he was gone.

My knees threatened to collapse under me. I held the table for support.

Poppy bit her lip and turned to her soldiers. "You heard His Majesty. Prepare what you need for the journey."

They nodded and left the canteen without a second glance at their unfinished meals. I couldn't understand him. He was letting me outside on a leash. I could try and find my friends if they fled to Northbrook. He must know that. But if we were caught, surely he would refuse defeat again.

Tears welled into my eyes at the thought of running toward but being unable to reach Fern in time. Just like Valerie. Poppy pursed her lips with a sympathetic look, but instead of saying anything comforting, she said, "Let's get you ready, Lieutenant."

CHAPTER TWELVE

Northbrook
NORA

———

We departed from Galdor Academy at dawn and headed east to Northbrook.

We walked on foot so I was forced to see Cassius's empire firsthand. Red banners cascaded over government buildings and businesses. More and more Anti-Gifted soldiers wore red uniforms matching our legion, and civilians who aligned with us wore red bands proudly around their limbs. Some girls were creative, intertwining red ribbon into their braids and ponytails, turning the symbol into a fashion statement.

As we crossed through towns and cities, Unfortunates filled the streets and walkways. They welcomed us with a great, endless cheer, often stopping and swarming like a parade around our troops.

Their troops, I had to remind myself. They put me in red and a newly fashioned lieutenant's jacket, but I was not part of his army. *Their legion. Their civilians.* My people...

Hands reached for Cassius on his horse, and he allowed their reach because my people looked up at him in awe, in a love and devotion that splintered my nerves. They wanted to touch their leading hero, their savior, fingers often molded in prayer. The display reminded me of when he freed me and other Unfortunates from imprisonment. How the other women bowed at his feet and whispered their praises. How he listened to each one with a gentle, feeding gaze, and how his eyes met mine when I wished he would.

Now my muscles tightened back when he inclined his head over to me. He made sure I saw my people—free and lively and appreciative—because of him. My anger must have been a flame because his smile deepened every time he checked on my reactions, as each new wave of supporters came rushing forward.

Ellie created murals along our path, too. Some intricate paintings of Cassius overlaid brick if we stayed in one place overnight. Always with the Iridion crown adorning his head and the Gifts along his wrist warming the background in beautiful colors. Other times she'd simply write lines or reference the Great Book in flowing script.

To discredit their meaning, Poppy and I continued to debate about the Great Book as we traveled, an easy way to distract myself from what I was seeing. She'd often read out loud with the rest of her battalion. *A way to get multiple points of views*, she insisted. These were my favorite moments because I could go against them in a more public display of disdain.

"So, this is what justifies killing people?" I asked.

We jumped ahead a little, reading several chapters about the Divine's promise to the Gifteds who followed Him and now the supposed fruition of that promise in three descriptive battles. Certainly not the promises I kept.

"No," Poppy asserted. "This justifies our movement. Don't you see that we're doing the same now? We're prevailing over our oppressors through a Diviner who exacts justice in His name."

"Besides," added Ellie, "the text says that the armies were wiped out and that mission was commanded *by* the Divine."

"But from the other stories we've read so far and what you've told me, that is contradictory to the Divine." I heard myself in protest. "What about the man and his son? When the Divine commanded the son be killed by his father, you tried to assure me that He would never actually condone that. So why is it different here?"

Poppy blinked at me, pleasantly surprised, and I found myself with the same expression. My first connection, each question pouring out of me in fast procession. I didn't know how to feel. Livened because I sounded educated and caught my first real argument against her? Or terrified because I was retaining our lessons? I found myself whirling with both.

The other girls glanced at each other in silence until finally looking to their leader for a good answer. After a full minute of unsettled heartbeats, Poppy said, "The Divine provided a ram in place of the son's sacrifice at the last moment. That represents Him as a provider and tells us that the father is absolutely devoted to the Divine and what He promises."

There was that word again.

She paused, her squinted eyes focused upward like she was searching for invisible strings.

"In this instance, I think because the Divine doesn't provide an alternative at the last moment to stop bloodshed, then His followers are justified in a holy war. He's more complex than what makes you comfortable."

I frowned and crossed my arms, "I think the Divine is more complex than what makes *you* comfortable, too."

***

We reached Northbrook on the third day of our journey. A week and a half passed since Cassius seized the throne. Since I saw my friends last.

There were no parades waiting for us in the dense forest. Silence filled the path, Cassius's army fanned out to avoid the trees. We neared the train station, occupied by awaiting Anti-Gifted members.

We approached and rested while Cassius spoke to the captain, a woman in a hat that distinguished her from the others. Poppy stretched; Bree fidgeted with her nails; Ellie played with her bow string; and Holly wrote something in her notebook. All restless except their general.

About ten minutes later, Cassius departed from his conversation and moved to the outside of our brief encampment. He turned toward us, still on horseback so everyone could see him clearly.

"All Gifteds are to be taken out of their homes and placed into the warehouse for judgment." He projected his voice, clear and direct. "If they resist, you have permission to use necessary force. Free any remaining servants, and if any of you find a Makan, send them directly to me."

Delilah, I thought but quickly tried to dismiss it in case Cassius heard me. He reared his horse, trotting in our direction. Fern's younger sister was a Makan. I would not let him take her.

While the other troops jumped into action, Poppy stalled

for her king.

He smiled at me; I scowled.

He dismounted so we stood on equal ground, though he was still taller than me. "I have something for you."

An object, heavy and carefully wrapped, was presented. I intentionally placed my hands where we wouldn't touch and pulled it toward me. Unwrapping the cloth, the blade poked out first, shimmering in sunlight. Stunned, I quickened to unfold the rest and clutched the helm in my branded hand. My sword. An extension of my arm returned to me.

"I'm glad you like it," Cassius said.

The smile on my lips disappeared. He gave me this sword. I bowed to him on that very day. The curve of his lips pulled as I recalled the memory.

"I could kill you right now," I blurted.

Poppy and her battalion bristled; the king chuckled. "What would that change?" he asked. "Both of us dead?"

My mouth tightened. I had no answer. If he died now, the AGM would still follow him as a martyr. The same was not true for me.

He climbed back onto the horse, and then he was gone.

Poppy watched me for several heartbeats before turning to her battalion, ringing out orders. They nodded, following their king with more purpose.

I needed to reach the Fairaway house before anyone else.

"Permission to go southwest." I pointed absentmindedly, but my heart already raced with a mix of longing and dread.

Poppy eyed me, "Granted."

My body positioned to run, but she found my arm and kept me in place. "Hold on," she warned. "Did you forget that I was once a servant there too? We go to the Fairaways together."

No. I almost whined but stopped myself. I hadn't forgotten, and I was foolish to think Poppy wouldn't notice.

We walked southwest together. My heart tore at wanting and unwanting. If Fern was here, then I would help her escape. If Fern was not here, then I still didn't know if she was alive.

The house stood still as we found our way up the tree the way servants did, on rivets that circled around the trunk like a ladder. I landed onto the porch with a loud thud, hoping that would announce my presence to anyone inside. The house remained silent and dark.

There were seven servants here. They wouldn't just vanish.

Poppy must have sensed that too, creeping ahead of me and light on her feet. She entered the door frame first, and I followed. The house wasn't wrapped anymore from the time Maya spent here. Wood creaked underneath our steps.

Movement flashed in the darkness, and Poppy grunted as she was thrown in the air by a large mass that entangled around her entire frame. She strained and gritted her teeth, thrashing her head until something covered her mouth and muted her screams.

Vines, I realized. Thick and sturdy.

"Fern!" I broke away from a defensive stance, hope rising in my voice.

The walls absorbed my call with no response. An ache carved out my chest.

"Fern is not with you?" Ms. Fairaway revealed herself, a cascade of vegetation brimming behind her, waiting to strike.

"No!" I answered louder than I intended. My voice lowered. "The AGM captured me while Fern and the others escaped. I was hoping she would have fled to you."

Sorrow filled her mother's voice. "If she's fled here, she has not reached me."

I cursed under my breath. *Where were you?* I wondered. *You promised me.*

Looking back up, Ms. Fairaway still met my gaze, her face more hardened and experienced than mine. If I couldn't help Fern right now, I could at least do this.

"You need to flee," I said, trying to match her intense look. "Cassius is rounding up Gifteds, and yours will be a prize."

"He will not get to me," she replied, matter-of-factly.

"He doesn't have to. He has an Animus Gift and can make you give it to him willingly." She blinked away as if to consider, so I pressed, urgent. "He's also asking for Makans specifically brought to him. Delilah is in grave danger. You must protect her and find Fern, too."

Several heartbeats passed. Every second we stayed frozen, the closer Cassius could advance at any moment.

"Go!" I stomped my foot on the ground, its ripple finding the Avlis in front of me.

"Come with us." She ushered me forward. Poppy shrilled, loud enough for it to hum through her restraints.

I glanced at the Unfortunate. "I can't."

The words came out easier than I expected, but they shredded at my throat.

"Why not?" demanded Ms. Fairaway.

"Because," I said simply, "that must be exactly what Cassius expects."

Realization came through as I explained myself. "We're telepathically connected. He's been connected to me ever since he got his Animus powers. If I were to go with you now, he would find us and he will *not* accept failure again."

A blossom of relief washed over my veins despite my words. This was the first time I confessed our telepathic connection to anyone, and I could speak freely about it now.

Ms. Fairaway nodded, her expression now careful and strategic. "Very well. I'm sorry you must remain a prisoner, but you're brave to do so. If you take my girls, will they be taken to the AGM safely?"

I nodded, grim. "Part of their mission is to free servants. They'll be safer outside of your hands."

On my word, the vines parted and pushed forward her servants. I caught a glimpse of blonde hair that denoted Delilah, but she remained obscured from view.

Six girls walked toward me in a cluster, stationing themselves near me but not beside me. Hesitation and fear filled their eyes just as they had when they asked how I escaped, if they should join the Anti-Gifteds Movement. Now they didn't have a choice.

Amelia, I remembered her as the head servant, clasped Ms. Fairaway's arm without fear of an attack.

"I'm staying with you," she declared.

"Amelia," Ms. Fairaway softened her name, "you'll be safer with the AGM than with me."

"I do not care. I have served you for far too long to stop now."

Ms. Fairaway patted her hand. "I'm sorry, Amelia."

Without warning, she used her Gift to wrap her head servant in greenery and move her to my side. Amelia released one stubborn yell before remembering her station and stormed outside to the patio.

Ms. Fairaway sighed, forlorn. She looked up to Poppy who was still bound to the wall. "I'll tie up the loose end."

The Avlis motioned her hand. The vines tightened around

Poppy's body and she screamed.

"No! Stop!" I yelled.

Ms. Fairaway ceased immediately. Her hand throbbed at the ready, but regret plastered on her face. All of these women were people she saved from other Houses. Poppy was still one of those women.

Ms. Fairaway swallowed and readjusted her form. She looked at me, her features sharpened. "Make sure we are not followed, Nora."

I nodded, not trusting my words to form a promise.

We watched the Avlis leave, hiding herself inside a web of vines and using them like spider limbs. Vegetation crawled up the ceiling in a dense clump and out the open window. The emptiness of the Fairaway house returned, mocking me in Fern's absence.

I sighed, unsheathing my sword and cutting away at Poppy's restraints.

CHAPTER THIRTEEN

Among the Trees
NORA

I encouraged the Fairaway servants forward while Poppy trailed behind, continuously rotating her wrists and stretching her arms. Whether she was restless or embarrassed by her inability to fight Ms. Fairaway, I didn't ask.

We brought the girls to central command, which was the empty field usually held for Northbrook's daily bazaar and the Flower Festival. The earth still split between grass and where Maya poisoned it to ash. We kept closer to the green side.

A makeshift barn also imposed as starkly as the Iridion Castle against the clearing and surrounding trees. A red wave of soldiers crowded in a crescent moon shape around its entrance.

I stayed with the Fairaway servants a few moments longer as Poppy snapped back into action and ordered they be accounted for and given roles.

I wanted to know their names, but they were already pulled away by AGM soldiers in other units. Poppy grabbed my shoulder and steered me toward the warehouse. I grabbed her back, halting us before joining the others.

"You do not breathe a word about Ms. Fairaway and Delilah's escape," I whispered harshly in her ear.

She severed the connection between us. "What gives you the audacity to give me orders?"

"Because I didn't let Ms. Fairaway kill you."

Poppy huffed, but she didn't refute me.

We entered the crowd. Ellie and Holly stood with us, but Bree was not in sight.

The door was open partway, and Cassius walked out, serious and concentrated. A few paces behind him but in time with his steps, a woman without a branded U followed him into the spotlight. Her bones clung to her skin in a ghostly outline, and her eyes fixated on her feet.

"Is he starving them?" I asked out loud.

Poppy answered casually. No different from telling me the weather. "It's how we subdue Gifts on our own without killing them. Get rid of their energy, get rid of their ability. She already looks like an Unfortunate, doesn't she?"

My mouth twitched, but I didn't respond. She did look like an Unfortunate, and we all watched her in a spectacle of anticipation. Her very own Choosing Ceremony.

Cassius stopped, and she stopped too.

He addressed us, "My kingdom, you witness Divine judgment in Northbrook. Those spared reveal themselves allegiant to our cause. Those who oppose us are returned to their Creator."

Claps and cheers enveloped my senses. Ellie whistled her approval, and Holly wrote furiously in her notepad, writing down his every word. The king smiled, savoring the applause. That was why he stood here—not for a righteous cause but for his own ego.

I stood alone, arms crossed, with that truth exchanged between us when his eyes caught mine. His jaw tightened alongside his smile, an almost invisible display of frustration.

Watch, his voice pierced my mind.

He turned back to the Gifted woman. She sank to her knees and tilted her head up to the sky, her movements stilted and resistant. I knew what she was going through all too well while possessed by his Animus Gift.

Cassius stood over her; AGM soldiers shuffled to get a better view. He made sure to tilt so I could see his thumb pressed firmly against her forehead. The rest of his hand cupped the top of her head and obscured half of her face.

Judgment came swiftly, as silent and absolute as the angel of death. They stayed connected for several heartbeats as Cassius recited a phrase he probably didn't need for concentration anymore but did need for highlighting his dominion.

"If you can see it with the mind of your heart, and feel it in the depths of your soul, then you will hold it in your hands."

In the next instant, Cassius stepped back and the Gifted crumbled to the ground.

A bright green light caught our attention, twirling between the king's fingers.

Two AGM soldiers ran over—I hoped in a moment of disillusionment—and dragged the body away.

"Next," Cassius commanded, and the next Gifted walked toward him.

After he pocketed the third Gift, I couldn't stand to watch anymore.

My nerves on fire, I readied myself for Poppy's confrontation, but it didn't come. I forced myself out of the crowd, colliding with each person in my path.

I continued to walk toward the tree line with no other purpose than to remove myself from this camp. I wouldn't flee—Cassius made that reality impossible—but I needed distance. I was that servant girl again, so withdrawn now that her return struck me with despondence and torn familiarity. Leaving the Montgomerys was impossible for her as she suffered alone on rainy days, holding onto a promise she didn't know how to fulfill. And here I was now, unable to tell her that we've changed—that things got better. That she had anything to hope for in her future.

Bramble and undergrowth entangled at my feet, but I continued walking despite the resistance. The trees stretched taller and further around me, the sun reaching me in fragments.

The silence deafened. I wanted to tell that servant girl *something*. Anything to convince her that we lived between then and now, servant and soldier. I did leave the Montgomerys, and I did keep Valerie's promise. I accepted a role at an elite Gifted military school, and after some time, I made friends with my Gifted peers. I wasn't always a good friend to them. I lied by omission about my telepathic connection to Cassius. I became so determined for things to go right that everything went wrong, and I wished I was a better leader too. One they could follow with full confidence.

A new sight—rocks and pouring water—steered me in its

direction. I found myself walking alongside its stream, hearing the rush of water, smooth and uninterrupted. Birds chirped to each other high above my head. The leaves and mud sank under my footsteps.

I inhaled a deep breath. *Where were you, Fern?*

Nora?

I halted, swerving my head around, back and forth. "Fern?" I whimpered. I heard her voice, echoing through my mind in all its calming beauty. "Fern!" I shouted, louder this time. I couldn't see her. I was alone in the middle of nowhere, but I didn't want to be alone anymore.

My feet propelled forward into a full sprint down the brook's path. *I would find you. I would find you!*

"Fern!" I shouted again.

Nora!

I heard her voice, loud and clear as the bright blue sky. Still, she was nowhere in sight.

I came to the water's end abruptly, and I stopped with it.

"Where are you?" I yelled, desperate.

At sea.

The sea? How was that possible?

Where are you? she asked.

Words continued to fall from my mouth despite her voice only belonging inside my thoughts. I needed to fill the silence. "I'm in Northbrook."

Northbrook? Did you find my mom?

"They're both safe. They fled, I'm not sure where." I sat down now, my hand running along the stream. "Fern, this is crazy. How are we talking right now?"

Static garbled in my ear, and Fern's voice became faint like she turned to talk to someone else.

Her voice returned, *Mr. Harris says that Prince Henry*

created a connection. What were you thinking about before you heard my voice?

A tightening seized my heart; my mouth went dry. I stared at the puddled water for a little too long.

Nora?

"I was thinking of you." A pause. "And the team and how I left things. Mr. Harris is with you? Who else? Did everyone—?"

Everyone is here, Fern assured me. *We even picked up Kai's mom and his doctor mentor in Stone Creek.*

I half expected them to say hello like we were all in the same room together, but the forest continued to surround me.

So Prince Henry was the reason. He was an Animus. He had the potential to speak telepathically to other people, but for him to create a connecting line between two outside individuals...

"I can't believe I'm hearing you right now," I said, unexpected tears swelling in my eyes.

Mr. Harris thinks it could be image association or a strong emotional tie.

I burst into sobs, the first in a long time. A strong emotional tie indeed. "You're alive! That's all I care about right now. Fern, I was so *worried*." My voice reached a high-pitched croak.

She heard my cries. *I missed you too*, she whispered.

I continued to lament as all of my anxious restraints loosened. Several heartbeats passed in silence.

We're on our way to you.

"No," I said, standing as the moment ended and fear returned. "You can't. I'm here, but so is Cassius and his army."

We can still get to you. Head south. We'll meet you on the coast.

"No," I tried again. "He uses his Animus Gift to telepathically connect with me, too. If we're close enough, he'll know where I am. He's done it before. You need to stay away. Find a place you can lay low and hope that Prince Henry's range for connecting us is far more reaching than Cassius's."

She didn't respond for awhile, long enough for me to worry we lost each other.

"Fern?"

I haven't forgotten our promise.

She caught me off guard. I folded my arms around me, my voice low. "I'm glad."

And we'll keep our distance until I can fulfill that promise.

A smile tugged at my cheek. "Thank you. I'll do what I can here. I'll—" ideas came in rapid succession "—convince the AGM that Cassius isn't their savior. I'll gain intel for you. I'll sabotage any plans I can. Fern, the world can't be turned over like this."

It won't.

I wished I shared her confidence. "The problem is I have no idea what the new solution would be. We can't go back to what we had before."

We'll figure it out, together.

Another smile. A flutter in my chest. I nodded like she was right in front of me. "Together."

There was a pause, and then a sharp pain of static cut through my ear. I winced. "Fern?"

She didn't respond.

"Fern?" I asked again, more urgently.

She came through in broken pieces, her voice far off and

concerned. *Wait...Isaac...why does he look...?*

"Fern?"

Silence. Disconnected.

Anxiety swirled within my stomach once more. The last time I saw Isaac was inside the castle after the siege. He was captured while frozen mid-action under the Animus Gift. What did Cassius do to him?

I sprinted back to camp.

Just as I reached the clearing, I caught a glimpse of someone and suddenly I was off course, spinning and hitting the ground hard.

Poppy groaned from her place in the dirt. I stood with her, nausea beginning to rise within me. I swallowed it back.

Ellie and Holly were here too, helping their general back to her feet.

"What was that?" Poppy demanded.

"Are you okay?" Ellie asked.

"Yes." I didn't have time to waste if Fern was in danger.

"Hey!" Poppy reached out and caught my arm anyway. "We're supposed to be allies."

I shoved her off. "I am *not* an Anti-Gifted soldier."

She shook her head. "I'm not talking about that. We're both Unfortunates—once bonded by servitude."

"I thought you didn't have a Choosing Ceremony."

"Nora."

I stopped at the abrupt use of my name, her voice sincere. A pause filled the space between us. Holly poked Poppy's elbow to encourage her to speak. She swallowed before adding, "I'm sorry you had to watch judgment. It's not...for everyone."

We stared at each other. Out of everything she could have said, I wasn't expecting her to apologize for something she believed in or for her soldiers to care enough to make her.

"You were coming to check on me?" I asked.

"That's what a general does."

I paused, hesitant. If she and her soldiers were trying to extend an olive branch, I could do the same.

"Do you think we can read some more? Later, that is."

Her eyes widened, and a big smile scrunched up her freckles. "Of course."

"You wanted me?"

We turned to find the king in our midst. Standing in front of him, the color drained from my face. I stumbled back. At the snap of his fingers, he could learn...I didn't want to even think it in case he was listening to my thoughts now.

"You have to stop doing that," I breathed, hoping he'd think that was why I was so startled. "And yes."

Cassius only smiled, pleasant with an undercurrent of hostility. "You left the judgment early."

I glared at him. "You can't expect me to watch you commit atrocities."

All three AGM soldiers shifted awkwardly in the corner of my eye.

"I want to know what you did to Isaac," I changed the subject before he could defend himself.

He tilted his head. "What's your sudden interest in Isaac?"

I forced myself to think of Isaac Winters as I did when he was taken away from the ballroom. "You had him under your control the last time I saw him. What did you do to him after the siege? Did you downcast him?"

He squinted, and I knew he was reading through my mind. Cassius stepped closer, his hand reaching toward my face. "Why can't I...?"

We touched, and I flinched. He ignored it, too focused on

something unseen. I became too focused on his fingers as they gently brushed my cheek, my forehead, through my hair.

"Interesting. Your memories. They're incomplete." He inclined my head as if that would change anything, but the gesture looked like he might lean into a kiss. His lips were slightly parted as part of his investigative expression. I watched as it changed into a mischievous curiosity. "What have you been up to?"

He couldn't see all of my memories? So, he didn't know?

"Know what?" His entire body stiffened as he held me in place, expecting an answer.

I pushed him away so we were no longer in contact. "Tell me what you did to Isaac."

Cassius's jaw twitched, suspicious, and then masked it with a shrug. "I brainwashed him."

"*What?*"

"I told you that I was practicing memory work," he explained. "I used Isaac as a test subject and twisted some things around in the process. You'd be amazed at how fragile perspective is."

"*You brainwashed him?*" Horror etched my face. "How can you do that so flippantly?"

"Nothing I do is flippant," he corrected. Hurt and anger surfaced in his gaze, but he maintained a confident voice. "His Gift is better in service to his king. He's on the hunt for those fugitives you call friends. It was that or I kill him."

"He'd probably prefer death to serving you." My words burst out, sharp and frightened. "Who else will you brainwash? Will you rearrange their memories and thoughts and feelings until their true nature is erased?"

I spoke, louder and louder, gesturing to Poppy, Ellie, and

Holly. I prayed that their bristled shoulders and lowered eyes meant that they imagined themselves as possible candidates.

"*Enough*," he demanded, low and firm. "I do what is necessary for this new kingdom, and Gifteds with great strength must be subdued this way. My soldiers never need to undergo such measures because they are already loyal to me."

Of course he had an answer—one that seemed reasonable on the surface. But I knew that once the balance slipped, he would have a new reason to hurt people.

"I'm not loyal to you," I said, resolve regaining more and more of my courage.

Cassius smiled then as if remembering something delightful. He held my stare as he walked closer, leering down at me until his hair brushed along my temple.

"When you kiss me again, it will be of your own free will. Just as you did when I freed you from prison. Just as easily as you killed that retched minister."

He pulled away, his next words loud enough for everyone to hear as he strode away. "I'm glad you're on this path with me, Nora. You're already a few shades brighter."

CHAPTER FOURTEEN

Friends or Froze

FERN

—

Night stretched into day and repeated itself several times over.

The sea stretched out in all directions. No land in sight. Roots far too deep underwater for me to reach. To be stuck in a place void of earth would usually make my skin itch, but I appreciated the rest it gave me. We needed to get to Northbrook. My mom taught me about strength, taking on the weight of protecting others. I needed her strength now.

The Mares took turns propelling our boat forward. Skylar periodically used the wind to our advantage to help push and steer. Right now, Ms. Lancer was on break while Kai and Dr. Hansen used their Gift at the back. Skylar also rested, the sails catching wind on their own. Kai's mom sat on the ledge to my right and held Prince Henry, humming to herself as he slept. We haven't had any similar episodes with him since Stone Creek. I wondered briefly if he would accidentally sink the ship if another fit caused an Animus Gift outburst and then distracted myself with something else. Better not to give him ideas.

Skylar sat in a circle with Leo, Molly, Persephone, and Mr. Harris. Leo found a deck of cards inside the cabin, so for the past few days, the twins taught everyone else how to play several games. It was a welcome distraction and passed the time well. I watched them from my seat along the ledge, finding it more entertaining to watch the game play out instead of joining in.

Molly partnered with Persephone, finally getting the hang of what Leo appropriately called Cheat. They shared a collection of red and black cards, obscured to everyone but me facing the same direction. The team rotated clockwise, so it went Leo, Skylar, Mr. Harris, and then Molly and Persephone. The rules were deceptively easy: take turns placing cards face down in sequence from 2 to Ace four times. The game ended when there were no more cards in play, or more likely, when someone claimed a cheater and that cheater was caught. After all, it was nearly impossible to always have a seven when you needed to put down a seven, so you needed to pretend. Someone could catch you in a lie if you lacked confidence or if they had enough sevens to be suspicious.

It wasn't a game where you really needed a partner, but Molly was always too slow either reacting to her turn or deciphering the correct sequence and gave herself away. Persephone directed her body language, pointed at cards, and whispered how Molly should play several steps before it came around to her.

Leo eyed his sister, trying to decipher if she was being genuine or deceptive when she said things out loud like, "Play your Jack. Yeah, that's a Jack."

A build-up of tension rose between the players. Leo laid a Queen down; Skylar claimed a King; Mr. Harris said two Aces.

Persephone poked Molly, and she shouted with a jolt, "Cheat!"

Mr. Harris gave her a surprised look.

"Show us those cards!" demanded Persy.

Our teacher chuckled, pleased, and revealed his cards. I leaned forward to see one Ace of Spades and one Ten of Clubs. The cheater was caught, and everyone dropped their concentrated facades. Molly gleamed as Persephone hyped her up, the two giving each other credit for the win.

They chatted all at once, revealing their uncaught lies or how they were going to play in the following round. Leo collected the tall pile to prepare the one-hundredth game.

I wished Nora was here.

Where were you, Fern?

My eyes widened, and I perked up from my slouched position.

"Nora?" I half-whispered.

Fern?

I gasped, so sharply I could hardly breathe. She repeated my name two other times, calling to me. I stood up now, looking at both sides of the boat in confused alarm.

Mr. Harris and I locked eyes.

"Nora!" I announced like a crazy person.

Everyone stopped talking now, staring at me with the same puzzled expression.

Where are you? Hearing her voice again was like pulling a heavy blanket over my torso. I forgot how comforting she was.

"At sea," I responded, giving no other explanation to the others. I turned myself away to face the water. "Where are you?"

I'm in Northbrook.

Northbrook? Really? A cheery smile lightened my face. "Did you find my mom?" I asked, hoping.

They're both safe, she assured me quickly. *They fled, I'm not sure where.*

I bit my lip. My mom and Delilah were safe, but if they fled...then we wouldn't reach them in Northbrook anymore. My mom was certainly formidable as an ex-military Avlis. She knew how to use her Gift to its fullest extent from earth to metal.

She could hold her own against the Anti-Gifteds Movement but if the Diviner caught her, she wouldn't stand a chance. She would go somewhere he could never find them. Somewhere I didn't even know.

Nora weaved through my worried thoughts. *Fern, this is crazy. How are we talking right now?*

"Fern, what's going on?" Mr. Harris asked.

I turned back to our team, shaking my hair as an answer. Red strands puffed out like a lion's mane.

"I'm talking to Nora right now. Is that something an Animus can do?" My words were too direct because Mr. Harris didn't blink for a little too long.

"You're talking to Nora right now?" he asked.

"She's in here," I pointed to my temple which didn't make me look very credible. "She's literally talking to me in my thoughts right now, Mr. Harris."

I placed my hands on my hips to stop myself from fidgeting anymore.

We all glanced at the baby Animus. "He's definitely

staring at you," Leo commented.

Those blue eyes didn't blink either. I would have been amused at how scary a baby could be if it wasn't directed at me.

Mr. Harris held his mouth open for a few breaths, his voice not quite reaching a conclusion. "I had to keep my Gift a secret, so I didn't hone it in," he finally confessed. "But considering what he's already capable of...he *could* create connections as he figures out the world. When did Nora start talking to you?"

"After I thought of her."

"And Nora?" Mr. Harris prompted.

I turned away from him as though to ask but only stared out at the ocean. "Mr. Harris says that Prince Henry created a connection," I finally answered, wondering if she heard my full conversation or only when I purposefully spoke to her. "What were you thinking about before you heard my voice?"

A long pause ensued. "Nora?"

I was thinking of you, she answered delicately. *And the team and how I left things. Mr. Harris is with you? Who else? Did everyone–?*

"Everyone is here." I turned to the team and gestured with a smile, forgetting that she wasn't here to see. I looked over to the back of the ship, "We even picked up Kai's mom and his doctor mentor in Stone Creek."

***

We continued to talk, me pacing the deck as the others stared and waited for context. Nora was in Northbrook but refused to come to the coast. Just like Prince Henry, the Diviner shared a telepathic connection with her. The idea disgusted me.

I ran tapping fingers along the boat's ledge as we figured out where else we could go that wasn't Northbrook. How could I stay away when we were so close? Where could we possibly go without Cassius and his army finding us?

I imagined the kingdom's map once again. All those little dots that were important to us. Below Norburn, there was a large stretch of mountains. It was the least populated area in the country due to its uneven terrain and its separation from main cities. The settlements there were far and in between, mostly made up of Auras who could find the best vantage point from the sky.

The Diviner should focus on attainable territory first, and he could even ignore the mountains entirely if it was too much trouble for his military. What threat did Gifteds living off the grid pose against his rule? Hardly any from what I could come up with. We could always go there. If I could dig through the rock, we could even make an underground hideout. Even Auras wouldn't be able to find us if we did that. I clawed the air absently, imaging the action. She was the only missing piece.

"I haven't forgotten our promise," I said resolutely, and I listened to her rattle off what she could do while a prisoner. I could have smiled if the last word didn't sting so much.

Our connection fractured when the shout of my name jolted a ripple of fear through me. I turned to face Persephone, the source of the voice. Everyone else was looking at something beyond the ship, out there at sea.

Fern?

I didn't respond, walking closer to get a better view. There. Water propelled on either side of something, someone—a Mare—coming straight for us. We all continued to stare, partly confused and dazed at the sight, until he got closer; I could see his pale skin and almost white hair.

Fern? she repeated, more concerned.

I squinted. "Wait, that's Isaac Winters."

His movements were sharp and precise, but a sinking feeling fell in my chest at the malice in his expression.

"Why does he look like that?" I was talking to our team present now, but I heard Nora say my name one more time before a silence snapped between us like a disconnected chord.

Prince Henry and the rest of us held our focus on the Ice Mare. Could Cassius have done something to him?

My fears were realized as he stopped suddenly, close enough now that we could see the deep red in his eyes, bloodshot like he hadn't slept in days. Ice formed as quickly as he halted, giving him a platform and a direct line towards our ship.

Skylar jumpstarted the sails, and our bodies lurched like a carpet pulled from underneath us. My palms hit the deck. We raced forward, but Isaac was quick to follow.

I bolted upright, noticing Kai hanging over the boat's edge. I ran to his side, passing by Ms. Lancer as she handed Molly the baby, telling her to hide in the cabin.

Kai slipped; I grabbed him by the ankles before he could completely fall overboard.

"Lower me more!" he demanded.

I didn't question him before, and I wasn't going to question him now. I lowered my arms down, my body firmly pressed into the boat's side.

Ice crept up the wood paneling, spikes jutting out of the water at either side of us from Isaac's hand. If he surrounded us on all sides, we would be at a standstill. I remembered our defeat against him in the Simulation Lab, but then he was merciful. Back then, it was a lesson. This? He was out for blood.

Kai's arms outstretched as far as they could go. His palm slammed the wood, and the ice melted back into water.

"Lower!" he called.

My wrists strained from his swinging weight. "I can't!" I called back.

He murmured something to the wind, continuing to palm the ice in his reach. He was delaying the freeze with the little ice powers he had, but this couldn't be a long-term solution, and he knew it. Kai's body relaxed, steading himself against the boat's side. The ice crept forward again, this time wrapping around his hands.

"Kai!" I shouted, struggling to lift him back to safety.

The ice melted from his fingers, and water trailed down the entire boat's side until the threat completely receded. Kai hollered a small victory, and I took the cue to bring him back onto the deck. I stumbled, heaving from the new relieved pressure, but Kai was already giving me a quick *thank you* and sprinting to help his mom.

Mr. Harris shouted orders. Ms. Lancer held her feet firm at the front of the ship, and Skylar was a small spot in the sky, hovering in the air as a guide. Green caught my focus. We were heading towards land and at a desperate speed.

A spike of ice, like a glacier, formed out of the sea. The boat slammed into its side. Chunks of ice broke through the paneling, and I rolled, sweeping my hand over to use my Gift for protection but nothing happened.

Our pace slowed to a cruel crawl as ice shredded against the ship. Leo and Persephone rushed over, the iceberg so close they could press their palms against it. Leo used his one good hand to bring its shape down while his sister stepped back, building a fire in her hands. She created discs out of flames before, but she stretched her arms further and further apart like she was molding clay until the fire disc was large enough to saw an entire section down with one throw.

We dislodged, the boat dredging forward and taking on water. Mr. Harris called for Dr. Hansen, and she wasted no time standing over the left-hand side—removed from any ledge—and directing the ocean from sinking us.

Molly sprinted out of the cabin with Prince Henry in hand, her clothes drenched and the baby crying. I noticed loose items floating above a new sea line before Molly shut the door behind her in a vain effort to keep it contained. She found Mr. Harris and stood close to him, struggling to keep her balance and the child in her arms.

I looked over to Isaac, still at sea and walking toward us, ice forming with each hard step.

Land was closer now. A stretch of sand and rock and trees lined the horizon. Civilization beyond the beach meant this wasn't the dense forest of Northbrook, but from where we were, I didn't see anyone on the coast witnessing our fight.

All three Mares were working in tandem, rushing us closer and closer. The wind howled with great effort by Skylar's aid. The sea sprayed in my face and blurred my vision. I watched land grow larger. I really thought we were going to make it.

Ice broke through the back with a splintering fracture, ripping a fourth of the ship from its body. In another instant, ice encased the underbelly and lifted us out of the ocean completely. The boat's nose slanted downward, enough to bring all of us into a cluster there.

Glancing to the beach, I could see we were practically at

the shoreline. A few yards of water rolled in small waves before us. My fingers twitched, feeling the earth close by.

Skylar landed back onto the deck with a thud, crumbling from gravity's weight. Dr. Hansen came over to her aid, propping her up against what we had left of a banister. She was panting, fatigued, and so was everyone else—either from using their Gifts or from sheer terror.

The boat settled, and then there was an eerie silence.

Frost crept on all sides; our breaths visible with each passing second. He was going to freeze us like he had at the Simulation Lab. Except this time, it was real. Certain death. We knew the Diviner could mind control people—seen it and felt it for ourselves—but if the Diviner was in Northbrook with Nora, then something else snapped entirely within Isaac Winters.

He revealed himself, ice lifting him to our position. I steadied my breath, concentrating as he landed onto what remained of the deck. He wiped the hair out of his eyes, panting.

Mr. Harris stood, all our attention deviating to his sudden movement. He kept a steady gaze on his former student, and Isaac returned it. I wouldn't let them fight. I just needed a few more seconds.

Mr. Harris jolted into a charging position, and I used the distraction to the fullest of my ability. Vegetation clung onto the remaining haul like a giant squid, and with a heavy groan, we broke away from our icy confinement. Everything I could reach—grass, branches, shrubs, flowers—wrapped around our frames to hold us steady. Mr. Harris, specifically, was held in place by an unbreakable ribbon wrapped around his feet.

The vines rolled us over the sand until we were within the

safety of a wooded area between beach and residential homes. We stopped, the others taking a few seconds to understand what had just happened and their new surroundings.

I stood, commanding hidden roots to sprout from the dirt and trees to lend me their leaves so I could entwine them into more vines. They had used all of their Gifts getting us here. Renewed, I would get them to our new home.

I slammed my foot down, and the earth collapsed and parted, creating a tunnel entrance. "Get inside!" I ordered, keeping my attention on the water. He would be here any moment.

They did, though I heard some protest from Leo, who was quickly intercepted by Persephone, and by Mr. Harris, who was yelled at by Ms. Lancer.

"The prince needs a mentor!" she shouted on her way down.

When I knew it was safe, a swipe of my hand closed the dirt's surface above them. Scraping my foot where I stood, almost looking like I was bored and started a tick, the ground gently parted further and further out so my team could run further and further away. Everything was so soft here, easy to direct. It wouldn't be this easy where we were going.

But first, we needed to lose Isaac.

Was there a point to try and reason with him? What Cassius did couldn't have been absolute, could it? Even if it was futile, I decided to try. If he still attacked, then I would do the same.

"Isaac!" I shouted out.

Isaac didn't bother stalking forward like he did earlier. He made his presence known—a tree exploded at its trunk and the others began to wilt from a covering of frost, living up to his last name. Even so, I could tell that his energy was waning. His body hunched over as he walked like he couldn't keep himself upright anymore, and the display was fierce but only a display.

"We're not your enemies!"

A cascade of ice launched my way. I blocked, afraid it would reach the hidden tunnel. The dirt iced over and hardened; I detached my hold and ran back into the open.

"Cassius did something—"

I cut myself off with a sharp gasp as he attacked me again with the same move. The ground shifted under my feet, helping me move with quick precision. Isaac leaned on a tree at this point, and I found my chance.

I halted and opened my arms out wide. The ground parted, and Isaac fell in. I brought my arms back to my chest in a sharp movement, crossing my ankles for added emphasis. The ground closed, and Isaac disappeared with it. Tree roots loosely snagged his form. I didn't want to kill him. His ice would make it difficult for him to dig back up, hardening in place with his manic touch. That was enough.

"I'm sorry," I murmured, reopening the tunnel's entrance for myself.

Turning away, I descended and closed us in once again beneath the earth.

CHAPTER FIFTEEN

Faywater
FERN

———

"Underground...again," Skylar smacked her lips in disapproval.

I didn't bother responding at this point, and if I could, my lungs were already threatening to give out. Dirt parted as quickly as I could walk, my pace slowing from a stomp to something brisk in the last hour or so.

The small city of Faywater bustled above us. I could feel the clatter of feet, of resting buildings in sunken places and of parks light and flowering.

I halted, my fingers brushing with clay. Too thick to go through right now. I patted the wall, deviating our path to the left.

"Fern." Mr. Harris put a firm hand on my shoulder.

Stopping, I realized how much clay caked my hands and mucked up my shirt. How frantically had I been pressing us forward? Turning, I noticed how their worn faces only worsened in the dim fire light in the twins' hands. He didn't need to say anything else.

"Let me find a safe opening for clean air," I suggested.

"Hey," Mr. Harris tried again, stopping me in my tracks this time. "Rest and tell us about your conversation with Nora."

I resisted the urge to tie my hair up, strands clinging to my neck in sweat. "She's in Northbrook," I confirmed, "with the Diviner."

"I knew it!" Skylar yelled.

"Not like that!" I waved my arms in dismissal. "She's forced to join him on his conquest. She said we need to find somewhere else to go—somewhere he can't find us."

"What about your family?" asked Kai.

I gulped. "They escaped, but we have no idea where they are now." There was a pause, eyes downcast. I created a crudely drawn Iridion map on the wall behind me. "But I think if we tunnel our way to the mountains below Norburn, we can hide out there. It's the last place the AGM would look."

Skylar whined quietly to herself.

Doubt laced Kai's voice. "Isn't that...far?"

"*Yeah,*" I stretched the word out in a sigh and then stood straighter, determination in my next sentence. "I can get us there. Let me get that air."

As I treaded a little further away from the group, Mr. Harris didn't stop me this time. I continued walking for several more paces and closed my eyes, feeling the earth around me. I imagined being below ground was like being in the sea for Mares. Comforted by the silence, swaying in the shifting waves of tectonic plates. How the surface warmed with sunlight and the bottomless, cold abyss.

Roots pushed through the tunnel walls like hands reaching for mine to follow. I let them guide me, their pulses beating in time with mine and leading me up, up, up to the surface.

There.

One root, so thin I could accidentally break it, belonged to a patch of clovers. There wasn't any movement nearby nor wind, but there *was* indirect lighting from above. Heavy objects laid dormant in an organized pattern. A shed perhaps? That would be the perfect place to bring in air without alerting anyone of our presence.

I crawled up its path and slowly poked my head out. A wireframe of aluminum formed a warehouse, and thin lines of light illuminated the people within, laying like stones on their sides.

I gasped, and several heads lifted to the sound. Metal rattled as they shifted and eyes opened, slow and full of sleep.

Muffling a scream with one hand, I shuffled backwards through my tunnel and ran back to the group.

"Fern?" I collided with Persephone, ignoring Kai's inquisitive voice.

"I found something terrible. *Come here*," I blurted, terror lowering my voice an octave. Pulling her along by the arm, she followed. The others did too, and I pointed at the hole leading to whatever nightmare I just witnessed.

Persy gave me a concerned glance before crawling through first. I was right behind her as she came to the opening, pulled herself through, and ignited a flame. Maybe I was imagining things. Maybe I really needed sleep. Maybe she would find nothing and think I was crazy.

"Oh my Divine."

Not crazy. Definitely *not* crazy.

I stood beside her, frozen in place as the others saw too. What I mistook for storage was really *people*. At least twenty of them, women and men of all ages, crammed together in the bare bones of a warehouse. The metal rattling came from chains binding their hands and feet to the ground. Most of them couldn't lift their heads for too long; heads plopped back onto the ground with an unceremonious thud. Their clothes hung loosely on their forms, and dirt and oil coated their hair.

"What *is* this?" Skylar demanded, hopping from person to person in brief examination.

They watched her fly, expressions of envy or longing trying to break through their blank stares.

"It's disgusting," spat Leo, his fire growing in intensity.

"It's the Anti-Gifteds Movement," Mr. Harris said. "Look at their hands. They're Gifteds."

Kai bent down beside a woman in her mid-60's and rotated her wrists with little effort. No branded U.

Molly hovered her palms cupped over her mouth. "How did they subdue your Gifts?" she asked, leaning to the slumped man in his mid-20's nearest to her.

"There were too many," a voice whispered. We turned our heads to a woman who was old enough to be my mom, and Molly ran over first, even falling to her knees to be at eye level. She clasped her hands over the woman's tied ones.

"Lancers, *water*," Molly snapped.

Ms. Lancer wasted no time, using the conserved water in the nearby clovers to provide enough for a sip. I feared she would use her Gift outside of the warehouse and alert any guarding soldiers, but the chained woman cherished even that little bit.

"Please tell us what you can," said Molly, her voice low

and delicate without the rasping hiss in her throat.

"Ask her yes and no questions so she can shake her head," suggested Mr. Harris, walking closer. "Did the AGM do this to you?"

The woman nodded in confirmation.

"Did they force you out of your home?" Molly asked. A prickle rolled over my shoulders. I could still hear their fists against Mr. Harris's door.

She nodded again. "So many," she whispered, looking down.

Faywater was known for its large Unfortunate population. Gifteds here could fight, but just as ants could overpower with sheer numbers, so could the AGM.

"Have you seen the Diviner?" Molly asked.

"He's king now," grumbled the man in his 20s. I crossed my arms over my chest, holding back a biting, *We know.*

Molly made a sour face before asking again, polite to the woman in front of her. "Have you seen the king?"

She shook her head.

"That makes sense," Molly noted, rubbing her pinkie finger against the woman's bruised but unbranded hand.

I remembered the night Molly lost her Gift to the Diviner. We were in a warehouse similar to this one. I could only imagine how she was feeling. All I could think about was metal meeting the flesh of Cal's stomach and locking into his ribcage. I forced my mind back to happy thoughts though those were few and far between at the moment.

"How long have you been here?" Molly brought me back to the scene at hand.

The woman put her hands up and shrugged in a way that said she didn't know.

Kai spun in a small circle, his head craned to the ceiling.

"It's a wait station," he announced. "Not just a prison."

"For what?" asked Persy.

Lines of Gifteds corralled into the castle. I knew *for what* before Kai even said it.

"Cassius is going to come and take their Gifts."

A small chaos erupted from our group as we turned to look at each other in dread. "How far is Northbrook from here?" Skylar landed back onto the ground, her Gift blossoming to life around her.

"He's at least a day's trek away," I confirmed, putting my hands up in an appeasing gesture.

"He might be at a wait station there," Kai added.

Skylar charged toward our tunnel. "We have to leave right now. He could be on his way, or we can be captured too."

"No!" Molly shouted among the murmurs. I jumped and stared at the entryway, fearful someone posted outside would hear us freak out. The chained Gifteds didn't even so much as whimper.

When the door didn't slide open, I looked back to Molly. Her eyes trained on each person, and I couldn't tell if she was going to cry or if she was finding her words.

"We can't leave them like this."

"Look at them, Molly." Skylar twisted back and mocked a presenting gesture. "How do you expect us to free all of these Gifteds and make sure they don't get recaptured or killed in the process?"

Protect all you can. "We can take them with us!" I shouted as loud as a whisper would let me. This is how I could fulfill her promise. Save Gifteds in wait stations along our route. Build an army to turn the tide instead of avoiding capture.

They paused, contemplating for a breath. Leo's light dimmed with the reflection of his frowned lip.

"They're too weak," he said. "They won't make it—they'll slow us down."

"Let them decide that," I countered. "They deserve the choice."

"They already have a choice." Skylar's voice and stare cut through me. Her fists clenched and her teeth bit down hard against her jaw like she was trying to contain her anger. "My father...my father had a choice. Pledge himself to the new king or downcast his family as Unfortunates. I'm sure their options are no different."

Mr. Stanton chose the king. Chose to keep the riches he had. Chose to look the other way. In some messed up silver-lining way, he chose Skylar too. That was what they must have talked about in his office the day we traveled to Caliel. While searching the mansion, we found Skylar's mom bound to a bed, blankets stuffed into her mattress. Molly knew before the rest of us. *Look at her eyes*, she demanded. Though the transformation was more obvious in Molly's eyes, going from an unnaturally bright red to amber, we could see how vacant Mrs. Stanton's eyes were. The twinkle was gone. The iris turned grey. The king's threat was serious. Of course, a man would not want the same fate upon himself and his daughter.

When I didn't respond fast enough, Skylar continued, addressing the chained Gifteds. "Who among you wishes to join us? Raise your hands."

Stillness.

She looked directly at me again. "There you have it."

My mouth opened to object but someone else said something before me—a small voice from the left corner. It belonged to a woman close in age to the one Molly sat next to.

"I...would like to go."

Persy zigzagged her way over. She pressed her index and middle fingers together, a bright yellow fire burning where her fingertips would be. With two swipes, the Gifted's hands and feet were free from their bind.

"Come with me, Celia." The woman extended a hand to another woman who vaguely resembled her. Celia nodded, and Persy freed her too. The two Gifteds supported each other as they walked toward us.

"Anyone else?" Skylar's voice didn't sound welcoming.

I stepped forward, the ground lifting up beneath me until I was on higher footing. I addressed the chained Gifteds with my hands on my hips. "Your Gifts and your lives are always in danger with him as ruler. We're going to a place the king cannot find us, and we *will* end his rule. We can't do that without you."

Some looked at me. Some closed their eyes. Some raised their voices, asking to go.

CHAPTER SIXTEEN

Gifted Spotlight
NORA

Sneaking around the tent was the only thing keeping me grounded and rational. As the latter half of a day passed and the moon rose steadily in the sky, anger still boiled in my chest and brought fire to my nerves. Cassius humiliated me during the best chance I had convincing his soldiers he wasn't their savior. He fed into their fantasy of us and then dared to tell me I was growing brighter.

My legs twitched with the desire to run—all the way to the coast like Fern suggested—but that victory would only be temporary. Either I led Cassius straight to my friends, or he'd catch me and I would remain locked inside the castle. Staring out a window waiting to be saved for an eternity.

I encircled the tent where all seven of Cassius's generals accompanied the king in one place, forming a war room. Each morning, Poppy would relay her battalion's duty but offered little information as to our full intentions or other battalions' assignments.

After hearing Fern's voice ten days since their escape, new hope blossomed with the rise and fall of my chest. I would find out whatever I could about upcoming plans and assist my friends. I would do anything to take Cassius down once and for all.

Voices muffled through the tent's fabric; too many to decipher individual phrases.

I shuffled to the next side of the tent and fervently pressed my ear again.

Cassius was speaking, but it took me a heartbeat to register his words. "Isaac will report once we move inland toward Faywater. There, we can resupply ourselves with everything. Food, soldiers..."

Laughter erupted behind me. I stifled a gasp, turning around but seeing no soldiers still awake and loitering about the camp. I shuffled closer to the tent opening just in case.

"What about my battalion, sir?" Poppy's voice rang out crisper than I expected. I retreated a half-step away from the tent, but no one was the wiser of my presence.

Cassius paused, and I kept my mind blank in case he detected me.

Finally, he spoke. "You are to move south. The insurgent Gifted students were spotted leaving Stone Creek by boat. Scour the beaches in case they intend to hide in the forest. You said that the Fairaways were already missing when we arrived?"

"Yes, Your Majesty," Poppy replied. I could practically feel her tilt her head down. "They must have fled sometime between our siege and your coronation."

I sighed a breath of relief, thankful that my demand for her secrecy was acceptable and maintained. In that moment,

I feared Cassius would hunt Fern's family down if he found out they were actively escaping Northbrook. But that had been hours ago. There was no chance of him finding them now.

"General Poppy." Cassius brought me back to attention, dark curiosity lacing his words. "Why are you lying to me?"

A spark of panic clenched my stomach.

I could hear Poppy stutter. "Sir?"

"I can review your memories," Cassius explained, as calm and clear as addressing his entire army. He wasn't just reminding *her* of his power. "Ms. Daphne Fairaway incapacitated you and fled with her Makan daughter. Why are you not reporting accurately?"

Poppy inhaled. "If you are reviewing my memories, Your Majesty, then you must already know why. My lieutenant requested that I don't tell you, and I decided the true chain of events made no difference to the disappointing outcome."

Her answer resounded with more professionalism than I ever heard her speak. She was excellent at switching between her servant voice and her carefree one.

Still, Cassius caught on to her word usage. "*You* decided?"

A soft thud rippled on the ground. Poppy must have kneeled and quickly. Her voice came from where I crouched and not above my head anymore. "I'm sorry for offending you, Your Majesty. It won't happen again."

Silence filled the tent, and even the outside world quieted until Cassius spoke again. "No, it won't. Rise so we may continue."

Footsteps indicated it was time to switch places again. I back peddled until I was behind the tent. I counted out the heartbeats in my head, waiting for whoever to pass before listening in on the war room again.

"What are you doing?" a whisper erupted in the stillness.

I stumbled but regained myself, ready to fight my way out of capture. Ellie and Holly faced me with inquisitive expressions, and I pushed down my fighting impulses.

"You're lucky we're not Bree," Holly whispered again, soft and careful.

"Or Poppy for that matter," added Ellie, her words more grave and consequential. "Now get up. Let's leave the general's work to the generals."

Ellie grabbed my wrists and pulled me up. I followed with little effort, neither wanting to cause a scene or to give them a reason to turn me in. I learned what I could tonight. If I connected with Fern again, I would relay what I knew to her. Cassius hadn't explicitly said it, but I knew him better than I cared to admit. He would *not* use me as bait at Northbrook's shoreline if they still landed here.

"I noticed that Bree wasn't at judgment," I said as we walked back to our campfire. "Or with you two right now."

"She's a very busy gal," Ellie said, shrugging.

"Bree's really good at wires and stuff," added Holly.

"*Wires?*" I didn't hide my confusion.

"Well, I write the speeches and the articles." Holly counted out on her palm.

"Don't forget the headlines!" Ellie jumped in.

"And the headlines," Holly nodded, "But Bree's someone who can broadcast to the whole country. She's very skilled with computers. Always tinkering."

The brutish soldier who threw rocks at me...was also skilled with computers? The idea couldn't fully process in my head, but these two didn't have any reason to lie about their comrade. A techie right under my nose. Poppy chose her soldiers well.

If we weren't at war, would they still pursue their current interests? I wanted to think so, even if logic told me they'd still be occupied with dirty dishes and piled laundry and Gifted guests. I could no longer deny the value the Anti-Gifteds Movement gave to my people, but what Cassius intended for evil could *still* be used for good.

Realizing I was internalizing a quote from the Great Book, I halted just as we reached our little camp.

"You look lost in thought," Holly commented. She reached for my hands and encouraged me to sway. "If you're feeling dull, how about we play a game to spend our time?"

A game? I didn't respond, but I didn't have to. Ellie latched onto the idea in a heartbeat.

"Yes! Oh, let's play Gifted Spotlight. Nora, you can be the Gifted."

A flashlight appeared in my hand within a blink of leaving Ellie's pocket. I stared at its cool exterior.

"Only if you want to," softened Holly.

I didn't want to play, but it was clear they wouldn't let me hover over the war room for the rest of tonight. Anger continued to alarm my senses. I wouldn't be able to sleep well either, especially if my mind continued to drift toward Fern's voice and the very real possibility Isaac Winters had attacked her somewhere at sea.

At least this way, a game could start a trust between me, Ellie, and Holly. Here was my opening to change an Anti-Gifted's allegiance.

I wrapped my fingers around the flashlight and clicked it on. Stark white light beamed, illuminating the trees in front of me and plunging everything else into darkness.

"Let's play." I managed to offer my warmest smile. "With conditions."

Both girls glanced at each other from the edges of my vision.

I continued, "If I win, you have to stop talking or insinuating or acting on *anything* related to a forbidden romance between me and the king. There is nothing between us anymore, and I'm a prisoner disguised as a lieutenant. Holly, you will write that down and both of you will stop others from gossiping too."

Holly nodded, earnestly.

"I like a wager." Ellie crossed her arms and tilted to one side, confident. "If we win, you have to share everything. Why the king is so fond of you. Whether or not he's a good kisser or flirt. How you came to Galdor Academy and became friends with Gifteds. *Everything.* And Holly will make sure to write down every word."

Holly squealed and clapped her fingers together. "Yes!" she exclaimed, louder than her usual cadence. "Every. Word."

Everything, I grimaced to myself, but sharing everything was worth this wager.

"Okay," I extended my free hand, "how do you play Gifted Spotlight?"

***

The rules were deceptively simple. Equipped with only a flashlight, I walked through the night forest in search of Ellie and Holly, who played as themselves. When caught, I needed to claim the red ribbon off of their bodies. If I managed to take both ribbons, I would be the winner. If Ellie and Holly evaded capture by the time the moon was at its peak or if they successfully stole my light source, they would be the winners.

Paranoia gnawed at my senses as I crept through the forest. Trees reflected back as harsh, ghastly figures. The flashlight swayed to each side, catching sight of bushes and shrubbery in the same stark glow. Absolutely no signs of life.

My ears pricked at the rustle of leaves and groaning branches. The two soldiers were given a ten second head start to run and hide, their barrier the edge of our encampment. I shifted to the left, following the subtle crunching sounds coming from that direction.

This game reminded me of training in a Simulation Lab. If I wanted to, I could pretend that I was still learning how to become a Royal Crest Knight alongside my friends. These trees imitated Northbrook. Fern was lurking somewhere above me, and she'd use her Gift any moment to surprise attack. This flashlight was actually my sword, and I'd slash away entangling vines as they found my ankle. She'd catch me when I was too preoccupied, and she'd reveal herself, laughing with cheerful amusement, as I hovered upside down in her trap. My deadpan expression would only serve to make her laugh more, and then she'd get closer, composing herself while the glint remained in her emerald eyes. Her eyelashes would flutter, and I'd watch her lips as she detailed out what just happened with all its flair and exaggerated glory. Her lips...some freckles dotted along her mouth so close to mine.

I wrestled my imagination away just as a branch snapped from my right side. The flashlight beam danced wildly in front of me; I caught movement at a nearby bush and heard a small giggle.

"Hey!" I raced after her, the small giggle rising into an unbridled cackle.

Holly came into focus, her loose blonde hair swishing side to side. We were evenly matched in our speed, our heights not different enough to make any significant progress. I continued until my breathing became uneven. I stopped, watching her form disappear past the light's beam. Looking up to the moon, its pale face greeted me at an acute angle. There was still time before the clock ran out. I wouldn't waste my energy on the first chase.

A bird cooed above me, and I searched for its source. Open air and thick layers of canopy greeted me. Shadows seeped into bark divots and light fragmented off leaves.

Panting, I trudged forward. Holly probably deviated to one side, but maybe I could track her haste.

Following the path, I glanced at the ground for any feet impressions and to each side for any disturbed foliage. For maybe another hundred feet, there was no indication. But before I decided to give up, I noticed an upturned root and pieces of dirt flicked up like someone had tripped over it.

I crouched down, inspecting. Wouldn't I have heard a hard thud or even a yelp?

A bird—the same bird—cooed above me. As my flashlight whirled upward, suspicious, Holly giggled right behind my back.

I jumped, my light beaming at disturbed leaves but no person. My heart beat louder in my ear.

Giggling resounded to my right, just behind the wall of shrubbery. Holly darted as the light revealed her, but this time, she tried to run across my vision instead of away. Determined, I stepped forward to catch her when I tripped over the root and slammed into the dirt.

The flashlight fell out of my hand. Laughter echoed again. A hand illuminated at the edges of darkness, ready to snatch my light away.

I gasped. Scrambling to my feet, I claimed the flashlight

first and held it fiercely to my chest.

Holly appeared like a phantom, clawing at my forearms. Her nails cut deep, drawing crescent-shaped lines of blood along my knuckle and wrist. I wrangled against her, managing to block with my left and hold the flashlight with my right.

I flashed the beam directly into her eyes. Her entire face scrunched, and her arms hovered over her sight on impulse.

There. Her ribbon tied around her shoulder. I snagged the fabric, but the moment I did, Ellie dropped to the ground from above.

"Revenge!"

I stepped back, but Ellie already had her fingers around the ribbon's knot. "Yoink!"

"No!" I pressed my palm, but the ribbon was already in the other girl's possession.

I reached out with my other hand—the one holding the flashlight—and I realized in that half-heartbeat how stupid and desperate I was. My light separated from me, and the two girls pounced.

Their laughter taunted me from above, their faces twisted in shadow from the flashlight swinging in their hand. I flailed, but one kept my arms pinned while the other weighed down my legs. I lost. I lost. I lost.

"Nora?" Holly hovered over me, all haunt removed from the way she said my name.

The flashlight steadied between us. I didn't realize tears washed over my face until now.

Holly's eyes widened, surprised. She slinked off me and gestured for Ellie to do the same.

I sat up, panting from anger and exhaustion and frustration and sadness and longing. The two AGM soldiers watched me behind the light's glow.

"Easy," said Ellie. "It's just a game."

Holly swatted her friend before turning back to me, her expression filled with worry. "Are you okay?"

My attention deviated from her to Ellie to the flashlight and back to her. The tension released from my muscles, slouching my shoulders.

"I'm sorry," I finally said. "I don't know what came over me. You, you weren't the one who stole my light."

Holly's face softened at the bizarre nature of my comment, and her smile deepened. "So poetic. I think I'll write that down, too."

CHAPTER SEVENTEEN

In Search of Commonality
NORA

———

We returned to our tents, but instead of entering mine as expected, the two soldiers burst into Bree's sleeping quarters.

A curse and the clatter of equipment followed, but that didn't stop our intrusion. Ellie encouraged me forward, and I sheepishly tucked inside.

I recognized a wrench, screwdriver, pair of scissors, and grey tape among the small tools scattered along the floor. Bree sat with her headphones pulled back on one side so she could hear us. A humming box sat in front of her, connected to the headphones with a single wire.

"What are you doing?" she demanded. "I'm busy trying to contact the king's special operative!"

Ellie sat down with a deep sigh, completely ignoring the urgency in her comrade's voice. "How do you expect to contact Isaac so late at night and so far away?"

"He should be in Faywater by now scouting out those—" Bree paused, remembering I was here with a steel glare. "I'm not discussing anything with our *lieutenant* here."

Mockery laced how she addressed me. The mention of Isaac and Faywater brought a sting of dread and hope. If my friends did encounter him and escaped, they could be only a day's distance away. Still standing, I placed my hands on my hips.

"As your lieutenant, I order you to tell me what you're doing and why."

Bree scoffed, "I don't take orders from you." She turned the radio off and removed her headphones completely before standing. Taller than the tent's height, Bree completely overshadowed me as she said, "Even if you were a legitimate superior, my job comes from my general or my king."

I remained assertive. "Then I'll have a talk with your general or your king."

Bree scoffed again before turning away and sitting back down, the intimidation over. Holly flipped through her on-hand notepad to occupy herself while Ellie leaned in Bree's direction.

"Take a break," Ellie encouraged. "Nora is about to tell us everything."

Bree groaned. "Why do you two care so much about our king's love life?"

Ellie found Bree's shoulders and shook her side to side. "*You can't tell me you're not interested!*"

"And besides," chirped Holly as she clicked her pen, "Nora is telling us her whole life story. Wouldn't you like to know how she became Iridion's first Unfortunate soldier?"

"Yeah," chimed Ellie, "she practically started our revolution."

"Wait." I lifted both hands for them to stop, heat burning my entire body. "What are you talking about? I didn't—I didn't start the Anti-Gifteds Movement."

"Sit down." Holly patted the ground, but I remained standing, my voice becoming more firm.

"I *didn't* start the Anti-Gifteds Movement."

"No," Bree agreed, for once on my side. "You were certainly the catalyst though. Imagine the horror on our faces when they introduced an Unfortunate pretending to be a Gifted."

My eyes narrowed. She was referring to Mr. Harris's pet project: recruit me as Galdor Academy's first Unfortunate student with the promise of becoming a soldier. I remembered when he introduced me to the Senior Circle and how much my presence infuriated everyone in that room—even Cassius. Though at the time, he disguised his dismay as genuine concern for my safety.

I remembered the photos taken of me during the Simulation Lab as I fought alongside my team members. The AGM coordinated their first large-scale attack after those photos were printed, and Mr. Harris's plan to satiate the rising tension failed. The AGM wanted equity, not a token representative.

My hands tightened into fists at my side, a simmer to set the record straight directing my actions. "Are you ready,

Holly?"

Ellie closed one eye firmly shut and rotated her hands together over the other eye, imitating a camera operator with a lens. "*I'm* ready."

"I'm ready," repeated Holly.

I stared straight at Bree, conviction in my every word. "I never pretend to be anything other than an Unfortunate."

***

Holly scribbled as I spoke, slow and thoughtful of my words.

"How far back do you want me to go?" I asked, politeness forcing me to ask the question. I agreed to divulge everything, but I'd rather start with Mr. Harris's arrival over anything during my childhood.

"Let's start with your Choosing Ceremony."

My nails dug into my palms, restraining any poor reaction from etching my features.

"We can skip around, but I'd like some background," Holly continued, too engrossed in her own thoughts to notice.

When she finally looked at me from her paper, I started. I described my frilly pink dress and hair pin, which prompted the girls to share similar outfits they wore at their selected Choosing Ceremony. When I mentioned being selected at ten years old, Holly commented at how young that was and glanced at Bree.

I looked to Bree too, catching the unspoken connection. "When were you chosen?"

She offered another hard stare in return. "I was eleven."

"When did you learn how to do all of this?" I gestured to

the radio and scattered tools.

"As a free woman."

"And you think that's with the AGM?"

"I don't think so. I *know* so."

A sigh loosened my shoulders. We wouldn't get anywhere without commonality. I sat down. "I'm not a hero."

Bree's lips thinned. Holly's pen halted. Ellie's pretend camera tilted down.

I continued, "I attended Galdor Academy to fulfill a promise to a servant girl who was killed by Gifteds."

There was a pause, and then Holly asked, "What exactly was that promise?"

Valerie formed in my mind, brightened with the idea of our impending future and then muted with her sunken, unmoving expression. I pushed through the memory.

"I promised her I'd escape servitude no matter what happened. At the first chance I received. Mr. Harris arriving to the Montgomery House was that first chance." I hesitated, but I finished my thoughts, "I'm sure if the Anti-Gifteds Movement arrived first, I would be tempted to join."

They were listening intently now, focused and solemn.

Ellie stopped pretending to be a camera operator altogether and equipped a sketchpad and pencil. "What did Valerie look like?"

A pit formed in my chest as I glanced from Ellie to the paper in her hands. I didn't know if I was ready to see Valerie in full detail outside of my memories.

"She was the color yellow. My sunlight casting away the clouds and the rain."

My voice softened as pencil scratched on paper, but I couldn't see what Ellie drew. Inhaling slowly, I shared our days. Our joyful, terrible days at the Montgomery House.

Molly's attack. Our promise. Our escape lost before it even began. How I spent so much time in routine, detached from any identity or purpose until Mr. Harris arrived and changed everything. Holly was on her tenth sheet of paper, and Ellie was on her third.

"I will not apologize for fulfilling my promise, and I don't expect you to apologize for taking your first chance out of servitude either. I'm just sorry that your first chance to escape was through such violent means, and I'm sorry we remain enemies because of our allegiances."

A prolonged silence swept through the tent, but the air didn't threaten to suffocate me. It was nice to finally speak to Anti-Gifted members without being in the throws of battle or tense interrogation. In this moment, clarity breathed in and out of my lungs. All of the puzzle pieces clicked into place except one: the true solution to our blight.

"Why don't you support the king?" Holly finally asked.

I expected Ellie to add a comment about the way he looked at me or our mandatory tea ceremonies or his insistence that I remain alive, but her head remained down in fervent concentration.

"I used to," I confessed, leading into our introduction, growing friendship, and budding romance.

"I even," I hesitated, staring at the sword tucked at my waist. "I even pledged my loyalty to him when he gave me this weapon."

Their forms leaned forward. I swallowed back my pride and my sorrow. "I thought he was worthy to be king at the time."

Another silence.

"What kind of leader is he to you?" I found my asking in return, fixing my sight on Holly. "Why do you support a

Gifted as your Anti-Gifted leader?"

I knew part of the answer, even if I didn't fully understand it. Poppy asserted that he was touched by the Divine to liberate Unfortunates and downcast Gifteds. As the Diviner, he led an entire army of Unfortunates with the promise of their equity and effectively flipped our system on its head without actually changing anything. But as the prince, he had every right to call a Determination against his sister and prove himself more entitled to the throne.

I pressed one more question. "Why not prove himself as heir and make change from the inside?"

Poppy ripped aside the tent's entrance. "You should be asleep."

Her three battalion members bristled to attention, and I turned toward her. She looked down at us, stoic despite the strain in her face.

"This wasn't my idea," Bree said emphatically. "They barged into my tent, and—"

"Everyone return to your rightful tents," Poppy interrupted. "We're heading to the coast at daylight."

Ellie groaned like a child. "But *General*, Nora lost a bet and I'm almost done with some of her life story sketches!"

She ripped away a page and presented it to me. In shades of charcoal, I saw sunlight streaming through a large window-pane and a young woman draped in tendrils of fabric like smoke admiring its warmth.

Within a few blinks, the paper crinkled and distorted as Poppy ripped it away at the center. I gasped and instinctively reached out, but the drawing was already rolled up in a ball almost as tight as Poppy's jaw.

"You will go to bed now or I will burn the rest in the fire. I will hear no more excuses. Goodnight."

"But–"

"Yes, General." Bree sat up, placing her hand on her comrade's wrist to stop her from speaking out again.

"Goodnight, General," they said in unison with varying degrees of defeat.

Poppy remained in the entryway until Ellie and Holly filed out, slow and begrudging.

She gripped my forearm as I tried to pass. "What do you think you're doing?" she demanded.

I imitated her usual, careless demeanor missing from her current hardened one. "I'm becoming more familiar with our battalion, General. I *am* their lieutenant after all."

While she was taken aback, I ripped away from her hold. Entering my own tent across from Bree's, I caught sight of two more pages. One atop my cot and the other slumped in the corner as though Ellie had thrown them in with haste.

Zipping up the entrance, I collected the paper and bundled myself under the blankets. The flashlight still in my possession, I waited several minutes before illuminating the space around me.

The first paper depicted various minimalistic scenes of the same young girl, though her dark hair and clothes clung to her frame as though perpetually drenched in rain. She slouched, bitter and despondent, as she did household tasks. The last one must have been me cleaning out the gutters the day Mr. Harris arrived because the servant girl was almost completely darkened with soot and grime, peering off the roof's edge.

And the second depicted the same girl decorated in armor and adorned with a sword. She stood as I did; her expression read determined but weary. Brave despite fear. I wondered if that was how I looked to those AGM soldiers or if that was a version of myself lost in defeat.

I turned off the light after several more minutes and pretended I was drifting off to sleep in our dormitory on campus. Tomorrow, I would wake up and you would be sleeping soundly in the bed next to mine—white peonies dotting red hair.

CHAPTER EIGHTEEN

A Dandelion Wish

FERN

I couldn't feel my arms anymore, and a permeant migraine brought my mind to static with the mental strain to keep urging the earth forward.

We left Faywater. A few days ago, by Kai's calculations. Heading northwest by Skylar's intuition. I could see the Iridion map like it was right in front of me. *The mountains*, I repeated to myself. *We have to reach the mountains.*

Soil stopped parting automatically with each step. Stomping my foot down softened the dirt, and pulling my arms apart strained and strained and strained. Our progress slowed but I refused to stop. The others volunteered to dig with their own Gifts, as futile as their efforts were, so I could spare a break.

"Let me," Kai urged, and I watched him, his mother, and Mr. Harris chip away at the wall as I caught my breath. Mud and oil caked our skin, our clothes, our hair. The smell of dirt mixed with our sweat and lingered in the air.

Skylar stopped complaining and even volunteered to braid everyone's hair after we all appeared disheveled. Anything to make our work easier.

"Let me," she said, weaving with twitched fingers. Most of her first efforts were too loose, probably used to servants modeling her own hair, but she got better with time. Securing each one by knotting at our split ends.

The more Gifteds we rescued, the more cramped our underground tunnel became. Molly and Dr. Hansen watched over our growing population, sometimes carrying people one at a time from checkpoint to checkpoint if they were too weak, old, or sick.

"Let me," Molly said, talking the most out of anyone so we could have something to distract us. A conversation. A story about her younger sister. A song that echoed through the chamber. Her voice was untrained, but none of us minded enough to tell her.

Every night, the twins would take turns tunneling out of our makeshift cave to find food, water, and clothes. When they reported back, we would know which town we were in and which direction to head toward next. We slept huddled together despite the growing heat, and we watched over the group in rotations. We would suffocate down here if we weren't careful.

Day after day, it took longer for me to drift into sleep. Dreaming wasn't enough for my Gift to replenish well, but Nora was there sometimes, talking to me in a some sort of connected dreamscape if our proximity was relatively close. Prince Henry acted as the dial connecting our frequencies. Once we discovered each other the first time, she mentioned how Cassius would enter her dreams sometimes while at the academy. She was so hesitant to share that I decided to press later when she was no longer his prisoner.

"Fern?"

I turned away from the rolling countryside and found her behind me, cheeks flushed like she ran here. The wind picked up, and I held my hair, clean and untied, so it wouldn't get in my face.

"Nora?" I noticed how her eyes darted about. "Are you looking for something?"

A cobblestone cottage settled behind her. Smoke puffed out of the chimney, and the smell of chocolate chips enveloped my senses.

Her mouth hung open. "I thought...someone else would be here."

I pouted my lip. "Is it okay that it's me?"

A smile overtook her face like she was trying to fight it. She scoffed playfully and walked down the hill toward me. Stepping on her tiptoes, she wrapped her arms around my neck. "I'm glad it's you."

And another night while we deviated around Galdor.

We sat across from each other—Nora straight and proper in a deep red chair and me lounged in a stark white one. She sipped on tea, though there weren't any plates or kettles or even sugar bowls between us. Just red and white flooring, sleek and soft at the same time. A bright blue sky with fast-paced clouds expanded above us. I stared for a while since I hadn't seen the real sky for at least a week.

She spoke rapidly about the war, all the details she could think of to tell me. "Ellie and Holly have opened up to me, and

I think Bree might be starting to. Poppy is noticing, and she's definitely working against me. She was your ex-servant. What can you tell me about her?"

She stopped, and I slumped my neck over to look at her. Patient and somehow jittery all over. I wanted to move and hug her, but the pain of reality followed me here. I remained in my chair.

"How are you?" My voice carried over like a dandelion wish.

Nora rubbed her fingers along the cup and stared down at her tea, saddened wrinkles revealing themselves in her reflection. "I'm...trying my best. How are you?"

"Tired," I confessed, "but I'm trying my best too."

The floor tilted with a gust of wind, leaning us toward each other. The teacup was gone. Red and white connected and so did our hands.

I gripped her palms tighter, my fingers aching. "I believe in us."

Nora gave me a faint smile.

The unity flower settled.

More time passed—we were so close now. A newfound energy encouraged me forward. But the Gifteds we saved were now grumbling, hungry, hopeless.

Both Leo and Persephone came back from the surface, shaking their heads with grim expressions. They hadn't found anything. We were no longer within any city limits. We were no longer near any available food source.

That was two days ago. They surfaced recently again in hopes of any change and hadn't returned yet.

Sobs cried out every so often but died down quickly; distressed people were either comforted by Molly or too dehydrated to produce tears. No one moved unless they had to, reserving their own energy as I depleted mine. We were right at the base of the mountain range. We had to be!

After picking up Gifteds in wait stations along the way, we had a conspicuous group of twenty-three. Three were Avlis, but we rescued them recently and they were in no condition to use their Gift to help me. Our tunnel remained long but narrowed. I didn't close it behind us anymore. There were too many of us, and I needed to use the last of my energy forward. They were counting on me. *Nora* was counting on me.

My knuckles slid against something new, something sharp. My flesh tore open, and blood spilled down my hand. I winced, stumbling back.

"Let me see." Kai was already next to me. He reached for my hands, but I pulled them back despite their throbbing and shaking. I needed to keep going.

"Fern," he said my name sternly.

I ignored him, pressing my palm against rock. My entire body started to convulse with an effort to express joy.

"We're here," I rasped. "We just need to..." The floor wobbled; I steadied myself against the mountain's rough surface, head down and eyes closed. "...get inside."

"Fern," he said again, this time sympathetic. His arms found my elbow, trying to keep me steady. "If we're here, let's take a break. We can take a break."

"I have to..." I was heaving now. Oh Divine. I wished Mom was here.

Eyes still closed, I imagined her teaching me and Delilah how to defend ourselves with our Gifts. Endless and sometimes torturous as a child but oh so dearly missed now.

Baby sprouts?

I gasped, my throat dry and itching from the inhale. My eyes shot open, and I turned violently, the most effort I could exert to gaze upon Prince Henry. Of course!

Mom? I croaked.

Kai's concern grew, and he stopped me before I could step forward. "Fern, sit down."

I tried to explain to him, but my thoughts loosely connected with my voice. I mumbled incoherently as Kai helped me to the ground.

"I need water." He ushered to his mother.

My head throbbed; I closed my eyes once more and concentrated despite the pain. Mom doing the dishes. Mom meeting my friends for the first time. Mom bringing Poppy home.

Mom, we're underground going toward the mountains.

Mom, we're going to the mountains.

Mom, the mountains.

A plastic bottle nudged my lips, but I bent my head lower, my palms resting against my cheeks. *Mom, the mountains. Mom, the mountains.*

"Fern."

Kai lowered himself so he could see my face, but I refused to break my attention. After several breaths, water carefully smoothed over my skin. The sensation was both relieving and distracting; I looked at Kai as he swayed water across my forehead, below my eyes, and down my neck and chin before dispelling it to the dirt.

We stared at each other for a long time, though time was becoming harder and harder to comprehend. I blinked slowly.

"Are you okay?" he asked.

"We're so close, Kai. I just need to…" I looked at the rock

ahead of us; my shoulders slouched.

One hand rested on my knee, halting my initiative to stand. "Let's wait for Leo and Persephone to return."

So we did. In agonizing silence. The occasional cough disrupted the stillness. My thoughts lazily repeated themselves until they became gibberish. I heard Mom. She called me by a nickname she created. She could be right above our heads. She could be as far away as Faywater if Prince Henry's ability to connect far outreached his older brother's. But I heard her. Which gave me greater hope than my doubts.

Fine work she's done. Step aside, soldier.

I stood, and my legs finally gave out from under me. Kai found my arms before I could fall on my face; the ground rumbled as it tore apart somewhere down the tunnel. Apprehension and fear rippled through our group until Leo's voice echoed off the walls, more cheerful than I heard in a while.

"Look who we found!"

Pushing through the crowd, I saw her—*Mom*—with Delilah at her heels.

She smiled at me. "You've done brilliantly, baby sprouts."

"Mom!" I tried to step toward her, but my muscles twitched uncontrollably. She ran forward, catching me in time for a hug. Delilah joined, and we were together again.

"We also found something else," prompted Persephone.

Craning my neck up but not releasing our embrace, I saw what Persephone was carrying in her arms. Squash and pumpkin and cabbage and beats—all kinds of root vegetables.

My face scrunched, the action to cry, but I only blubbered. They must have found a farm. Finally, we could eat and finally, *finally* we could reach our destination. Alive and together. Alive and okay.

My mom hugged me tighter against her chest, laying me down. I tried speaking again, but the weight of everything became too much. My eyes fluttered shut, and the earth's sweet darkness greeted me with rest.

CHAPTER NINETEEN

A World Worth Fighting For

NORA

———

We traveled to the coast after Northbrook and stayed there, watching the sea ebb and flow. The horizon remained open for the rising and setting sun. I found myself glancing back to the ocean every time I tried turning away, both worried and hopeful that a ship would crest over the end of the world or would suddenly ambush the shoreline behind our backs.

I stayed up for as long as I could, imagining Fern in case she was close enough for a connection. I imagined my hand reaching out into the darkness and remembered the memories we shared. Dancing with the utmost freedom in a field of unity flowers. Dressing up for the Flower Festival. Training hour after hour. Sharing meals and stories and laughter. Even to the very beginning, when I found her a little odd for embracing me so quickly and still embracing me after finding out I wasn't a Gifted. I sighed every morning when her voice didn't resonate with new information, but I refused to let that deter me. Just as I had to hope when they first escaped, I had to hope they escaped again.

After three days, a messenger sent word that Isaac Winters had encountered my friends at sea, and their last known location became Faywater.

Arriving in the small coastal city, Poppy wasted no time shoving me in front of the king. We were in a large white tent with a circular table mimicking the one senior members sat at in Galdor. Cassius wore a simple black and brown outfit that reminded me of a soldier, but he still held the composure of his status.

What caught my attention, though, was Isaac Winters standing perfectly still in the corner of the room as though he was a statue. He didn't react to my presence, his stare as icy and indiscernible as ever. He appeared freshly cleaned with a few bruises purpling his exposed skin, and I wondered what he looked like when they found him.

Cassius's eyes glanced up, examining, and then his mouth pouted. "She doesn't know their whereabouts."

With a wave of his hand, he dismissed me and looked back down at the map in front of him.

Poppy pulled at my arm, but I wasn't going to waste this opportunity to learn what he gathered from Isaac. They must have escaped, but what did Isaac do to them?

I yanked but when Poppy's grip tightened, I thrashed. A guard inside the tent came to her aid, but my blade dug into the ground between his toes. He froze, shocked and face down, but before he could process I hadn't actually stabbed him, I lifted the hilt of my sword straight into his nose. Blood splattered against the back of my hand, and he stumbled back, covering his wound.

Poppy reached out for my hair, but I only felt the wind behind my neck. Charging forward, I pushed the table but Cassius gripped his side and forced a stalemate. I stopped wasting my energy, opening my mouth to speak when Poppy grabbed my wrist and twisted hard. I screamed, releasing the sword in my hand. I tried to turn around, but her other hand was already wrapped around my waist, ready to lift and forcibly remove me from the king's presence.

"Wait." Cassius lifted his hand.

We stopped struggling. Poppy released me but shoved me forward with an angry jab. She'd probably punish me later with drills or spars against her mallet, but I would bear the consequences.

Cassius smiled as though he was impressed, and I wondered what I looked like to him today. "It seems I've been rude. Was there something you wanted, Nora?"

Isaac hadn't even flinched during my burst of violence. He hadn't taken a step forward either to protect the king or to attack me. I glanced from the Ice Mare to the Animus.

"Release your hold on Isaac. I wish to know what he saw of my friends."

"I don't have to use my Gift on those loyal to me, remember?"

I frowned. *Because you brainwashed him*, I thought. "Then you will have no problem if I talk with him."

I began walking around the table, but Cassius blocked my path and made a *tsk* sound. "Alas, he is not loyal to you. He will not speak to anyone but me."

Convenient. "Will *you* at least tell me if you've captured or killed any of my friends?"

Cassius thought the question over. "All of the insurgents

escaped custody," he said, stirring the bitterness inside me by refusing to address them as the people closest to me. "None were killed, but it sounds like one harrowing ordeal."

I bristled. He must've chosen his words carefully, holding all of my attention for as long as he could. Cassius grabbed the map with one hand and my belt with the other, bringing both of us closer to him. The action caught me off guard, and I stumbled closer to his body than I wanted.

"They went underground." He tapped Faywater's location with his index finger. "If we don't find them soon, they might suffocate or starve to death. You wouldn't want that, would you?"

He gently placed my hand onto the map's surface, directing my index finger to our current location. "Where do you think they would go?"

I stared at the country, appearing so small condensed onto paper. There was Cherryville, where I spent most of my life serving the Montgomerys. There was Thunder Bay, my hometown, so close to Stone Creek, and the heavy Avlis populations at the furthest points of the world in Northbrook and Ironcrest.

Every dot was a place full of people—Gifteds and Unfortunates who had either already succumbed to their new ruler or were still living out their lives with some semblance of peace. Marks inked the page with his conquest. This was the world I was fighting for. This was the world Cassius was destroying.

In all honesty, I didn't know where Fern was. She hadn't told me where they'd go next instead of Northbrook. The last thing I wanted to do was to give him a guess, even if it was a complete lie, and be proven correct. Cassius watched me intently, reading through my struggled thoughts and waiting for an answer.

My flat palm turned into a claw, and I scrunched up the map in my fist, tossing it onto the floor at his feet. It was a childish move, but one where Cassius would have to bend down and pick up the trash. Poppy's shoulders rippled, aghast.

I scowled at the king, "If Fern has led them underground, I know they are safe."

He held my gaze. "Don't be so sure. As I was casting judgment here, some of the Gifteds saw them arrive above ground and take anyone who wanted to go with them. If you ask me, that's a lot of people to hide."

I smiled when his words meant to strike worry. "Then that's a lot of people safe from *you*. I trust Fern completely."

Cassius's jaw twitched.

"General," the king addressed, "you may escort your lieutenant out of the tent now. Fulfill your duties to show her our point of view, or I will be greatly disappointed. It seems like she's getting on with *others* in your battalion but not yourself."

Alarm crossed Poppy's face. She nodded quickly, snapping at me and gesturing to the tent opening. I obeyed this time, smiling at the thought of Fern out there somewhere, keeping her promise to me.

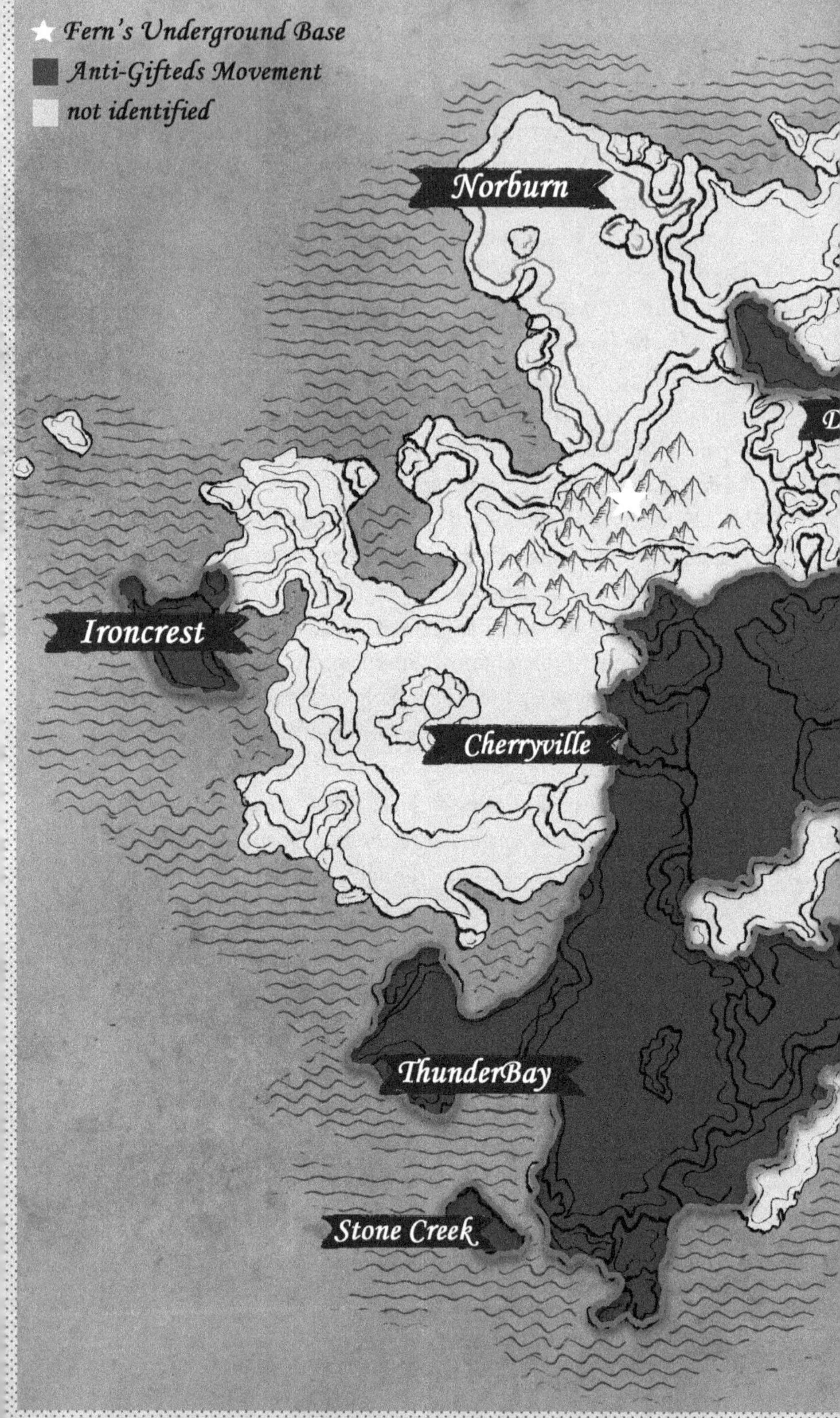

Fern's Underground Base
Anti-Gifteds Movement
not identified
Norburn
Ironcrest
Cherryville
ThunderBay
Stone Creek

1 Month Later
Caliel
Bellhaven
Osthall
ldor
Northbrook
vater

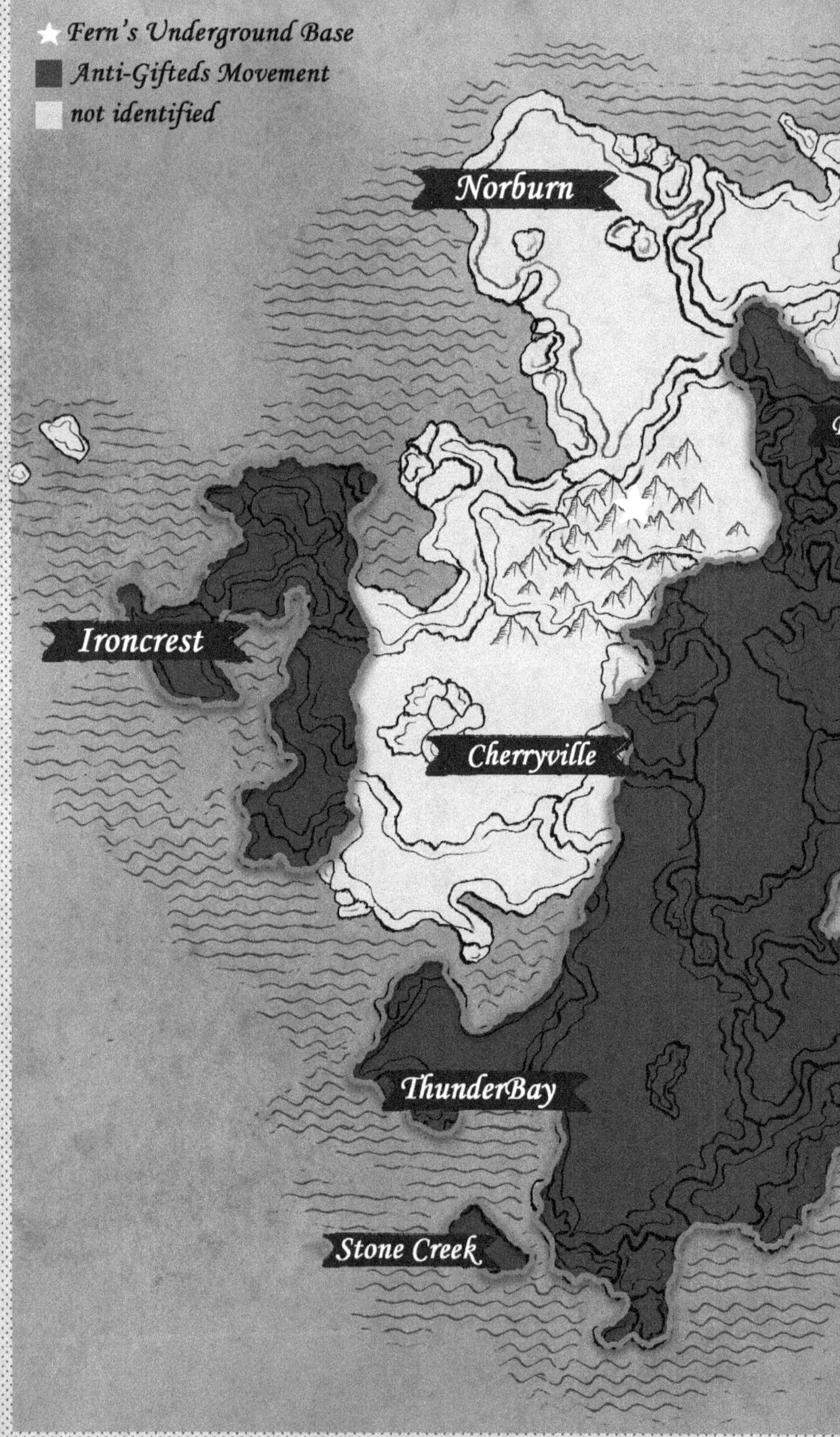

Fern's Underground Base
Anti-Gifteds Movement
not identified
Norburn
Ironcrest
Cherryville
ThunderBay
Stone Creek

2 Months Later
Caliel
Osthall
Bellhaven
aldor
Northbrook
water

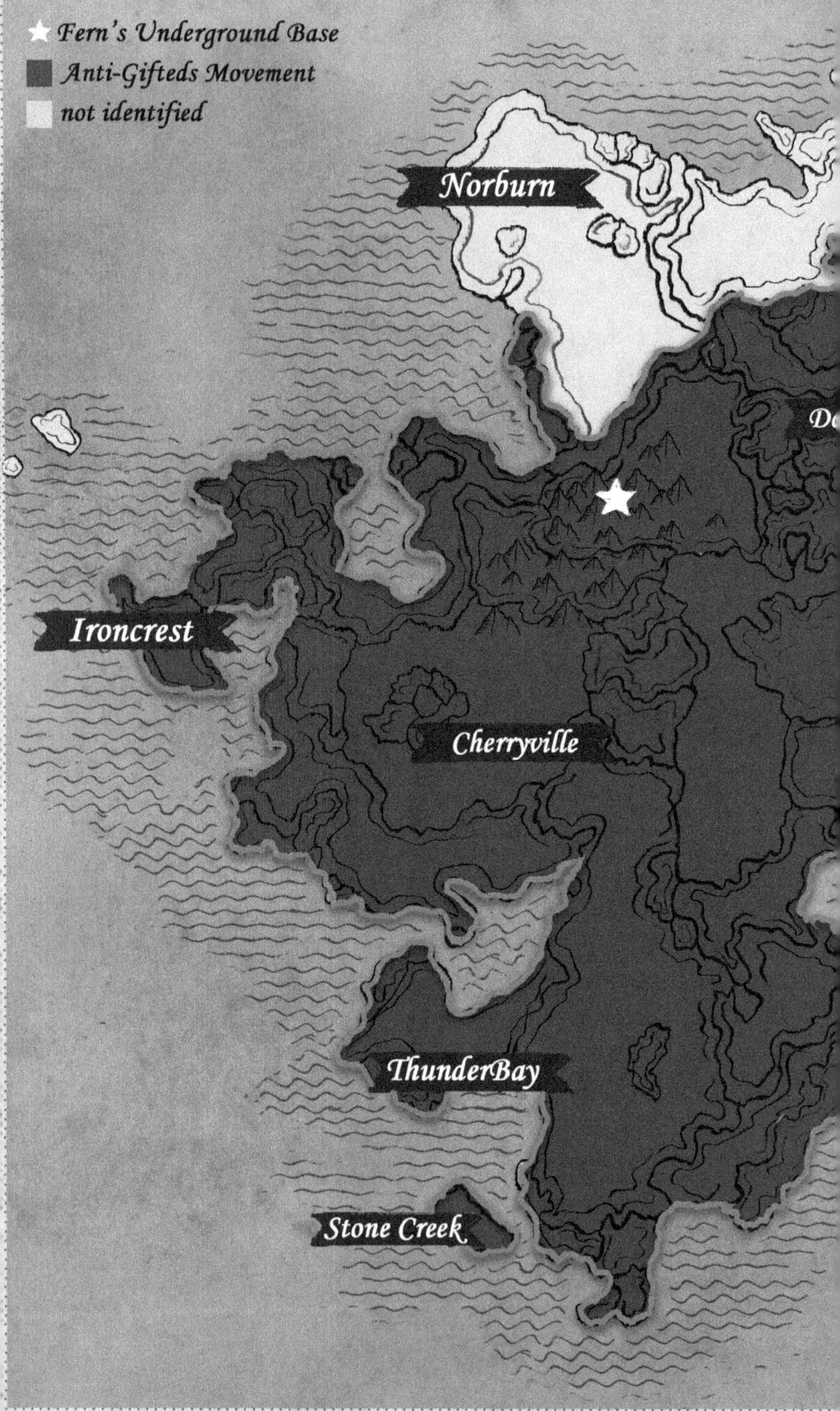

Fern's Underground Base
Anti-Gifteds Movement
not identified
Norburn
De
Ironcrest
Cherryville
ThunderBay
Stone Creek

3 Months Later
Caliel
Bellhaven
Osthall
ldor
Northbrook
water

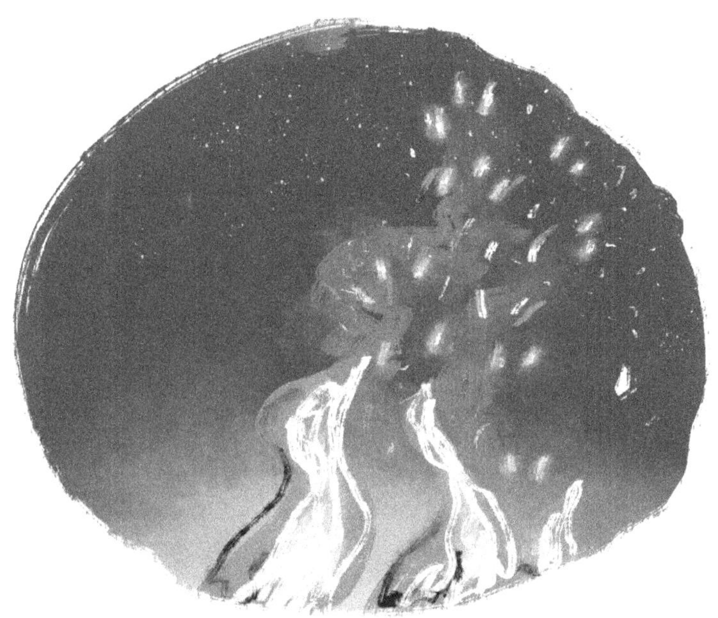

CHAPTER TWENTY

By the Fire
NORA

—

For the next three months, we traveled up again to Galdor, through smaller towns within the eastern forests, down the coast again, all the way up to Caliel, and back down again toward the country's center. I tried documenting as much as I could within the margins of the Great Book so Poppy would think I was taking notes. I was doing both.

Every time Cassius left to go back to the capitol, I noted when and for how long, and if he traveled with a Gifted-turned-Unfortunate who didn't die during the conversion. Every judgment, I forced myself to stay longer and longer so I could write down how many were downcasted and how many were deemed saved. The largest number of downcast souls in one place went to a mixed city called Belhaven: 3 wait stations, 126 Gifteds killed, 4 saved.

I wrote out Cassius's phrase when the first Gifted prisoner was downcast, hearing it repeated in every city and town the AGM controlled or occupied: *If you can see it with the mind of your heart, and feel it in the depths of your soul, then you will hold it in your hands.*

When I heard Fern in spare moments, I informed her of what I knew and what to avoid. I listed out when I heard her, where I was, where she could be, summaries of our conversations, and strange dream details. Unity flowers doodled at the page corners.

For the Great Book, color drew attention to the text more than my pencil markings along the sides. Every time a passage confused me, which was often, I highlighted it in orange. When I liked something, which was just as surprisingly often, I highlighted it in pink. When a theme reappeared, and I noticed it then or later in discussion, yellow illuminated the words. In three months, my copy hardly had a white page anymore.

We were stationed in Osthall now. I had never been to Iridion's second largest city before, but the war didn't appear to be here. On the surface, at least, Gifteds deemed loyal to the king traversed freely. But rich socialites still needed their comforts, so Unfortunates under the AGM banner worked in the common black dress servants wore. Poppy explained that not everyone was fit to be an Anti-Gifteds soldier but these girls had a protection they hadn't before: a watchful eye to make sure Gifted Houses treated their staff fairly or face downcastment.

I knew Valerie would approve. If I didn't know the terrible things the AGM and its leader did, I would approve too.

Why did we have to do terrible things to get what we needed? All this bloodshed and heartache and resentment could have been avoided if we received those needs in the first place.

"You got your thinking face on," Poppy noted as she probed the fire with her stick.

Stars lined the night sky above us. The AGM army rested across the city park, maintaining their own fires or huddling in their tents. A blanket wrapped around my shoulders, and I held it tighter to the wind. Bree, Ellie, and Holly were already asleep or at least silent in their tents, leaving us to the slow passing night.

"I'm just looking for the answer," I replied, delicate because I knew what would come next.

An outburst. "There you go again about finding an answer," Poppy teased, prodding the firewood with more enthusiasm. Her words were mean, but I knew by now that she wanted to know more. That she said everything that was on her mind and appeared hostile for no other reason than because she liked the confrontation. "What is it this time?"

I matched her smile. "Obviously I don't want Cassius in power."

She matched my words with a draw of sarcasm. "Obviously."

"And the Anti-Gifteds Movement abolished."

A roll of the eyes. "*Obviously.*"

She picked up a can near her chair and tossed it to me.

I caught the drink and spoke as she retrieved another for herself. "Come on, Poppy. Before the AGM, what do you want in your future?"

The can opened with a snap, and Poppy slumped lower in her chair as she sipped. After a few heartbeats, she rested her elbow and held the can up as she thought my question over.

Finally, she looked at me with a shrug. "I just wanted my House owner to die, and that's what he got."

She tipped the bottle to me like she was giving a toast and held her head back to drink more.

"You belonged to the Fairaways though."

She emitted a sound of protest before swallowing. "Not originally."

"Then what after that? After killing your first House owner?"

She wiped her mouth. "That's it. I would have died, or I guess I could have escaped to Norburn. With the AGM though, I got my revenge and now I liberate other Unfortunates in the same boat."

"Revenge. Liberation. They're all so meaningless when all we're doing is—" My arms were out wide, and I was looking at the ground, not sure how to finish my sentence.

"Doing what?"

"Doing the exact same thing Gifteds do to us! It doesn't feel right."

Poppy finished her drink and threw the can in the fire. It crinkled and shrank and became nothing. "It feels right to me."

We stared at each other for several heartbeats, the fire reflecting in our eyes. "Your Great Book says differently," I said at last.

A smile pulled at Poppy's lips. "What have you been

learning?"

"There are full chapters about caring for one another. Even in these orange sections talking about Gifted masters and Unfortunate servants, they're both called to respect each other. Minister Gabriel intentionally focused on how we should serve Gifteds but never how Gifteds should do the same for us."

"I'm not like Minister Gabriel." Poppy wasn't smiling anymore.

"You must see it too," I pressed. "We can't put Gifteds lower than us. We're equally human in the Divine's eye."

Poppy adjusted with a long sigh, resting her hand on her cheek. "Then what is the answer?" She sounded bored now, a little worn.

The answer was always at the tip of my tongue. My lips always started to form a letter, though it could never decide on what and rested open. I tried to reiterate what we already agreed on.

"We want the ability to live our lives as we choose. The way Gifted are free."

Poppy chuckled. "What do you think we're doing here? Causing chaos to cause chaos? Killing to kill?"

I scoffed. "You are doing a lot of that."

"Hey, Gifteds wouldn't give us the light of day otherwise."

"They might have."

"What? With you as Iridion's first Unfortunate soldier? A Galdor Academy student? Ridiculous."

"Mr. Harris was trying something, and it failed," I admitted. "But it only failed because you didn't like me."

"I like you!" She reached over and smacked my arm. I jolted but recognized the gesture as friendly.

"You as in the whole Anti-Gifteds Movement." I smacked

her back. We giggled like younger girls.

"Stuff like that is too slow." Poppy opened another can with a hard pop. "Look at the world we're creating now. Unfortunates won't have to stand in line to be chosen. Won't have to separate themselves from their families. Won't ever have to leave their future behind for a Gifted family that treats them like shit. Are you really telling me you want to go back to that?"

I shook my head. "No, I don't want to go back. I just wish...that this wasn't how we move forward."

I opened my can and took a small sip, drinking in the silence.

"Before getting wrapped up in Mr. Harris's failed plan," prompted Poppy, "what did you want in your future?"

I stared at the fire for a while. "I wanted...to escape servitude with the girl I loved."

"Valerie, right?"

"Yeah."

She poked at the fire. "Where would you have gone to?"

"Does it even matter now? She's dead."

Even saying it out loud stung my heart. I looked down to the ground, below the earth where both Valerie and Fern were. I...shouldn't compare the two. Not when one was alive and in my dreams and saving the world in my absence. Not when my track record for love was so terrible.

Poppy stopped, sitting back into her chair and speaking in a softer tone. "Where would you have gone if she was alive?"

I thought about our plan and wondered where we would have gone. Which sign would entice us.

"Anywhere no one could bother us," I confessed, too self-conscious to admit to the cottage I liked to imagine. Some details Poppy didn't need to know. "But I don't know anywhere that's really like that. And I don't think about her as much as I used to."

"Who do you think about now?"

I bit the inside of my cheek, thinking about red hair and white peonies, about tall oak trees and chocolate chip cookies, about green eyes and freckled lips. "No one."

Poppy considered my answer before blurting, "I'd take my mom to Ironcrest."

My eyes lifted to hers, startled by her statement. "Ironcrest?" My voice spoke before I could properly come up with a response. "There's hardly anything there except a maximum security prison."

"It's the furthest point away from Northbrook." Poppy stretched her hand out. "*All* the way to the west."

I scoffed. "If you wanted to get far west, you could always take your mom to Thunder Bay. It's safer there with the Unfortunate population."

"If my mom was alive, she might be inclined to agree."

"Oh." We both took a swig.

"You're not going to ask how?"

"I wouldn't want to rehash how Valerie died."

"I'll tell you anyway."

Poppy stretched back, legs and arms long and worn. "My father." She looked to the sky and then added, "He was an Avlis."

My throat clenched, and I started to choke in a loud struggle to compose myself. Poppy leaned forward, patting me on the back. I grappled with all the possibilities running through my mind. This Unfortunate revolutionary who escaped servitude through the AGM...was half-Gifted? What can you say after that? Thankfully, she continued for me.

"He owned my mom, and then...he owned me. Do you understand what I'm saying?"

I nodded, still heaving and grappling with her confession. She handed me water, and I drank away the burn. "Being his daughter didn't mean anything to him," she said. "We were just used as collateral for each other, and one day I tried to fight back and well, she died for it."

She died for it, I repeated in my mind, wincing.

"Valerie!"

I pushed Molly aside, but the damage was already done. Blood poured out of Valerie's left arm, and she sank to the floor, holding onto the wound in a futile effort to keep it steady.

I rushed for the first aid kit and wrapped gauze over the bite mark, cleaning where I could with a washcloth.

"We can't keep living like this." Her eyes met mine, so puffy and red from tears but also so resilient. She didn't regret her decision.

I rubbed her tears away with the washcloth, making sure Molly had already left before saying, "Then let's go live somewhere else."

Her eyes widened, and she grabbed my hand with her uninjured arm. "Are you serious?" So resilient, and so hopeful too.

"Yes," I whispered even lower. "We can go."

She squealed, a spark of energy causing her to jump up and down. "We can finally be free!"

I covered her mouth, holding her in place in case any of the Montgomerys were still close. I understood why, though. Excitement bubbled in my chest, too.

She stopped and tapped my hand to tell me she would be

quieter. I released her. Valerie beamed, "I'll go if you promise me something."

I knew all too well what it meant to fight back. Valerie knew what it meant too, and she made me promise to continue fighting—even if that meant fighting without her.

"I'm sorry," I finally said.

A messenger came into view, running and stopping when he reached our little encampment. "General Poppy," he announced.

She turned to him, shifting from melancholy to authoritative. "Yes?"

I jolted before he could speak, hearing Fern yell, *Find Nora!* in my skull. I winced in response, placing my palm against my forehead. The general and the messenger looked in my direction, but I gestured for him to speak, feigning a headache.

The messenger looked back to Poppy, "There's a Gifted insurgence in Doverly."

Standing now, I listened with bated breath. She had to be close.

"By order of the king, your unit is to return to Galdor Academy at once. More orders will follow your arrival."

Doverly

FERN

Deep red and orange leaves hid our forms and blanketed beneath our feet. Cold morning air refreshed our lungs and awoke our senses. Birds chirped in the last warm places among dormant trees.

My Gift held limitations as fall turned into winter. Plants were less coaxed into sprouting and branches grew brittle.

At this moment, I waited patiently for something to

happen.

Skylar came into view, a blue and blonde spot in the sky. She pointed and mouthed *northeast*. I acknowledged with the slightest of nods and looked to my right. Leo was already in that direction.

As though on cue, a wave of heat and smoke broke the silence. Spooked footfalls zipped away from the scene, heading closer to my right side. I shot up from my position, my arms raised high above my head. Earth erupted from its resting place at once as an enclosed pin.

"Looking good," Skylar announced, lowering to peer inside.

Leo and I ran to the uprooted wall. Our patience paid off. Though I couldn't see the deer, I could hear its circling hooves in search of an escape. I made sure there wasn't one.

Skylar hovered over Leo as he passed a bow and arrow to her, a weapon we collected off an Anti-Gifted soldier in a brief confrontation near Cherryville.

The Aura huffed a disgusted sound. "I can't believe I have to learn this."

She said that every time. I replied the same every time. "I'm not crushing it to death."

"Or burning it alive," Leo added. "Here, you got this."

He pulled her down like one would a fairy, stepping closer with an encouraging smile and reminding her the basic steps as she did them.

"I know, I know," she repeated but smiled as she spoke.

Skylar fired twice, and I released a sigh of relief that it was over.

Lowering the walls down, I morphed the earth into a platform and looked away from the deer's fallen body. "Skylar, would you mind checking the area for any Anti-

Gifted soldiers?"

"On it." The weapon exchanged hands, and they lingered for a breath too long before she disappeared into the direct sunlight.

We waited for a few minutes, and the Aura returned already on the ground. "Clear."

Nodding, we made our way back to camp. Out of the three of us, only I could feel our place underground. My foot fell and the reverb indicated a hollowed-out cavern.

Here. I halted, centering myself and imagining a rectangular platform beneath us. The earth indented and then lowered us down, down, down to our top-secret, underground base.

Between the workload of five Avlis, we opened up a large space for everyone to gather for meals and conversation. I lowered us down to that very place, returning the dirt to the surface after we stepped off the platform. My mom and her allies sprung into action and took the deer into a carved-out room where we found a salt deposit. Perfect for preparing and storing meat.

I looked around. Rooms resided in front of me and on either side. At this point, we were doubling and tripling up to save on space. I didn't mind myself, considering how the dorms at Galdor Academy grouped an entire class of students together.

Kai read in the back corner of what we designated as the living room, and Persephone was missing, probably getting some rest.

Molly sat in a circle with a large group of Gifteds we rescued from wait stations. Our numbers had grown from twenty-three to thirty-eight. A Lux we rescued from Belhaven had her Great Book tucked inside her clothes, and she held it up now, its bound leather jacket unsettling my stomach.

I walked into their conversation as the Lux woman holding the book said, "—or else the word is lost."

Molly opened her mouth to say something.

"What's going on over here?" I asked, resting my hands on my hips.

"They think losing their Gift means they're damned," Molly said curtly.

"It's true!"

"Yeah, but then you're saying *I'm* damned." Molly stood up and ripped the book out of her hands as she said the word "damned."

"We must protect our Gifts at all costs," the Lux insisted.

Molly read to herself the section she was hung up on with a scrutinizing glare.

I spoke up in the silence. "'At all costs' doesn't sound very good. Sure, we could die losing our Gift and Molly here is a rare case, but I wouldn't use fear to dictate my actions like that. I mean, if you're going to die anyway, you might as well choose it in an epic way."

The Lux woman huffed, and I folded my arms over my chest. *You know what?*—I hadn't kept my promise protecting Unfortunates in this war but I could at least protect Unfortunates in this debate.

"What's wrong with being an Unfortunate?" I prompted.

Molly scoffed at me, her glare burning into my skin like the brand on her hand.

The Lux woman took her opportunity. "*Thou whom cast hence mine own Gift shall be forever condemned to an Unfortunate soul.* Meaning if you use your Gift unwisely or against the Divine, He'll take it away."

"It's what the Diviner does, too," another Gifted perked up.

I rubbed my elbow, trying to bring the hair down. She quoted Minister Gabriel from that terrible day in Galdor Square when Gifteds and Unfortunates laid waste in a massacre. He held onto that quote with an iron grip and continuously taught what we deemed true: Unfortunates were marked with sin. Corrupted souls in need of an unending redemption.

I refused to believe an evil soul could laugh the way Nora did.

"My mom always said that this quote focuses in too much on Gifteds," I replied calmly. "It actually has nothing to do with Unfortunates, and even if it did, that doesn't mean we should keep them under our thumb. How could they receive grace if all we give them is strife?"

"Ha!" Molly handed the book back.

The lady didn't like that gesture. I lightly kicked Molly's knee to tell her to back down. She made a disapproving face but didn't say anything more.

"How can it have nothing to do with Unfortunates? It's right there." The Lux gave the book a hearty slap.

I teetered on my feet. "I'd have to give it a re-read just to be sure," I confessed, "but it's easy to misinterpret. He's addressing Gifteds specifically, not Unfortunates. I think it's more about 'hey don't defy your God' than 'hey don't become an Unfortunate.' They were already in existence before this point."

The Lux made a musing sound, flipping through the book and not looking at me. "I suppose I can give it another read," she said with a hint of irritation.

"Great. Let's do it together, hm?"

She didn't respond. My feet continued to teeter, ready to turn away when I felt a new pressure closing in. I embraced the air behind me, and Delilah materialized with a start.

"How do you do that?" she protested, ripping away from my hold.

"I'm your sister. I always sense you." I successfully ruffled her blonde hair.

She slapped me away.

"Good afternoon, Delilah," the group greeted.

"Hey y'all." She waved her hand and then looked at me expectantly. "Can I go topside next mission?"

"What? Why would you want to do that?"

"*Please*," she whined like I was Mom. "I'm not doing anything down here."

"Delilah's a Makan, right?" one of the Gifteds butted in.

"I am," she said cautiously. My arm wrapped around her shoulder, bracing myself for his next words. Makans were already seen as lesser, cowardly Gifteds, and the Diviner was not making their reputation any better.

"Maybe she could learn what the Diviner does."

That was certainly not what I expected him to say. My hold loosened in surprise while Delilah's eyes twinkled. "Do you really think so?"

I fake laughed, pulling my sister's hoodie over her face. "Absolutely not."

"Hey!" She protested, her hands too busy ripping off her hoodie to stop me from dragging her away from the group.

I released her in the room we shared. Delilah huffed, putting her hands on her hips and mocking my stance. "That was a good idea!"

"That was a *terrible* idea," I refuted. "No topside for you, and especially no emulating the Diviner."

"But mom always says to make yourself useful."

"You are being useful as my not-dead sister."

"Don't say that." Delilah turned away from me, pouting with her arms now crossed over her chest.

"I'm sorry." And I meant it. Hugging her from behind I said, "You have to understand how dangerous all of this is. Nora even says the king is looking for Makans."

She didn't respond, sinking against my weight.

"*Delilah*," I sing-sung.

She sank further.

"Delilah..." I stretched.

"It's not fair."

Her mumble was barely audible, but I heard her as loud as a shout. At the gravity of her words, I stopped playing games and released her from the hug. It wasn't fair because she was born with negative connotations already nicking at her skin. It wasn't fair because she couldn't go topside and I could. It wasn't fair that the Diviner proved Makans to be the most powerful Gifteds in the world, and she couldn't use it. There were plenty of ways that none of this was fair for her.

She turned back to face me, looking more distraught than I'd seen her in a long time.

I sighed, kissing her on the forehead. "I know."

✳✳✳

We left for Doverly at 4am: me, Kai, Leo, Persephone, Skylar, and Molly.

Tunneling to different cities became second nature over the past three months. We came up with a method of making things easier. I already carved out tunnels during previous missions, so the ones we repeatedly needed to use (like entering and exiting the base) remained open but could close with the same hand motion used to close a sliding door.

Doverly was in between Galdor and Osthall, so we took what I called a highway tunnel toward the second largest city in Iridion until we needed to deviate off course. My Gift parted the dirt around us toward the town, wasting little energy with other tunnels already set in place.

I relied on tree roots to reach the surface, sturdy and sage in the cold weather.

There.

Stopping, I turned to the others and pointed upward. They stopped too, but someone unseen stopped half a step too late.

"Delilah!" I shouted.

She appeared out of the emptiness with a groan, cheeks burning from the attention. "I thought you'd be too busy to notice."

"I don't need an excuse. You need to go back home this instant. How did you get past Mom?"

"You know she's a heavy sleeper."

"Delilah!" I could not believe her. I tried to calm my voice to be more stern. "Go home. Right now."

"I don't want to go all the way back by myself *in the dark*," she protested.

"You should have thought about that before you snuck out."

She stepped closer to me, pleading and half-screaming. "I can do this! Just once, Fern! I'm already here."

I opened my mouth to object again, but she was right. We didn't have all day to remain gridlocked like this.

"Stay here," I pointed to the ground she stood on. Before she could protest any further, I lifted my index finger for her silence. "When we drop down Gifteds, you start leading them down the tunnel. Understand?"

"But—"

"*Understand?*"

Delilah groaned, "I understand."

"Good." I sighed. *One time*, I thought to myself. *She gets one time and I'm molding her feet to the floor when we return.*

Inhaling for one breath, I encouraged the earth to rise beneath our feet and separate above our heads like an elevator. We ascended and surfaced along the far wall of a makeshift warehouse.

Morning light streamed through the open door. King Cassius held a chained Gifted by the chin, his eyes lifting to meet ours. Isaac Winters, hands itching for violence, and Ebony Nique, throat crackling a pleasured laugh, flanked him.

Recognition set in.

"Look at that." The king guided the Gifted's head in our direction; our reflection blurred in the prisoner's teary state. "They're here to save you."

CHAPTER TWENTY-TWO

Two Sisters

FERN

———

My breath held at the sight before me. Until this very second, I didn't realize how lucky we were. Hitting wait stations when they were dormant, the Gifteds inside still had a choice to make. Now three pairs of antagonistic eyes sliced right through me. And now I've put my sister in the worst situation she could possibly be in.

"But they can't save you."

The Diviner brought the Gifted back around to meet his gaze. A bright light, the hue of lavender, erupted where his hand connected with the Gifted's jaw. We winced, covering our eyes from the momentary glare. And then the light disappeared, the Gifted fell face first into the ground, and the king admired a marble of the same color thrashing in its container.

The Diviner flattened his palm and let the marble slide onto the floor. He stood, addressing the chained Gifteds.

"The only person who can save you is me."

With one intentional step forward, the marble crushed beneath his boot and the Gift inside vanished with a harrowing crunch.

We could run away. We could go back into the tunnel. I could collapse everything behind us. But we were caught in a snare. If we ran away, he could take half of us before we squeezed through the tight space. If we did reach the tunnel, what was stopping him from following us all the way back to base? We would doom everyone. And worst of all, with the clench of his fist, any one of us could become putty in his hands. He could easily freeze me in place so I couldn't use my Gift to do anything.

I glanced to either side of me. The twins were both to my right alongside Skylar. Molly and Kai were to my left. Everyone was rigid and tense. This was my call. I was the only one who could lower us back down. Our underground operation was worth protecting, and besides, I wasn't one to back away from fights.

We could collapse the tunnel and sacrifice ourselves, but there was still Delilah...

The Diviner must have understood this, must have read my thoughts, because he stared and *stared* and then tilted his head.

The world wobbled as an icy feeling crawled up my spine like cold hands stilling my body in place. My arms relaxed to their sides despite my hair standing up in alarm. All other noises muffled except for the chilled words that came from the Diviner's throat.

"Bring your sister up."

His command blocked out any other thoughts or actions.

I sensed Delilah beneath us. As I called to the earth, my

hands shook violently, unwillingly. Dirt shifted under her feet and ascended her to the surface.

"Fern!" Kai said my name, but my sight fixed angrily on the Diviner's.

A cheer. Delilah's cheer, right next to me, cut abruptly short. I couldn't even turn to look at her, my eyes fixated angrily in front of me.

"What's going on?"

The world snapped back into focus. My jaw hurt from clenching so tightly in effort.

Delilah was above ground now, cowering behind my sleeve.

"Stay behind me." I ushered her further away from his sight.

Thinking of my next action before I did it, the Diviner lunged as I raised my foot off the ground.

I gasped, my concentration fracturing. His hand—with all its power to take—closed in on me.

A blur of auburn hair. Molly cut in, taking my place as the Diviner latched on. "It's funny, isn't it?" she asked, stepping forward and pushing him back. Her voice rang loud and clear for the chained Gifteds around her. "Once you turn us into Unfortunates, you no longer have any leverage over us."

Isaac, his fingers tight in a fist and frostbitten, drove toward Molly. But Kai was at the ready, grasping Isaac at the wrist with a pick-on-someone-your-own-size look.

Skylar launched into the air, tackling Ebony in one swoop. Pinned down, Ebony's features shifted to look like a boy who died young. A horrible screaming sound emanated from her disguise, and Skylar stumbled back, bright red and horror-stricken.

Leo and Persephone sprinted in opposite directions—the

Mati sister to my right and the brother to my left—breaking the chained Gifteds free. They encouraged them to the back of the warehouse and away from combat.

The king shoved Molly aside and charged for me. My original intention was to send Delilah back down so she would be safe no matter the outcome, but I realized in that moment I lost concentration, the earth swallowed back up. My sister was now stuck; half of her body underground and half above ground.

I planted my stance, commanding the earth to rise. A wall formed, and I propelled it back—all the way to the other side of the warehouse near the entrance. Earth slammed into the aluminum framing, but the king swerved out of its path, casually pivoting on his feet.

Aluminum.

Kai went on the defensive, shifting ice shards back into their original state and creating a whip out of the collective water. He blocked any advances with a snap, breaking ice apart into fragments and absorbing it into his weapon.

Ebony, with Cal's likeness, stood; the wide smile the only indication of the false appearance. Skylar used her Gift to quickly move further back and used her momentum to find footing. She stood slightly hunched, her chest rising and falling fast.

"Aw, do you miss me?" Ebony's voice came through, the one thing she couldn't replicate from photographs along a dresser.

"You're dead!" The wind picked up around Skylar's shout.

The Aura hurled the Mute straight into the left-hand corner of the warehouse. Ebony shifted back into herself on impact. She moaned, struggling to connect her nerves with her body.

Skylar inhaled with her lips fixed in a tight O shape. Ebony's hands wrapped around her own neck, choking and wheezing with eyes wide. The Aura stepped closer, and the Mute clamored up, mouth wide and thrashing in a vigorous effort to restore airflow.

Skylar grabbed Ebony by the throat and forced her to remain still. Two, then three, then ten breaths went by, and the Mute's struggles ceased. Her hands fell onto her stomach, and Skylar released her hold, panting and weeping all at once.

Space closed between the two Mares. Kai attacked Isaac head on. The whip made contact with Isaac with a crack. Water turned back into ice and snapped in half.

Kai returned what was left of his weapon into a free form of water circling behind his back. Isaac clenched his fist. The water hardened around Kai's hands and both dropped like a heavy stone. He fumbled with his restraints as Isaac stepped closer.

Leo watched, frantically releasing another prisoner before flinging into action. He stepped in between the two Mares. Fire breathed along his shoulders, and his right hand intertwined with Isaac's.

"Go help Persy!" Leo shouted to Kai.

With those extra seconds, the ice around Kai's hands turned back into water, and he slipped out of the restraints.

"Are you sure?"

The Ice Mare stood off against the Mati, their right hands clamped down on each other. "I'm sure," Leo managed.

Kai nodded, running off to help free more Gifteds.

Isaac flexed his fingers. Icicles coated and crawled up Leo's entire arm. His skin turned a deep blue. Leo clenched his teeth together, collapsing to his knees. Blots of frozen blood formed underneath the sleet coating as Isaac added pressure until both ice and flesh shattered.

Sweat and strain dotted Leo's face. He panted, looking up at his assailant with a weak, wiry smile. "Wrong arm, fuck-o."

Leo swung his left arm—the one clean of third-degree burns. A rage of blue flames like a tidal wave pierced Isaac's face. He wailed, doubling back and holding onto his eyes. His muscles tensed like he was trying to summon his Gift, but the temperature rose and boiled his skin in a deep red. He hit the ground with a resounding thud, passing out from the searing pain.

My fingers reached upward in search of the earth within the aluminum frame. Traces small but durable.

The king closed in, despite my effort, and our hands collided.

"*Fe—*" Delilah's voice cut off as her body stiffened, her mouth hung open. At the helm of the Diviner's will, her hands clawed at the soil in a frenzy.

I wanted to scream at him, but my mouth remained tightly shut as we struggled against each other. I couldn't let him grab my face.

A thin layer of earth separated our touch. With a wave of my hand, rock jutted out in a cascade and the force threw him to the left side of the room.

Molly ran toward me. "Fern! You need to open the tunnel!"

"What?" I looked from her to the Diviner. Persephone was confronting him. I turned back to Molly as she tugged my sleeve.

"Open the tunnel," she repeated. "The Gifteds are all in one place."

She gestured to the back wall behind me. There they were,

twenty or so, in a line. Ebony was dead, Isaac was incapacitated, and the king was distracted. This was our chance. I nodded, lowering the earth in one long stretch with the push of my hands.

I started closing it up when Delilah successfully freed herself. Her nails caked with dirt, and her eyes searched in a craze. I ran over to her, unsure how to stop the madness, when she bit my arm.

"Ow!" I reeled back.

"*Persy!*"

My attention deviated back to my left. Yellow, as bright and as warm as the sunshine, filled the warehouse in its glow.

Time seemed to slow to a taunting stop as the Diviner released his hold and Persephone collapsed beneath him.

Molly shrieked, so long and painful. The only sound in the universe. Her hands, one branded over the other, cupped Persephone's head before it could drop, drop, drop like a fallen tree. Molly cradled and rotated her in a gentle sweeping motion, laying her on the floor with more dignity than she had when she succumbed to the Diviner.

He held Persephone's Gift in his hands like a trophy. My sister calmly walked over to his side.

Then the next sound in the universe. Leo's denying cry. He charged—we all did. The Diviner watched and readied.

Molly's head perked up to Leo's voice, and she jumped up. I watched, waiting in agony to see who connected first. Molly's hand smacked against the king's wrist, and the yellow marble went airborne. She caught it in the next breath and grabbed Leo with her free arm, swinging him off course before the Diviner could take him too.

I arrived; Skylar and Kai to the left and right of me. We were all on one side. All except—

"Give me back my sister you bastard!" I screamed, the earth shifting on all sides. The metal frames rattled from their foundation.

The Diviner had stepped to the warehouse's opening, Delilah stopping when he stopped. His voice remained neutral, almost business-like.

"I'd say this is a fair trade. For now, at least."

"Fern!" Both Kai and Skylar held me back, but it was Kai who was speaking. "Persy needs medical attention *now*."

He wouldn't just let us get away. He wasn't that kind of person!

"I'm not leaving my sister!" Tree roots, as old as the country, churned along the earth's surface.

"We don't have a choice!" Wind howled, water whirled, Leo's fire threatened, and Molly pleaded.

I bit down hard. "I'll find you!" I yelled, hoping my words would tear through her now blank expression. "In the meantime—" my friends pushed me into the tunnel opening—"find Nora, D!"

The king's eyes flared at the mention of the name, but I didn't care. I repeated myself one more time, "Find Nora!"

He shifted then like he was about to attack anyway, and I locked the earth above us.

CHAPTER TWENTY-THREE

Alabaster

NORA

The train screeched to a halt. When I first came to Galdor, Mr. Walton was still alive. Mr. Harris was still a secret Animus. Molly was still an Imitation. And I was a terrified servant who had no idea what was in her future here.

Looking out at the sea of red that greeted and directed us, I didn't like the outcome.

Poppy stood, and we followed her out. Unlike Osthall where Gifteds roamed freely with their Unfortunate servants, everyone in the capitol seemed to be a soldier here. Women and men in red uniforms guarded red-draped buildings and patrolled empty streets.

Few people wore their own colors the closer we got to Galdor Academy. I assumed they were Gifteds who pledged allegiance to the new king, but no one used their Gift. Not even in the casual ways I would often see around the city. No Auras quickening the distance by sky. No Mati or Feras performing in the square. The sidewalk was bare of Avlis flower shops and vegetable stands. No Mare children playing by public water fountains or fire hydrants. Even Imitations somehow hid their animal attributes.

We entered the academy through the black gate. I stared at the walls—those impossibly high walls I noticed the first day I arrived here. Black ash and dirt smeared its original pristine from hundreds of Anti-Gifted soldiers pouring in during the queen's ball. Inside, cracks traced crooked outlines from my nightmares. I traced them with my hand to make sure they were real. Its maintenance had been neglected for some time before the AGM took over, only catching my attention now.

I stopped, bringing my hand back to my side. Turning to look at the rest of the Grounds, I saw a familiar figure, though I hadn't seen her ever wear a short dress in all the time I've known her. Maya sat on one of the vacant training fields, stroking the grass blades with her harmless touch.

Poppy approached her; the rest of us clumped behind.

"Oh, Nora!" Maya waved enthusiastically at me despite my best effort to stay obscured. "I'm so glad to see you. How did you like Osthall?"

She spoke like we just went away for vacation. "It was...fine." I tried to push aside my immediate frustration. "How have you been?"

An exasperated sound erupted from Poppy's mouth. "We don't have time for idle chit chat," she snapped. "We're awaiting orders after an insurgent attack. Where may I find the king?"

"Haven't seen him," Maya replied, remaining casual with a shrug. "He picked up two new Unfortunates not too long ago—you know, Gifteds-turned-Unfortunates—but he left soon after. And you know what? I haven't seen them in a few days either. Cas must be hiding them from me."

The Gifted insurgence had to be Fern and my friends. Did they run into Cassius while he was away from the main conquest?

"Speak of the devil." Maya pointed to the academy entrance.

"Don't call him that," Poppy hissed, even if it was just a turn of phrase.

We turned. In a silent rage, Cassius led a small group of AGM soldiers.

Quick movement drew my eye; one stretcher sped to the infirmary, Isaac almost unrecognizable behind the bandages over his face and body. Another stretcher was pushed at a slower pace with a blanket over whoever was inside. It must have been Ebony. Both Gifteds were the only two missing from his ensemble. I watched her gurney slip into the back of the infirmary where the royal morgue resided.

I returned my focus back to the king as he charged toward us, holding onto a viscously defiant girl tied by rope like a dog.

Now I understood why Fern asked someone to find me. *Delilah.*

Bree, Ellie, and Holly saluted while I unsheathed my sword. "What do you think you're doing?"

Charging forward, I sliced the leash away from his hand. Her mouth and hands were bound too, so I held onto her, defensive. Recognition reflected in her hazel eyes, the specks of green reminding me of her sister. Delilah stopped struggling all at once and remained by my side.

"The alternative was to use my Animus Gift against her the whole way here," Cassius replied, easing his fist and releasing the rope to the ground. "I didn't think you wanted to see her like that."

I untied her remaining restraints. What could he want with Delilah? He was searching for Makans sure, but this was also his greatest opposition's sister. I held us closer.

"I'm taking her on as an apprentice," Cassius responded to my thoughts. "If she tries to run or doesn't meet my expectations, I'll have no choice but to pass judgment."

"Apprentice?" I challenged. "You could take on any Makan. Why Delilah?"

"Makans are few and far between these days. Besides, she wants to learn."

"What?" I turned to Fern's younger sister who rubbed her hands in an effort not to look at me.

"It might be useful," she replied, far more meek than her entrance.

"Useful how?" I demanded, but Poppy was already speaking.

"Your Majesty," she cut in. "What are our next orders?"

"Relax, General." Cassius warmed his voice. The muscles in his face and body relaxed. "The insurgence has been taken care of. I actually called your battalion back because I have a calling for you specifically. Are you willing to accept?"

Despair threatened to tear at my heart as Poppy saluted, full of excitement. "Yes, sir!" she exclaimed.

"Then accompany me to the east wing. We don't have a moment to lose. Delilah—" he turned on his heels—"you rest up with Miss Nora here. You've had a very trying day, but if you'd like to get a head start, remember that Gifts are not visible by natural eyes."

The insurgence...had been taken care of. Delilah was captured. Oh, Divine. What if...what if—?

Cassius's eyes like sapphires, clear and cutting, found mine. He breathed in all the fears running through my mind. He breathed out all of the panic and dread and frustration stitching my face. I still didn't know what he was doing in the east wing of the castle. I certainly didn't know why he was taking Poppy there. And I couldn't force my hand and make him take me there too. I couldn't leave Delilah by herself or worse, bring her somewhere she wouldn't be safe.

"You know, you're almost there," he began, pensive, "but Poppy is brighter than you."

A cold front swept in the silence and muffled their steps as they left. I watched, and I wondered how different they would be the next time we saw each other face to face. The other soldiers eased.

"Fern said to find you," Delilah finally said once they were gone.

"I know." I gripped her hand tighter.

She seemed to understand that answer without explanation. "What do we do now?"

Maya stood from her position on the ground with a relieving stretch.

"He can be really biting sometimes. Would all of you care for lunch?" She glanced at everyone expectedly.

My eyes narrowed. "You can't be so casual about all of this."

Maya shrugged, "What else do you expect to do?"

I inhaled, squeezing Delilah's hand again for comfort. "Are you hungry?"

She nodded, and we all made our way to the canteen.

Delilah walked between me and Maya with Bree, Ellie, and Holly flanking behind.

She observed the remnants of our school as we walked,

and I kept a steady hand in hers as she irregularly flickered in and out of visibility. Anti-Gifteds peered at her curiously.

"Does your Gift reflect how you feel?" I asked as we passed by the entrance and took our place in line.

"Why don't you say that louder?" Delilah ripped her hand away and crossed her arms, flickering faster.

It had been a while since I managed a tween.

Ellie snickered. "She could be your little sister, Nora."

"You'll learn to control your Gift better with time." Maya answered before the tension grew. "I wished I could see my brother grow up with me. He could have pretended to be a ghost appearing and disappearing like that. Have you scared your sister before?"

"Hardly!" Delilah grabbed a tray. "She's always catching me. Says my footsteps are too loud."

"That's an Avlis for you," Maya smiled, serving herself and then Delilah a helping of mashed potatoes.

"Is Fern alive?" I asked as we passed down the line. I had to know. I had to know this instant.

Delilah remained visible, though her voice came out soft and trembling. "Fern is alive, but he took Persephone's Gift away."

Relief washed over me momentarily thinking about Fern but vanished with the news about Persephone. A heaviness sank within my heart, and I forced myself to stay quiet as we found a table.

Delilah leaned into my side as the others stepped ahead of us. "Should I be saying any of this out loud with *them* here?" Her eyes danced between the AGM soldiers.

I bit my lip, weighing the risk. "Yes," I whispered back. "Just be careful. Don't share anything that could hurt Fern, and only answer my questions. Can you handle that?"

"I think so."

We sat down at a round table. Bree, Ellie, and Holly sat side by side to my left. Delilah sat to my immediate right, and there was a visible gap between Maya and Holly.

Delilah continued. "He did something to me that made me go numb. My hands were so dirty, but he washed them afterward."

She looked at her hands now, clean and red with the nails filed down.

Maya frowned, unfolding her napkin over her lap as a way to keep her eyes down. I opened my mouth to assure Delilah that she was safe now. That she wouldn't have to feel powerless against his Animus Gift again. But I couldn't lie to her.

"Is Persy okay?" I asked instead.

Delilah shook her head, "I don't know. I think that Unfortunate girl took the Gift back."

"Molly?"

"Yeah, that's her name."

That made sense. I could still see her Gift, a black marble with the red snake eye shape in the middle, turning to grey and dust when it broke open on the floor. Molly wouldn't let another friend go through the same fate, but was restoration even possible?

I eyed Maya but she sipped on her tomato soup. The other Unfortunates ate in silence but eyed their new captive with varying degrees of interest.

"Delilah," I prompted. "Please tell me about your Makan Gift."

She wiped her mouth with the back of her hand. "What do you want to know?"

I handed her a napkin. "Everything you can tell me."

"Well, I can turn invisible but I can't move through things. I tried plenty."

Ellie chuckled again, and Holly nudged her with a disapproving face.

Delilah smiled warily from the attention. "Oh, and I can still see everyone. Even other Makans when they're invisible."

"Do you have to be invisible to see them also invisible?"

"No. We can see each other no matter what. When Grandpa was still alive, he could find me when I was a baby. Mom finally just put me in a pin."

A plethora of small smiles unfolded at the table, though the AGM soldiers tried to hide their mouths.

I let her eat a few more bites of macaroni. "Can you see light in other people?"

"Like the minister?"

"No, not him," I corrected. Minister Gabriel claimed to see the auras of those around him, but he thought I was a Mati before I was revealed as an Unfortunate. Just another lie from that man. "I mean...can you see other people's Gifts? Colors inside people? Anything like that?"

She pursed her lips in thought. "No."

"No?" The disappointment slumped my shoulders. What Cassius said returned to me. "Gifts are not visible by natural eyes. Do you have any idea what that means?"

Delilah shrugged, eating more. "The natural is the visible plane. It's what I see while invisible, too. *Wait.*" She stopped shoveling food in her mouth. "Let me try something."

She disappeared from sight for a long time. Everyone fixated on the empty seat.

The Makan reappeared with a loud, exasperated inhale. "Oh. My. *Divine.*"

"What? What is it?" Holly blurted.

"I can see it!" she shouted and then covered her mouth with her hands.

I leaned closer and touched her shoulder. "What do you see, Delilah? Describe it to me."

"Well, I don't see any Gifts because everyone here is an Unfortunate. I tried to look at Maya and imagine she vanished from the visible plane too. She became a dark silhouette with a grey circle sitting where her heart is, and so did everyone else in varying degrees but you—" she pointed at me with her fork—"Nora your circle is like alabaster. Makes your silhouette a little brighter than the rest."

I tried piecing together what she was saying as the others exchanged quiet looks. What Cassius told me before was true: Unfortunates were void of light but I wasn't. Why though? Why wasn't I void of light like the others? Why wasn't Poppy?

"Delilah," I prompted, more hope sparking inside me, "you said everyone else was grey in varying degrees. What do you mean by that?"

"Exactly what I said," she chirped, pointing to the three AGM soldiers with her utensil. "She's a shadow grey. She's a soft grey. And that one..." She squinted at Holly. "You remind me of a dolphin's coat."

"A dolphin?" Holly blushed as Ellie teased her. Bree remained silent; her eyes narrowed in Delilah's direction.

Cassius saw something change in me after he won. He demanded where my light had gone, but maybe it just dimmed or almost diminished. If I wasn't the only one capable of being bright, with Poppy as our prime example, then there had to be a reason why we fluctuated. I just needed to understand *what* that reason was.

Before I could ask Delilah any more questions, Maya

wiggled her fingers excitedly. "I would very much enjoy your company Miss Fairaway if you would like to show me what else you see as a Makan."

"*Maya.*" I drawled, "This is serious."

"It's a simple invitation." She began listing off activities they could do together. All the freedoms she could enjoy while my friends suffered for our mistakes. Persephone could be dead right now, and I wouldn't know. Her Gift was taken away by Cassius's hand, and I refused to pretend that didn't happen. Ugh, this was hopeless.

Delilah vanished and reappeared again while looking at me. "Oh wow, you're definitely darker now. Not at all like alabaster. Hey, how are you doing that? Are you a Lux or something?"

Maya stopped talking, and a hush fell over the table. The dethroned princess cleared her throat, settling back into a neutral posture. Old habits crept over my movements too, even as my mind whirled with the color change within me. I folded my hands over my lap and stared down at my food.

"No," I said, though I didn't sound confident. "No, I'm an Unfortunate."

The Unity Alliance
FERN

I closed all of the tunnels and sensed all of the earth colliding back into place. He would not chase us. He would not find us.

We flooded the underground base, and every Gifted and Unfortunate there turned from their laughter, their conversation, and their cooking; they fell speechless at what they were now seeing. Leo leaned onto Molly's frame. Water and blood began to drip from his arm. Skylar and Kai carried Persephone, slumped and eyes closed. And I came without a younger counterpart, ushering in the starved Gifteds and already-turned Unfortunates with the earth pulling beneath their bodies like sand.

My eyes met Mom's, and with a hard push, we closed the last entryway in on ourselves like a tomb.

Dr. Hansen came forward first, then Ms. Lancer, Mr. Harris, and all the others we rescued and were since rejuvenated. A cascade of shouting orders.

"Get me all the blankets," Dr. Hansen said, pressing her hand to Persy's forehead and then her chest. Mr. Harris ran off into the sleeping corridors.

"Let me see that arm." Ms. Lancer examined Leo; Prince Henry cried in his backpack carrier. Gifteds found their starved counterparts and offered encouraging words.

Mom stormed up to me, frantically looking around to no avail. I knew what she was looking for, but I wouldn't tell her until she asked. She grabbed my shoulders, "Where is your sister?"

My face crumbled into an uncontrollable sob. Her grip went to my back, and she pulled me into a big hug. Tears and snot drenched her shoulder. "What happened, baby sprouts?"

"De—de—" I gasped for air, and then it came out all at once. "Delilah's been taken by the Diviner! We got there. And he was already there. And then he took her. Mom, he has her and *it's all my fault.*"

She cooed me as shadows sprinted around us. "Hey, hey, let's get you water and you can start from the beginning. We need you right now, okay? Your sister needs you right now, too."

She led me to the kitchen area away from the chaos. I sniffled, "You're not mad?"

"Oh, I'm furious," she corrected quickly. "I'm *livid*. If the king doesn't kill your sister, I will when we find her."

She handed me a cup of water as I wiped my eyes. "But not really, right?"

Her voice softened, "No, not really."

Through the endless crying, I told her everything that happened.

Blankets littered the space as makeshift cots. Dr. Hansen and Kai went to each person, investigated their issue, gave them what they needed, and listed out absent supplies. The two Mares worked nonstop and were only a third of the way through reaching everyone.

Persephone laid still with two blankets bundled tightly around her body—the same way we had found Mrs. Stanton. She needed an IV at the very least, which we didn't have the equipment for. Molly watched over her, promising to alert the doctor if something new happened.

Leo's breathing regulated. A cotton shirt clogged his screams after Mom used her own prosthetic limb to create a metal saw and Dr. Hansen sliced away what remained of his right arm. Skylar gripped his remaining hand during the vicious procedure. I kept my eyes away while holding his legs steady, but the sound was vicious and unbearable.

Another Mati we rescued was at the ready, cauterizing the open wound on Leo's shoulder. Kai wrapped a towel over the amputation and covered him with a collection of spare clothes to keep him warm. Skylar still sat next to him, playing with his hair with bruised fingers and keeping him awake with light banter despite his closed eyes.

"How is my sister doing?" he asked.

Skylar looked over to the cot right next to him. He could have reached out if he still had an arm there. She stared at Persy's matted hair and still features. "She's a fighter. She'll get through this. Worry about your recovery first."

There was a long pause.

"How dare you touch me," he whispered.

"How dare you tell me to stop." She made a whirlpool with her finger for good measure.

He mumbled a laugh.

"You were really brave today." She shifted back to seriousness while his lips pulled into a smile.

"You were brave too. Did you *kill* Ebony Nique?"

"Why would you—?"

"The famous Gifted killer? *You?*"

"It's—"

"I can't believe you killed her."

"*Leo.*" Her lips quivered now as she tried to trade playful aggression for solemnness. "Yes I did, but you shouldn't make light of it. Especially because she, you know, looked like someone else."

"Hey." He waved his left arm around with terrible aim, his eyes still closed. She caught it, leaning closer as their hands clasped. "It was just an illusion, okay?"

"I know. I know." She exhaled, looking at him with a reassuring smile he couldn't see. "I'll try."

Prince Henry garbled with a gummy smile around Mr. Harris's feet. Sitting up, he clapped his hands, and like magic, a live painting of watercolor played a clip of Skylar and Leo leaning into each other with eyes closed, lips pressed. As soon as the image appeared in my mind, it disappeared, and everyone in the room halted, speechless once more. The only professional was Dr. Hansen who paused for a breath and then continued her work.

Skylar's face flushed the deepest shade of ruby red. She straightened her back and lowered their clasped hands against his stomach instead of seemingly on display.

Leo's eyes opened, and he slightly sat up by the color in Skylar's face. "Did the baby just snitch on us?" he asked, beaming like he was impressed.

Prince Henry rolled onto his side and beamed back.

"Yeah, I think he just broadcasted that to everyone in the room."

New energy rose within me. "*When did this happen?*" I practically screamed.

"Maybe it's not the best time to talk about it," suggested Skylar.

"What, two weeks ago?" Leo looked at her for confirmation.

She held her mouth open for a breath until she registered how well he looked. Very much himself. Skylar's lips formed a soft smile, and she gave a quick kiss to the flat side of his hand. "Yeah, about two weeks."

His smile became teasing. "You dare kiss my hand in *public?*" he exaggerated. "Do you have no shame?"

"Shut up." She returned, but her voice lacked any real scorn. "Lay back down. I'll make you do math problems if I have to."

"Anything but that."

He leaned back down, and the milliseconds drew back in as Dr. Hansen and Kai moved to the next person. The moment subsided.

Mr. Harris picked up Prince Henry and walked over to where my mom and I sat. Mom had since washed away the blood and reshaped the saw back into her leg prosthetic.

"We need to get supplies for Persephone." He stated the obvious.

"How do you suppose we do that?" I asked.

"We go to Norburn. Topside."

I chuffed. "You want us to go rob an abandoned hospital?"

"Not exactly." We watched the baby play with his fist as he clenched his fingers and then eased them. "We're at our limit underground. I think you know that."

I did. Until now, we relied on Nora's intel but our connection was spotty and inconsistent. And after what happened in Doverly, our numbers totaled to a cool sixty. It would get harder and harder to keep ourselves hidden even if the Diviner didn't just attack us and kidnap my sister. It was time to change our approach.

"For someone who isn't a mind reader anymore, you're spot on," I finally said.

A dry laugh resounded in his throat. "I think we can get support from a group in Norburn."

"A—" I made air quotes with my fingers—"*group?*"

Norburn was notorious for its criminality. *Group* was a mild term for what he was really saying.

"It's a possible source," he insisted. "They're made up of Gifteds and Unfortunates. They'll have the resources we need to take care of Persephone, and anyone else who needs help, too."

Not exactly my first choice for getting supplies since it was probably highly coveted by whomever owned it, but if they had what we needed to save Persy, then the risk was worth the reward.

I stood. "Let's go."

"You want to go out right now?" My mom stood up too.

I looked at Persephone. "There's no time to lose. Mr. Harris, are you good to go now?"

He stood and nodded. "We can be on our way in five."

I turned to my mom. "I'll be right back."

She gave me a warning glare. "You better. I'll keep the fort steady." She then looked at my teacher and snapped her fingers, "Peter, you better bring my daughter back to me."

She didn't have to say that she had already lost one daughter today for Mr. Harris to understand. "Yes, ma'am."

He hurried off, and I made my way over to Persephone's cot. Molly kept a sacred vigil. She deserved to know. "We're going to get her help."

Molly nodded absently. "If you find a Makan, bring them too."

"What?" I wasn't expecting that response. "Why?"

She held her hand out and revealed the yellow marble she took from the Diviner. Persephone's Gift.

Molly's voice cracked, "I don't know how to give it back to her."

My arms folded around me at her words. We'd seen the Diviner crush Gifts into his hand and absorb their power. Aura, Mati, Avlis, Nox, Animus. Divine only knew how many times he switched when he wasn't fighting us. When he was a mere Makan in our midst. When he tricked Nora into caring about him.

Was it even possible for us to regain what was taken from us? Or to obtain a Gift that didn't belong to us? The idea of having anything other than an Avlis Gift chilled my spine.

I leaned down and planted a firm hand on her shoulder despite the uncertainty. "I'll see what I can do."

***

Mr. Harris and I headed to Norburn in relative silence.

We found ourselves at the deserted train station where the welcome sign was graffitied to warn people away. I noticed the city map and the black ink that rubbed out the Lilac District. The smear reminded me that this was where we first discovered the Diviner. Where he first attacked all of us and killed someone I couldn't save. I looked away.

Mr. Harris didn't stop to look at the map, and I followed his lead straight ahead.

Even though we arrived with plenty of daylight, the city remained a horrid place. Trash glistened along gutters and alleyways. Cardboard boxes carved out sleeping places for ashen people. Cracks created shards in the sidewalk, and grime coated brick buildings a muddy red color.

"You know your way around?" I asked, side stepping around a trail of ants leading to whatever fresh kill was hidden in the shadows.

Someone shouted something incoherent above us. I flinched and sped up to walk alongside Mr. Harris, wrapping my arm around his in a secure gesture.

"Don't look at anyone directly," he instructed. "And always look like you know where you're going."

"Do you actually know where we're going?" I whispered back.

He tilted in the most subtle nod. "I do."

We continued on, noticing people but hardly crossing their paths. A group of black suits and shoulder pads walked into a restaurant together in front of us. An old woman with a nothing-to-lose face inhaled a cigarette on a balcony across the street. Loose pavement almost tripped me several times, worn down from what I could only imagine were Gifted duels and gang wars.

Finally, when it felt like I couldn't take being out in the open anymore, Mr. Harris pivoted and we entered into an oak wood building. A bar.

Glasses clinked. Chairs teetered and scraped against wood paneling. Patrons leaned into one another, chatting and raising their voices in unison. A man in the back of an open kitchen yelled "Order-up!" to the woman wiping her hands on a towel. She retrieved a tray.

As we entered, eyes peered at us and then away, disinterested.

"Take a seat anywhere," the woman said quickly, passing us carrying a tray of fries, burgers, and two beers. The scent of food, real *enjoyable* food, watered my mouth.

A small smile twitched at the corner of Mr. Harris's mouth as he nodded and led us to the bar stools facing the kitchen and all kinds of fancy levers. I sat down beside him, swiveling back and forth. He remained still and straightened his posture.

Two women sat idly to our right. They quieted, absorbed our features, and then went back to their conversation. I made sure to keep my attention straight ahead.

The waitress came back and threw her braid over her shoulder. "What can I—?"

She stopped as she looked at Mr. Harris, unblinking and then blinking rapidly.

All of the hustle and bustle in her demeanor melted away as she leaned against the counter and rested her cheek on her wrist, a hostile smile forming on her lips.

"You look like shit, Peter. To what do I have this *esteemed* honor?"

The two women next to us halted and looked over at us

again inch by brutal inch.

"I became an Unfortunate," he said to her first statement, displaying his brand. Her intimidating smile fell, and her hostility changed into one of sympathy.

She pulled back and looked down, occupying her hands with dish work. "I'm sorry to hear that."

"I'm alive—that's what matters," he muttered, shrugging it off. "And I'm here to ask for your help."

"*Help?*" Anger brimmed her question, so unexpectedly I couldn't help but jump. She raised an eyebrow. "Why would I help you?"

"You're the only one we can turn to right now," said Mr. Harris. "We need the Lady Lilacs."

I didn't hide my surprise, snapping my attention toward my teacher to make sure he spoke correctly.

"The what?" I said out loud. I turned back to the waitress in front of me, though she was side glancing to the two other women sitting beside us. I turned to them and then back straight ahead again. "You're all—you're all *really*—?"

I couldn't even say the name, completely floored.

"I thought...I thought..." My mouth hung open, trying to connect the dots. The Lady Lilacs took up a brief moment in the history books—an all-women gang that operated in the Lilac District of Norburn. The exact place we went to catch the Diviner two years ago and lost our first teammate, Cal.

The woman stared at me, deadpan. "You thought we were all dead? We are. Who is this scared girl you bring into my bar anyway, Peter?"

"I'm not scared," I tried to counter, but Mr. Harris talked over me.

"Fern, this is Lady Sanchiko. Lady Sanchiko, Fern is one of my students."

I paused, staring at the unimpressed Lady Lilac. "Nice to meet you," I managed, pulling out my arm to her.

She turned back to my teacher, and I slowly retracted. "The Lilacs are not at liberty to help the royal government. Don't you have *armies* for that?"

"Lady Sanchiko, you must know that Prince Cassius has taken over as king."

The dishes clanked as they flew back into the sink. "Do not say his name in my presence."

The chef called a new order. Lady Sanchiko used the opportunity to walk away from us.

When we were alone again, I whirled on him. "What am I missing here? The Lilacs are disbanded, in jail, killed! *You* lead that charge like a decade ago yourself. I'm so intrigued, but I'm very confused. Tell me right now!"

Mr. Harris sighed, unable to match my energy. "They're a lot smaller now but not truly gone. King Daltus wanted them stopped because they were getting too powerful—threatened his power. He was still a new king. Everything was a worry. But I could read their thoughts and see what they've been through to help others. I made an agreement with the Lilacs to keep their operations subdued, arrest a couple for publicity-sake, and ensure my brother was none the wiser."

I listened to him intently. "You'd make a good king, Mr. Harris."

He scoffed, "That ship has sailed."

"But this one hasn't," I finished. The Lady Lilac came back around the bar. "Lady Sanchiko," I blurted assertively, "we request your support. We need your help to take down the king."

She studied me. "I said no."

"*Please! We* can't do this alone. We've rescued sixty

Gifteds from the king's hand, but we lack the space or resources to continue growing."

"It can't be done."

"*Please!*" My voice whined even sharper, desperate and causing a scene. I didn't care. Persephone needed me. "My friend lost her Gift. She might die if we don't find her better medicine."

The two women next to us curled, bristling for a fight. Lady Sanchiko gestured for them to stand down. "A lot of friends die here, Miss Fern." She filled a glass full of water and passed it to me. "What is your friend's name?"

I didn't realize I was crying. Raising the glass to my trembling lips, I tried to regain my normal voice but I sounded like a child. The heat in my face continued to rise. "Persephone. She's a Mati. She needs an IV and some other things."

My words mixed together. Lady Sanchiko tilted the glass in my hand, gesturing for me to keep drinking.

"Cassius took my Gift, too," she said quietly. She gave me a pained smile and nodded to Mr. Harris. "Probably why your teacher here thought he could soften me up."

"But your hand," I mumbled, pointing as I took another gulp.

She examined her unblemished hand, a few rings dazzling in the light. "I'm in Norburn, honey. I don't always follow the law."

That was fair enough. I responded with a thumbs-up as I continued to drink down the glass.

Lady Sanchiko sighed, letting out all of her irritation. "Tell you what," she started, gesturing to the two neighboring women, "Lady A and Lady H can help get you the hospital supplies for your Persephone."

"*Really?*" I gurgled.

Mr. Harris leaned forward. "*And?*"

"*And,*" Lady Sanchiko rolled her eyes at him, "I'll ask the other members what they want to do, but I make no promises. What do you call yourselves?"

I finished my drink and stared at the empty glass, thinking. We didn't have a name. It was always just the team. Us.

When we were still at Galdor Academy, I tried giving everyone nicknames with the title "Protector." They didn't stick, and I knew they were childish the moment I proposed them. I made sure to keep thinking through my answer. If the Lady Lilacs were going to take us seriously, we needed a serious name.

Memories pulled on my heart. I replayed our moments, dancing in a field of red and white. Our shared dream: you on the left and me on the right. We did this together even while apart.

"We call ourselves the Unity Alliance."

CHAPTER TWENTY-FIVE

The Answer
NORA

Morning sun poured in from the window. I awoke with a chill, shared blankets now bundled completely over Delilah. Tugging to no avail, I remained awake and looked at her closed eyes and delicate face. She saw the light in me too. I focused so long on Cassius's Animus Gift, I hadn't investigated his Makan one. A Gift they both shared.

My priorities shifted; I needed to protect her from him. I didn't care that she was interested in learning what he could do. I wouldn't do that to you, Fern.

A knock came from the door. Delilah's eyes squinted open, and she groaned in protest, stretching. I propped up on my side as the door opened, expecting Poppy to check in on me. Maybe I'd get her to talk about the east wing and gain a few clues about what was happening there.

Cassius walked through the threshold instead; I scrambled to my bare feet. "Where is Poppy?"

"Good morning," he smiled, completely ignoring my demand. "I've come to invite you to tea. I'll give you a moment to dress out of your pajamas."

A yawn undercut my stern intentions. "I'm not leaving Delilah."

"She'll be in safe hands. No one will disturb her."

"She can accompany me for tea."

"That will not do."

I stepped forward, my words already formed in my thoughts before I said them. *And how are you going to stop me?*

He lifted his hand in a halting gesture. *Act carefully*, he weaved. *Your disobedience can harm others.* He gestured back to Delilah who was rubbing her eyes, oblivious to our silent conversation.

My mouth wired shut. He noticed and bowed, "I'll be waiting outside for you."

When the door closed again, I cursed under my breath and stomped over to the dresser. I grabbed the first dress my fingers caught, putting the garment on in a hurry. Wrapping the sheath over my waist, I tucked my sword into its holster.

As I found socks and shoes, I snapped at Delilah as she found my pillow and pulled it close to herself like a plush.

"Do not leave this room," I ordered.

She didn't respond, eyes closed. I frowned, torn between fully waking her up to tell her not to leave or letting her rest. I forced her to stay up for as long as she could bear, asking about her sister, how they were surviving, and any upcoming plans. Cassius had to already know plenty of information sorting through her memories, and I refused to stay in the dark. Already I imagined myself hanging from the ledge while he stood poised at the center of our playing field.

I let her sleep.

Walking over to the bookshelf, I scribbled a note in case she woke up before I came back.

After a deep inhale, I swung the door open. Two guards stood along the wall, and Cassius faced me directly.

"Are you ready, Miss Nora?" He was more triumphant than usual. Almost like his old self. His *fake* self, I reminded myself.

He ignored my thoughts like he hadn't read them. I eyed the guards. "I thought Delilah wouldn't be disturbed."

"They will ensure just that," Cassius replied.

"They are not to enter."

"You have my word. Now come along."

He outstretched his hand, and in my sleepy haze I slapped the gesture away. But then I remembered what he said about disobedience, and fighting every other instinct in my body, I forced myself to try again and clasp our hands together. I shivered by his touch, and he smiled as though my reaction meant something else.

We walked to his office with Mr. Harris's namesake still there.

Inside, a porcelain tea set paired with a large portion of eggs, sausage, buttered rye toast, peppered grits, and a sugar-coated muffin. He poured loose-leaf tea over the strainer on my side and then his.

I sat down, cautiously staring at the large meal. "What's the occasion?"

He sat across from me. "We've made a lot of progress since the last time we met like this. It's cause for celebration."

I took the creamer before he could and started pouring in his cup. We watched as his black tea turned into a pale brown color, filled to the brim, and spilled over the side.

"Define progress."

"You're just trying to keep yourself dark," Cassius said, unfazed. He snatched the creamer back before I could drain it completely and make a bigger mess of the table. "But it won't work. You're too hopeful."

I bit the inside of my cheek. As I wiped my hand with the napkin, he delicately sipped at his tea in an effort to reduce its contents.

"Is that what my light means? That I'm hopeful?" I asked, dry and bitter.

"That's been my conclusion so far. The Unfortunates in my service display a range of resolve. You were the first I noticed, and the brightest by a mile." He was looking at me now with the same enraptured interest he displayed when we first met.

"I guess I'm not that special anymore." I tried to deviate his attention from me, but hearing myself say it stung more than I expected. I really was just an ordinary girl doing what she thought was right and what others thought was ridiculous.

"I would disagree," he said, words far warmer than his usual tone.

I watched him pour the remaining milk into my cup. "Then what do you want from me?"

"I *want* you by my side. I liked when we were both on the same side. Don't you remember that at all? I even thought that maybe you'd..." He trailed off, a red shade rising from his collar.

We both didn't want him to finish. "You should have thought of that before you destroyed all of my progress in the first place."

"That was never my intention."

"You can't want me by your side and hurt the people around me. I know what you did to Persephone."

His fork hit the plate with a metallic snap. "Your friends chose their fate, and you continue to choose yours."

"You talk like the Divine," I said like an accusation. After reading the Great Book, I recognized it reflected more and more in his words. A copycat.

"Your people say so."

"That doesn't make you divine."

"No," he agreed, drinking more tea. "But it tells you something, doesn't it? In all that time interacting with them and learning the Word, you still don't understand what I am?"

I opened my mouth to respond, but I hesitated. I knew him as a prince who kindly defended and protected me during my first year here. I knew him as the Diviner who tricked me into leading my friends into danger and rattled this country in two. I knew him as the king who judged Gifteds based on their loyalty. I knew him as a Makan who could see light in Gifteds and in myself and in Poppy and wanted to prove himself stronger to those who underestimated him.

I wished I could separate him out—make him two different people. One I could despise with my entire being and one I could support and comfort. If he wasn't one person, I might have understood him better.

He read my mind, but I responded anyway. "I don't."

***

A week passed by in a slow drift.

After I incapacitated a guard asking for Delilah, Cassius

came to my door to fetch her personally. They'd be gone for half the day, and Delilah would tell me what they did at lunch. I listened carefully to what she told me, though it was as cut and dry as training got. She was right in her instinct to see people within the invisible plane, and Cassius was helping her hone in that skill, taking her to see loyal Gifteds in the city or turncoat Gifteds inside the castle walls.

She taught me, in turn, what each Gift looked like. The elemental Gifts were closely related to their power: Avlis were distinctly green and brown; Auras were shades of blue and grey; Mares were shades of blue and green; and Mati were warm colors of red, orange, and yellow. Imitation and Feran Gifts were uniquely patterned to reflect their animal, hence why Molly's had a snake eye.

Luxes were typically the brightest to look at in hues of white and yellow in stark contrast to the inky black color within Noxi hearts. I remembered when the Determination Arena filled with black rays as Cassius gave himself that Gift. Used it to almost kill Mr. Harris. Mutes reflected the rainbow in an effort to replicate any of the other powers, which made me think how nonthreatening Ebony Nique actually looked in his eyes. Animus held a deep purple hue, and Makans were similar to Unfortunates with a grey-toned glow.

"And he didn't say anything that was weird or ask you about Fern?" I asked every time.

Delilah shook her head. "No, I think he has all the information he can from my mind." She tapped a finger against her temple. "But I never went topside, so he only knows they're somewhere in the mountains."

That was still too close for comfort. If he got a turncoat Avlis to investigate, they might be found within a few days. If he hadn't already found their hideout. I counted down my heartbeats to subdue my panic. He'd tell me if my friends were discovered. He'd gloat. He'd tell me I had no reason to fight him anymore because everyone else was taken from me. My mind continued to race with little comfort.

I shifted into old habits to distract myself. Mundane tasks from my time in servitude. Cleaning my room. Straightening the bookshelf. Folding my clothes in perfect squares. Organizing them by color. Organizing them again by season.

I practiced with Bree, Ellie, and Holly until our bodies trembled from ache.

On the seventh day, I walked into the canteen kitchen and started washing dishes. I needed something as endless as my contemplation. The three girls found me there and got to work too. Holly stood beside me at the sink while Ellie dried and Bree put those items away.

Unfortunates wanted to live freely. That much was obvious, but what did "freely" mean? It meant to do what we wanted instead of what Gifteds required of us. If we wanted to be a servant, that was living freer than servants chosen at a ceremony. If we wanted to pursue an education or run a fishing business or become a soldier, then we could. No Gifted person or institution would stop us based on our Unfortunate status. It wouldn't even be a factor.

I passed the silverware to Ellie. Holly handed me a rogue fork.

Gifteds feared losing their power. In a literal sense with their Gifts and in a figurative sense with the advantages gained from having Unfortunates beneath them. What advantages? Freedom for one. If they wanted to pursue an education, Galdor Academy was an option for those interested in the military. Every city held at least one primary school for their youth, and Gifteds weren't taken out when chosen for servitude or to support their family. There were inner prejudices against certain Gifteds like Mati, Mutes, and Makans, but those weren't justified either.

Bree returned to a fresh collection of cups and began stacking them for the cabinet.

There had to be a way for both of us to live freely without fearing each other at the same time. No Unfortunate above a Gifted and no Gifted above an Unfortunate. No downcastment either. Gifteds could remain Gifteds while also respecting and caring for their Unfortunate counterpart. We shouldn't bring Gifteds down to our level. We should be elevating ourselves to theirs. Abolishing the Unfortunate Laws of Servitude. Setting up a government made up of both Gifteds and Unfortunates. We couldn't force people to love one another, but we shouldn't force us apart either.

Right?

I stopped washing a plate and looked to the fluorescent light above, waiting for the Divine to respond. A sign that my inner ramblings held merit. My answer to improving this world without destroying it.

"Boo!" Poppy's voice startled me. I gasped, my reflexes causing soap water to splash over my hands and apron.

She laughed, "I was wondering where you all were! Did you miss me?"

I turned around, her hands padding my shoulders like she couldn't get the energy out fast enough. Holly wiped her wet hands on her apron, and Ellie folded the towel down. Bree finished putting away cups in one of the taller cabinets she could reach.

They glanced at each other, a confusion spreading over their faces. "We were wondering where you went too," Holly said, much calmer than her general.

"It's good timing too. I think I finally found the answer," I noted.

Poppy nodded her head but clearly wasn't listening, "Mhm. Mhm. I have something to show you!"

I hesitated. "What is it?"

"Check this out." Poppy took a step back and snapped her fingers.

I squinted, staring at her with her hands on her hips. "I don't think anything happened."

The girls murmured in agreement.

"Really?" Poppy looked at her arm and then down at herself. "Hold on."

I blinked as she tried to figure out the issue, and she disappeared from sight. Holly sucked in a breath while the rest of us stilled. We could still hear her, murmuring to herself.

"General?" Bree asked, her voice rougher than the rest of us.

"Ah!" She yelled and reappeared in front of us with a new triumphant pose. "You see? Or rather, you don't see?"

My eyes widened. "What did Cassius do to you?"

"Our *king*," she corrected, "gave me a Gift. I'm a Makan now. Isn't that cool?"

"He did *what?*" Proper words failed me. Anger and horror plastered my face. The others hid their expressions better, glancing more obviously at each other as if to ask who should react first.

Poppy flickered in and out again with little control, bouncing around the kitchen space so fast she looked like she was teleporting.

"Keep up Nora," she teased. "I'm a Ma-kan."

"But that's not possible!" I blurted, though the evidence

continued to contradict. I pivoted, "Why would you do that? I thought you hated Gifteds. Why would you *become* one?"

Poppy shrugged, though I only saw her start the action. "I do, but if this is His plan, then I'll accept it, you know?"

"His plan?" I gripped the sink for balance.

"Yeah, Cassius has been trying to implant a Gift into Unfortunates for a while. Why are y'all acting so surprised? Bree, you had to know perfectly well what you were setting up in there."

"I absolutely did *not*," defended Bree, serious and grave.

The rest of us remained in stunned silence. *The east wing.* He was experimenting on Unfortunates in the east wing. But surely I would have noticed a sudden increase in Gifteds wearing red uniforms.

I gasped, pulling myself forward and grabbing her by the collar so she couldn't slip away. "Your new Gift, where did you get it from? Where is Delilah?!"

She wrangled me. "Easy, easy! It was already a Gift Cassius had on his wrist. Delilah is perfectly safe for now."

At her words, I released her and stepped back towards the sink, grateful for the sliver of good news. I pressed on, worried to know what her next answers would be.

"Poppy," I started. "Were you the first successful subject?"

She became cautious, defensive. "Yes."

"And what happened to all the others?"

We stared at each other for a long time.

"They all died," she said, matter-of-fact to cover any hint of remorse. I knew her well enough now to know she was burying her true feelings deep down for Cassius's message to shine. "It was too much for them to take on a Gift, and they perished. His Majesty asked if I'd volunteer because I was the brightest Unfortunate in his court. He had a theory that was the missing ingredient. A strong-willed soul within a strong-willed person."

I hated how in this very moment, I wanted that bothersome title of his brightest Unfortunate. I could have stopped this. I could have prevented this. I would have torn that room into ruins.

I managed to press further. "And you knew about the experimentation for how long?"

"I've known what's been happening in the east wing since we first carved it out."

A bile taste filled my mouth. "You let Unfortunates walk to their death Divine knows how many times—for what? Your messiah? You're more of a Gifted than I realized."

It was a low blow. Something I wouldn't want Fern to overhear because out of everyone, she was the exemption. My only consistency in this fight. But it was what Poppy needed to hear. I didn't regret how her face turned sour.

She paced, on the verge of storming off, when she clenched her fist and teeth. "By the way, we're leaving in an hour without *you*, Lieutenant Nora."

Her declaration pierced through me. My anxiety rose at the implication. Cassius made it clear that if my light didn't "improve" or if I stepped out of line, I'd return to Galdor Academy as a prisoner of war. I hadn't stepped out of line far enough, but Poppy was brighter than me now. She held a resolve I couldn't because everything she hoped for had happened and continued to happen.

I swallowed a deep breath, "What reason do you have to leave me here and away from my soldiers?"

"Oh, don't pretend you care about my battalion," Poppy snarled. She glanced to her best Unfortunates. Ellie and Holly shrank back, but Bree remained stoic.

"I apparently care more about Unfortunate lives than you do," I retorted. Her new Gift reflected her anger, violently flickering in and out.

"This is the next step!" Poppy shouted. "We serve a mighty force who can take Gifts and give to others! We should be *celebrating* this development." Her voice cracked at "celebrating," and Holly stepped forward to comfort.

So many times now, Cassius had warped people's perspective or struck so much fear into their hearts that they twisted against their very nature or their cause or their morality. His damned excitement this morning. We were celebrating a supposed immense progress since the last time we met for tea.

"Do you really believe that or does Cassius?" I asked, staring straight at her now.

Poppy's eyes twitched as she struggled to respond. I wondered if she saw my light right now too. If it was something she could even do so early with her Makan Gift.

She regained her fierce composure for one more instant. "We're finding the Gifted insurgence," she sneered, "and you won't be able to warn them this time."

I exhaled. Fern. They found her.

"No!" I ran forward, but Poppy vanished from sight. My fingers grabbed at the air.

She stormed off, her shoes clicking against tile and reverberating through the kitchen. The door swung open and slammed shut.

My breathing irregulated as my heart quickened.

"Poppy!" Holly ran after her. Ellie did the same, but Bree paused, watching me hyperventilate.

"I need to warn them," I whimpered, not bothering to keep my thoughts secret. "Oh Divine, no."

The floor swayed beneath my feet, and I fell onto the ground to avoid vomiting. I tilted my head back up to the ceiling, whispering "Oh, Divine" over and over again. I found the answer, but Cassius had found his own too. My fingers were slipping off the ledge. I looked to the endless universe below.

"The shipment code is 865790."

My eyes found Bree as she teetered off the playing field to catch me. She stared back, her arms crossed and mouth drawn in a begrudging up-curved line. A shipment code meant there was an convoy. Access meant I could stowaway on this mission. Reunite with my friends. If not warn them, then fight with them.

"I don't understand," I croaked. "Why are you helping me?"

The Anti-Gifted soldier looked away, her arms tightening against her chest. "Because my general and my king have done something unspeakable, Lieutenant."

Slowly, I inched my way back up to my feet and by such a miracle, I was standing at the edge of the playing field with Bree beside me. Before I could think too much, I fell forward and embraced her into the largest hug I could muster.

"Thank you," I wept. "Thank you."

Her entire body tightened at the gesture, and she only let me cry for three heartbeats before she broke free.

"Hurry," she warned, "They're likely counting inventory now."

I nodded, wiping away tears as a new concern rose within me. "What about Delilah?"

Bree shrugged but her words haunted me. "I cannot help you there. That's for you to decide."

CHAPTER TWENTY-SIX

While Delilah Is Away
NORA

That's for you to decide.

My hand gripped the inside panel of the armored truck, repeating Bree's words in my mind as they rang true. I had less than one hour to mull over the new power given to me, and I crouched, silent and frustratingly indecisive.

Delilah was out in the city with Cassius. There was no time to reach her, free her away from the king without suspicion, and sneak her onto an convoy on its way to her sister. There was only enough time for me to sneak in with Bree's helpful code number and think as the minutes dwindled. Cassius made it clear that my disobedience would bring harm to Delilah, and warning Fern of an attack was by far the most declarative disobedience I could enact.

Fern. I couldn't stand the thought of losing her or losing any of my friends to something I could prevent. I had complete control of the outcome, so the more I sat in silence, the more my heart *ached* for her. A burning sensation rose in my chest at how close I was to seeing her again. If I closed this door right this moment and sealed myself inside, I would see her again. Not just a phantom in my dreams but right in front of me. I could completely vanish into her embrace and feel her heartbeat where my ear met her chest.

But if Delilah was harmed once I went missing...I would be effectively choosing one sister over the other. Fern had every right to hate me if that happened, and I didn't want her to hate me. I wanted her to... My fingers brushed the door. No. I shouldn't entertain the thought.

I cursed to myself. What was the point of Bree helping me if I let this opportunity go to waste? If I left, Fern would be warned and Delilah would be punished. If I stayed, Delilah and I would remain under Cassius's thumb and Fern would be blind sighted.

I brought my hand back to my lap. Seeing that the door remained ajar, I turned away in hopes of coming to a decision. The AGM were only taking one supply truck with them, indicating that only one or two troops were on this mission. A discrete tactic or an arrogant one. I hoped for the latter.

I stood, my form pressing into the crates stacked as tall as my eye level. Slowly, I pried the top off the nearest crate with my blade, unsure if there were any passing guards. Then carefully, I reached my hand inside and felt a thin layer of plastic. Finding an individual item, I pulled it out and examined a wafer ration, wrapped in the same cheap foil that came with the twins's secret stash. *Hmm.* I tilted the box slowly and found it full of food for the journey.

Opening another crate underneath it, the same contents revealed themselves to me. Hope blossomed as more crates revealed more food. They didn't have Fern's precise location yet, or else there would be no need for the surplus. It could be days or even weeks until they found her, but the implication was clear: they would not stop until they *did* find her and my friends.

I looked at the door again, a thin sliver of light streaming in from its small opening. If I couldn't stay without damning Delilah, then maybe there was still a way I could help Fern.

They would not find you. Not until they starved. Not until they had to come back, empty-handed and weakened.

Taking each ration in hand, I unwrapped their seal and crushed the wafer in my fist and between my fingers until a dust littered the floor. I stomped over crumbs as I made my way inward, squeezing between columns and discovering new supplies like water and weapons. Adding the water to the floor, it sponged up the dry bread and absorbed into the wooden boxes at my feet. Weapons I could damage, I did so with the hilt or blade of my sword.

Glee captured my attention as I did everything in my power to hinder the AGM and give our insurgence another chance to thrive. This armored vehicle became my own playground to wreak havoc like a Gifted child. I wished my friends could see me right now. Fern, Leo, and Persephone would help me in the chaos. Kai, Skylar, and Molly would watch, appalled. We would banter back and forth as they disapproved of our methods. *Do you have a better idea?* Leo would point out, and they wouldn't.

My sliver of light vanished as the door shut with a hard shove and the automatic locking mechanism clamped into place.

"No!" I shouted, breaking the silence. I rushed over, but I stopped myself from banging my fists against the door. If I was caught now, they'd resupply the truck while still in the academy and my efforts would truly be wasted. I paused and waited, hearing muffled shouts and then the engine roaring to life.

No. I paced, glancing up at the ceiling and to the disarrayed crates. I couldn't leave! I fulfilled what I could do for Fern; I had to still fulfill my responsibility to Delilah.

The vehicle reversed, and everything shifted from the movement. I fell back, landing hard against the door. A stack of crates rushed my way, and I shifted to the right to avoid being pinned in place. A narrow stretch of room allowed me through, and I pressed myself deeper into the truck.

There had to be an emergency exit of some kind. Looking at the wall that separated me and the driver, I realized that the paneling was uniform with the rest of the truck's interior which meant I couldn't reach the wheel. That left the ground.

Closer to the center of the vehicle, I examined the floor to the best of my ability, kicking up excess water and soggy bread in the process. My fingers brushed along the ground, but it was as smooth as the ceiling.

We were driving forward now, for how long I couldn't be sure. My heart beat too fast for me to count, and the containment's rumbling drowned out any other sound. Desperate, I launched myself on top of the nearest crate stack and crawled my way over to the left side.

The wheels gained speed, bumping over something that resonated like a crater. The boxes jumped and shifted positions; my body slipped and fell over in a mangled heap. Pain struck my sides and knee, and I inhaled before squirming out of the uncomfortable, sunken position.

Crouching now, I brushed my hand through the darkness where I was and came up empty. I pushed forward but nothing indicated an escape hatch. That left the passenger side as my only hope.

The crate in front of me was light enough, so I tossed it with all of my might and carelessly navigated to the right side of the vehicle. The accelerator roared, and I used more energy than was necessary to push aside everything covering the ground. My hands waved blindly, the hum of the back wheels vibrating through my palm.

A latch, I thought. *A latch!*

My finger snagged on metal, and I gasped. Both hands wrapped around the latch, I pulled but the opening caught on the heavy items around me. I stayed low, refusing to lose my escape's location. Scrunching my body into a ball, I kicked the bottom box in front of me with all of my strength and pushed it as forward as possible.

Lifting the latch again, a rectangular hatch fully opened. Pavement sped forward and the back wheel rotated endlessly. This emergency exit wasn't meant to be opened while the vehicle was still active.

I watched as the road continued to stretch, trying to imitate Kai's calculating stare despite the futility. I crouched and carefully patted the exterior wall around the hatch, hoping to find a grip for me to hang onto. Nothing. Only a smooth surface. If I jumped now, I would collide with the tire.

I huffed, resigning myself to my new destination. Cassius would soon return to the academy and find me missing and Delilah... He could kill her with his hand or steal her Gift or brainwash her into being his lackey like Isaac Winters or simply torture her until she begged for every other option.

Maybe I deserved to jump off the ledge and resign myself to that endless sinking sky. I stared as the wheel whirled and the world raced without me.

Brakes screeched, and everything tumbled forward. I gasped, closing the hatch before another decision was made for me. The crates behind me pressed into my back, and some toppled over my head from the sudden force. Paper filling and broken weapons slammed onto the floor around me, and I stilled for a few heartbeats, catching my breath and realizing I was still alive.

Shouts erupted from outside the truck. Their words cleared at the driver's side, her and another soldier conversing.

"Mission number?" the soldier outside asked.

The driver listed it off.

A pause. Faint tapping. "Battalion and personal ID number?"

Shoving loose items away, I opened the hatch again and silently thanked the Divine it didn't make any metallic noise. The pavement and the wheel waited, stationary. Gathering my courage, I jumped down into the narrow space and found myself crouched underneath the convoy. I glanced around, finding feet at the driver's side and a plethora of walking and standing soldiers further ahead. Poppy was somewhere among this troop, hidden by the uniformity of the AGM pants and shoes.

We were at a checkpoint, I realized. Guard rails and train track lines indicated we were at the Galdor city limits. I exhaled, thankful we hadn't driven too far. I could still make it back to the castle with two hours of careful travel on foot. I just had to stay undetected.

Glancing behind me, intricately planned buildings and

sidewalks and trees beckoned. I slipped out from under the truck at its back, the open air chilling my spine almost like Cassius's Animus Gift. I cautiously removed my jacket, the one that easily denoted me as a lieutenant, in case anyone caught the movement.

Folding the wet material against my chest and without an alternative hiding place to duck behind, I walked back into the city on a tightrope straight line without once looking at the checkpoint—hoping, *praying*, that the armored vehicle's position was enough to cover me for the first hundred yards.

The hustle and bustle of Galdor worked to my advantage. As people crossed the street, I followed them timidly to the sidewalk before dipping into an alleyway and then behind a dumpster.

My heart beat so loudly, I thought I might faint. I sat there for a few minutes, counting down the seconds until my breathing evened out again. I waited in case anyone spotted me. I waited in case I needed to run.

Though I lacked a mirror, I knew I looked terrible. The water I had dumped onto the floor now splattered over my uniform, especially drenching me at my ankle. Food particles clung to me too, and I spent several more minutes patting away any evidence of my destruction. I smoothed back my hair, tangled and matted, and placed the strands into a tight, low bun.

My time as a servant didn't fail me now. I treated myself like I did when I had to clean the gutters and pretended that was exactly what I did to deserve such a disheveled appearance. Cuffing my pants until they reached capris-length and removing my over shirt completely to reveal a white, dryer and cleaner tank-top, I folded the two worst layers and laid their better side over my forearm.

When I returned to the academy, I vowed to take a long bath while Delilah recalled her day through the bathroom door.

My features morphed into a proper, neutral expression as I returned to the sidewalk. Keeping to the far right. A shadow. Unimportant. Unnoticed and off duty.

A glance or two pierced my way, but I kept my eyes on the Iridion castle and ducked away from city guards as they too weaved through the crowd.

Excuses formed in my mind as I closed the distance to Galdor Academy. I could escape the truck unnoticed, but there was no way I could scale that wall without sounding the alarm. The front entrance was my only option and the boldest.

I belong here, I thought to myself. *I am the king's brightest Unfortunate. I am the king's personal favorite. I am the king's key prisoner. Let me through.*

Two guards stood just as they had when I first arrived to the academy, except now they wore red uniforms and the distinct Royal Crest Knight pin was missing on their lapels. *I belong to him*, I thought in spite of myself. *They will let me through.*

They bristled as I neared, so I stopped about five feet from the entryway. I stood even straighter and spoke in my soft, neutral servant voice.

"It seems I have lost my way. Please allow me to return to His Majesty at once." The two men didn't lower their guard. I tried a sterner expression, a sterner tone. "Do you know who I am?"

"We are aware," the left one drawled.

"Then you shall have no problem letting me through," I snapped and then dared to add, "unless you want to keep your king waiting."

"His Majesty has not returned to the castle," the right one said. "*You* can wait here until he does. I'm sure that won't be a problem."

I overplayed, but I refused to show him the distress tugging at my nerves. If Cassius saw me as I was—outside of the academy grounds and in my current attire—then I was doomed.

"Not a problem," I lied, chirping my voice an octave. "I just want to wear something…more appropriate when I see him."

I gestured to my bare skin and wrinkled clothes since they were already scanning me suspiciously.

"You can wait here for his arrival," the right one reiterated.

I clutched the hilt of my blade, on the verge of breaking. Time to go on the offensive. "What is your ranking, soldier?"

The two men, already at their weapons, gripped theirs tighter. "We're guards, ma'am," the left one answered.

"I am a lieutenant under General Poppy's command," I barked, unsheathing my sword with a metallic hiss. "Let me through as your superior."

The left one bit the inside of his cheek. Before he could speak, either to approve or to deny my request, a new presence prickled at the back of my neck. The men saw him before I did, loosening their hostility and bowing before their king.

"What is the meaning of this?" Cassius demanded, stepping closer to my side.

Caught, I retained my fighting stance. "These *soldiers*," I spat, "refuse to let me through."

Cassius looked bewilderedly from me to his guards.

"Explain."

"She was outside of the academy, sir," the left one answered. "Asking to be brought to you. We asked her to wait for your return."

Cassius raked me over, but I refused to look his way. Instead, I fueled all of my anger and frustration at the two men before me, thinking repeatedly of their hindrance.

"Nora," he said in a soft tone, gently placing his hand over mine on the sword's hilt. It took all of my energy not to flinch from his touch, to keep up my story. "Lower your weapon please."

He didn't use his Animus Gift to command me; I placed my sword back into its sheath of my own accord. I turned to him finally and looked into his eyes. He held me in his stare, and I reached for all the memories that we enjoyed. Our dance in his bedroom. His kiss on my cheek and on my lips. When we looked at each other for too long in his private training room. Anything I could pull so his Animus Gift would focus on that and not on my most recent memories.

Cassius's mouth twitched and his throat bobbed, and I knew I succeeded.

"Why are you outside of the Grounds?" he demanded, hiding the fragility underneath.

I smiled slowly, mischievous and difficult for very different reasons than he assumed. "I wanted to see you," I mused, wrapping my free hand over his arm. He jolted but didn't step back.

I chuckled as I rolled soft circles along his skin, "I guess I became quite feverish, too. Please forgive me for my appearance and display."

He gulped more audibly now, and I focused my attention on nothing else. No one else. I pulled away before his ideas became their own actions and kept my smile as assurance.

Finally looking around our vicinity, my façade faltered as Delilah wasn't there. Was she invisible? Was she using her Makan Gift to hide or to scare me like she did her sister?

"Where is Delilah?" I asked in the most nonchalant voice I could muster.

A shadow cast over Cassius's face, twisting from pleasure to restraint. My smile fell and my voice hardened. "Cassius, where is Delilah?"

He glanced back to the main road where I came from, and though the transport was too far away now to be seen, I recognized what he didn't want to outright tell me. I tried to step back, but my heel caught on stone and I collapsed.

Any false dignity I had left vanished as the information raced through my mind too quickly, too impossible to grasp onto with its full weight. Delilah was taken onto the mission to apprehend her sister, and I ran back to him. To *him*.

If I stayed on—if I had known—I sprung to my feet and shouted. "*Delilah!*"

I stepped forward, but the guards swarmed my form before I could flee. "Delilah! No! *Delilah!*" Shock limited my actions; I thrashed but together, they picked me off the ground and carried me through the gate.

CHAPTER TWENTY-SEVEN

Us and the Weapon's Rack
NORA

"*Delilah!*" I shrieked, ignoring how the soldiers along the academy grounds halted and watched my plight.

I bit the hand firmly covering the hilt of my sword, and the guard's grip tore away as he yelped. He then slapped me across the face as if an impulse response, and I sliced my blade across his chest. Blood spewed out from the large gash, and both men dropped me hard onto the ground.

Soldiers in wait sprang into action, either to aid their bleeding comrade or to apprehend his assailant. I stood, ready to beeline directly through the black gates when Cassius's form blocked my exit. He stood several paces back with his hands behind his back like an instructor, reminding me too much of Mr. Harris when he refused to place me on the Diviner task force. He wanted what, a show? A demonstration of how much I would defy him?

In that momentary hesitation, someone grabbed me from behind and I drove my sword past my shoulder. The blade met resistance, sinking into thick flesh. Blood poured over my back, and an acrid smell overtook my senses. I freed my sword through an upward motion and refused to look at what I had done to another person.

Several other hands were already clawing at my clothes, and I cut at their fingers wildly. I couldn't hear their screams over my own as more hands replaced retreating ones like I was fighting a mythical creature. Cassius's entire army descended on me.

I needed to get to the mountains. I needed to get to the Fairaways! I needed to escape him.

Someone burrowed their fingers under mine, and the sword disappeared from my hold. I was on my back now, swarmed by shadows obscuring the sun. I squirmed, but more hands firmly kept me in place.

"*No*," I croaked, sobbing now. My sword returned as a blade against my throat, cool and sharp and covered in an inky red substance.

"Enough." Cassius's voice discerned itself from the violence, calm but stern. I couldn't see his face, but he must have seen mine. "Take her to my private training room. I'll watch over her until she's calmed down."

Exhaustion pushed through the adrenaline, and I only cried as those uninjured carried me inside the castle while those with missing fingers and gashes made their way to the infirmary.

***

I was dropped unceremoniously once we reached his private training room, and Cassius snapped the door shut behind him. It was just us and the weapon's rack now. Sprawled out on the floor, I offered a throaty laugh that imitated Ebony Nique's insanity.

He pretended not to notice, rolling up his sleeves. "You killed three of my soldiers and injured a dozen more," he noted, but I couldn't place his voice. Dark but also matter-of-fact.

"Sounds like it's punishable by death," I suggested. *But you stopped them,* I thought. He let me maim his soldiers but refused to let them retaliate in the same way.

He scoffed, "Is that what you want?"

"No."

As I sat up, crimson beads rolled off my skin, sleeves, and hair, creating a ring around my fallen form. Unfortunate blood stained my hands in a pursuit to save Gifteds. If Holly saw me right now, the headline would write itself.

"It's not what I want, either," he confessed.

"I don't care what you want," I snapped. "How could you do this?"

His lip pulled into a smile, but he stopped himself. "Do what?"

I stood, despising how he leered down at me, and snatched a knife from the weapon's rack. "Where do I start?"

Fresh fire helped me close the distance between us in swift strides, and I swung the blade at his head. He swayed to my left, dodging but not moving away as I struck the door.

"I know what you do in the east wing!"

I contemplated twisting the knob open, but he grabbed both arms before I could dislodge the knife and twisted me around. My back pressed against the door now, his body too close to mine and my arm raised high against his grip. The knife hovered above our heads.

"How many of your soldiers died before Poppy's success?" I demanded.

"28."

"That's vile."

"It's Divine work."

I clenched my teeth, bile rising in my throat. As I loosened my fingers, he registered my intentions and ripped himself back. The knife clattered to the floor, and I swiftly picked it up.

"Was that your plan for me? To turn me into a *Gifted?*" I shouldn't have been so upset with the accusation, but surely that goal couldn't have been the only interest he had all that time ago.

His face turned sour, "Of course not. I had no idea it was even possible until I tried on my own general."

I stepped forward, the blade pointed straight at his heart. He swallowed, his features softening into sorrow and his hands up in appeasement.

"Nora when we first met, you were blinding. Absolutely radiant. I had no intention of turning you into anything you're not. But if I can offer that to others, then I will."

"It was their choice then, was it?" Doubt laced my words. Counting out the carnage in my notebook, I recalled 18 within its pages. That still left 10 of his own soldiers. "The Gifteds-turned-Unfortunates you brought back to Galdor— you experimented on *them* too, didn't you?"

Cassius didn't deny it. "All of their sacrifices were in service to their country. You out of anyone should know what that means."

I wobbled forward, the world tilting on its axis. I blinked

and refocused, thinking of Persephone whose Gift was stolen by him and how none of his experiments survived.

"But it didn't take. Why?"

He clenched his jaw, but he answered anyway. "I didn't return their own Gift. I gave them other Gifts or their same power from a different subject. Returning their original Gift is the last hypothesis I need to test."

I took another precarious step forward, ignoring how the muscles in my arm shook violently. How splotches of red, purple, and black bruises overtook my limbs. Time seemed to dwindle. I changed subjects, unable to do anything else for Persephone.

"What are your plans for Delilah? Don't you *dare* lie to me."

"She's more useful as a bargaining chip," Cassius replied, stepping closer in my direction. I adjusted my knife's point in warning, but my eyes squinted, suddenly heavy. He continued, "This is war, Nora, and that means I need your friends to cooperate and surrender."

I blinked more, a headache pounding in my skull, urging me to rest. Refusing my own body's plea, I turned to the door. To the outside world. To Fern.

"I need..." I whispered, but I slipped before I could fully rotate and finish my sentence.

Cassius caught me before I could crumble, and I willed my hand to lift, for the knife to puncture him, but it laid numb by my side. His fingers pulled my hair away from my face, and I willed my arms to slap his touch away but they remained still. I panted, willing my body to move but it didn't.

This wasn't his Animus Gift overtaking my body. This was exhaustion mixed with an incredibly heavy pain, pure and unrelenting. His face blurred as my eyes struggled to stay open. This reminded me too much of our connected dreams, where he either killed or haunted me. I wanted nothing more than to wake up and return to my dorm room. For Fern to come to my bedside and guide me back to reality, sensing my nightmares even though she didn't know what they were.

This was real, I desperately reminded myself. *This was real and she wouldn't be there when you awoke. Stay awake!*

My will weakened. I was falling, further and further into sleep.

Fern, I thought, calling out to her, to wherever she could hear me. *Run, Fern. Run.*

My eyes closed, and I drifted off into the warmth that enveloped me. Trees and stone blurred past as I ran, ran, ran, after tuffs of red hair.

CHAPTER TWENTY-EIGHT

Below the Mountain
FERN

Mr. Harris and I returned to our secret base in the mountains with a plethora of medical supplies: bandages, cough syrup, packets filled with invisible nutrients, and a few needles. We carried it all on our backs, looking the part of hiker to any suspicious figures.

Lady Sanchiko would introduce our Unity Alliance to the collective, and if we joined forces, they would come of their own accord in two weeks' time. As a gesture of trust, I shared our hideout's location, and as a gesture of goodwill but no outright promises, they gave us what we could carry.

Fresh water in plastic bottles swished as we ascended on foot instead of racing there with the ground shifting beneath our feet. We couldn't make it obvious that one of us was an Unfortunate and one of us was a Gifted in case we were spotted. The earth hummed beneath my feet anyway as it always did when I was this determined and elated.

Soil opened as we stood above our home, and we descended to eager hands and faces. Molly, though, grabbed my wrist first and pulled me toward her like a vine finding a branch. She led me to Persephone, whose face was scrunched and pale.

"Did you find a Makan?" Molly asked, her face burned with urgency. Had she slept at all since we left?

I didn't want to give her an outright no. "The Lady Lilacs will decide if they're willing to help in two weeks," I replied. "She wouldn't tell me if they had a Makan until then."

Molly shook her head, "She needs help *now*. She's starting to—"

Before Molly could finish, movement flashed in my peripheral. Persephone convulsed in sharp movements, her eyes closed but moving behind her eyelids with an agonized expression. Dr. Hansen rushed to her left side, and I was upon her right, unzipping the backpack in one swift movement.

Molly hovered overhead for a breath before she sat on her knees and used her shoulders to elevate Persy's legs up in the air. This mustn't be the first time she had to help in this way.

"Leo!" Molly shouted.

Instinctually, I handed the doctor one of the packets with

an enclosed needle, and she examined the label.

Leo arrived, falling close to his sister's head. Heat radiated off him, violent at first like a fireplace first ignited, before calming to a consistent simmer. He placed his one hand over her chest where her heart thumbed wildly and snuggled his face in the crane of her neck, warming but also restraining her there.

Dr. Hansen punctured the bag at its corner, filled her syringe with its liquid, and grabbed ahold of Persy's forearm.

"Keep her still, Miss Fairaway," the doctor urged, and I pressed down on her right arm and laid my head on her stomach.

I didn't watch the needle meet her skin. Instead, I focused on the desperate rumble in Persephone's stomach and the tremors subdued as they arrived. Her breathing became more shallow.

She might survive with new medicine, but she might already be too weak. And even if she did last another two weeks and the Lady Lilacs came as I hoped and they had a Makan as I hoped, how would they know how to give her Gift back?

An idea formed, however stupid, and refused to leave. I wasn't a Makan, but maybe...just maybe you didn't need to be a Makan to give Gifts. I watched the Diviner crush Gifts in his palm, watched how they absorbed into his skin, watched how he used them to hurt us. What if I saved her? What if I killed her? I was not one to dwell on the what-ifs for terribly long.

Persephone continued to convulse and burn with sweat; Dr. Hansen cursed.

I threw my open palm out to Molly. "Hand me her Gift."

"What?"

"Now."

Molly dug into her pocket.

I barely registered its weight before slipping the yellow marble into Persy's limp hand and squeezing her fist shut.

***

I replayed what happened next as I squatted perfectly still in the trees, lying in wait for the Lady Lilacs like a feline on the prowl. Two weeks passed, and if they were coming with their assistance, it would be today.

The marble fractured; yellow light as blinding as the sun illuminated through her fingers. Persephone's blankets caught flame near her arms, and Dr. Hansen pulled the needle back as its metal tip singed bright red. Leo sprang into a seated position as Persy inhaled a large breath, her eyes opening. A yellow glow continued to emanate from the veins in her wrist as we patted out the small fire at her waist; Skylar made quick work to dissipate the smoke. Leo continued to stare down at his sister in disbelief.

Feet shuffled as a crowd formed around us. Dr. Hansen placed the back of her hand over Persy's forehead, paused, and then asked if we had any water.

I handed her one from the backpack. "Tilt her up, please," the doctor ordered.

Planting my knee squarely against her back, I held her neck gently with my right hand. Dr. Hansen uncapped the bottle and brought the lid to Persy's mouth. I tilted her neck as she swallowed, her breathing regulating with each successful gulp. Leo repeated her name over and over again in a soft whisper, resisting the urge to wrap around Persephone's frame and hug her. Some of the Gifteds whispered their own prayers over her, and most others just watched in awe.

She was safe and a Mati again, and it was all a miracle. I wanted to share the news with Nora—wanted to ask if Delilah had reached her and how they were fairing together. Had it already been two weeks since Delilah was kidnapped? That was too much time.

Uncertainty threatened to tear at my heart, but I focused on what was around me. Distractions have helped so far, and today would be no different.

The final leaves of fall cascaded to the ground as the wind picked up. I thought about how the trees would be bare in a few days, and I wouldn't be able to hide in their branches anymore. I thought about how grey the sky was, and the threat of a storm. Had it been raining in Galdor at all? *Where were you, Nora, when it rained nowadays?*

I thought about our time at the Flower Festival, her in that beautiful purple butterfly outfit and me dressed in green and brown casual attire. I thought about weaving baskets and how she snapped at me, which was so unusual I didn't mind, after I asked about the rain. I thought about the unity flowers I bloomed with her watching and cheering me on, and I thought about that name I gave to the Lady Lilacs.

The Unity Alliance. Hopefully the name alone would provoke action, provoke change. Hopefully they would come today.

The crunch of leaves brought me back to the present. Excitement soared through me. Could it be them?

Someone emerged, a woman who looked younger than her years and a sword loosely held in her hand. I stared down at her blonde scalp from a bird's eye view. She glanced around her surroundings but didn't look up. She wasn't a

Lady Lilac. A bright red headband designated her an Anti-Gifted soldier.

They hadn't scouted out this far before, though they must have become bolder, more assuming with Delilah's limited information. I remained still and silent, and she did the same like she was waiting for someone. I didn't like it. I needed to leave this spot. If she discovered me now, more would circle this location and hover right over our hideout. If I could move a few trees over and capture her attention, she'd deviate course. Investigate elsewhere.

I crouched even lower, my body condensed into a ball to avoid making any sound. My hand adjusted down the branch slowly like a sloth, and my foot aimed to follow when a bird cooed to my immediate left.

I jilted my head up and made eye contact with an arrowhead pointed straight at my face. The archer released the arrow, and I barreled out of the way, using my Gift to slide to the ground.

Poppy emerged, holding her giant mallet in one hand and dragging a weight behind her with the other. It was Delilah, her clothes torn from a struggle and one eye closed shut with dried blood. The sight sickened me to my core; the earth rumbled in fierce warning to those above and to those below. The trees bent lower and encircled us in a web of branches, blocking off the reinforcements running up the hill.

My ex-servant smiled at my dismay as her two operatives, the archer and the blonde, flanked her sides. The blonde's sword landed a few inches from Delilah's neck. My sister didn't wince or strain or flinch. She just looked at me with her one good eye and an apologetic face. My sister was useful right now for all terrible reasons.

"Reveal your secret base," Poppy ordered.

I didn't respond for a breath, encouraging grass to overgrowth around us. Poppy watched me, her smile falling as she repeated. "Reveal your secret base, or your sister dies. It's a simple trade."

I'd say this is a fair trade. For now, at least. The Diviner's words rang in my ears, though it was my own remembrance instead of his influence. Our escape for her capture. Now, our surrender for her safety.

The blonde inched the blade closer to Delilah's neck, a glimpse of begrudging in her movement. Flexing my fingers, a stem wrapped around the metal frame, and she froze in place, probably anticipating an attack. A flower bloomed instead, and the sword drew no further.

"There's no need for that," I said, gesturing Poppy forward with my hand and the earth obeyed.

She and Delilah shifted closer as the soil beneath rolled them toward me. The archer and the blonde tensed, but Poppy gave them a halting hand of her own. We now stood an arm's length apart.

I would not bring my sister fear or harm. I would not draw this stalemate out. I was risking a lot of people, but if I could time it just right...

Dirt softened and sank around us, descending into our underground base. The two AGM soldiers tried to follow, but grass caught their ankles. Before they could free themselves, I already knit the earth back together above our heads. I made sure no one could follow, and I tried not to smile at how seamless that move worked.

Poppy glanced around at the expanse around her as refugee and rebel eyes noticed her stark red presence. She still had a scar, however faint, right under her jaw where split skin had been bandaged during her arrival to the Fairaway House.

You could easily miss it with the lighting and the tilt of her head, but I remembered its healing. A slow process. In stages just like her namesake flower.

We stood in the center of the living space. Two weeks ago, she would have seen a litter of weakened Gifteds receiving treatment. Now, there were only three sick patients, and they were safely tucked in their own room. Persephone sat at the far corner with her brother, alive and recovering.

Enemies surrounded Poppy on all sides, at all exits.

My foot stomped, urging the ground to wrap around her legs. Immobilize her. But she snapped her fingers at the same moment, disappearing from sight. My eyes widened—*what?* A gust of wind rustled my hair; Kai and Molly shouted out in surprise as they were promptly pushed aside by an invisible force. Poppy's form flashed from one breath to another, and the impossible was realized.

A new Makan freshly coming into her Gift. What on earth did the Diviner do to her?

Everyone braced, their eyes darting around for a glimpse of her reappearance. But I could hear her running across the ground. Just as I could a hundred times with Delilah.

There. My left. My eyes darted for what she was running to: Mr. Harris holding the baby prince.

I waited until her foot fell into a rhythm, and soil broke away from its source, surging up and capturing Poppy mid-stride. She yelled and clawed at her restraints, throwing dirt off in clumps before it hardened all around her. She flickered in and out like a waning candle until she was completely exposed again.

Mom encased her further, ordering the earth to wrap and constrict her neck until all Poppy could do was look up and flare her nostrils in case she needed to hold her breath. Mom wasn't cruel enough to kill someone she took in as her own. That much I trusted, even if Poppy didn't.

Dr. Hansen and Kai were already upon Delilah's crumpled body, examining her injuries and measuring her responses. After securing Poppy further, mom wept openly beside her daughter. She was home, but she was not safe. None of us were.

I strode over to the Anti-Gifted general. Nora told me how the king made her a lieutenant under Poppy's battalion. The two of them spent many days together. Many days I wished to get back.

Though I was tall, I made myself taller by lifting the ground beneath my feet so Poppy could look me in the face from her prison.

"Did you torture Nora too?" I asked.

Poppy raised an eyebrow and gave a sly grin. "You've captured a general, and the first thing you ask about is my *lieutenant*? If I told you I killed her, what would it matter—?"

Her smile strained, and she choked on her words. I realized with horror that my knuckles were so clenched they were white, and *I* was the one harboring her voice. I released my hands, flexing them by my sides where Poppy couldn't see, but she knew. She must have known too well how an Avlis could hurt her.

"I'm sorry. She's not though, right?" I urged. "She's alive? In Galdor?"

After a fit of coughs, Poppy answered. "As long as the king favors her, she is alive."

That assurance had to be enough for now, even if the statement continued to burn inside me. *As long as the king favors her.* How long could that last when she remained against him—when she helped me during our connected meetings?

I swallowed and focused on the interrogation. "Did the Diviner give you a Gift?"

Poppy sneered, using all of her facial muscles to achieve the action. "I remember when you'd pick red poppies in the spring and give them to me in a small bouquet. You wouldn't even create them yourself."

I blinked and pouted. Going on tangents or not following the conversation in a linear path was something I often did. At a time where I needed to be serious, she steered us elsewhere. Fine. I'd match her. It would take Unfortunates hours to dig us up. We had plenty of time.

"I remember when you spoke for the first time. You'd been with us for what, an entire year, before you said your first word? I think it was a whispered *'thank you'* when I offered irises instead."

"What would you offer, Nora?" Poppy prompted, the sly smile returning. "If she was your servant?"

My mouth wired shut as the general stared, waiting. "She's not—" I stuttered. "I've never seen her that way."

"In what way then?"

I looked around, aghast and my face flushed, but if people met my gaze, they were too far away to hear us. Mr. Harris successfully moved to the other side of the cavern, doing his due diligence to keep Prince Henry from capture.

"What would you offer her?" Poppy brought my attention back, teasing.

I put my hands on my hips, narrowing my eyes in challenge. "A unity flower."

Poppy considered my answer, twisting her mouth like there was a bad taste inside.

"What?" I demanded. "Were you expecting something else?"

"I wasn't expecting them to take so long." The earth rumbled above our heads. Poppy sighed as best she could in her state. "There it is."

I looked up along with everyone else as something—correction, *someone*—ripped the world at its seam. Recognizing my Gift and the Anti-Gifted's relief, there must have been a turncoat Avlis among their ranks. Someone who pledged their loyalty to the Diviner. Someone we couldn't save at a wait station or in that dreadful throne room.

Our hours suddenly turned into mere minutes.

Screams and shouts echoed through the cavern. Mom was already at the tunnel entrance, her voice commanding above everything else.

"This way!" She beckoned the Gifteds to safety but I remained where I was. Our team remained too.

Voices muffled as everyone else retreated. Mr. Harris with Prince Henry. Dr. Hansen with Delilah. Ms. Lancer ran up the rear with stragglers. I locked eyes with Mom and nodded. She bit her lip and closed the tunnel in front of her.

Poppy strained, hoping the distraction would weaken her prison, but my hold kept her in place. Molly and Kai stood to my left; Skylar, Leo, and Persephone stood to my right. There was a space, I noticed, beside me where Nora should have resided.

"Ready?" I breathed.

They nodded, jaws clenched. I nodded back. The barrier between us and the Anti-Gifteds Movement thinned. Tremors rippled through the cavern like a burrow dug up, but I was not waiting prey.

I inhaled, deep and slow before flailing my arms,

mimicking a wave. The dirt beneath us softened, churned, until it mimicked a wave too. We ascended, our secret base breaking apart and collapsing in an avalanche of soil. My feet swayed with the tide, my body encircling my friends and our hostage. I focused on our small patch like a hurricane's eye. The ground would not swallow us up but keep us upright, balanced.

The turncoat Avlis successfully broke through; the sky greeted us in a greyish haze. We pushed ourselves up to the surface, and with a commanding halt, the earth settled back into place below our feet.

We were surrounded on all sides. My initial barricade was removed and given back to its original source. The turncoat Avlis stuck out like a sore thumb among the Anti-Gifted soldiers. He wore a dark green coat over a black shirt and pant combination, standing with his hands hidden in his coat pockets. He also sported a few moles along his face and neck, and the streaks of grey in his hair surprised me.

I prepared to fight an old man. *An old man working for the AGM*, I reminded myself. *Never underestimate your opponent.* I could practically hear Mom's reminder.

Less than half of the Anti-Gifted soldiers brandished weapons, too. An odd enough observation to point out. Their overconfidence in our surrender would be their downfall.

We all stared at each other for several breaths, each waiting for the other's move. Without Nora, orders fell onto me. I'd do her proud.

I turned to my right side, talking to Skylar, Leo, and Persephone. "Head north. Split the army and circle back around when you can."

Skylar lifted off the ground immediately. The twins nodded, though Leo looked skeptically at his sister. She *just* recovered from a terrible battle. I silently wished she escaped with my mom and the other refugees instead, but I also silently guessed that Leo would not let Persy fall to the same fate twice.

They broke off to the north, and a fourth of the soldiers broke off to chase them. The rest stayed, glaring at me, Kai, and Molly.

I didn't reveal anything else, charging at the turncoat Avlis in front of me. Molly replaced my original position, blocking anyone from freeing their general. Kai flanked me, attacking anyone who dared steer me away from my main target.

The turncoat Avlis stepped back, his hands freeing from his pockets and twitching at the ready.

I swung a right hook, a square of hardened earth following in time with my movement. He clenched his hand into a fist, and my attack shattered against his knuckles.

The ground uprooted underneath my feet like a hook. I caught the impending action, jumping as high as I could into the air. With the wave of my hand, the reaching soil sliced in half, and I threw the disconnected portion at his head.

He braced for impact again, but the weight was heavier than my first attempt. He fumbled to the side. Landing back onto solid footing, I felt the root of a tree beneath us. With a rising motion, I lifted the root to the surface—just enough to trip him.

He fell—the worst scenario when fighting an Avlis—and I lifted both arms up to the sky, my hands arched like claws. The root snapped to attention, breaching the ground's surface and twisting around the man's frame. Its grip tightened and loosened as the man fought back as he too commanded the root to obey him. My eyes narrowed in concentration; a sting of pain erupted from my brain. I had already used so much of my Gift already.

I focused harder and harder on the tree. So much so I didn't notice how the grass around me began to lengthen and slither around my ankles. I gasped at their wiry touch, and they latched on, ready to ensnare.

Kai swooped into the fray, his arms spread wide. He grabbed my arm with his left hand and swiped down at the grass encircling our feet. Water stripped away from the grass and the dirt and hovered over his palm, leaving the ground dry and weakened. The greenery fell over, limp and grey.

I stepped out of the loose hold, smiling as the root successfully covered the man's body and dragged him closer to the tree trunk. One of the heavier branches lowered, bonking him on the head and rendering him unconscious for good measure so he wouldn't use his Gift to escape.

"Thank you," I breathed to Kai.

He patted my arm before releasing me. The water lowered to hover and hide his upper body as he charged at more Anti-Gifted soldiers.

Molly screamed, "No!"

My head snapped in her direction. She was pinned down by a heavy-set woman with purple-dyed hair, but she was more focused on something else. I followed her line of sight; the blonde soldier was actively pulling Poppy out of her encasing. Clusters of dirt and rock littered at their feet. If I wasn't so out of breath, I would have cursed.

I bolted toward Molly, forming a giant mallet out of grass and sticks that rivaled Poppy's own weapon. Using the momentum from running, I swung as hard as I could against the AGM soldier's side. My mallet met bone; she soared several feet and collapsed in a heap.

I didn't stop. Instead, I charged straight for my ex-servant. The blonde soldier noticed and quickly handed Poppy her mallet before running toward another part of the fight.

We connected, my handle over hers in an X formation. To her credit, Poppy held her ground even as her feet skidded an inch back. I didn't use a weapon very often, but I reached my limits with using my Gift. This final creation would have to suffice drawing her back.

Through her concentrated expression, she had enough energy to taunt me. "You know...if you let me kill you now...then the king doesn't have to do it in front of *Nora*."

With each pause, I increased the weight of my offensive. But when Poppy mentioned her name, I unlatched our stalemate and swung for her head. She dodged with a laugh, "You know you might've had a chance. She has such a soft spot for Gifteds."

I swung at her again with no luck. "Shut up!"

Her face darkened, and she exchanged a blow. I leaned back, teetering. "*You* don't tell me what to do anymore!" Her mallet swiped at my feet, and I fell.

She giggled, snapping her fingers and disappearing from sight. My weapon held across my chest defensively, I sprung into a crouched position. Hearing Poppy's mallet zip through the air, I blocked as best as I could. Rubber ricocheted off my handle, and I retreated a step back.

I felt her step out wide to my left, and I blocked from that direction as her mallet whooshed by again. The handle to my weapon broke in half, wood splintering apart and jagged now on one end. The muscles in my legs throbbed as I maintained an apprehensive stance.

Poppy reappeared with a wicked smile, way closer to my face than I estimated, and jabbed me in the stomach with the blunt end of her mallet. Momentarily stunned, I held where she hit me as she used her Makan Gift to hide again, her arms gearing up to swing.

I rolled out of the way as the mallet came down. Dust flew into the air as her weapon hit the earth.

A pocket of loose dirt, almost like sand, brushed between my fingers. Poppy let out a frustrated scream. Though I couldn't see her, I heard her clattering back to a standing position, mallet heavy behind her. I waited several breaths for her to get closer again, my Delilah-finding powers activated. Poppy would be no different.

She halted a few inches away from me. With a fist full of fine dirt, I chucked it at her. Her Gift came undone immediately as she howled, dropping her weapon as she wiped at her eyes. She cursed at me, her face bright red in humiliation.

I sprung up to my full height, panting.

Poppy was heaving too, slouched as she stood like a cornered animal. Two forms arrived; Kai and Molly stood by my side. The Anti-Gifted general blinked rapidly, her attention darting between the three of us. She inhaled, her face turning a darker shade of red. But before she could give any more orders, a horde of soldering feet crested from behind her.

We stepped back, alarmed, but so did Poppy. She whirled around to see Persephone leading a charge of women, at least twenty, each with a distinct tattoo on their exposed right shoulder. The Lady Lilacs. They came!

I noticed Lady Sanchiko at the front line and couldn't help myself from waving at her. She saw me but didn't wave back, her acknowledging smile cut for war.

Poppy took a step to the left, away from both sides, and

stumbled. The blonde soldier and the purple-haired one who fought Molly rushed over to their general, tugging her away even further.

Poppy snapped her head from the Lady Lilacs to me, her eyes still swollen and irritated from the sand. A mixture of shock and fear defined her features. I found all of my satisfaction in her shock and none in her fear. I placed my hands on my hips and gave her a challenging expression. *Your move.*

The two aiding soldiers whispered something to their general, and she wrangled away with a screech. Her chest rose and fell rapidly, and we waited breathlessly for her decision.

"Fall back!" Poppy growled, and the AGM—whoever was conscious or unrestrained—retreated.

CHAPTER TWENTY-NINE

Hidden in the Lilac District II
FERN

With shaking limbs, I found my mom and the hiding Gifted refugees. Maybe she found me with how much I wobbled down the hill in search of them, buried deep within the earth.

Two Avlis Lady Lilacs helped pull everyone out, my limbs and mind exhausted. Together, we looked like an army. A group just over eighty. Us at fifty-eight and them at twenty-three. Night approached quickly, disguising us from any spying eyes.

We made our way to Norburn in silence, the uncertainty of our new company making us all eerily quiet. Who would speak first? Who was in charge and were each of us trustworthy? I wanted to break the silence—desperately—but in this moment, gestures were simply enough information. We mimicked Unfortunate servants, silently saying, *Come this way. It's okay. We're together. The AGM are gone.*

"Where are they taking us?" Ms. Lancer finally asked as we passed the Norburn unwelcome sign.

I had no idea, but instead of sharing that sentiment I chirped and said, "Our new home." Loudly. For everyone to hear.

I doubted it would be an actual home. Seeing Norburn in the daytime made it difficult to believe real, warm homes even existed here. But since the Lady Lilacs came, that meant we were now in an alliance. We would join them just as much as they would join us. The only thing we all knew for certain was we couldn't hide underground anymore.

We steered toward the Lilac District, that black spot on the station map. The Gifteds huddled closer together as the Lady Lilacs led the way. I made sure to elevate my stance so everyone could see me as we walked, and the rest of our team matched my energy. Skylar gave herself a boost so she could make it to the top of a rooftop and scout from there. We separated the same as we did on the battlefield. Leo and Persy flanked the right side as me, Kai, and Molly walked along the left. The LL's didn't stir or bristle at our strategy, giving no indication of fear or apprehension toward us. I absentmindedly looked for Lady Sanchiko since she was the only familiar face, but I couldn't see anyone in much detail in this dark.

The remnants of the Lilac District still staggered my mind. It didn't take long for Skylar to realize her wasted effort as many of the remaining buildings had unstable or caved rooftops. She landed back onto the ground and strode side by side with Leo.

I watched them for a moment. Skylar pushed her hair all

the way to one side so they could see each other better. She tried to keep her attention ahead with a straight face, but his stare and sheepish grin was obvious. Her lips struggled to stay neutral, and she glanced back with the same smile.

They spent so much time hating each other for their status. Arrogant heiress and arrogant street rat as Leo once emphasized. But they shared arrogance, knowing each other fully without fully knowing each other, and spent their time despising one another together, drawn to interact with pestering, name-calling, teasing.

A callous part, a very small part of me that didn't have a proper place within my body, wanted to say that they wouldn't last long. That they were too different from each other. That their closeness had caused some sort of short-lived fantasy, and the flame would die out as quickly as it sparked.

Their hands intertwined, and I noticed the way Skylar visibly relaxed from his touch. Even if that callous part of me was true, it wasn't trying to convince me about them. I was thinking about Nora and all the times we gravitated towards each other and held hands and glanced at each other with that same expression. She'd always freeze up from our initial touch but relaxed over time. We'd share an endless stream of conversation, and I loved her laugh.

I did that, I thought. *I brought her joy.*

I looked away from the new couple and back to what was in front of me. A school stared back from its silhouette in the darkness. A central tower-like entrance and boxy brick body. We shuffled inside, on the brink of a swarm with how many we were. The inside wasn't any warmer than the winter air outside, but the temperature rose steadily as we all filed in.

Dim light imperceptible from an outside glance

illuminated the reception area and impending hallway. A Mati Lady Lilac lit a steady flame in her palm for better sight, and four others among their ranks created similar lanterns.

The Mati moved to the front and led our path down the corridor.

One of the Mati Lady Lilacs, a woman who appeared to be in her 40's, gestured for Mom in a different direction. Mom carried Delilah the entire way here; my sister's eyes closed and sleeping soundly from a body shut down.

"Where are we taking her?" my mom asked before I could.

"The nurse's office," the Lady Lilac responded with a whispered, kind voice. "You may stay with her."

A line of fear tried injecting itself into my heart at the idea of separation again, but I pushed it down. Out of all of us, Delilah needed the most medical attention. Because Poppy tortured her. Beat her into a red and purple pulp. Threatened to take her life after who knew how many hours of pain. Anger blossomed within me at the recollection and my own imagination. The earth pulled toward me, but I breathed in and out a few times and let those negative emotions retract. This was not the time to explode. This was not the time to overexert myself further.

Mom must have come to the same conclusion. She nodded. "Please help her if you can."

The Lady Lilac nodded again, and they disappeared down the first hallway to my right. In a flash of light, I saw the sign for the library. I hadn't been in one since starting Galdor Academy, and I made a mental note to go later.

Schools always seemed to replicate each other no matter where they were in Iridion, but the white-painted brick was vacant of its usual posters and classroom creations. I didn't want to speculate where those children were now or focus too much on the ghastly shadows framed at the edges of our vision.

We passed an opening to our left that expanded into a cafeteria. A cascade of rows and empty seats laid dormant there. The kitchen itself was blocked off by a gate, but that was all I could see of its existence.

We came to the end where the hallways split to the left and right. We went to the right, past a bathroom with a dolphin mural, and into the gymnasium. The double doors creaked open, its sound echoing across the vast space. Two Lady Lilacs clicked the doors in place so they remained open, and we proceeded to file in.

Bleachers enveloped each side of a basketball court. The fire light shined off the sleek wooden floor, revealing white and yellow lines. This must have been an Unfortunate primary school. Gifted schools would have equipment to practice training techniques in their gymnasium. Open earth for Avlis—maybe even its own horticulture section or greenhouse. A pool for Mares, split in half to work with fresh and salt water. Plenty of high-rise ropes and balance beams for Auras. A boxed-in chamber for Mati to safely play with fire and fringe their hair. Imitations and Feras would work in pairs in their own corner, and Makans and Luxes would hone in their Gift without the need of equipment.

This room, in stark comparison, was empty of all character. And its size suggested primary school because it was bigger than necessary. Since Unfortunate girls were required to enroll within the Choosing Ceremony from the year of their tenth birthday onward, their classroom enrollment dwindled drastically after fourth and fifth grade. I'd never been in a secondary Unfortunate school, but I imagined it would be way smaller, if it existed at all. What other schools would Unfortunates play against?

The fact that I had these new burning questions and no new answers flustered me. I should know. I should ask Nora, even if it was a guess for her too.

Some Lady Lilacs directed us to the bleachers. All on the left side. None on the right.

I sat on the first row, directly in front of Lady Sanchiko who hadn't acknowledged me again since the mountains. My friends followed suit at my sides, slumping onto each other for support. The AGM fight and the walk took its toll on us. Persephone was already weakened from losing and then regaining her Gift, leaning on her brother with an expression more muted than usual. Skylar and Leo were the most physically okay, their hands still clasped together and resting on Skylar's thigh. Molly sported a few abrasions, including one particularly bad one around her neck that wrapped around almost like a brand. She breathed with intention beside me. Kai had a few cuts and surface level gashes scattered along his body from AGM soldiers who succeeded past his defenses. I couldn't see how I looked, but my headache reached a constant simmer like fizz on soda pop. The muscles in my limbs felt sore and torn. I wanted to be smaller, shorter, so someone could hold me in their arms.

Mr. Harris stayed standing with Prince Henry bobbing on his hip, but Lady Sanchiko snapped her fingers—a sharp whip in the silence—to tell him to sit down. He did, right at the edge where the seat met the stairs. The baby sank into his lap, wiggling around so he could mimic standing and play with Mr. Harris's face. Our teacher didn't mind, smiling as Prince Henry's soft giggles amplified through the gym. They were alright. Maybe a little worn from the spike of fear Poppy brought, the quick evacuation, and the walk here but very much alright. Through the hurt, I knew I would do it all over again for all their safety.

The Lady Lilacs sat down too. I observed them as they passed. Women with the same exposed or hidden shoulder tattoo of a lilac. They held no other markings like pins or hats or colored bands that indicated rank like the Royal Crest Knights or the Anti-Gifteds Movement. What stood out most was how the oldest members remained standing at the edge of the athletic court and how out of twenty-two women, one Lady Lilac was distinctly male. A soft boy with a medium build and dark ruffled hair that was long enough to obscure his forehead and almost his eyes, making him appear even younger than I could estimate.

The woman next to Lady Sanchiko stood out as the de facto leader. Sharp dark eyes washed over the assembly, an indiscernible expression on her face. Her lilac tattoo flourished against her bronze skin, and a few pieces of gold decorated her ears and wrist.

After a few breaths, she spoke in a neutral, authoritative voice. "I am Lady Saleema. Let me make one thing clear: you are not here out of charity. Lady Sanchiko has pleaded your case, and we have agreed to a tentative alliance."

Starting strong, Lady Saleema.

"We will provide our numbers and supplies for one counterattack against the crown and its military," she continued, oblivious to my inner thoughts. "If we're successful, then we may continue as a united front. In return, the new sovereign will grant freedom to all imprisoned Lady Lilacs and grant a two-year clemency for our operations."

One counterattack, I thought. If we could turn the tide together, then our alliance could continue. Her terms seemed reasonable, all things considered too, even if it was vague and possibly conniving. Two years was a lot of time to give a criminal organization clemency, but out of all the condemned people of Norburn, I'd choose the one who specialized in separating the abused from the abuser.

Mr. Harris, however, stirred in his seat. The new sovereign. Would that fall to Mr. Harris or Prince Henry? If our teacher wasn't the estranged brother to King Daltus, we would have pledged our allegiance to King Peter Iridion instead. It wasn't something we actively talked about.

"Lady Sanchiko," Lady Saleema gestured to the woman in question, "please call on the Unity Alliance members who gave you their proposal."

Lady Sanchiko stepped forward so she was beside her leader and clasped her hands. "Mr. Peter Harris and Fern Fairaway, please stand."

We did. Ms. Lancer reached for the baby prince and took his weight off Mr. Harris.

All eyes inclined in our direction. But it was Lady Saleema who made me go skittish, her icy examination rivaling Isaac Winter's Gift. I wondered if she was a Mare; she hadn't given any hints to her own Gift.

"Mr. Harris," Lady Saleema mused. "We know you well. But Miss Fairaway—" her stare was solely on me now—"we are unfamiliar with you. Tell us, what is your idea for our first counterattack?"

Out of all the usual questions she could have asked to know me better—age (20), Gift type (Avlis), birthplace (Northbrook)—hers hadn't made the list. I was on the spot now, thrown into making a heavy decision without much consideration. But Lady Saleema wasn't misguided in her query.

She could be testing my reaction, how long it took me to

answer, and most importantly, if I could give her a good one.

"We destroy the weapon factory in Ironcrest."

When a silence followed, I felt compelled to continue, piecing everything together as I spoke. "We are the Unity Alliance, and we want to do exactly that. We will defeat the AGM but not by behaving like them. We will focus on acts of liberation with minimal casualties —without killing anyone if we are able—and bring people together, including those who oppose us. That starts with destroying the crown's main means of creating weapons. Besides," I finished with a cheeky smile, "if we go to Ironcrest, we can also free any Lady Lilacs imprisoned at the penitentiary there."

A small curl of Lady Saleema's lips betrayed her hostile façade, but it was gone in the next instant. *Just enough though*, I hoped. *Just enough to be the perfect choice.*

After a few more heartbeats of silence I refused to ruin, the leader of the Lady Lilacs turned back to Mr. Harris.

"Mr. Harris, if we succeed at destroying the weapon factory in Ironcrest and freeing our members, will you do everything in your power to uphold our request for clemency?"

Mr. Harris swallowed. My fingers twitched from the roaring excitement replenishing my nerves. I succeeded in winning her favor. It was all up to him now to seal the deal. We stared and waited.

He chose his words as carefully as she had. "If I am reappointed as the 1st Senior Royal Crest Knight, you have my word."

CHAPTER THIRTY

A Hesitant, Unspoken Yes

NORA

———

In my dreams, I chased after Fern—to warn her of the impending attack—but the mountains were endless, and I didn't reach her in time.

Each morning, I tried reaching out to her again through Prince Henry's Gift to no avail. Every drip of sunlight haunted me with my what-ifs. Days stretched on like this, my wrist firmly clasped to the bed frame so I wouldn't hurt anyone else.

Then, finally, the door to my room creaked open and I inhaled a deep breath of fresh air just for the company. Meals came once a day while I slept, so this simple action broke the monotony. Maybe I'd even receive news—Cassius or Poppy here to gloat but grant me closure nonetheless.

Isaac Winters wore a red bandana over his eyes, his hand thumbing the door and then the wall as he walked in. Bree, Ellie, and Holly entered behind him without their general.

Holly took Isaac's free arm and led him near my bed. No one said anything as we watched his hand trail the bed frame until he met my restraints. Ice covered the metal until it became fragile and snapped apart.

I brought my hand to my chest and sat up in quick movements. Too quick because Isaac's mouth twitched at the sound of the bed creaking. A shard of ice glistened razor sharp in his hand.

"She's just sitting up," Holly assured, gently placing her hand around his strained one. Her fingers turned bright red from his frosted touch, but she didn't react.

"We can take things from here," said Bree.

"Thank you, Mr. Winters." Holly trailed her hand down to his wrist before guiding him back to the door. He grimaced but didn't object as she helped him through the room.

She released him at the entrance. We watched him struggle to find the knob and then close the door behind him. His gait was heavy as he maneuvered down the hallway. I wondered for a moment who among my friends destroyed his eyesight before turning my attention to the battalion.

A sudden, dreading sickness threatened to overtake my chest. Cassius was smart to use them. I was far less inclined to violence, and from their weakened appearance, they must have fought my friends, but my friends fought right back.

Holly had a black eye, and Ellie's arm was in a cast. My eyes focused on Bree, who held her side with an open palm. She gave me the access code that helped sabotage their mission. Delilah was the only reason I didn't stay on the journey, but it turned out she was used as a bargaining chip all along.

My eyes narrowed. "Did you know?" I demanded. "About Delilah?"

Bree's lips flattened into a line, and she shook her head. "I thought I was helping you."

I huffed, expecting a fight. It would have been easier to stay mad, but that simple confession was enough for any resentment to leave my body.

"You did what you could, and I'm thankful for it."

"You could have saved *one* box of food and water though," Ellie chastised. "We almost starved on the way back."

"Sorry." I shrank back, a thread of guilt weaving into my heart. "Does that mean...you don't approve of your king anymore?"

They glanced at each other, a wariness etching their features. A hesitant, unspoken yes. If he looked into any of our memories from this day, he couldn't know their outright answer.

"I see," I said, standing on my feet. My back stretched with gratitude; my feet still ached with a manageable soreness. "Where's Poppy?"

"Still in the infirmary," Bree began. They took turns detailing what happened: how they found Fern in a tree, how Molly gave Holly her black eye, how Skylar and Leo's combined effort broke Ellie's arm, how Fern cracked one of Bree's ribs, and how in the most unexpected turn of events, Poppy ordered a retreat. "The Lady Lilacs, or at least that's what His Majesty concluded."

My jaw dropped several times, but especially at the end. *The Lady Lilacs*, I thought. Mr. Harris must have pulled something up his sleeve, having supposedly vanquished them over a decade ago.

"What about Fern?" I asked urgently. "And my friends? Are they all alright?"

"None killed," Holly assured.

"Not without a lack of trying," Ellie noted as she bitterly waved her cast. "They almost had me for a moment."

"And me," Bree agreed.

I gingerly folded my hands at my waist, my smile muted. "Hopefully, you can forgive them. The next time I connect—"

I stopped myself just before it was too late. I hadn't confessed out loud to my and Fern's bond, and if Cassius were to shift through and hear this damning conversation already...

"They won't harm you next time," I finished.

The Unfortunates glanced at each other again in a silent conversation we all understood. Even if I didn't outright confess it, they picked up the pieces.

"I'm going to publish the article!" Holly suddenly blurted, her face scrunched with determination.

"Oh." The word slipped out of me, surprised and a little embarrassed. I thought about everything I had to share that night after losing their game. Why I came here, my relationship with their king, and my Gifted friends. I wanted to ask if revealing all of that now would be helpful, but I already knew that the answer was a resounding yes.

The anxiety of being read, being *known* by strangers—Unfortunates and Anti-Gifted members—would be the only hinderance. If my point of view could be published in the Divine Observer, that could sway public opinion just as much as it had with Cassius and the AGM. I kept quiet despite my hesitation.

"And *I'm* going to be the distraction." Ellie beamed, wrapping her arms around Holly's smaller frame with an encouraging hug.

"And this is yours. It's a copy, so it won't be missed." Bree stepped forward, grabbing my hand with her folded one. Something cylinder-shaped and plastic rubbed against my palm, and I kept it firmly there as she retreated back. I didn't open my hand in front of them, nodding instead with an unblinking stare. *We could trust each other*, I silently expressed. *I'm scared but I will trust you.*

We continued swapping useful information for a few minutes longer, though I realized that the sun changed positions drastically from the time they came in. Morning had shifted to midday. I waved them goodbye, Ellie hollering that she'd be back with a tray from the canteen, and watched the door click closed.

Several heartbeats passed, but my heart didn't slow. Looking down, I inhaled and uncurled my fist to reveal an ID chip with General Poppy's name and ID number written along its side.

✳✳✳

I stayed in my room for the rest of the day voluntarily, firstly to figure out places to hide my new ID chip where I knew it would be safe and secondly to figure out all the ways I could use it to its full advantage without drawing suspicion. Despite all the options, I couldn't sleep without the ID clutched in my hand underneath my pillow to know that it was always there.

Drifting off, I fell into Fern's dream. It had to be hers because I stood in a library, a place I hardly recognized except for its concept. Books. Shelves and shelves towering above my head. So many words and stories I didn't know could exist.

The air was warmer than I expected, bringing me a comfort alongside its vague wood smell. I trailed my hand along colorful spines and peered out into the median. Soft yellow lights hummed in a constant rhythm above my head, filling the emptiness with its drawl. Its quiet atmosphere made me want to keep it undisturbed, so I tiptoed carefully from aisle to aisle without any clear direction.

I think the word is "skimming", I thought.

I turned onto the next collection of romance stories—a path I should probably avoid—when I noticed Fern standing among the S authors. She was almost as tall as the shelf, her head tilted down as she examined an open-faced book in her hands. I couldn't see its cover or its contents, but her gaze was transfixed on the page until her eyes shifted and she was suddenly fixated on me.

Heat rose in my cheeks as we stared at each other, but I tried pushing it down. Why did I feel like I caught her in an awkward moment? In an awkward place?

"Oh, Nora." She closed the book with more speed than necessary, putting it back onto the top shelf where I couldn't reach. She closed the distance between us, enveloping me in a hug that lifted me off the ground. "Thank the Divine. I missed you so much."

Her voice drifted softly in my ears, lulling me more into her embrace. She released me, but our hands stayed connected.

"I missed you too," I admitted, examining her exposed arms. Here, her skin was clear and smooth. Her hair a vibrant red so long it wrapped around her elbows. Her face a spray of freckles and eyes gleaming green. How did she really look? What couldn't I see?

"Are you okay?" I asked.

Her smile faded, and she looked down, waving our hands in soft, hesitant movements. "We're okay."

"I'm asking if *you're* okay."

Her eyes flickered back to mine, lips pulling back into a weak smile. "I will be. We're in a Norburn school now and way better off than before."

"With the Lady Lilacs?" I probed.

"Yes," she breathed. "They're ruthless but know how to be kind too. Did the AGM tell you?"

"My battalion did."

She stopped swaying our hands. "Your battalion?"

My eyes widened, and I gripped her tighter in alarm. "I mean the battalion I'm assigned to. I have great news. The three girls Poppy introduced to me? They're on our side now."

I expected some push back, suspicion, but Fern wasn't that kind of person. "Tell me how."

We sat down across from each other as I shared everything I possibly could. Her hand rested on my knee as I recalled my struggle in the armored vehicle. Between saving her or saving Delilah. How the choice was rigged in the first place.

"You made the right choice with the information you had," she assured me. "Your efforts were not wasted."

I sighed, relieved to hear her say that. My hand overlaid hers. A ripple shot through my nerves as I recognized the action, but I didn't pull away. She didn't either.

"I can do more," I said. "Bree gave me a copy of Poppy's ID chip. If I go to the Information Square, I should have unrestricted access to every AGM operation and schedule. Just like we did when we stole Mr. Harris's."

Fern beamed. "Really? That would be wonderful!"

She rushed into the retelling of her limited time with the Lady Lilacs and how she—yes, *she*—convinced them to attack the Ironcrest weapon's factory as their debut counterattack.

"I'll do everything I can to help you succeed," I promised, a fire burning deep in my core.

This was happening. This was really happening. No more running or hiding or endlessly wondering where she was or if everyone was okay. The Unity Alliance would be loud, the constant talk among AGM soldiers, and most importantly, triumphant. Fern couldn't have picked a better name.

"I know you will," Fern said, softer again. "Just promise me you'll be careful too. We—*I'll*—be devastated if we succeed without you."

We stared at each other for several unshakable heartbeats, the correction not lost on me. In truth, I would be just as devastated if we succeeded without her. But I've been down this path before with devastating results.

"I can't promise that," I admitted, patting her hand before releasing mine. "I don't expect you to do the same. You're already doing so much to fulfill your first promise to me."

She noticed my withdrawal and did the same, tucking her hands between her crisscrossed legs. She teetered in her seated position to fill the returned silence. I wanted to apologize, pull her back to me, clarify that I *would* be careful but would also be drastic when necessary.

I looked up, saying her name and seeing how the edges of my vision were now slipping away. A library disappearing into the void of space.

"Fern, I—" My hand reached out.

Fern looked up, but darkness overwhelmed her.

The door slammed open, and I awoke in my bed with a

terrified jolt. Lifting my head up, I kept my hand underneath my pillow, the ID still tucked in my palm. Cassius turned on the light, revealing himself as the source of my disconnect. I winced, blinking rapidly with a fresh wave of urgency.

His heaving slowed as seconds passed. I tried to process his features. This was the first time I saw him since we fought a few days prior. He was in sleek black pajamas now, a weird sight. His eyes were heavy but frantic from a lack of sleep.

"I couldn't reach you," he finally said. "I thought..." He trailed off, regaining his breath. Did he run here?

"I'm still here," I reassured in a flat tone.

"Right." He glanced around the room, curious. "That's...a relief."

When he found nothing out of the ordinary, he looked back at me with a struggled smile before turning off the light again. "Goodnight, Nora."

He left as quickly as he arrived, but sleep evaded me. I remained restless with the ID tightened in my grip.

CHAPTER THIRTY-ONE

Ironcrest

FERN

————

The last thing I remembered was Nora reaching out to me before the dream cut out like a film, and I awoke in the library—the *real* library—of the school we now inhabited. I stared at the ceiling for a few seconds, catching my breath. My fingers thumbed the carpet, keeping me grounded. I tried reaching back, dreaming of her again, but she was gone.

We departed for Ironcrest four days after arriving at the Lady Lilacs's safe haven.

It wasn't enough time to completely replenish my Gift— only halfway—but we needed to act faster than the AGM. Four days was plenty of time for them to scour the mountain and Norburn to find our new location. Mom protested my involvement, but Lady Saleema determined all six of us needed to be there to fulfill the mission and prove ourselves as capable allies. My actions had to match my words— something Mom instilled in both daughters. In the end, she joined us.

We were a group of twenty, leaving the other sixty-one at the abandoned school. Kai was already making all possible scenarios and war strategies after winning Ironcrest. *The west side*, he kept repeating to any attentive ears. *The west side is bound to be ours.* His optimism helped offset any bubbling nerves as we made our way to Iridion's furthest west point.

The eleven Lady Lilacs stayed close to their leader like magnets. Lady Sanchiko and the male Lady Lilac (whose title turned out to be Lady Mika) were among them. The weakest of us were confined into the middle, me included.

I'm the last defense. That thought kept me useful.

I need to see Nora again. That thought kept me walking one step at a time.

Mom and Mr. Harris rounded the back of our squad. Our teacher's actions had to match his words, too.

The Ironcrest weapons factory was a huge complex out in the middle of nowhere. Before Iridion was a country, people depended on external weapons, even as Gifteds first came into their power and hadn't quite honed it in. Dormant for long years, the factory became newly active for the AGM's use.

"The weapons available at the academy are remnants of a by-gone era," Kai finished his little speech, sounding very pleased with his textbook knowledge.

"And a costly wall decoration," added Leo, which prompted a plethora of scary scenarios for the life he led in Norburn.

"I've never seen the appeal," Skylar replied, exaggerating the nasal in her voice.

"You like themes, though, don't you?" Leo pressed.

A glint shone in both of their eyes.

"Of course."

"Then make one room themed around the past and the archaic. The Stantons are stuck there already, right?"

"Hmm," she pretended to ponder. "I *should* hang up a blade or something ridiculous like that in our home. Maybe then you won't be the only thing out of place."

"*Oh,* you're inviting me over to your place?"

Molly groaned with fake annoyance, though I was sure it was partly real. "*Please,* you two. How are you more insufferable this way?"

Skylar glowered but Leo winked, and the anger washed from her face. I imagined she would have to be fiercely protective of her decision to pursue him. Their kiss replayed in my head. I needed to be fiercely protective too.

I need to see Nora again.

We journeyed onward.

The only other notable landmark for miles was the Ironcrest maximum security prison that Ebony Nique broke out of, which felt like eons ago. There used to be a small military base too, but the AGM bombed it to oblivion in the same sequence of attacks. They would receive a taste of their own poison today—but unlike their victory, ours would be cautious of the death toll. An antidote, then.

We saw the smoke and pillars before we saw the factory.

Nora used her general's ID chip to shuffle the guard schedule and left a vacancy at the entrance gate between 1 and 1:30am. As intended, the gate was defenseless.

We charged, our steps surprisingly silent. Mom bent the metal apart, and we broke the gates wide open. There wasn't anything we could do about the cameras beforehand, so we kept a quick pace through the courtyard. At the actual doors leading inside, Lady Sanchiko entered the code gleamed not from Nora's new unrestricted access but from her subordinate Bree, who worked on most AGM technology upgrades. After a breath, the light turned green, and we flooded inside.

Finding ourselves at a landing, I couldn't help but remember the warehouse where the Diviner attacked us. Always that damned place. We now stood where he did, the factory line stood below us. The whirl of machinery snuffed out our footsteps on the metal grated floor.

We split into two groups. Mom led me, Persy, Molly, Lady Sanchiko, and five other Lady Lilacs down while Mr. Harris, Leo, Skylar, Lady Saleema, Lady Mika, and the last five Lady Lilacs stayed on the landing. They headed toward the manager's office tucked in the corner.

I watched as the secretary noticed their impending presence and screamed, though I couldn't hear her. Three Lady Lilacs surrounded and consoled her, keeping her seated with a firm grip but talking to her with gentle faces. Mr. Harris opened the door to the manager's office, and Lady Saleema strode in first. The glass obscured any onlookers, so I stopped watching and focused on my own task.

Mom waited for me at the end of the stairs. I caught up, the machines whirling louder and the air thicker with heat. A neat row of turning cogs and metal arms and burning iron stood before us. Workers in all-black uniforms were stationed at different points of the weapon-making process, though what they did and for what purpose eluded me. All that mattered was how their backs faced us and how our movements remained muffled over the droning *clinks* and *clanks*. I couldn't see the workers on the other side of the assembly, so I hoped they couldn't see me.

Lowering myself into a crouch, I followed the others

toward the machinery. Suddenly, as fast as a Makan turned invisible, all of the cogs and metal arms halted and the fire extinguished. A shrill alarm took over the mechanical rhythm, and the factory flashed a red hue.

The workers stopped, twisting to look around and catching us in the process. Most went rigid with fear, eyes wide. Some even opened their mouths to scream and bolted to the far walls on either side of the complex.

We stalked forward, intimidating the ones who stayed near their stations. They stepped away as we stepped forward, their hands up in an appeasing gesture. I stared at one masked person in particular who was closest to me and Mom; I was ready to react in case he tried anything funny.

Mom widened her stance and planted her feet firmly on the floor. She lifted her arms out in front of her and curled her hands like she was holding onto an invisible bar. Exterior parts, thin metal extremities, started to twist until they bent out of shape. I watched in awe at how easy iron and steel listened to her command. My most successful practice was when I peeled the floor out from under our feet in the Simulation Lab against Isaac.

Even though I wasn't at my best, I tried anyway. Mimicking mom's stance, I reached out to the microscopic pieces of rock hardened and refined. But even as I felt its presence, curling my hands did nothing, and the strain threatened to overwork my mind. I pulled back for a few breaths before I tried again.

My headache returned and its ringing blended in with the blaring alarm. I closed my eyes, pretending that what was in front of me was the earth from home. Soft. Malleable. Is that what a kiss would feel like?

I opened my eyes. My mind drifted too far, and I hoped

Nora was too far away to hear. But maybe she was the key. If I could recall the same urgency to protect here, then maybe something as cold and indifferent as steel would meld for me.

I tried again, reaching out to the machine and to the last time we saw each other. The desperation to pull her to me. I curled my hands, feeling resistance as though I was actually holding onto the metal frame. My arms strained, but I pressed harder against the invisible force until it caved and I stumbled forward.

Opening my eyes again, one of the larger tubes connecting one machine to the other was completely wound-up like the end of a candy wrapper. I repeated myself several more times until fatigue overwhelmed me. As I stretched my arms and swayed on my feet, Mom split a cylinder-shaped part in half and Persephone scorched the equipment.

The doors slammed open, loud enough for me to hear in-between the alarm, and we snapped to attention. Soldiers in red uniforms swarmed together at the entrance, looking down at us and then to the left-hand corner. I couldn't count their exact number from my position, but I knew there were more of them than us.

Mr. Harris's subgroup engaged first, offering time for us to finish our damage. There was still one thing left to do.

I ran over to the end of the assembly. Nora sent an urgent order for explosives this morning, and to my relief, they already filled several crates with grenades and rounded bombs.

Molly came to my side, picked up a grenade from the top, and pulled the pin. She reeled back and arched her throw so it would land on the other side of the machinery. It hit a gear instead and bounced back in our direction.

It skidded on the floor and stopped several feet to my left.

Dread filled my lungs.

I waved my hands, *commanding* with a frantic urgency. It lifted too slowly off the ground, and I released it as quickly as I could in its intended direction.

The grenade ignited mid-air, knocking us on our backs. Shrapnel pierced the air, a large piece cutting into my shin.

Through gritted teeth, I stood. Blood spilled down my leg, but I could hobble. Molly rushed over, her head zipping left and right at things I couldn't see. My sight was still on the box of remaining firepower.

She said something too quickly for me to understand. I patted her hand to tell her I could manage on my own. She looked at me and mouthed, "Are you sure?"

"Go," I mouthed back. "Get everyone out."

She hesitated for only a second before nodding and running off. I moved to the box and pushed it closer to the middle of the assembly line. No one stopped me, and I imagined they were either fighting someone else or fleeing. We'd all flee soon.

Satisfied with its new position, I picked up a grenade, pulled its string, and placed it back in the box.

I spun and tried running away, but a sharp line of pain brought me to the ground. Cursing, I sprung back up against the ache in my knee and limped to the stairs.

My hand gripped the railing with all my might, hopping on one leg one agonizing step at a time. I made it to the top of the stairs and propelled myself toward the entrance. The door swung open, and the night air iced my lungs. Most forms were already past the courtyard.

I tried following, changing into a run. Distress shot through my entire leg with each stride, but I still wasn't fast enough. The ground betrayed me as a wave of my hand did nothing to sweep the dirt below my feet.

I could feel the tension swell with my heartbeat, how the air thickened with dread. The earth warned me but did not help me.

"Fern!" I heard Mom's voice and felt my body propel toward the gate when the factory exploded.

***

A constant ringing muted my ears. The smell and sight of smoke blurred my sight, and heat singed my skin. But I stood anyway because I refused to give up on this mission and its promise.

I was thrown close to the gate, which was flat on the ground. Fire consumed the factory behind me. I turned around to survey the courtyard. A few bodies lay dormant in the grass, but none were any I recognized. Other people—coated entirely in ashes or burns that left their allegiance unrecognizable—stumbled away from the chaos. They didn't attack, so I didn't retaliate.

Turning back to the gate, I caught Mom's form as she raced to me. We clasped together, and I coughed as soot permeated the air. Leaning on her, we walked further away from the flames. My feet twitched uncontrollably, which usually caused my Gift to blossom in wild, unfocused ways, but the earth remained hard and unyielding.

"*Mom*," I panicked. "The ground is gone. I can't—Mom, the ground is gone."

"It's still there baby sprouts," Mom promised, right at my ear so I could hear her. "You're okay. Just overworked. The ground is still there."

I whimpered, feeling like a child all over again. Tears

displaced the dirt along my face, each step agonizing, but we kept moving anyway. The ground was dead, a companion so lost to me it was now a stranger. I trudged through the grass, crying at its indifference to my presence.

The Lady Lilacs and Unity Alliance were regrouping further into the forest, the trees now imposing instead of inviting. I convulsed, and Mom held me tighter. But then I caught sight of Lady Saleema, sporting the red AGM lieutenant's jacket like a trophy. She stood at the tree line, leaning all of her weight on one of the trunks. I saw her, and I remembered that we weren't finished and that we still needed to press on.

I gently released myself from my mom and walked over to her. Mom hovered, but she didn't touch me.

Once I hobbled over, Lady Saleema said, "You look like hell."

"Are you ready to free your fellow Lilacs?"

A cold smile crossed her face. "This alliance means that much to you, doesn't it?"

"Is that a yes then?"

"Yes. All we're waiting for is Leo. And to get that patched up." She gestured to my leg. "The rest are heading back to base. If we come back empty-handed, then you must leave us."

The threat was obvious, but I didn't care. I nodded and regretted the dip of my head. "We won't return empty-handed."

Lady Saleema didn't respond. Kai appeared and removed the shrapnel from my leg with a pair of tweezers in his emergency bag. After the wound was cleaned and wrapped, it still hurt like crazy, but I managed to keep up with the others on the way to the Ironcrest maximum security prison.

The window of time that Nora gave us passed, so guards stood at the entrance and heavy movement patrolled the perimeter. They probably were on high alert after the factory explosion. But we prepared for this possibility. We acquired the name of the current captain here as well as the lieutenant whose jacket Lady Saleema now wore.

She stood abruptly and grabbed my elbow. I faltered to my feet at her whim, instinctually pulling away as her grip tightened around my arm. Mom and Leo stood too, startled and ready to attack our ally.

"We don't have all night," she growled.

Mom narrowed her eyes. "You will show my daughter some respect."

"*Mom*," I tried to appease. "It's okay."

"It's not." She focused all her attention on Lady Saleema. "My daughter is helping you save some of your comrades. You *will* show her proper respect now *and* after we complete this mission."

The two women glared at each other for several breaths before Lady Saleema huffed. "If we get out alive with my family, then I will be...a little more agreeable. Now bind your hands together. Make it look like you're cuffed and weakened."

Appearing satisfied, Mom morphed metal around her and Leo's wrists until they were interlocked.

Lady Saleema nodded before stepping out of the underbrush and yanking me alongside her like I was the largest threat. Maybe to the AGM, I was.

We walked straight to the entrance. They caught sight of us quickly, bristling and readying themselves for our arrival. Fear prickled along my limbs, and I made sure it showed on my face. Mom and Leo stayed so close; I could feel them along my back and nipping at my heels.

Soldiers in red uniforms or red-affiliated bands peered at us from every angle, but I kept my focus on my leg, careful to make sure blood didn't seep through the bandage.

A soldier with a red hat denoting him as captain met us a few feet from the entry.

"Captain Womack." Lady Saleema shouted more so than greeted.

"Lieutenant," the captain acknowledged with a tip of his cap. "What happened at the factory?"

"Some Gifted insurgents bombed us. Sneaked in during a shift change." Her reply came out raspy and low, fresh from the fight. "Found these in the rubble."

She yanked me closer to her side when she said "these," and I almost toppled over in my already weakened state. The ground still felt detached from my touch, leaving me more defenseless than ever. The soldier eyed me and then the other two in our little caravan. I put my head back down to act more demure.

"I need to put them here until General Poppy arrives," Lady Saleema continued.

"Why is this one bandaged?"

"She's the leader." I appreciated the lack of hesitation. "Figured the king would want her alive for questioning."

"Understood." Captain Womack gestured us forward. "Follow me. We have few cells available, but we can group up."

He started walking. As we followed, four guards flanked us. Two grabbed Mom and Leo and pushed them forward in time with the captain's pace.

As he entered the pin we already knew from Nora's intel, he asked, "Do you know their Gift types?"

Lady Saleema looked at me with pure disgust. "*This* one is an Avlis. The other two are Makans."

The captain made a pondering sound as he took in our features again. I looked exactly how you'd imagine an Avlis. Mom had the same features, and he stared at her prosthetic leg for a little too long. Probably deciding if it was worth confiscating. Leo pressed his hands into my back, so the captain couldn't see his obvious Mati markings.

"Makans," Captain Womack repeated, and I figured he was starting to get suspicious until he flashed a smile. "The king will be pleased to have two more."

"He will indeed."

We entered through a heavy, thick door that locked from the outside. The prison rooms laid out before us three stories tall. I squinted, the fluorescent lights too bright and dizzying.

I understood why Lady Saleema lied. If this operation failed and they detained us, Mom and Leo could easily break out of a Makan cell. Our intel indicated that each room was designed for Gifteds. Avlis, Auras, Imitations, and Feras were placed in an air-tight box with just enough room to breathe and eat meals. Mati got the same set-up but with vents intended to snuff out fires just like a training facility would in an emergency. Mares were tied and suspended in their sealed cages and given water on a schedule to make sure they were too weak to wield it. Old school metal bars lined the first floor where Gifteds unable to free themselves were detained like Luxes, Mutes, and Makans.

He led us across the first floor. Prisoners yelled and hollered as we walked by, and I couldn't hide the fear and rage gnawing at my heart. These people were in maximum security prison for a reason, and to them, I was fresh meat. The concrete beneath me was just as indifferent as the grass.

If this operation failed, protecting myself would prove difficult.

We finally came to an empty cell near the end of the corridor. The captain snapped at one of the guards with his hands free, and she started to rummage through the keys.

Now, I thought. *While we're isolated from everyone else.*

As if sensing that this was the perfect time too, Mom and Leo detached from each other with a hard snap. A blue fire ignited along Leo's shoulders and arm as he burned the guard holding him. The guard's scream was short-lived as Mom wasted no time knocking him out with a headbutt.

"Lieutenant, get back!" Captain Womack pulled who he thought was his comrade closer to him. Lady Saleema released me to stand surrounded by the AGM, their weapons drawn and her hands arched as though ready to melee.

The captain retrieved a walkie-talkie from his belt, but Lady Saleema slipped it out of his fingers. He barely had any time to process her betrayal as she threw the device to the ground and stomped it in half. He withdrew a knife in the next instant, but a dark mass began to crawl up his legs. His attention deviated, and he screamed—we all screamed—as we realized what was enveloping him.

Cockroaches.

Fat sleek brown bodies, hundreds of legs, and searching antennas.

"Get them off me!" The captain flailed as he tried to kick, swipe, and toss layers aside. The other AGM soldiers remained motionless, distant despite his pleas as though touching him would spread an infection.

Mom and Leo took the opportunity to knock them out in their shocked state.

Lady Saleema flexed her fingers, a small smirk on her face.

The bugs all dropped from the captain's body in unison and encircled him in a ring.

So she was a Fera. One of the worst Feras I could possibly imagine, though there was no way I was going to tell her that.

"You're disgusting," spat Captain Womack.

"Where are the Lady Lilacs?"

"In their cells."

The cockroaches closed in.

"Alright, alright!" The captain tried to make himself smaller. "Lady Beatrice is in 330!"

That answer must have worked. The cockroaches backed away and dispersed to unseen cracks and corners of the prison, released from their master's control.

Lady Saleema grabbed the captain by the collar and threw him against one of the cells.

His head connected with metal. The thud rippled through me with a jolt, and Captain Womack slumped over.

"Hey, hey!" I touched her shoulder. "We don't kill if we don't have to."

"He's not dead...at least I don't think he is."

I huffed, releasing all of my frustration. Leo leaned closer. "We'll start freeing Lady Lilacs. Who is Lady Beatrice?"

"She's our true leader." Lady Saleema's shoulders relaxed.

"And how many Lady Lilacs are we looking for in total?" Mom asked.

"Nineteen."

Mom and Leo nodded, running off in separate directions while Lady Saleema and I searched the first floor.

"Lady Lilacs?" we hollered.

Mom and Leo made it to the second floor when the prisoners caught onto our search. They shouted, begged, and hollered over each other for the chance of escape.

"Over here!"

"Come back!"

"I'm a Lady Lilac!"

They became a chorus of supposed allies. Already too loud, some started to bang against their restraints in hopes of grabbing attention.

Mom remained on the second floor while Leo ran up to the third.

A rush of guards burst through the entrance. "What's going—?" one yelled and cut himself off at the sight. We stared at each other, unbreathing.

Mom raised and scrunched her arms in front of her chest in one quick motion like a workout rep. Metal screeched as the bars on the first floor bent inward and left gaping holes for convicts to slink out of.

"Get back in your cells!" one AGM ordered, but prisoners walked free and they would remain that way.

But these were Gifteds who were deemed powerless enough to be held behind metal bars. We needed more. I rested for what—three hours at this point? *Plenty of time to help*, I lied to myself.

The AGM started to advance. Mom prepared herself, and I reached out to the only thing in the room made from sand and rock and earth.

Glass cracked and then shattered, so loud and violent it reverberated through my entire body. Everyone stopped, or rather the world did.

My brain turned fuzzy. The smell of iron filled my senses, and the taste of blood entered my mouth. I wobbled but kept my balance, squinting at the black spots eroding my vision. Prisoners ran down the stairs in a stream of bright orange, and I heard a fight far away. My eyelids fluttered, threatening an everlasting sleep. I needed to move, but nothing happened.

I realized why Nora couldn't promise to be careful, though the thought was slipping away, and I tried to laugh, though I didn't feel it happen. Neither of us would be careful.

We would fiercely find our way back to each other.

The prison became empty just within a few minutes. Mom supported my weight and wiped the blood from my face.

"I'm so proud of you baby sprouts," she whispered.

Forms appeared, though it was hard to focus on their details. All I could focus on was *not* throwing up. They crowded us and talked with feminine voices. The only thing I caught was when Mom gently said, "We're going back to base, baby sprouts. With the Lilacs here, your alliance is at an even one hundred."

She lifted me into her burley arms.

"A hundred?" I whimpered, pressing my head against her chest like a baby.

"One hundred."

I paused, hoping to say something cool or victorious like, *Let's take back Iridion!* But fatigue snuffed out all of that and what I said instead was,

"Nora's going to be so happy."

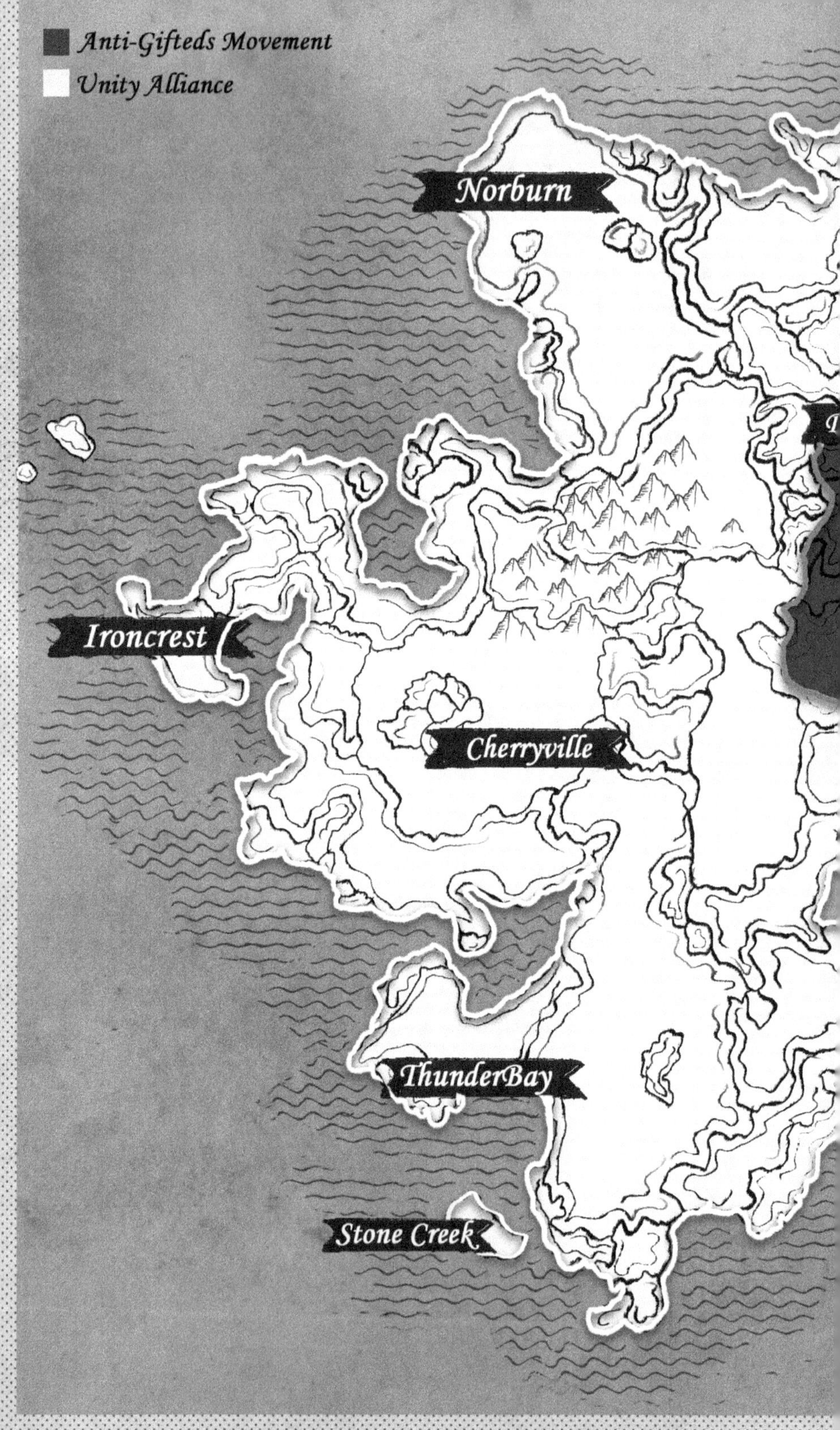

Anti-Gifteds Movement
Unity Alliance
Norburn
Ironcrest
Cherryville
ThunderBay
Stone Creek

1 Month Later
Caliel
Bellhaven
Osthall
aldor
Northbrook
water

CHAPTER THIRTY-TWO

Three Movements

NORA

——

The final red-tipped leaf wisped off its tree and spun, spun, spun to the ground. The air shifted and stirred in a howl through the barren branches. A grey haze permanently dimmed the sky and threatened rain.

The year neared anew, and Fern was taking back territories in a wave unprecedented. When we were in range of each other again, I could hardly hold back a beaming smile. I worked with her day in and day out—anytime we could connect, I found ways to help claim the Western front.

Once Thunder Bay turned, taking on other Unfortunate cities like Faywater turned soon after. She was keeping her promise, and I would do anything to see my promise through.

Every Anti-Gifted soldier trembled on edge. Cassius used any excuse to take more Unfortunates into the east wing. Any remaining after a defeat. Any hesitation or hint of disobedience.

I found every excuse to sabotage. Was this the fifth or sixth time we altered the Information Square to our advantage?

I twirled the copy of Poppy's ID card in my hand, staring at the blue screen with intent.

"There's a supply run on its way to Faywater," I said, clicking on the vehicle icon to see its exact travel path. The captain's name popped up, and I read out how many AGM members were in the convoy too. "It's grain, actually."

Oh, Fern said with delight. *This will be easy.*

I exited and scrolled down. Several red highlighted rows caught my eye. Clicking on the first one, a new page displayed a different transport. The early morning air shivered to the bone and rattled out my words.

"There's a counterattack heading to Faywater, too."

How many?

"Thirty." I exited and looked at the other two. "There are two other troop convoys. Another thirty are reinforcing Northbrook, and twenty others are heading to Caliel. They ship out tomorrow. Would you like me to reroute or delay them?"

I'm heading to Caliel tomorrow, Fern noted. She remained quiet for longer than a pause.

In her absence, I slowly turned my head side to side, checking to see if anyone was nearby. Wouldn't want any new Makans lurking in the shadows.

I made sure to come here right before daybreak when everyone was still asleep and huddled under their blankets for warmth. I tried to keep myself as still as possible, stationed at a pillar nearest to the instructor housing. My form hid entirely from the entrance West watchtower, and I hoped I was short enough to remain obscured by the infirmary in front of the South tower.

Fern came back, comforting and warm in comparison to my surroundings. *Mr. Harris suggests rerouting all of them to Caliel.*

I hesitated, "Isn't that a little dangerous?"

Yes, but he thinks it's better to blow up the trucks all at once and away from large trees.

I could trust her, but I asked anyway. "Just the trucks, right?"

Of course.

Alongside the Lady Lilacs and rescued Gifteds, the Unity Alliance was more than capable of holding its own against the Anti-Gifteds Movement. Cutting off transportation was their first priority.

Once trucks were inoperable, Anti-Gifted soldiers were placed in the same warehouses they caged Gifteds. Except they were kept well fed and looked after while Fern encouraged them that they were not enemies. Just thinking about it made my heart swell.

I tapped on the drop-down for destination and typed in Caliel for the trucks not already going there.

"It's done," I confirmed. "They're all taking the same route. Interstate 25 all the way up."

Perfect. Fern eased. *Is there anything else we should be aware of this week?*

I returned to the main scheduling page. "Looks like Poppy has a lot of war meetings today. I'll make sure to avoid her and Cassius as best I can."

That sounds smart.

"No kidding." Sunlight stretched through the clouds and fog. "I have to run. Be careful in Caliel."

Only if you're careful in Galdor.

I chuckled, my breath puffing light smoke. Even though I couldn't promise to be careful, I still wanted her to be safe. The phrase came out on instinct, and she carried the same sentiment.

"Deal."

The more we interacted, the easier our ability to connect and disconnect became. I diverged my attention to the sky and focused on its grey haze. A few heartbeats passed; our connection pulled away from my mind the same way a thought slipped away from the moment.

Click. Disconnected.

I exited out of everything and made sure to go through the necessary steps erasing my history. The Information Square dimmed and then became transparent. Pocketing Poppy's ID, I slowly stepped away, trying to appear casual. I walked closer to the infirmary, hugging its walls. Then, I walked out from its entrance and toward the castle. In view of the South watchtower, they'd think I just came out of the hospital instead of the Information Square.

The sun rose steadily. A few soldiers greeted the morning with a sluggish, yawning pace. I averted attention by walking down the hallways to my room.

Bree, Ellie, and Holly turned the corner at the opposite end, walking toward me at a unified pace. We collided, and I twisted myself around to join them. We did this effortlessly now. The group gave me witnesses, deniability.

We chatted loudly so anyone who looked our way would see us together. Ellie used her dreams as the easiest conversation starter, and I half-listened as we made our way to the student canteen.

"I left my dog in the training room, and I frantically tried to get her back," Ellie explained.

We were half-way across the Grounds, now brimming with life. Despite the chilling air and permanent grey sky, the sun emanated a soft light hue. Was that the color of my light at this moment? Almost white but not quite there?

"Your dog?" wondered Holly.

"You don't have a dog," Bree noted.

"My House had one. A fluffy little guy. I had to get him back before they noticed he was missing."

A familiar form caught my eye, and Poppy stood there, trailing our movements with her stare. I looked away immediately, thankful that we were already at our destination. I swung the canteen's door open and gestured for them to walk through. They did, smiling and waving around me and not their general.

***

After a breakfast filled with House anecdotes and secret business, I returned to my room and took a shower. Stepping out of the bathroom, my skin warm and clear of any evidence I was outside, I didn't expect to see Poppy sitting in my window alcove.

I avoided her ever since she became a Makan. I couldn't stand seeing what Cassius did to her. I didn't want to remind myself of what he was doing day in and day out to my people. Out of everything I could sabotage, the east wing was no longer a viable option. I was careless, but I wasn't keen on what he might do if he trapped me there. Once he was defeated, then his experimentation would stop too.

Poppy was visible at least instead of disappearing out of thin air.

"I'm starting to understand why you like your shitty view," she said. Her chin rested on her wrist, making her voice sound even more dejected.

"What do you want, Poppy?" I was done circling around conversation after conversation.

She turned toward me. Thankfully, I was already presentable in a long-sleeve red dress.

"You're certainly getting what you want," she replied, though the accusation didn't hold any bite. She waved a newspaper lazily drooped in her fingers. "Got *this* slammed in my face today."

I recognized it immediately as the Divine Observer, the AGM newspaper that they used to inform the public of their movement and war progress. Holly wrote and published the article about me, though when she tried showing me earlier this morning, I refused to have it read out loud to me. No need to rehash my life twice.

When I didn't say anything back, she narrowed her eyes to slits and opened the pages with more force than necessary. "Let's see. 'Iridon's first Unfortunate soldier continues to fight for her country while in custody. She fights for Gifteds and Unfortunates alike, even taking on interest that goes beyond her station.'"

My cheeks flared at the last comment about my "interest," but I still refused to say anything.

Poppy's voice strengthened, laced with frustration and panic. "Holly tries to distract the reader with your love life, but I know my soldier well. You're in *custody?* Fighting for Gifteds and Unfortunates *alike?* This never should have passed printing. Are you trying to get her killed?"

"No." That answer, I was certain.

"I saw you with them today. Are you trying to get all of

them killed? You understand they don't have the same protection that you do, right?"

My anger flared. "We understand fully. They see what I do. You're the one missing something."

Her mouth wired shut, and she looked out the window again. Despondence weighed her again. "His Majesty knows my report before I can even get to his office. We're failing out there."

A hint of sympathy pouted my lips. "You'll still get what you want with the Unity Alliance. Unfortunates will still get their freedom."

"You were right, you know," Poppy said suddenly, like what I just said didn't reach her. "I don't want to be a Gifted. I just..." She trailed off, flexing her fingers. "I just followed orders."

Silence.

"Nora." She whirled her head around, voice desperate as she stood, "Are we just servants forever? Can we ever break free of it?"

Startled, I stared at her, unblinking. Poppy became a mirror, a reflection of my own constant questions. I finally had the answer, and I could finally tell her.

Stepping forward, I clasped her hands in mine. Steady and concrete, my eyes met hers. "You are free, and you bind yourself to what sets your heart on fire. You bind yourself to what matters. What matters to you, Poppy?"

"It matters that I live in a world where I don't have to feel so scared all the time."

I held her hands tighter. "Are you afraid of the Divine?"

"No."

"Are you afraid of the Diviner?"

Her answer didn't come. Instead, she stared and stared

and stared, tears brimming but refusing to pool over. I stared back, every hope etched into my face that she would finally see that Cassius was not who she should bind herself to. He was not who I wanted to bind myself to any longer.

"I gotta go," she said, tearing herself abruptly from my hold. "This was a mistake." She found the door in a whirl and slammed it shut, leaving me in the stillness.

***

The next day, news spread of the grain truck overturning in Faywater. The UA stationed there fed the people instead and locked the soldiers in the wait station as expected.

Cassius invited me to tea.

I didn't get to see Poppy again. Isaac Winters was the one who escorted me to his office. He confiscated my sword easily; I wasn't inclined to slice Isaac to ribbons to keep it.

Paper scattered across the desk, and Cassius sat with both hands wrapped around his skull. A servant was already inside, delicately trying to find a place for the tray among the stacks.

An irritated huff escaped his lungs. Cassius looked up and pierced through her. The servant's body immediately stiffened, and she rigidly placed the tray down on an empty chair off to the side. Once she was done, he flicked his finger toward the door, and she left in five quick steps.

His arm fell against the desk with a loud thud, and the other rested his chin. "Leave us."

Isaac nodded; his movements more fluid this time. The door clicked closed, and I was once again trapped in a room with *him*.

His eyes met mine, and I averted my gaze. Catching sight

of the tea tray, I beelined to its location off in the corner. I occupied myself with filling the cups.

"Nora."

I ignored him, measuring out the perfect milk and sugar ratio. A prolonged silence followed, and I thought he went back to the items on his desk.

Turning with the cups in hand, he towered directly in front of me. Startled, I yelped and tried adding distance, but I slammed into the wall. The tea spilled over and burned my hand. Wincing now, the cups fell from my hold and clattered to the floor.

Cassius bore into me, his intense expression unwavering as he collected napkins and gestured for me to extend my hand. I grabbed the napkins from him instead. His mouth twitched but he didn't object. Some tea pooled into my brand, and I bit back a wince as I pressed down in that already-tender area.

"Nora."

He tried to brush his knuckles along my cheek, but I slinked away. I didn't want to look at him, blocking out my thoughts with the objects around me. A door. A desk in disarray. The ruined carpet.

"I want to believe that we can still change this world together."

A burn blighted my chest. *Together.* That belonged to someone else. My thoughts deviated to her, but I quickly snuffed it out and pretended to be very interested in a red book among the others.

He pinned me to the wall, the action jolting me into a rage. I tried to push him away, but my arms were scrunched at my chest. His eyes, as blue as the sea, crashed into my soul. I realized what he was trying to do, so I forced my gaze to look left in a blinking frenzy.

"You've been in and out of my Gift a lot more recently."

His hands cupped my face and guided me directly in front of him. We locked eyes again. Searching. His expression remained taut and his presence unyielding.

"Is there something you'd like to tell me, Nora?"

I strained to turn my head—to look away—but he kept me firmly in place. To look straight at him. To face that abyss I mistook for the sky. I focused on the abyss and nothing else.

"No," I managed.

"Hmm." He pulled away and stepped over the teacups. I exhaled, rubbing out the nerves along my hands.

Cassius organized the papers on his desk into a half-decent pile and pushed the chair in. I noticed the Divine Observer laid neatly below the rest.

"Let's test that answer." He sounded almost manic with the thread of mischief in his voice. "I'm heading to Caliel."

Any relief vanished in an instant. "Whatever for?" I blurted.

He strode to the door, but I blocked his path. He arched a brow in mock curiosity, "*Was* there something you'd like to tell me?"

My mouth went dry. "No."

He smiled, malicious, and side-stepped around me. "Then to answer *your* question, a leader must fight to protect his kingdom. I read somewhere that we have that in common."

CHAPTER THIRTY-THREE

One Step into the East
FERN

———

He knows. Fern, he knows.

I jolted in my seat as Nora's alarming voice entered my mind. The unassuming caravan rocked all of us back and forth, so my action hardly brought attention. My eyes landed on Prince Henry cradled in Molly's arms. His blue eyes punctured into my soul.

"What happened?"

Several people straightened in their seats and glanced at

me. Even Skylar stopped writing on a pad of paper with interest. I continued to stare at the baby prince.

Nora panted like she was running at full sprint. *He knows! He must know about our connection or my sabotage or both. He's on his way to Caliel now! You must turn back.*

Fear gripped my heart like her emotions entangled with mine. Weariness grew on my face as I processed what she was telling me.

Fern! Her voice rose an octave. Was she crying? *Oh Divine. Fern, can you hear me?*

"I'm here." I held my hand out to comfort her, but it hung in the empty air.

A whimper echoed in my ear as she tried to compose herself. *He's coming to Caliel. You must fall back. For a day. Or for however long it takes. Fern, please.*

"Nora." Her name rolled softly off my lips, my voice low and concerned. The caravan sped forward. "Where are you?"

I'm at the Information Square. I'm...I'm logging in.

"How long do we have until he arrives?"

She sniffled. A few breaths passed in silence. *He'll be in one of the convoys. They'll get there in five hours at most.*

"How long until we reach Caliel?" I turned to Kai.

"We just passed Osthall so..." He worked out the math with his fingers, "We have two and a half more hours."

I stood from my seat, my back flush with the roof. Lady Sanchiko and Mr. Harris resided as the driver and co-pilot respectively. "Speed up. We're getting to Caliel in two hours."

"Bossy," Lady Sanchiko noted. "I like it."

Her foot pressed harder against the petal. I returned to my seat and clicked the belt in place. Prince Henry continued to stare, eyes wide and absorbing the world around him.

"Thank you for the warning, Nora," I told her gently.

"We'll prepare."

You're not backing down, are you?

If Kai had a telepathic phone line to Nora, he could go on and on about how important it was to claim a stake of the east side. How important Caliel would be as the religious capital of the world. How we were on the verge of turning the tide in our favor.

But none of that paled in comparison to how I felt about her and how I would be as reckless as possible to just see her again. Cheerful and unshackled from his snare.

"Never."

She exhaled, sounding like she was coming back to her senses. *How can I help?*

I pressed my finger to my lip in contemplation. "Once we win Caliel, we're doing a march on Galdor. On the first day of the new year." It was an idea jumping in my mind for a while now, and I finally convinced the Lady Lilacs to approve the move.

A march?

"Yeah," I trailed off, suddenly hesitant myself. "A peaceful protest. Something that the whole kingdom can join. We march, from wherever we are, to the capital as a unified front."

There was a prolonged silence. *You're beautiful.*

"What?!" I exclaimed so violently I sprang from my chair and slammed back down in an embarrassed heap.

I mean your mind is beautiful, she corrected, but the earnestness in her voice stayed. *That's a perfect idea.*

My fingers twirled the ends of my hair. "Thank you."

So, what can I do?

I sighed with relief knowing that she wasn't crying anymore. "Figure out a way to share the march with the country. We need as many eyes and ears on this as possible for it to work."

A peaceful march on Galdor at the start of the year?

"The very first day. January 1st." I needed the date to be perfectly clear. "828 AA. That's After Alston. Double A's. Double means two."

I know how time works, she laughed.

Good. I could still make her laugh.

I'll see what we can do while he's away. If he knows... Her voice sobered again. *I don't know why he didn't confront me as bluntly or put an end to my sabotage right here and now.*

I knew why. We both knew why, but neither of us wanted to actually say it. I would anyway. My ears burned as my words resounded through the car for all to hear, too.

"Because he still loves you. In his own twisted, obsessive way. He doesn't want to let go. And..." I forced myself to keep going. "I'm the villain standing in the way of your twisted, obsessive happiness."

I hoped my outlandish words softened what was otherwise a confession. I closed my eyes and pretended that we were alone, sitting across from each other at a kitchen table. Somewhere we were both familiar with.

Please be careful, Fern. I don't— She stopped herself and tried again. *I want to see you when you march on Galdor. I'll find you among the masses. I'll cheer you on even if I can't reach you.*

A smile swept over my features. I probably looked like a maniac with my eyes closed and my lips curved, but I didn't care. "Only if you're careful in Galdor."

We always ended the call with the same tag:

Be careful.

Only if you are.

I wondered if Nora realized how much it sounded like a promise despite her initial insistence not to make any more promises. I took this vow more seriously than anything else in my life, only second to our first promise ushered during the palace siege. A sentiment I'd keep as we continued barreling toward Caliel.

***

Skylar, Leo, Persy, and I reached the Stanton House, which felt just as imposing as it had been when we first arrived last year. It stood as its own entity separate from the smaller buildings outside its gated yard.

Skylar entered the passcode so we could walk through with her. To my surprise, her passcode still worked. Maybe her father always hoped she would join him.

That was not the case today.

The Stantons, as Skylar explained with great hesitation, kept their fortune through the church. Somewhere down the line, a cut of donations was given to the family in exchange for grant charity. New benches. Long-term mission trips. An entire new cathedral that made even the worst singers into angelic voices. *Give a little, receive ten-fold* as the Great Book proclaimed.

That present was meant to be from the Divine, but the people of Caliel gave credit to the Stantons. More money arrived from churches wanting the same splendor. She wouldn't budge more after that. All that *really* mattered was overtaking those who aligned themselves with the Diviner and hopefully, we would also gain allies from the church once we revealed its soiled roots.

We closed the distance to the grand staircase and entered

the foyer. Six Lady Lilacs accompanied us. Half of them fanned out to align with the three impending hallways. Nora's intel claimed soldiers were stationed around the estate, but we couldn't be too careful in case there were some housed inside too.

No one greeted us at the door or in the foyer. Skylar mirrored her movements when she came home the last time, using her Gift to navigate down the central hallway to her father's study.

"*You!*" Skylar shouted.

We caught up to her pointing at the poor servant who dealt with us last time we were here, though her number was erased from my memory. She now wore a simple red dress and at the sight of her mistress, she sheepishly cowered against the wall. A servant turned affiliated. Not a soldier.

Skylar swept over to her, clasping their hands together. "What is your name, 24?"

"Ma'am," the girl shook. "It's a pleasure to see you again. Let me notify your father, and—"

"Your *name*, 24. What is your name?"

"Katherine, ma'am."

"It's nice to meet you, Katherine." Skylar shook her servant's hand with a smile. "No need to announce me, Katherine. Just tell me where the Head of House is."

Katherine nodded but still looked weary. "He's in his study, Miss Stanton."

"Of course. Keep up the good work."

She sprinted off, and we did the same. One Lady Lilac remained in the hallway; she eyed the servant to make sure she didn't run off and notify anyone of our presence. Katherine remained silent and eyes down.

Skylar threw her arms out and the doors to her father's

study swung open with wild abandon. Mr. Stanton stood from his chair, startled beyond belief.

"Hello, father."

"Skylar." He placed a hand to his chest as if to manage his heart. "I thought—I thought for a moment you were—"

"The king?" She stomped inside. "Trust me, I'm worse."

Persephone and I closed the door behind us. He looked at his opposition: his daughter, two Mati, the leader of the Unity Alliance, and two Lady Lilacs. He looked as sharp as ever with a navy pinstripe suit and silver-blue accents, but dark circles rimmed his eyes and worn wrinkles sank his skin.

"What is the meaning of this?" he demanded, but it lacked any real authority.

Skylar stepped forward until she was on the other side of his desk. "You've proven yourself incapable of running the Stanton House with love, stability, or honor. I am taking over as Head of House."

He scoffed like she was joking, but she only glared. When he recognized her stillness, the humor vanished from his face.

"You can't be serious." His voice became stone. "I've maintained our House for almost forty years!"

"And where is my mother?" Skylar cut him off with a slicing neutral tone. "Where is the woman you swore your life to?"

He opened his mouth but hesitated. They stared at each other for a few unblinking moments, both struggling to keep their composure.

Skylar swallowed, "I thought so. You disgraced us the moment you gave into fear's hand. *I* will not do the same."

"*You?*"

"I am the heir."

"Skylar, this isn't the time—"

Wind picked up despite being indoors, swirling around its caster. "I don't think you're hearing me correctly. You are no longer making decisions for the Stanton household."

Her dad shifted but didn't back down. "What I do—"

"You do for this family, so you've told me." With a storm at her back, Skylar waved her hand and threw her father into the closet on the right side of the room. She flicked her fingers and the lock set in place. "You betray yourself. It's not a legacy I choose."

She sauntered over to his fireplace, found a rod, and threaded the metal through the closet handles. Her father's fist bashed against the wood, but the Lady Lilacs held his prison in place.

Skylar hummed to herself as she walked over to the desk and rang the bell.

The servant from before, Katherine, meekly revealed herself in the doorway with the Lady Lilac close behind.

"Yes, ma'am?"

"Dear Katherine, help these women take this armoire to the wait station. It no longer has a place in my household."

Mr. Stanton screamed something muffled but absolutely undignified.

Skylar kept her attention on the servant with sharp eyes and a disinterested expression. She already looked like the Head of her birthright.

Katherine stammered but nodded, ushering the Lady Lilacs forward. As they lifted the armoire off the ground, Skylar nudged the air beneath it for assistance. We watched the closet wobble down the hallway and finally disappear.

Skylar exhaled, her face softening and hand brushing the desk. She pulled a crumpled piece of paper that named other rich Houses in the area who pledged their allegiance to the king and studied it for a long time. Leo shifted to her right side so he could wrap his left arm around her waist. She leaned into him but continued looking over the list.

He whispered in her ear, but his voice still carried for everyone to hear. "If you want to run away right now, we just need to raid all the treasure chests first." A light laugh escaped her, and he continued. "I'm serious. Do you know how much your stuff would go for in Norburn? Someone might even kidnap you for ransom."

"How romantic." She rolled her eyes. "Would you come save me?"

"Absolutely, but when I get there, you'll already be the new leader of the Letter Boys. On a throne and everything."

She pondered the fantasy before slowly separating herself from his hold. "That won't be necessary." Trailing her hand along the desk, she carefully sat into the matching mahogany chair. "This throne suits me enough."

He mocked a bow to her.

Persephone and I looked at this interaction with reddened faces. They certainly had no qualms flirting right in front of us, but I guess they never had any qualms fighting in front of us either.

"The Diviner is getting here in an hour and a half." My voice punctured the air. I didn't want to hedge my voice with a *maybe*. Nora's terror was too certain. "We should meet with the others."

The twins nodded.

Skylar stood up with the list in her hand. "*I* am going to arrest these men. We needn't waste our time trying to appeal to their senses."

Leo scoffed, "How long have you been waiting to say

'needn't'?"

Skylar danced over to him. "Ever since my father said I *needn't* a prize horse for my birthday."

He did a double take as she twirled past him toward the door. "Wait, *what?* You're joking, right?"

She shrugged but didn't give him a finite answer. Once out of the office, her posture returned into a strait-laced state. Leo ran after her; Persy and I followed quickly behind.

***

Skylar and the twins walked casually down the sidewalk to the first House on the list. I broke off from them in a sprint, needing to reach the outskirts of Caliel in time for the trucks' arrival.

Falling into a rhythm, I tried connecting to Molly or Mr. Harris who were both at the frontlines of the supposed surprise attack. *Come on Prince Henry*, I thought with each stride. Pulling from my strongest memories, I pictured Molly when she first turned into an Unfortunate and when she stepped out in front of me as a shield against Cassius's touch.

The connection clicked into place.

She must have tried connecting with me too. Before I could breathe a single word, her voice erupted in my mind.

The trucks are here! They're in our sight now!

"What?" I quickened my pace in disbelief. "That's impossible!"

I'm telling you what I'm seeing!

"Okay, okay." My thoughts scrambled as I neared the city's left-most entrance. "Is everyone in place?"

Just missing you.

If I wasn't running, I would have bitten my lip. They

didn't necessarily need me, but we were all safer together than apart if the Diviner showed up. "Follow the plan as usual without me. Watch out for each other in case—"

Understood.

Molly disconnected, and I braced for what would happen next.

I made it to the edge of town, apartments and churches lining the street on both sides. The road stretched into open plains. Three armored vehicles drove in a line down its path. A rocky beach resided to the road's left where the Unity Alliance laid in wait.

A figure—Mom—raced out from her position. She halted and threw her arms in a sling-shot motion. A giant boulder dislodged from its resting place and soared as though light as a feather, landing directly in front of the first vehicle.

It crashed; metal contorted with a shriek. Grey smoke lifted into the air where the hood of the car used to exist and began swarming the entire wreckage.

The two other convoys swerved out of the way—the third deviated course toward the beach and the second sped straight for the city.

I aligned myself with the car, preparing to derail it once the AGM soldiers were close enough. My feet wide apart, I tried to straighten my back but realized I couldn't. Cold chills ran down my body and rooted me in place. *The Diviner.* He was here, and he was about to run me over.

I saw myself in the reflective glass, a mix of terrified and resolute, when I was lifted into the air like a mouse caught by an owl. Skylar strained as she held my dead weight. She gasped, and her body stilled too. Gravity took hold and we dropped.

My body crumpled on a grassy lawn, unable to break the

fall. Skylar landed somewhere I couldn't see, but she didn't scream either. We were unable to make a sound with the Diviner's hold on us.

The truck screeched to a halt; I heard running and Leo shouting Skylar's name.

The Diviner's attention must have waned because all feeling returned to my arms but not my legs. Lifting my head up, I saw Skylar lying in frozen pain to my left and a church entrance right in front of me. I didn't wait for him to notice. Digging my nails into the soil, I crawled up the stairs and was just tall enough to turn the knob. I could cry tears of joy that it was unlocked.

Leo shouted one last time before it died out in his throat. A car door opened and slammed closed. I managed to slide my body inside.

The white-painted hallway was bare. At the end were bathrooms, and a short distance to my left were two double doors leading somewhere deeper into the church.

Gritting my teeth, I pushed myself forward. Behind me, I heard nothing which only made me more frantic with fear.

Then, a distant thud and all feeling returned to my legs. I shot up from the ground in an instant, bursting through the double doors and into the sanctuary.

I almost made it down the aisle before my lower body gave out again. Collapsing in a heap, I made a quick note of my surroundings. Red carpet. Rows of pews. Stained glass windows. An altar. A ramp leading to a closed door all the way to my left.

I made quick work pushing my body down the nearest pew to my left. Only the aisle had carpet, so I had to propel myself forward with my palms against the cool floor. The pew seemed to stretch on forever, though I imagined it was only seven or eight feet long. Just enough room to hide myself.

The church's entrance knob clicked open and the door creaked, though it hadn't when I squeezed through. He could take over my entire body at any moment. I've seen him scramble brains until they altered or popped. I've seen him make people do what they never wanted to. This was intentional—it had to be. That vile man. He could kill me just for being in range and he decided to hunt me down instead.

I made it to the end of the pew. Twisting my torso upright, I pulled my legs until I was in a sitting position. My knees pressed against my chest and my back flushed with the pew's end.

The double doors swung open. He entered the sanctuary.

I closed my hands around my mouth so tightly it was bound to leave an imprint. He became imperceptible; his footsteps were light along the aisle carpet. But I could feel him, scanning, searching. A terrible creeping shot down my neck more poignantly than his Gift. My breathing quickened, already panting from effort.

A soft thump rang out like an explosion. My heart beat so loudly in my chest I swore he heard me. But I heard him, too. He paused two pews behind my position before he continued walking down the row.

I needed to move! But even what little control I had didn't want to listen. Any flinch and he could spot me.

Get it together! I yelled at myself, feverishly angry that terror could grip me like this. I wanted to tell myself that fear came with the isolation. In every other interaction with the Diviner, I was with our team. But I also knew, rising just below a gasping breath, that I didn't want to die without freeing her.

Mustering my courage, I swung myself around until I faced the altar in the first row. Nothing blocked my path in front of me. My eyes glanced back and forth between the door to my left and the altar to my right. The door was the safe choice—the careful one that could lead me to safety. But I didn't promise to be careful.

I lunged myself as far as I could to the right, crawling forward, every nerve on fire. If I could reach the stained glass—my hand outstretched to the image of God.

My hand fell limp, disconnected. The Diviner charged; several pews skid across the floor in his wake. He was at me in three strides, gripping my hair and throwing me down at the altar. He took over my body but not my mind, giving me the terrible privilege to scream without a single sound leaving my mouth.

I watched him wrap my hair around his fist and pull me from the ground. I couldn't feel the pain, but just looking at how close he was repelled me.

He dropped me, and I fell on my back, sprawled out on the stairs like a sacrifice. My neck lolled, and I saw the stained-glass upside down. One of my hands rested on my chest and the other lay dormant on my side. I couldn't reach the earth even though it was so close in range.

Pressure clamped down on my left side. The Diviner snapped his fingers, the sound echoing through my ears. My neck lifted to face him like a dog hearing its owner. I hoped he could see the disgust seething through my eyes. The pressure was *him*—his left foot dug into my arm as though he needed to keep me in place. He leaned down, crushing me. My only reaction was in the form of heavy breathing, and his mouth curved like he wanted more.

But that meant releasing control, which was something he

would never entertain. *I hated him. Dear Divine, I hated him.*

He studied me with those signature blue eyes. What did she see in blue eyes anyway?

His mouth broke apart into furious laughter, his body convulsing like he couldn't contain the dark glee within himself.

"I don't know what she sees in you, either," he jeered. "Look how pathetic you are—all alone."

Despite his appalling breath and disturbing taunt, my mind—free of his influence—drifted to the Flower Festival. Making a misshapen basket next to a pretty girl wearing a purple butterfly outfit when she said that no one truly does anything alone.

As if my thoughts were spoken, Cassius reacted by placing all of his weight against me. His laughter drowned out with fresh wrath. Yes—I would call him Cassius from now on— he wasn't a messiah who wielded the Divine's Gift. He was just a boy with too much power playing in the sandbox of our lives.

He bent down lower until he had his hand wrapped around my throat. I stayed perfectly still as we stared daggers at each other. His nostrils flared; his grip tightened and then loosened. Regaining his composure but still brimming with sinister intent, he tilted my head side to side like he was inspecting me.

"How should I kill you?" he mused. The sun shone through the stained-glass windows and illuminated him in all the colors of the world. All the Gifts he has stolen for himself.

"No," he chided as though I gave him an idea. "I need you to die in a way that leaves no doubt for Nora to hope. Your Gift means nothing to me if it's not ripped away right in front of her."

He lifted my head with his hands, "I could sever your head and bring it back to Galdor." He stared for several breaths before he thought better of it. He dropped me back down with a hard thud. "No, she'd be scarred for life. I can't have her thinking about you forever."

He *tsked*, looking away as he pondered my death.

My neck bent awkwardly, but that meant I could see the stained glass again. I stared at its pieces until my eyes seared with pain. *Shatter*, I thought. *Shatter.*

"I could always bring you back in pieces. A little broken but well enough to keep her happy," he teased. A thumb brushed over the edge of my lip, his voice lowering. "But I don't like sharing."

He raised his fist; I could make out his shadow.

"Cassius!"

I recognized Mr. Harris's voice. Hope bloomed in my chest; I focused more intently on the glass.

Cassius whirled his head to the sanctuary's entrance. In the next breath, the pressure on my left side released. Molly screamed with all her might, tackling Cassius somewhere away from me.

Sensation returned to my limbs, my nerves, my words. I yelled with sudden pain. Glass imploded, shattering over us like rain. Small cuts embedded themselves in my skin, but I was grateful to *feel* again.

I sat up, less than careful. Mr. Harris stood firm at the end of the aisle closest to the double doors. Prince Henry was in his arms, his eyes watching all of us. Thank Divine.

Cassius ripped Molly off of him, and she stumbled between us, blocking a direct path to me.

He tried to use his Animus Gift, piercing through Molly, but she stayed exactly how she wanted to. His eyes danced to me. My arm swelled with color, but nothing was broken from what I could process. Carefully, I weaved the glass pieces into a large shard right in front of him. Confusion mixed with what I hoped was fear paled his face.

He turned back to Mr. Harris, and a cry whimpered out of Prince Henry. The baby dug himself closer into our teacher's chest. Cassius fumed, an understanding clicking into place.

Within a blink, Cassius vanished from sight. His Makan Gift.

"Mr. Harris!" I warned.

Our teacher ran down a left-hand side pew while I prepared to strike. I could always hear Delilah. I could hear Poppy. He would be no different.

I aimed and fired; glass whizzed through the air and collided with the back wall.

Cassius materialized centimeters from its touch, shock halting him in place.

He tried to mind-control me again—whether out of habit or hopefully out of desperation. I prepared another shard, this time thinner with a sharper point. My arm gave more resistance, but I held firm. I would strike him right in his monstrous heart.

As I took aim, the entry rattled open, and someone ran toward the sanctuary.

"Wait!" I shouted, but it was too late.

Cassius claimed their mind and body, freezing them right behind the double doors.

Lady Sanchiko walked through with an unsettling calm and expressionless face. She was originally stationed at the beach with the Unity Alliance. She must have followed behind Molly and Mr. Harris for back-up, unaware that they were protected by Prince Henry's Gift or simply hopeful she would be protected too.

Mr. Harris took a step back as her body faced him, her focus on the baby in his arm.

I tried attacking again in the stillness, but Cassius was ready for me. He vanished from sight again, roaring, and Lady Sanchiko launched at Mr. Harris.

She bellowed furiously, tugging at Prince Henry with all her strength. Molly ran to our teacher's aid as the Lady Lilac punched him in the face and desperately tried to pry the baby away. Prince Henry slipped to the ground.

Cassius shouted through the sanctuary, his laughter and rage echoing off the walls like he was all around us. I tried searching for him—to hear his footsteps—but the commotion was too loud. Prince Henry's wailing intensified.

"*Fern!*"

I turned to see Molly losing against Lady Sanchiko as she, twisted with violence, tried to step on the baby below her heel. Sprinting over, I used the momentum and my weight to topple Lady Sanchiko over while Molly grabbed the prince off the ground and pressed him tightly against her chest.

Mr. Harris and I pinned Lady Sanchiko down: his left and my right. She shrieked and kicked and clawed at us. I supposed she mirrored all the rapid fury and jealousy of the one commanding her. We looked down with pitying, sad faces.

Terrible apprehension bristled at my neck. *If I can't kill you*, Cassius hissed through my mind, *then I'll just make Nora forget you altogether.*

A door slammed shut, reverberating through my bones. Lady Sanchiko's crazed state softened until she was a panting mess.

"Oh Peter," she cried. "Peter, I'm sorry. I—"

"Hey, hey." Mr. Harris gently held her cheek in his hand, wiping away the tears as they streamed down Lady Sanchiko's face. "Regulate your breathing. You didn't cause any harm."

She stammered, trying to apologize again. I lifted myself off and stumbled back, almost falling over one of the pews. Cassius's threat rang through my thoughts, haunting me. I tried to connect to Nora. I thought about cookies and butterfly outfits and dancing in a flower field and her hand on mine and training together and waking up beside her and every single second I could remember.

Nora! Nora! "Nora!"

"Fern?" Molly was already in a crouched position, ready to run at any moment in case I was now under his control. She looked at me with grave concern, the prince tight against her side.

My breathing came in short spurts. I couldn't reach her; I knew I couldn't reach her. She was too far away and the baby wailed, consumed with the terror of what just happened. Cassius's final words threatened to consume me with the same terror.

To forget me, he needed to alter Nora's mind. What was stopping him from changing her into a puppet like Isaac Winters? What if the next time I saw her, she was no longer herself but entirely his?

CHAPTER THIRTY-FOUR

National Emergency Broadcast

NORA

I stared earnestly at the fireplace as the flames grew, consumed, and brightened. Ever since Fern disconnected, my nerves raged; I wanted to do more. I wanted to cause more ruin. We waited until nightfall, eager to do just that.

Bree and Ellie sat with me, all three of us sitting on the floor since I didn't have enough chairs. If I allowed myself to drift toward impossible things, I would pretend we were having a sleepover. Though, I realized, it felt like most of our time together was comparable to one large sleepover. Gossiping about lovers. Swapping relatable stories. Discussing our hobbies and dreams.

We were in relative silence now.

I allowed myself to drift toward other impossible things. I closed my eyes for longer than a blink, imagining a faraway house hidden just beneath the canopy and filled with sunlight, strange outfits, and the scent of chocolate chips. Or huddled together in a hammock and talking about our day as the sun gleamed its last rays. Or just taking her hand and running off to wherever in the world. *Her* hand wasn't Valerie's hand anymore, though I still couldn't bring myself to admit it.

"Nora?"

I opened my eyes. Both girls were looking at me, but it was Ellie who spoke. "What were you dreaming about there?"

"Oh, I wasn't dreaming." I waved both hands to dismiss the idea.

"You better not," Bree said, sharp as ever.

"I wasn't."

"You had your eyes closed for at least ten seconds," Ellie chided.

"I was day…" I paused as I realized what my next word was, "dreaming."

Ellie glanced at Bree with a cheeky smile, but before she could pry, I spoke up again. "What do you wish to do? When all of this is over?"

Ellie pondered for a heartbeat while Bree offered her answer.

"I'd like to learn from an Avlis. They can bend metal into strange shapes, and I could try to piece it all together. Imagine if a single radio could encompass the entire country. Or how fast something transmits with a curly wire compared to a straight one, if there is a difference to be found at all?"

Slipping into tech talk, most of her words were lost to me. But I saw her enthusiasm, how quickly she was speaking, and her passionate gestures. A soft smile formed on my lips listening to Bree, her initial rejection of me well past us.

"I'll have to introduce you to Ms. Daphne Fairaway," I suggested. "She's an excellent metal Avlis and would probably love that sort of challenge."

"She's your friend's mom, right? The one?"

My face puckered in an attempt to stop a flush of pink. I swallowed that anxious, tingling feeling in my chest. Down, down, *down*. "The one and the same."

Bree considered and smiled.

Ellie shared her answer. "I'd honestly go back to painting, as expected as that is."

"There's nothing wrong with the expected," Bree encouraged.

"I *know*, but I guess it doesn't sound as exciting."

"You like painting sunsets, don't you?" I jumped in. "Blues, purples, reds, and—"

"*Oranges!*" Ellie chirped, fluttering her orange-painted lashes. "I'll paint an entire building orange if they'd let me."

She wrapped her arms around herself in a self-imposed embrace now that she didn't have a cast, giggling. My shoulders relaxed to its sound. Much better than the silence.

The door clicked open, and her laughter snuffed out. We froze until we noticed Holly walking through the threshold.

"Please, do not stop on my account," she smiled. She closed the door behind her with careful fingers and stood at the edge of the carpet. "What were you talking about?"

"Orange," Ellie beamed.

"Oh, of course." She thumbed the ends of her blonde strands. "It's done, by the way. We're ready to go onto the next."

We chose our words carefully, spoken and unspoken. Cassius was still in Caliel, so our unspoken words were free, but the minutes before his return dwindled. The risk was necessary. Holly added the Unity Alliance march details into the AGM newspaper right before the new edition went to print. The changes went right over her editor's head and in an odd place tucked between other propaganda. Once released, it would be difficult to retract.

The *next* involved all of us, even more blatant than Holly's successful mission. My lips thinned as its reality set in. Poppy's warning ran through my head. Whether I wanted it or not, I did have more protection than they did. Even worse still, I remembered my own warnings in Northbrook. They were not loyal soldiers anymore, which meant Cassius would have no qualms hurting them. Changing them, like he did with Isaac.

"You can back out now," I blurted. "I can go alone. You won't have to put yourself in danger any more than you already have."

They looked at me, concerned and confused.

"It's a little too late for all that," Bree scoffed.

"Agreed," Holly nodded.

"Why are you in knots now?" asked Ellie.

"I just..." My chest tightened. "I'm just so tired of having people help me only to have it all fall apart. What we're about to do—you will be blatant traitors to the AGM. If I go alone, then there's still a chance you can slip through the cracks. I can take full responsibility. He won't...he *might* not hurt me."

They looked down and then at each other.

"We no longer know our king," Holly said, somber. "And therefore cannot continue as faithful servants."

✳✳✳

We headed to the Galdor broadcasting station.

Using Poppy's duplicate ID, we reached the academy gates with ease under the guise of patrol work. The guards radioed the West tower for confirmation we knew would be there. This ruse was practiced and performed so many times so there would be no hiccups.

"We must also confirm with the general herself," the entry guard said.

I stiffened, holding in any retort that would be suspicious.

"You must?" Ellie raised an eyebrow.

"Surely there's no need," added Holly in her sweetest passive voice.

Bree remained quiet, probably holding back her intimidation.

"I'm afraid so," he apologized, resolutely *not* sounding sorry. He pressed some buttons on his walkie-talkie and asked the person on the other end if they knew General Poppy's whereabouts.

"I'm right here."

Poppy emerged from the shadows. We jumped at her sudden closeness, collectively taking a step back in surprise. She glared at me, the darkness rimming around her eyes. How long had she been stalking us? Did she know we were leaving for a fake mission to be here now?

"Ah, General." The man stumbled over his words. "It looks like some of your soldiers are assigned to a city patrol. Galdor Square. Is that correct?"

We held our breath.

"Yes, that is correct."

We exhaled.

"Great." He stepped aside. "Go right through."

"Actually," Poppy took another step forward, lifting her finger. We gulped down another breath. "I'm going with them. Make a note, will you?"

The guard grumbled, unsure, but Poppy didn't waver, didn't even blink as she waited for him to follow orders. Once he did and the glow of his screen died out, Poppy glared at us until we started shuffling past the gate.

The Galdor broadcasting system was near Galdor Square, hence our "posting," so we headed there. Once we rounded a corner and out of the guard's sight, Poppy grabbed my wrist with the same tightness as cuffs. I stopped in my tracks as Poppy used her height to tower a full head over me. The other girls halted too, alarmed and hesitant.

"What are you *actually* doing?" she demanded.

I found no use in lying to her. Craning my head up, I glared right back. "We're broadcasting the Unity Alliance's next move. To anyone who can listen."

Her fist still ironclad around my wrist, she turned to her soldiers. "Do any of you understand what you're doing? This would warrant *public execution*, not just a slap on the wrist!"

Holly flinched, and Ellie blanched. Bree held them between her, rubbing their arms for comfort.

"I warned them the same thing," I said.

"I'm not talking to *you*."

"Poppy." Bree caught her attention. Out of everyone, she was her general's true second. "He is not our savior."

The sharp anger in Poppy's eyes dulled to sorrow as she processed the words. She looked just as despondent as she had when she asked me if we could ever escape servitude.

Poppy swallowed, "Then...show me what I don't understand."

The three girls exhaled, relief washing over their faces.

Poppy tore her hand away from mine, shoving me away from her for good measure. Her anger seemed to still fester but I didn't blame her.

The broadcasting station was the tallest building in Galdor, second only to the Iridion castle. Large antennas jutted out from its flat roof, reaching out to televisions and radios within the capitol and its surrounding areas.

Bree explained that even though the station couldn't reach the entire country, there was a system in place for connected stations to broadcast in their range and so on and so forth. We agreed—well before now—that the confusion would spark the message to travel regardless of its initial outcome. Besides, Galdor needed to know that they were about to be at the forefront of this war.

The first several stories had reflective windows so passersby couldn't spy on the news station working there. As we walked along, I stared at our distorted figures and shivered.

Soldiers stood on each side of the entrance, but when they noticed my lieutenant jacket and Poppy's general insignia, they let us right through. No questions asked.

The first floor was a wide, expanding space with comfortable-looking sitting areas scattered about. Even though the AGM soldiers walked about in red uniforms, the couches and chairs were still in the royal purple, gold, and white colors. There probably wasn't enough time to manufacture everything needed to match the new regime, but I claimed it as a sign anyway. We couldn't be erased. It was not too late to share the same space.

Passing a large secretary desk, we headed straight to the elevators. Poppy selected the up arrow, and I folded my hands to keep from fidgeting as we waited.

The bell chimed, and the doors slid open. A few people dispersed into the lobby. I obscured myself from view, but

Poppy nodded at them as they noticed her.

We filed in after. Bree chose the 11th floor while Poppy discreetly pressed the closing icon until the mechanism obeyed her. I allowed myself to breathe when the elevator shut, and we were the only ones on.

Holly's mouth quirked like she was on the verge of vomiting. The anxiety built in my stomach too, so I stared at her and silently said, *It's okay. You're not the only one nervous.* She inhaled slowly through her nose, and Ellie placed her head on top of her friend's.

The bell chimed again, and the doors opened to the 11th floor. The tallest point. The master control room that would override whatever they were broadcasting in one of the lower-level rooms.

We faced another door with a keypad needed for entry. Before I could retrieve my copy, Poppy strode forward and scanned hers over the keypad. A green light flickered, and the door unlocked. She glanced at the pocket of my lieutenant's jacket where my hand still resided.

"How did you expect to get inside without me?"

The general narrowed her eyes at Bree. The techie avoided Poppy's gaze and quickly swung the door wide open for the rest of us to enter. To my surprise, Poppy walked through without further confrontation.

Entering after her, my mouth hung open in shock. Master control was so much larger than I expected with a tremendous amount of television screens implanted along the far wall. Every channel played something different: a commercial, a re-run, a brand-new episode, the weather. My eyes scanned but gathered no information from the constantly changing lights, angles, and muted laughs. A giant timer stood above it all, counting up the minutes. For what purpose, I wasn't sure.

In the room's stark darkness, I barely perceived the outline of one person lounged at a desk that stretched out further than six feet. He stared at a screen right in front of him that duplicated somewhere on the TV wall. He switched between two other monitors on his left and right, and I noticed two empty desks closer to our position.

Some larger displays had a rectangular bar next to its broadcast, ranging from green to yellow to red. With each heartbeat, the bar flashed in a green hue. When one flashed yellow, he spun a dial and the bar flashed green again.

I stood rooted in place, dumbfounded, but Bree charged forward, clearly in her element. In only a few strides, she had the crook of her elbow pressed against the master controller's neck. After several painful heartbeats, she laid him gently onto the floor and pushed the chair out of the way.

Holly and Ellie removed the monitors off the empty desks, lifted one, and headed to the entrance. Snapping out of my trance, I moved out of their way and helped Poppy clear and move the other empty desk.

We barricaded the entrance with tables, chairs, and anything else that was heavy and detachable. My throat tightened as I thought about how we were barricading our only escape, too. We would broadcast for however long we could and then promptly be arrested.

I glanced at Poppy who feigned a neutral expression, but her silence betrayed the façade. Perhaps that was why she didn't demand I give up the copy of her ID. She fully expected to die today with her best soldiers.

"Are you ready?" Bree asked.

I offered Poppy my hand. She didn't take it; instead, she walked away and stood at the very end of the panel with her arms crossed. I stood next to Bree directly at the center. Ellie brushed my left, and Holly hovered close behind.

"Ready," I breathed.

Bree pressed a button, and a red light flickered to life. All of the televisions, every single one, unified into a black screen with white text.

National Emergency Alert
The Unity Alliance implores all citizens to march in a
peaceful protest on Galdor
January 1st 828 AA
Message approved by the Crown

Though the master control room was deafening in its silence, all national emergency alerts blared through its speakers. Right now, every household in Galdor, Osthall, and its surrounding towns was thrown to attention. If the system worked properly, the same broadcast was reaching all the way to Caliel, Northbrook, and Faywater and those stations delivered the news to Cherryville, down to Thunder Bay, and to Stone Creek.

I imagined Melanie Montgomery running right up to the television in the entertainment area and pressing her face so close she could see each individual pixel. I imagined servants standing stone still in the hallway and gathering what was happening based off their Gifted owner's reaction.

I imagined a dense cluster of businessmen and women halting their busy schedule to stare at display televisions in shops all across Galdor.

I imagined Fern cheering so loudly that the people around her had to cover their ears.

I imagined the world stopping—taking a moment to

breathe and listen.

Of course, this message was not approved by the Crown. That was the default closing for national emergency alerts. Hard fists slammed against the doorframe. After several heartbeats, someone must have swiped their ID; the latch clicked.

Holly sprinted to close the door as it met our barricade's resistance. Curses and shouts entered through the crack before she had the door closed again. More knocking followed, urgent and furious.

The door unlocked again. This time, a few fingers poked through. Poppy sprang into action next as the desks scratched the floor. She twisted fingers to retreat while Holly pushed the barricade back into place.

The giant timer reset when Bree pushed the button. We've been broadcasting for two minutes, thirty-four seconds.

I watched it count up in agony.

"Do you know which stations are broadcasting right now?" I asked Bree, hoping to distract myself.

"I notified all surrounding stations to prepare for a national alert, but there's no telling if they kept it on after reading it."

Something heavy and metallic hit the doorframe. I whipped my head around, my hand already around the hilt of my sword. Poppy and Holly jumped back, but nothing came through.

Bree chuckled, the sound out of place. "If they are keeping it on, the AGM are probably flooding their control room right about now."

I looked back at the clock. "Is three minutes enough?"

"Plenty."

The AGM used weapons now instead of their fists to

demand entry. An ID scanned; the latch clicked again. Several hands clamped down on the door and pushed. Poppy and Holly heaved against them; Ellie joined next to help in the effort.

Four minutes.

Five minutes. Six.

The AGM got the door just wide enough for someone to squeeze through but Ellie angled herself to look straight through the breach. Illuminated in the sudden light, she pointed her arrow and fired. A woman screamed, and the door slammed closed again.

Seven. Eight. Nine.

An unsettling silence swept over us. No more knocking or cursing or shouting. No scramble of feet or clatter of weaponry. Were they regrouping? Was there a secret entrance we didn't know about?

Ellie rejoined my side, her bow loose in her hand. She must have had the same thought. Our eyes danced about for any openings in the ceiling.

We hit the eleven-minute mark when the elevator chimed behind the door and icy tendrils overwhelmed my senses. I stifled a gasp, my resistance there and gone in a single heartbeat before his power clamped around my body. My fist slammed against the panel's red button, and the broadcast cut off. We plunged into darkness.

"What are you—?"

My sword unsheathed with a metallic hiss and sliced Ellie in half. Straight across her torso. Her scream pierced through my ears; her bow thudded to the ground. Blood spilled over the broadcasting panel, and she slipped trying to hold herself steady as blood pooled over her arms and poured down her legs.

All I could do was watch, just as horrified, as she collapsed under the desk with a meaty thump.

I'm sorry! I wanted to scream, but my mind and body were disconnected from each other—one belonging to me and one belonging to him.

Two screams caught my attention. My head snapped and trained on Holly and Poppy.

Poppy retreated from the door, viciously covering her head with her hands and choking on some great, unseen pain. Did he get in? No, that was impossible! Then why—?

Holly covered her mouth, her horror pinned on me. My legs bolted toward her with fast, methodical steps. She shrieked again, jumping back and colliding with the barricade. She wept, her hands shielding her eyes like a child too innocent to meet her demise instead of brandishing her sword. My arm lifted to slice her down when a large arm wrapped over my shoulder and around my neck, pulling me away.

It was Bree, choking me into submission. My sword slipped from my hold as I thrashed. Relief mixed with my ferocity. If she subdued me, he couldn't control my body anymore.

I continued to struggle despite my internal protest. Finding flesh, I bit down *hard*. She roared but didn't release me, her arm pressing further into my neck. My lungs clenched for air.

"Your sword, Holly!" Bree yelled.

Blood drooled down my chin, my teeth tearing into more skin. My arms reached for her head somewhere behind me, but I was too short.

"Holly!"

Trembling with eyes so wide and full of tears, Holly peeled

herself off the wall and reached for her weapon. The back of Bree's knees pressed against the broadcasting panel. Ellie lay unmoving beneath us.

I'm sorry! I'm sorry! I'm sorry!

The moment Holly's hand touched the hilt, she stilled. Her crying ceased, so absolute her voice no longer existed. She unsheathed the sword slowly, almost dully, under what had to be Cassius's control.

Poppy yelled again, though the sound was no longer painful but instead a battle cry. But instead of striking me, Poppy swung at Holly's head with incredible force. The sword clattered; Holly didn't move, didn't not even flinch, as the blow struck her skull and killed her.

"No!" Bree shoved me to the ground and sprang toward her friend.

A scream of my own clawed at my throat, but a clog swallowed it down like he had his hands around my neck. I heaved air back into my lungs, glancing frantically at my surroundings. Ellie's blood puddled around her and soaked into my hand, but I didn't feel its warmth.

Poppy and I lunged for Bree. She managed to dodge Poppy's swing, but my sword entered through her back, shredding her stomach and piercing her heart. Her words garbled, incoherent, and when I withdrew, my weapon was coated so thickly with blood I couldn't see any steel.

Bree slumped over, and silence filled the space between us except for our labored breaths. I expected to fight Poppy next, but she was as much under his control as I was. The only indication of her sorrow was in her eyes, overflowing with water.

We did what he commanded. Calmly, we stepped past the three Anti-Gifted soldiers I dared to call friends. This was all my fault. If I hadn't tried to convince them of their king— If I shouldered every sabotage— If I could have fought his mind control—

We removed our blockade with the same calm demeanor as rearranging furniture.

Blood dripped on the door handle as I swung it open.

The king stood directly in the frame, his dark suit a shadow and his sharp eyes a raven. Tears spilled down my face then, but my mouth stayed wired shut and my limbs remained his. My fingers didn't even twitch despite my desire to kick, strangle, and stab him.

We should be dueling. Blood should be spilling from our wounds. Only one of us should be dying. Not them. Never them. I stayed at the door like a servant greeting a guest at the Montgomery House.

Anti-Gifted soldiers crowded behind him, but they remained out of focus. Insignificant. My eyes fixated on him, though I was sure I would have done that with or without his influence.

We regarded each other with fury, though the more he took in my appearance and the way I looked at him with complete hatred, his shoulders fell. Defeated and disheartened. For what he did or for what he saw reflective in my sight, I hoped both.

"Seize her so I can stop," he asked rather than commanded.

"Yes, Your Majesty."

The AGM soldiers surrounded me, tying my hands behind my back with no effort. A few others did the same to Poppy. They held a tight grip as sensation returned all at once, the icy feeling running down my spine in retreat.

The scream clawing at my throat freed.

CHAPTER THIRTY-FIVE

The East Wing

NORA

———

Double doors once sectioned off Princess Maya from the rest of the world. Thick, black-tinted plastic loomed in contrast to the palace's marble walls and white wooden-carved entries. We were in the east wing of the palace—where the only person to come out, alive but changed, was Poppy.

She choked on sobs. I had since run out of tears, dehydrated and head splitting, but disgust continued to rip my body apart. Bree, Ellie, and Holly's limp bodies replayed over and over in my head.

The soldiers who apprehended us gripped me tighter as Cassius entered a code, obscured by his jacket, and pulled the door open.

An exchange between Poppy and Bree flourished in my memories. When I found the answer while washing dishes.

Bree, you had to know perfectly well what you were setting up in there.

Bree's voice rang in my mind, and I realized I'd never hear her again. *I absolutely did not.*

A fresh well of sorrow bubbled in my throat, and I wept as we entered.

Anything that denoted a bedroom was removed. Instead, a clear vase sat atop a table—filled to the brim with marbles of all colors and hues—and illuminated the darkness in a brilliant rainbow. In any other circumstance, the display would be beautiful, enchanting. But these were Gifts stolen from the king's judgment. Each one represented a person violated and likely dead.

Past the vase were bars flush with the wall creating six cells: three on the left and three on the right. All stood empty but at some point were used to hold Gifteds and Unfortunates prisoner for experimentation.

The soldiers tossed me into the first cell on the left. Suddenly free, I launched back to my feet. The door closed a second before my hands reached the bars.

They tried tossing Poppy in the adjacent cell, but she kicked and thrashed with new energy. "Wait! *Wait!*" She stretched her neck to look at Cassius. "My king! I am still loyal to you!"

He lifted his hand, and she writhed out of their hold. "You helped the traitors enter the building and kept the authorities from entering the master control room. Why should I believe you?"

She collapsed to her knees and bent her entire body to the floor beneath his feet. "It's true. I have offended you a second time and believed my soldiers over you." She lifted her head up with reverence, "But they were wrong. Nora led them astray, and you have dispelled any doubt with their judgment."

He watched her for a long time. I imagined he was reading her thoughts, weighing what she said with what she actually believed. In the broadcasting room, he forced her to kill her comrades in cold blood. How could she crawl back to him? How could she refuse to see how cruel that "punishment" was?

"Rise, General," he ushered.

She did, bowing to him for a long moment before whispering her thanks.

"You've pleaded for forgiveness, and I'm giving you mercy," he continued. "If you fall out of line again, I will have none to offer."

She swallowed, "Yes, Your Majesty."

"Bring Maya here."

"Yes, Your Majesty."

She paused, tilting as though she planned on looking at me, but decided against it. She left the east wing with several guards tailing her.

"Leave us." His voice echoed through the chamber. The remaining soldiers bowed and left as quickly as they could. The doors closed with a thunderous finality.

Cassius observed me from a safe distance. A ringmaster inspecting the lion.

"You lied to me." Something teetered at the edge of his words. Not an outburst but on the verge of one.

"Did you kill her?" I didn't care for whatever sympathy he was looking for. He returned to Galdor without any indication of what he left in Caliel. Above everything else, I needed to know what happened there. If he mind controlled anyone else to...to...

His jaw tightened. "Would you like to finally explain what you were discussing with that Avlis?"

"Her name is Fern."

His fist slammed against the bars, rattling my cage. "I don't care about her name!"

I stumbled back but thankfully remained on my feet. His face contorted as he tried to compose himself. He pushed sweat-stained hair from his face, huffing, but his hand still gripped the bar. His lips quivered as he forced a quieter voice, "Nora, I'm only going to do this *once*. Do you love me?"

Red darkened my face. "What kind of question is that?"

"Nora, I—" His palm pressed deeper into the bar like he couldn't get close enough. I stepped back, the wall brushing along my back. "Nora, I love you."

Time halted but the world spun, faster and faster. Words failed to form, every combination rotating on an axel until all I could think was: *How dare he.*

"You don't love me."

"I do." Resolve strengthened in his voice. "I've wanted no one else by my side but you. Ever since we met, I wanted that for us. And I think...I think I'm at a breaking point."

I observed his matted hair, his shallow breathing, and his knuckles white. "*You think?*"

"Nora." He held his free hand to his chest, our eyes meeting. "I want you to be my queen."

A scoff escaped my lips before I could compress my guttural reaction. Those three little words continued to flash: *How dare he.*

"*Your queen?*" I spat. "You—" I couldn't get the words out fast enough—"*just* made me kill three innocent women. Unfortunates you promised to liberate! And you're...you're proposing?"

My mind couldn't wrap around the absurdity.

"I meant it when I said I want to believe we can change

this world together," Cassius continued. "I want to believe that you still love me, too."

I didn't scoff this time. I laughed. A strangled, twisted laugh that sounded so removed from myself that for a second I pretended I wasn't laughing at all. I was someone else completely different, distant. Anywhere but here. I could not bind myself to him.

"I don't love you," I finally said, composing myself. "I love Fern."

My words hung in the air, and I paused. A shocked expression drained my face in contrast to his mournful one.

"It's true, isn't it?" I asked, the admission still surprising me.

I remembered dancing together in a field of unity flowers. How the pink hues in the sunset sky softened her features. How the world faded away when I was by her side. I've known for a long time; my mind and thoughts and actions all steered toward her. A love that only strengthened with each passing heartbeat. A love not new but everlasting, rooted in friendship and trust and faith.

Cassius stepped back and looked down as he read my thoughts, his question as slicing as a knife's edge. "There's no way I can change your mind?"

I shook my head. "At one time, I would have chosen you. But what I love in you is a lie. Fern has never been a lie. Now tell me once and for all, did you kill her?"

He lifted his eyes to meet mine. I held my breath.

The door opened, and three forms stepped through.

The sight of Maya brought a fresh wave of dread. Poppy positioned carefully behind her so she couldn't run away, and Isaac Winters led her to the cell next to mine. Maya remained quiet, but her face was flushed with confusion and worry.

Silence thickened the air.

"Haven't you done enough to her?" I asked, my voice now hoarse.

"Hardly," Cassius replied, glancing from me to his sister. His voice became teasing. "Oh Maya, you're about to be useful again."

The king walked over to the vase, shoes clicking with each step. His hand delicately moved through the Gifts, finding and plucking out a pitch-black marble. A Nox Gift. Most likely her own.

My stomach lurched as he walked back and passed my cell without even so much a glance. Maya tried to stand straighter in her brother's presence, lips quivering.

He didn't bother using mind control as he unlocked the gate and opened it enough for him to slip through. She stepped back, pressing against the wall for support. He closed the door behind him with a loud rattle. We flinched.

"What's going on, Cas?" she whispered, shivering with her hands lifted in appeasement.

She looked just as feeble and helpless as she had lying in her own throne room, a new Unfortunate.

"Nora," he said, cold and smooth. I faced them, my hands wrapping around the cage. "What is the Unity Alliance planning against my kingdom?"

He stepped closer, the black hue twinkling between his fingers. An uncontrollable shaking throbbed my limbs. My mouth went dry.

Maya stared, eyes wide. "Don't do this."

The king stepped closer anyway. Maya clung to the corner, desperate to create more distance.

"You already know what they're doing," I blurted. "A march on Galdor. *That* is what we broadcasted."

"*Details!*" Cassius bellowed. "Give me details!"

My voice hitched in my throat.

In a flash, he grabbed Maya's arm and pushed her into the wall. They struggled against each other. He forced her palm open and held the Gift between them. All he had to do was crush the marble into her flesh, and it would likely kill her. At least twenty-eight people died in this very room. Many were Unfortunate experiments who used to be Gifteds. Maya wasn't nearly as bright as me or Poppy. And even if she did survive as Persephone did...she would be exactly what she hated most.

"No!" I yelled, reaching out between the bars to no avail. "I don't know! It's peaceful. A peaceful protest happening in three days. There are no other details!"

"*Peaceful*," he repeated as a taunt. "How stupid is she to choose peace?"

Something clicked behind Maya's eyes. She heard his words. How stupid she was to choose peace, too. Suddenly, Maya was screaming, intense and fearful. She shoved her brother with all her might, grabbing the marble between them and pressing it into *his* skin.

Light broke open. Cassius stumbled back, jaw slacked as he gripped his hand at the wrist in disbelief.

A new Gift—poisonous to the touch—now encompassed his power alongside his Makan one. I've seen him switch between Gifts before, carrying only two at a time. Poppy cupped her hands over her mouth, watching in astonishment and flickering in and out of the invisible plane.

The king recoiled, stumbling back again and holding his chest with unsteady breaths. With a swipe of his hand, the Nox Gift materialized again and fell to the floor. It shattered on impact, igniting darkness and then turning into glass and ash.

I stared at the dust. Could that mean...could that mean he still had his Animus Gift?

He regained himself, wrath consuming his entire body. Maya panted and stood more regal than ever, staring back with a hardened expression. "You are a disgrace, Cas."

A surge of hope blossomed in my chest. This is what I always wanted her to be. A queen. A protector of her people instead of her throne. She was exactly that for one shining moment.

The king huffed, pulling out a hidden dagger from his boot. In one stride, he closed the distance between them. An incomplete gasp. A deep slit just below Maya's neck.

"No!" I shrieked.

She stumbled in shock, clutching her wound. Blood pooled at her chest, dampening her clothes in a deep red. Her dilated eyes found me, and she collapsed.

Another person was taken away, and I was powerless to stop it.

"Maya." I fell to the ground with her.

I reached out through the bars again. One bloodied hand released from her neck and found mine.

Her eyes blinked slowly, and her lips moved without her voice. *You're warm.*

Her fingers relaxed. Her body slumped over.

My sobbing strengthened, my hand still clasped with hers. Her eyes, still partly opened, looked like glass. Like beads emptied of their Gift staring right back at me.

"I swear," I heaved, loud enough for the Divine to hear, "*I swear* her actions today will be recorded in history. And *you*—" I pointed at Cassius with my free hand as he cleaned his blade—"you will be nothing but a warning. A nightmare figure to scare children into good behavior."

He kept his back to me, but I could see his shoulders bristle.

He left the cell, not bothering to close it behind him. I gently laid Maya's hand down and moved over accordingly.

The heat vanished from my body as he took over again. He unlocked my cell and threaded through, closing the distance between us and answering my frightening question. He managed to keep his Animus Gift. It didn't vanish with the additional Nox power.

I tried to fight the mind control—to back away, to run, to spit. The knife flashed in my vision for a heartbeat before he put it back in its sheath.

His hand reached out; Poppy stepped forward. "Your Majesty."

His fury transferred to her, teeth clenched. "*What?*"

"You've made your point, sir. We should begin preparations for the impending attack."

Poppy was...protecting me. Her wavering voice and deceptive expression told me so. I imagined Cassius didn't need to be an Animus to see that she was covering her reason for intruding. Had she lied to him earlier to stay out of imprisonment too? No. When she tried to lie once before, he caught her easily. Surely, I was only wishing.

He only looked at her for a heartbeat before turning back to me. "It's a peaceful protest, General. Nothing to fear."

So Fern was alive. She had to be! He tormented me without a definite answer. His thumb brushed over the edge of my lip, and I feared he would lean into a kiss that no longer belonged to him.

A smile curved along the edges of his mouth, but his face didn't soften. "So, there's no way I can change your mind."

There wasn't any warmth behind his touch, no real love beating in his heart. Only a challenge. A desire to break. "We'll see about that."

His palm connected with my temple in a blaze of startling white.

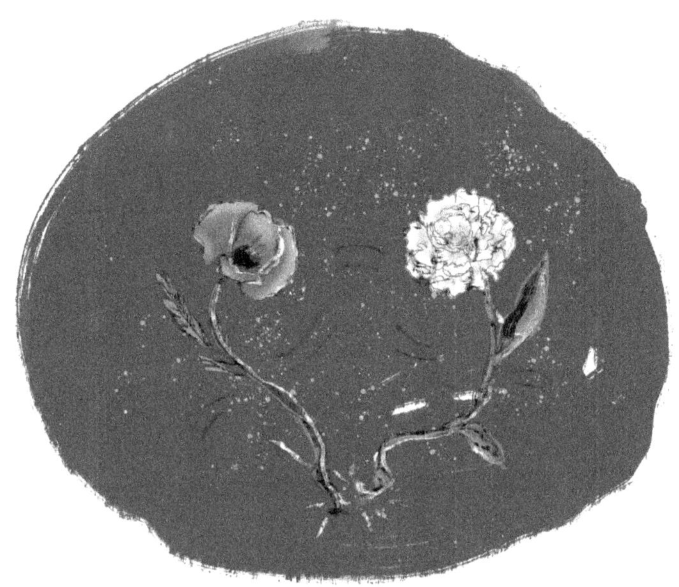

CHAPTER THIRTY-SIX

Disconnected
FERN

———

"We have to start the march sooner!"

I pressed my hands firmly along the pew's backrest to keep me rooted in place. Lady Beatrice, Lady Saleema, and Mom joined us in the church I almost lost my life in. We hadn't left; we regained our strength while the rest of the Unity Alliance claimed Caliel. Skylar and Leo were relatively intact after arresting the other rich Houses on her list and bullying the heirs into severing ties with the AGM. Cassius didn't touch them. He was only after me.

Everyone stared with less-than-urgent faces. Someone needed to talk this instant, or I'd explode.

"The broadcast said the march would take place on the first day of the year. No one will join us if we start sooner." Lady Beatrice's voice was too matter-of-fact. Too logical.

Mom walked over to my side and squeezed my hand, but I only dug my nails into the wood.

"But that's *three* days." I said through clenched teeth. "Nora needs me *now*."

"We're not compromising our own march so you can save your girlfriend." Lady Saleema mirrored her superior.

A fracture ripped through the bench. I stood straighter. "Leave in three days then! I'll go ahead and bring her back."

Lady Saleema narrowed her eyes; Molly bobbed Prince Henry on her hip with cooing reassurance. Lady Sanchiko sat upright, still on the floor, with Mr. Harris holding her hand.

Mom pushed my hair away from my face. "Fern, you almost died alone against him."

"*Cassius*, Mom!" I swatted her away, regretting the action but refusing to show it. "Call him Cassius. He's just a man."

"If he's just a man, don't let him get to you like this." Lady Saleema did not back down. "You'll have your chance to confront him again in three days."

"Nora might not have three days!" The reality of those words struck me like a lightning bolt. I held my palms to my temple, my breathing uneven. "Mr. Harris, do you know anything about altering someone's mind? What happened to Isaac Winters?"

Mr. Harris shook his head.

"It's a risk we'll have to accept," Molly chimed in.

"Molly!"

"*What?*" she challenged. "You think you have capital on fear? I know Nora, too. She's already lost someone who protected her. She wouldn't want you wasting your life either."

I tried firing something back, but it stopped in my throat. "What do you mean she's already lost someone?"

"It means we used to have another servant when I was…different. She's talked about her before. A girl named Valerie."

I racked my brain for several silent breaths until that name clicked somewhere in my memories. At first, throwaway comments about another servant she worked with at the Montgomerys.

And then basket-weaving. She threw me off when she said she wasn't used to doing everything by herself the way I often did. *When Valerie was brought home, my life as a servant became tolerable. I could depend on another to help me…*

Oh Divine, how foolish I was. How foolish I would continue to be.

"How can I do nothing? She needs me." My voice teetered on a whimper.

"She needs you to lead this march." Mr. Harris stood, looking wiser with a serious expression masking his distress. "You've come too far to give it all up now."

I stared, absorbing his words and his features—all their words and features. I gulped, shaking the nerves from my hands but they continued to fester.

Nora, I thought desperately. *Even if you forget, I'll fulfill our promise.*

She didn't respond.

***

We geared up for the march on Galdor in three days.

I needed to connect to Nora. Focusing on her like a moth to a flame. Clinking in place like polar magnets—or whatever simile I needed to use to hear her voice in my head. I needed to know that she was safe—that Cassius's threat held no merit. Each passing second spread fear down my spine, sometimes so acute I could throw up.

Nora, I reached out like leaving a voicemail. *It's Fern. Are you there?*

The wind whistled through my ear. No response.

I breathed in the cold winter air, wandering through our camp to distract myself.

A group of Gifteds and Unfortunates worked at a craft table covered with every marker type in the world. It was nice to see the Gifteds we rescued fully restored and ready to serve for once. They wrote on sleek white boards with precise strokes. Molly stood at the head of the table, directing everyone while Delilah stood to her right, filling in a letter with black marker.

Molly saw me and gestured me closer. I did, braiding half of my hair in a coping mechanism.

"Anything yet?" she asked, looking at my messy plait instead of my eyes.

I shook my head. "No. I'm—"

"*Lady Mika!*" Molly snapped her fingers, head swerved to look at the young man further down the line. He looked up at her with bulging eyes. "Let me see your sign before you put it in the finished pile."

Timid, he lifted his sign to reveal his work. Red ribbon, flowing and folding like the real thing, formed into a noose with blood dripping off the end for good measure. Simple but effectively disturbing. I grimaced, touching my neck. I could still feel Cassius's hands around my throat.

"Excellent work," Molly smiled. "Make a few more just like it if you can."

He nodded and added his creation to the finished pile at the end of the table.

Molly passed a new board down the line and turned back to me. "You were saying?"

I started braiding the other side of my hair. "I'm still trying."

"Good. Would you like to make a sign?" She gestured to the table, but there wasn't any room to spare.

"I'm okay." I looked at my sister's work. She finished bubble lettering the phrase: *AGM*. "How are you doing, D?"

"Fine. Pass me that red marker?"

I found the one she pointed to and gave it to her. She slashed the initials out with an X. I watched her for several breaths, thankful that she was right beside me.

"Delilah," I prodded.

"Hm?" She passed the sign down the line and retrieved a new one.

I bit my lip, fearful of the answer and how she'd react. "Did Cassius ever…hurt you?"

She stopped forming her *A* but only for a moment. "I guess so. It was really freaky when he mind-controlled me. I couldn't move! But he kind of acted like Grandpa after that. Helping me with my Gift and buying me ice cream."

"He—he bought you ice cream?" Our grandpa was a Makan, too, and cherished Delilah while they were together. I would never in a million years compare him to Cassius.

"Yeah, we ate it while I tried to see people's Gifts." She finished the *M* and started coloring in the letters with dark ink. "He's mostly weird—a little scary."

Molly, undoubtedly listening in, wiped her eyes. Cassius held her sister hostage before, too. I made the connection, and my face fell. "Molly, I'm sorry."

"No, no." She tried to hide her tears, but I was already holding her. "I can't say that I didn't want to know, either."

"I'm still sorry," I said from her shoulder. "There's no excuse."

"What happened?" Delilah asked, looking between us.

"Nothing." I gestured at her poster, not willing to share Molly's business. "Keep working. You're doing great."

Leaving their station, I watched people get rations and water ready, some Lady Lilacs jogging in a group, and the twins teaching some unfamiliar faces a card game.

Nora, I pictured her in my mind. *It's Fern. Are you okay?*

I heard myself breathe for a full minute. No response.

I found Kai busy with a pen and clipboard, walking alongside the rows of trucks we had at our disposal. His lips moved as he tapped the butt of the pen to his chin. I heard him as I got closer, running numbers with intense care. I imagined he was scribbling the calculations within the margins of his paper.

"If we recruit forty people in Doverly and then let's just say 100 total on the way down, then that'll..."

"What are you doing by yourself?"

"Just finished counting inventory, so I'm playing around with our march numbers now." Kai managed to steady the pen behind his ear and investigated my appearance. "How are you doing?"

"Crappy," I laughed half-heartedly. "Please tell me we're going to win."

Kai smiled. "The odds are way greater with that broadcast,

but it's still a guessing game. We have no idea how many people will actually walk with us."

The broadcast. I twisted my hair into buns without any ties. That morning was the last glimpse of her mental connection with me. Eleven minutes and then nothing.

"We're going to win, Fern," Kai said in the silence.

"You just said you have no idea."

"It just sounds like something you'd say."

I let go of my hair, leaned down, and hugged him. "Thanks, Kai."

"Here to help." We broke apart. "What are you going to do in the meantime?"

I watched the sun already setting. "I'm going to find a unity flower."

Kai chuffed. "Good luck this high north. But who knows?"

"Who knows," I agreed, and then I wandered off.

He was right, of course. Unity flowers didn't grow in Caliel and certainly not with this border-line freezing weather. But that was why the Divine created Avlis. We could cultivate flowers in our palm so long as we had the seeds or even the seed structure.

I found my own patch of heaven where no one else occupied and spent the evening blooming unity flowers in existence. White peonies and red poppies intertwined in a tangled heap all around me by the time stars lined the sky.

Nora, I prayed. *It's Fern. Please be safe.*

Mom found me. Persephone stood beside her with a ball of fire in her palm as a guide.

"These are beautiful, baby sprouts."

"Thanks, Mom." My torso deflated as worry filled my mind again.

"Let's hand these flowers out as we march."

"That sounds like a great idea, Mom."

"Excellent." She picked up a mass in her arms. "I'll add them to inventory. You'll make some more tomorrow?"

"Sure."

Persephone helped Mom navigate to a truck still open at this hour, and I dragged my feet to the Stanton mansion.

I should have been ecstatic to sleep in a real bed again and one with an expensive thread count. The blankets coddled me, but I tossed and turned anyway. The empty room mocked me with her absence.

Nora, I pleaded. *Nora, it's Fern. Hold on for a little longer. I'll be there soon.*

The mansion creaked as it settled. A hole carved in my chest. I rolled over, facing the wall.

I love Fern.

The words rushed past my thoughts, so sudden I whipped my head around the empty, dark room like I'd find them there. Like I'd find her there.

"Nora?" I whispered and then yelled, "Nora!"

But the connection was there and lost like she was nothing more than a ghost.

CHAPTER THIRTY-SEVEN

Awake

NORA

———

Wake up.

A snap followed, and I awoke at once. White walls and sterile air formed the infirmary. Pristine bedsheets restrained me from sitting up properly, and a rhythmic beep noting my heartbeat echoed to my left. To my right, I locked eyes with Cassius. None of it made any sense.

He gently squeezed my hand. "You're awake."

Confusion scrunched my face. My focus flickered to the wall where General Poppy stood rigid. I looked back to Cassius. "What happened?"

He exhaled, deep and mournful. Alarm pushed past the exhaustion in my limbs. I could not recall what led me here; all that remained in its void was a deep sense of fear, sorrow, and despair.

I gripped his hand still entwined with mine. "What happened?" I asked again. "How long...how did...why can't I remember?"

"Easy." His other hand cupped my face, but I continued to speak in fragmented sentences. He cooed, rubbing his thumb along my cheek. "I'll answer one at a time. But first, what *do* you remember?"

I steadied with a gulp, nodding.

"I know my name," I offered.

"Good. And you know me?"

I studied his face. His features were worn, but there was still that sparkle in his eye. A glimpse of starlight that permeated all of our interactions. Meeting each other on the Grounds through his own initiative. Speaking out during Senior Circle meetings as our leaders failed to meet expectations. Dancing together in the rain. All of those memories came back with gentle familiarity.

"Of course."

He sighed with great relief and squeezed my hand.

"You fought valiantly for the crown, but you were overpowered by some Gifteds. General Poppy got you out before they could do any more damage than they already did. Do you remember her?" He pointed over to the general who avoided looking at me.

"Yes." I was her lieutenant. We were friends. "But I don't remember fighting. Who is 'they'?"

"A Gifted insurgence," Cassius explained. "Calling themselves the Unity Alliance but it's a false name. They want to reestablish the old order, but you, my dear, refused to let that happen."

The Unity Alliance. What a lovely name except for the added detail that it was a misnomer. I blinked and pouted, trying to recall what he was telling me to no avail. Did I hit my head? Did the Gifteds nearly kill me, and I was resuscitated?

Cassius read my thoughts and answered me, looking absolutely miserable. "You were in a coma for the past four months."

"*What?*" My mouth fell open, shocked. *"Four months?"* I've been away from active duty for far longer than I could ever believe. Four months was enough time for the seasons to change, for the tide of this conflict to turn. My legs became jittery, ready to sprint into another battle at the thought.

I flipped off the covers and tried to stand.

Cassius grabbed my wrists and stopped me from reaching the floor. "Not so fast! You still need time to heal."

"I've wasted too much time!"

"Nora, please." He spoke so softly I stopped fighting him immediately.

From his seated position and my elevated hospital bed, I looked down to meet his gaze. Four months. He couldn't speak or interact with me for all that time. I loosened out of his grip and kissed him, soft and slow before easing back into my cot.

"I'm sorry. It's just a lot to take in." There was a pause before I tried for encouragement. "How have we been doing against this Unity Alliance?"

Poppy fidgeted in the background, and Cassius averted his attention. Not well by their reactions. "They've gained enough momentum to strike Galdor in three days."

The disparity between four months and three days clenched my jaw. What could I have done if I wasn't rendered in this state? What would have happened if I hadn't awoken?

Bile threatened to rise, but I swallowed it down. I needed to look at the positive. If I could get better in a few days, then maybe I can defend the crown again and this time, savor the victory.

"I'll be right by your side," I declared.

He smiled. "I wouldn't have it any other way."

We stayed like that for a few more heartbeats, holding hands and relishing in each other's company before he sighed, released me, and stood.

"In the meantime, rest. I mean it."

I nodded even though I loathed the idea. "Would it be okay if Poppy stayed with me? I want to thank her properly and ask some more questions about the battle itself."

He glanced wearily from me to his general. She stepped away from the wall. "I'll make sure she stays in bed and rests, Your Majesty—"

"You may guard the door." Cassius interrupted her so sharply that we jolted.

He turned back to me with an apologetic expression. "You just awoke to a lot of news. You two can go through the finer details later."

I huffed but didn't press. There *would* be plenty of time for us to share the gruesome details after this threat was demolished once and for all.

Satisfied with my silent acceptance, he left the room.

Poppy bowed as he passed and followed him out.

The door closed, and I counted out the heartbeats before getting up. There would be plenty of time, but how could I possibly rest with my head spinning like this? I took my covers off again and swung my legs to the floor. A chill ran up my bare feet, but I found walking easier than I expected after four months of hiatus. In fact, most of my muscle mass retained itself. A blessing of science or a blessing in general, I'd take either.

Carefully, I navigated the IV stand alongside me to the

exit.

Turning the knob, I peered out into the hall. Cassius placed me in one of the few private rooms, so the only person in my sight was Poppy, guarding me as commanded.

She noticed my appearance and eyed me without turning. "You're supposed to be resting."

"I can't sleep."

"You need to try harder than two minutes."

I leaned against the door frame for support. "Thank you for saving me. It must have been a terrible fight."

Her lips pursed at the comment. "It was," she finally said. "And don't thank me."

"Why not?"

"Because you're here."

"Yeah, but—"

"Get back into bed, Nora." She cut me off, but she still remained stoically in place.

"I will." I threw my hands up in appeasement, though she couldn't see most of my display. "I'm glad you're here."

I stepped back.

"You remember the lesson we learned about the Fall?"

I stopped just shy of the door closing, a crack so thin only one eye peeked through.

Her fists clenched at her sides. She was referring to our original Downcastment. When the first Gifted used her Gift for her own interests and not for its intention. To choose evil, knowing it was wrong and going against the Divine's request anyway. It was why Unfortunate girls spent their lives in servitude. A never-ending repentance and reminder of the first downcast soul.

The Divine meant to perfect humanity, and when they failed, we were created as punishment. But when we read the

Great Book for ourselves, we learned something crucial. Why bring it up now of all times?

"Yes," I said slowly and then explained myself. "The Fall was never meant to happen, but the Divine acted accordingly and it's our life's work to mend the bond between Him and us. Not just Unfortunates but Gifteds as well."

That was what Gifteds conveniently left out. They were still held accountable for their actions, charged with keeping to the Divine's will. After all, at that point in history, a person had to be a Gifted in order to become an Unfortunate.

Poppy bobbed her head in agreement but still didn't look at me. I saw only half of her face, eyes so lowered I could only see her lashes. Her mouth though was a tight line as though she was holding back—something she never did since I've known her.

After several heartbeats, I filled the silence. "I never got to thank you for sharing the Great Book with me in its proper form. You're doing a lot of good with our king."

She turned her face completely away, flinching so subtly I could have missed it if I wasn't so focused on her form.

"Our king..." she mused in a soft tone that implied more.

"Did I say something wrong?"

There was so much time missing in sleep. I hoped to give her a compliment, but now I feared I was hurting her in some way I couldn't understand. Had she and Cassius got into an argument of some kind? A rift perhaps?

"No, just..." Poppy lifted one of her hands and observed her palm. "I fear the king has done something he wasn't ever meant to do. Multiple somethings."

My stomach curdled from everything she wasn't telling me. What had Cassius done in my absence? "Poppy—"

"I just wanted to know if you remembered." She cut me

off again, finally looking at me with a smile masking pain underneath. "I'm glad you do. Keep remembering and get some rest."

She nudged the door closed and left me to a torment of anxious thoughts.

CHAPTER THIRTY-EIGHT

March on Galdor
FERN

Three.

Two.

One.

The morning came. Like flowers blooming to the sun's rays, we rose.

I was already awake, watching white cut through the twilight. Nora's one comment replayed in my head, over and over. *I love*, she said. Not "I like." Not "I tolerate." *Love*. It was almost too good to be true. My only regret was the inability to say it back.

I would tell her today.

Kai found me first, the early riser he was. He helped prepare our final supplies as our first 100 members readied at the edge of Caliel's southern limit. The train station resided in silence, surrounded by Unity Alliance and Lady Lilac soldiers.

I caught sight of Mom and Delilah passing out unity flowers and Molly handing out signs with Persephone. Further into the streets, Skylar hovered through the air to visit each church congregation as they stalled traffic, and Leo directed the news cameras as they hounded him.

All Anti-Gifted soldiers and movement-affiliated citizens were locked in Caliel wait stations scattered across the city. The only red abound were the poppies intertwined with white peonies. I hadn't counted how much I made but guessing from their prevalence, I made plenty.

To occupy myself, I braided two sections of hair and pinned them over my head like a crown. Fiddling with my fingers, I created a unity flower, untwined them, and tucked each flower alongside the loose strands near my ears.

Skylar's form whooshed past and then hovered over us, her smile like that of a hostess.

"Everyone is getting antsy to start and the cameras have been *rolling*. Are there any hold ups?"

"No, we're all set," Kai assured. He turned to me. "Are you ready?"

I exhaled, looking composed but wanting to sprint. "I'm ready."

Skylar clapped her hands, launching in the air and screaming, *"Let's march!"*

***

Fear prickled along my arms as we walked from Caliel to Osthall. The broadcast said exactly what it needed to: we would march—peacefully—today on Galdor. But the journey between the two cities was relatively vacant, safe for small towns, farms, and outposts. Our number grew in the single digits, and we hadn't encountered any other mass of people from the east or west. Nothing to suggest that the country was moved to action.

The small voice in the back of my mind told me that what we were doing was embarrassing. A loss. A disaster. Every flash of a camera worried me how they'd twist the words in print. *Unity Alliance is underwhelming. March on Galdor is a total failure.* I wasn't meant for writing headlines, but I knew they'd be clever.

Mom strode beside me. Kai, Molly, and Persephone were in my peripheral. Lady Saleema, Lady Sanchiko, and Mr. Harris carrying Prince Henry walked in a tight pack. I never let that small voice win, and I wasn't about to today. Mom helped me grow stronger in my Gift. My team was with me every step leading to this moment. Mr. Harris and I managed to obtain an alliance with a group once thought eradicated.

Even if it was just us, I would count this march a success. Even if it was just us, I could face Nora with pride. I would fulfill my promise to her today.

We made it to Osthall around noon. The glittering second city to our destination.

I never walked through Osthall before. We never stepped through during our claim to the west and our claim to the east was Caliel. Osthall's location and identity was too well tied to Galdor to take it over successfully.

Nora told us that the city appeared untouched by the war. Gifteds still lived their lives as comfortably as they had under King Daltus's rule with the new watchful eye of AGM guards and banners. Aligning with Cassius meant that you weren't taken to a wait station. Your Gift remained yours so long as you complied. Osthall didn't have any wait stations for this exact reason.

Seeing it from afar, I could only make out the skyscrapers jutting out from downtown. Up close, I could see the people and they could see us.

Red thickened the streets like the city was soaked in blood. Anti-Gifted soldiers in clean-pressed uniforms stationed themselves at balconies and rooftops. They blended themselves in with the clustered, anxious citizens along the sidewalk.

I could feel the march behind me pause and hesitate. But I refused to show my fear. *This is a peaceful protest*, I screamed to myself so I wouldn't scream out loud. *We are peaceful. Anyone who strikes first will be to blame. It will not be me. It will not be me.*

I walked ahead, feeling the cold emptiness at my back. I was an Avlis on a mission. Just a girl going about her day.

A thousand eyes burned into my flesh, the temperature rising inside me despite the winter air. I stared straight ahead, my mouth in a tight line so I wouldn't give way to crying, my hands fisted at my side so I wouldn't squirm. My footsteps echoed along the path, the only sound I could focus on.

Thankfully, the earth rumbled beneath my feet as the march started to follow, congealing on the road.

A rogue pebble flew through the air and clattered somewhere behind me. I flinched, but the projectile didn't strike me. I continued walking forward, a little unsteady. A shout rang out from the same direction, and I clenched my teeth to keep my expression neutral.

We are a peaceful protest, I reminded myself. *I am peaceful. I will not attack first.*

The temperature burned, threatening to choke me as we winded our way through the streets. Red blurred at the edges of my vision. Servant girls in black uniforms adorned their necks, waistlines, and ankles with red ribbon next to their masters who sneered at our signs and murmured obviously to each other. Soldiers fidgeted with their weapons, waiting for an order or for an opportunity. I refused to give them one.

I wondered how everyone else was fairing, though I didn't dare turn around. I could only hope that they held firm. The moment this peaceful protest turned into a riot or a massacre, everything we built ourselves on would crumble away. We had to reach Cassius first.

Someone brushed my side, breaking my concentration. I stopped and turned to see Mr. Harris, no longer carrying Prince Henry in his one good arm. He must have passed the child closer to the march's center where he would be the most protected and hidden.

The third royal's existence wasn't widespread news, but Mr. Harris was one of the most recognizable figures as King Daltus's 1st Senior Royal Crest Knight. More people murmured; movement caught my eye as onlookers weaved through the crowd to follow us—but not join us.

Mr. Harris and I guided the march down more roads. The same tension followed us our entire journey through Osthall, but not a single person followed us out.

✳✳✳

I kept my head high, but my spirits waned. Despite myself, I wanted fanfare. I wanted to show Cassius that he didn't have the world in his hands. That people could still move and act and say *actually, no I don't like what you're doing and I won't tolerate it any longer.* I wanted the Unity Alliance to mean something outside of myself. It could resonate with strangers the way it resonated with Lady Sanchiko and the other Lilacs. I wanted my promise to Nora to spread like ivy, be as grand as an oak tree and just as strong. She deserved a thousand people. She deserved the world.

We reached Galdor in the late afternoon, which in wintertime was just about sunset. My favorite time of day, which seemed more important now than ever.

I stopped in my tracks as I realized that we weren't at the edge of Galdor or anywhere near the train station that marked the entrance. We were at the edge of a congregation.

A mass of people extended out from the city limits and surrounded the capital on all sides. Avlis came from the southeast. Mares and Feras and Imitations continued to pour in from the furthest reaches of west and south. Mati and Auran and Lux Gifteds resided beside us from the northwest.

Even Unfortunates were in the mix, sticking out in their Sunday dresses or servant uniforms. They clumped together, tense with apprehension but nonetheless here. It was a circle. A *huge* circle we absorbed into.

Iridion came. We were just the northeast group. I wondered how much faith everyone else held while walking here. If they too were worried about being the only ones to show up and came anyway. The uncertainty of it all. If I had all the time in the world, I would hug each and everyone here.

One of the last things Nora said to me came back. *I want to see you when you march on Galdor. I'll find you among the masses.*

I searched for her likeness among every face despite knowing she wasn't there.

I'll cheer you on even if I can't reach you.

I prayed that a small part of her would cheer despite not knowing me at all.

Mr. Harris kept walking, and I came out of my trance.

The crowd noticed our arrival and lightly parted as we weaved through. Mr. Harris was more recognizable at face value, but I liked to think I looked striking too with my brazen display of unity flowers and confident stride.

It took several minutes to reach the front, which was dense with more people. Mr. Harris stopped in what would be the equivalent of a second row, and I stepped out in front of him.

Anti-Gifted soldiers stood to attention just as they had in Osthall, but they formed a barricade with their bodies and blocked us from entering Galdor. Their weapons flashed in a confrontational display, ready to strike instead of itching to get there. No one I could see past their line wore civilian clothes, and I prayed that the broadcast sent them out of the city. Osthall let us pass, but this was Cassius's stronghold. I was not foolish to believe we could walk in without consequence.

A few yards separated us from each other. My feet twitched, feeling the disturbance that came with buried objects. Rectangular and heavy. No doubt bombs, ready to destroy us before we even began.

We are a peaceful protest, I reminded. *We will not strike first. It must be him. He must show his true nature once and for all.*

I trained my sight on the Unfortunate in front of me. There was so much I wanted to tell her. I wanted to say, *I understand why you dawn this uniform.* I wanted to tell her that whatever happened to her as a servant didn't need to define her.

And most importantly, I wanted to cry, *I'm sorry. I'm so very sorry for how Gifteds treated you and I'm incredibly sorry that we have to fight at all now. I hope you survive this. I hope* no one kills you, and you can live in peace once this is all said and done.

She merely stared back, watching and waiting in silence. The crowd stirred, morphing into one body behind me.

I took one step forward, and the world ignited at its center.

CHAPTER THIRTY-NINE

Attack on Galdor

NORA

The infirmary walls rattled violently in warning. I gasped, wide awake, sitting up and clutching the blanket for support. Looking around my room, I tried processing what brought me out of sleep and felt the churn of the earth recoil my stomach. Another bomb. The city was under attack. The Unity Alliance was here, and my rest had to be complete.

I could hear the commotion outside, growing louder and closer with each passing minute. Smoke rose into the sky, blocking out the last rays of sunlight. Night was growing upon us and with that, a disadvantage against our enemy. A Lux could see what we couldn't and help direct the Gifteds in their slaughter. All the more reason we needed to act with precision. My heart thumped loudly in my chest, bright as ever.

I rushed across the Grounds and into the castle. Soldiers

barked orders to each other and ran to their own marks. They parted for me as I bolted, my focus intense.

Throwing my bedroom door open, I almost shrieked at the sight of Poppy sitting at my window alcove. "What are you—?"

"Close the door," she said urgently.

I did, striding over to my dresser to find proper gear instead of my current pajamas.

"What's going on?" I asked her, hoping for more information. Were we going to fight alongside each other once more against this movement?

"Nora, I need to tell you the truth."

I paused and then completely froze when I noticed my sword in Poppy's hand. The words came out carefully. "What are you doing?"

"We don't have much time before he discovers that I'm still in the castle and not at my post."

My bedroom became smaller. I lifted my hands, considering. "What is it?"

Poppy spoke desperately, too fast. "You are *not* on good terms with the king. He brainwashed you into a version of yourself that he wants, not who you truly are. He had us kill Bree, Ellie, and Holly—if you even remember them at all."

My hands lowered in confusion. "Brain—what?" I couldn't even fully comprehend. No. *No.* That was impossible. Cassius loved me. He would never—I woke up with no recollection, but he would never!

I stepped back, "You're one of them, aren't you?"

"What? No, *you* are, and *you* helped me realize that he's not a savior."

With each pointed *you*, she flashed the sword at my heart. Confusion flashed to anger, threatening to choke my voice.

I started shaking my head, but she continued, "He's just a man. A terrible man. I'm doing you a favor before you hurt someone you *truly* love."

Poppy threw the sword onto the ground, its crash startling me back to the present. She lifted her giant mallet high.

"No!" I collided into her, and we tumbled onto the ground.

I reached for my sword, fingers flexing as far as they would go. Poppy kicked it toward the door, found my hair, and yanked my head back. Pressing the staff of her mallet to my neck, she locked me in place in front of her.

"Cassius took the throne from his sister and trapped you here!"

"She—" My voice came out rough and strained. "She gave up the crown willingly!"

I managed to stand; Poppy stood with me, her body pressed against my back.

"He took the crown, and he took you!"

"No!" Maya begged him to take the crown—I remembered. But what happened after that? What happened between then and now?

"You were friends with Gifteds!" Poppy insisted.

She released one of her hands to dig around in my jacket, but I didn't have any hidden blades. We teetered as we fought for control, stepping toward my bed.

Friends with Gifteds? That didn't make sense either. My time as a student was in isolation. No one offered me their friendship save for Cassius. I remembered training with him, improving and growing stronger together.

"And when he trapped you here, you became friends with *my* soldiers! They died for you! Bree! Ellie! And Holly!"

Three forms tried to connect with the names, but all I

could see was a blur. Contorted silhouettes.

She screamed, pressing harder against my throat. "Remember Fern then! A red-headed Avlis. She's been with you since the beginning!"

"I don't—" We stumbled back as something did connect. Someone patting my head. A weight on my shoulder and red hair cascading down my face. A strange introduction? I wrenched it away, afraid of what would flash next, and slammed Poppy against the wall.

She grunted, her grip loosening. I broke free and ran to my sword. The hilt slipped in my hands, but I managed to point at Poppy. From what I could remember, we trained together too. Side by side. We traveled through Iridion together and spread Cassius's rule. I would even consider us friends up until this moment. So why?

"Why would you lie to me?" I demanded. "Were you hoping I would betray Cassius if I believed you?"

She steadied her own weapon and positioned herself back to the window. "I hate you so much for finally turning me onto your side just for you to fall into his arms!"

Tears fell down her face, and I flinched from the scorn.

"This war can end tonight, and if you believe me even for a *second*, you have the power to finish this." She pointed straight at my heart. "And if you don't believe me, find the red-headed Avlis. Cassius will want you to kill her the most."

"*Nora!*" As if summoned, his voice boomed somewhere down the hall. Footsteps ran toward us with incredible speed.

Poppy jumped onto the window ledge. "Goodbye, brightest Unfortunate."

She swung her mallet, glass breaking. Cassius burst into the room, but she was already gone.

I wanted to run after her—to kill her or to get more

answers, I wasn't sure. The wind rustled loudly through the new opening. Cassius spat a string of curses. Shaking, I managed to put my sword back into its sheath.

"What happened?" he commanded, charging over and grabbing my shoulders. "What did she tell you?"

A grimace marked my expression as I felt him read through my mind, the sensation more apparent than ever. By the time I started squirming to get away, he was already finished.

"I'm sorry," he panted, moving his hands down my arm. "I'm sorry. I just—" He released an exasperated sound, "I can't believe she tricked me for so long."

"Is she the only one?" I asked, my voice so much quieter than his. "Have I...?" I couldn't bring myself to ask the full question, but he understood.

"No," he said with certainty, bringing me into an embrace. "No, she's just trying to tear us apart. You're still mine." He repeated himself, and I wasn't sure if that was for my comfort or for his. He kissed the top of my head.

I leaned closer into him, but the ripple of another explosion reminded me that we couldn't stay like this forever.

I stepped back, my hand instinctively thumbing the hilt of my sword. A present from Cassius when I first started Galdor. Despite Poppy's attempt otherwise, I would make him proud today.

"Tell me what you've planned in place."

***

The Senior Circle room was just as I remembered it. All of the generals were absent, probably already in the fray, including Isaac Winters who guarded the northern wall.

We studied at a map sprawled out on the table, our sides pressed together. He pointed to the train station at the west-most side.

"The attack started at the train station, but most bombs have denoted by now. See these dots?" His finger danced in a circle around the city; I nodded. "We lined Galdor with landmines as a first defense before they can reach our barricade of soldiers."

"How far have they advanced?" I looked at a second dark ring closer to the castle where most commercial businesses resided and the crown at the very center.

A crash ripped through the sky, so fierce we could feel it through our entire bodies. Pencils, pens, and other small objects rolled off the table and clattered soundlessly to the floor as more tremors threatened our foundation.

Cassius grabbed me and pushed us back from the table as it teetered to the other side of the room. We stayed motionless as the collision continued for far longer than it should have. Even after everything settled, I continued to shiver.

"What the hell was that?" I rubbed my shoulders as we separated and walked back to the table.

Cassius cleared his throat, composed himself. "Our third barricade." He gestured to the dark inner ring but didn't elaborate, biting the inside of his cheek. "They're closing in."

"Do you know what direction?"

"If my instincts are correct, it'll be north."

"Then it's time we get out there, too." I stood upright. "Permission to assist Isaac Winters at the north wall?"

Cassius shook his head, "No. You'll stay with me as the last line of defense to the crown."

My mouth drew a line. I understood why Cassius wanted

to protect me—I just returned to my senses—but I was feeling brighter than ever. He couldn't afford to protect me today.

"But Cassius—"

"I'm not losing you again." His voice cracked from the weight of his words, and any ire I had faltered. He clasped his hand in mine and kissed the scar that marked me as an Unfortunate. "You're staying by my side."

I exhaled, resolute with everything that just transpired. "Okay, but I must insist that you have more than just me as your last soldier. Permission to station ourselves behind Isaac's line?"

"Granted."

That was a relief. I smiled, hoping my determination shined through. "Let nothing stand against us."

CHAPTER FORTY

Our Final Stand
FERN

———

A bomb scorched the earth somewhere to my right. Screams lifted into the air alongside smoke. And while most heads turned to look at the horror, I did not.

The Unfortunate in front of me turned her face, and I yelled, charging forward. People rushed in beside me, some running even faster ahead, the invisible line tethered and trampled in our wake.

I could feel the landmines buried under our feet. As I avoided them, someone anchored themselves along my back. It was Kai, and a quick glance revealed the rest of my team following my exact path, linked together in an unwavering chain. To my immediate right, Mom targeted and disabled each threat under the earth and various Lady Lilacs blocked anyone from setting them off as she worked.

I turned back, facing forward. Within a few strides, I knocked my first AGM soldier to the dirt.

More sulfur and gunpowder littered the air, clinging to my skin as bombs continued to go off anyway to the left and right, some distantly across the cityscape and some so close I feared the worst.

An Unfortunate in a red uniform swung at me; I sprayed dirt in his eyes, tripped others over roots, and dodged when they came too close.

Knowing help was at my heels, I focused solely on those impending points that made the Iridion castle. Cassius would keep her as close to him as possible. I would not fail her.

An arrow flew through the air, rushing past my torso and striking the ground to my right. I forced myself to keep running so I wouldn't lose momentum. My left arm hovered over the dirt, and the earth lifted just over my open palm. I created a shield against the onslaught of archers stationed in buildings I couldn't see. Their arrows knocked against the plate. Loose dirt and sand cascaded off, but no weapon pierced through.

The earth churned, and a shadow loomed over my head. Looking up, a shifting wave of dirt shielded our entire team from harm. Mom sped up until she kept pace at my side. I let go of my defense and it accumulated with my mom's creation.

We rushed past a large building, no longer in the archers' line of sight. The barrier came down, and we ran, faster and faster. My heart beat loudly in my ears; my breaths came quick and unrelenting. The city became a stranger to me. All I cared about was getting to the academy—to Nora.

Sprinting into an intersection, something hit me with enough force to knock me down. I spiraled and scraped my elbow on the concrete. I looked up to see a brute of a man— an AGM soldier who was just as tall and two times wider than myself. I sprang to my feet, contemplating if I could outrun him but contemplated too slowly.

He closed in; I called onto the trees that lined the city sidewalk. I watched in panic as the branches didn't reach out as fast as him.

A whirlwind of friends came to my aid. The twins stepped out in front of me, as if they rehearsed this very scenario, and scared him with breaths of fire. The soldier stumbled back just in time for water—moving in the shape of a lasso—to wrap around his burly neck and pull him further back. Kai stood firmly behind the man, clutching the reins.

"Keep moving!" he yelled.

"And save your Gift!" Molly pushed me along.

We sprinted toward the castle once more, Mom and Skylar taking the lead. Someone closed around my wrist, and I recognized the sound of her footfalls before her body revealed itself to me through her touch. *Delilah.* My little sister was guiding me through the chaos.

Her Gift fully in use, we were invisible to everyone else around us. We made it several blocks following our team, a secret among their visible troop, twisting past AGM and UA soldiers alike from the sidewalk's safety as they fought for us.

Every time someone broke off to keep us moving forward, I had to rebel against the useless feeling in my chest. They provided me an opportunity to be at my fullest once we reached Nora. I gripped my sister's hand tighter, reassuring.

As we moved away from the residential homes, an eerie emptiness swept the night. It made sense that Cassius would place most of his forces along the city limits. That would stop us before we could even begin. We were the ones that slipped through the cracks, but that didn't mean we were safe.

Everyone in our team had returned as our current

defense. Delilah inhaled loudly, her legs stammering. A child out of stamina. Mom and I caught on immediately, our own steps faltering.

"Delilah." I slowed down with her. When we came to a complete stop, she collapsed unceremoniously in the lawn at our side and our hands disconnected. Her face was a deep red, her chest rising and falling in quick precession. Mom and I exchanged a worried look now that we were visible.

We could run ahead, but there was no way I was leaving her alone. The battle raged on, seemingly far away, though seconds seemed to eat away at my chest.

"What should we do?" I looked to Mom for guidance. She spent most of her life in the military. Surely, she would have an answer even if the situation was personal.

"I can keep going," Delilah protested, though her legs visibly wobbled when she stood.

"I'll take her out of the city," Molly volunteered.

"No." Mom waved her hand, stepping forward. "I will."

Distress lathered her voice, and I understood why. Mom always hated when it looked like she was choosing favorites, and she was (in her mind) effectively choosing to protect one and abandon the other in the most literal life-and-death scenario.

"I'll be fine," I promised, and that seemed to satisfy her nerves.

Mom reached for Delilah's hand, and she accepted. We locked eyes again for one more second before they vanished from sight, and I realized that the moment passed too quickly. That could have been the last time I saw my family. If we didn't succeed...I shook the thought away despite tears already threatening to bring me to shambles. No. If I started crying, it would not stop.

We pushed our bodies back into running, gaining some distance when a cry called out from the alleyway.

A young woman in a red dress stumbled out into view, terror overcoming her limbs as she flailed about. I recognized her.

"Amelia," I breathed.

Amelia was our head servant at the Fairaway House. She wore a red bandana while she cleaned. She learned to never let me in the kitchen while she made desserts because I'd sneak another half-cup of sugar into the bowl. She was taken from our home by the Anti-Gifteds Movement when they seized Northbrook. She wasn't an AGM soldier, but she was about to be killed by a Mati for looking like one.

I deviated from our path, "Amelia!"

Both figures turned in our direction; I barreled toward the Mati while Molly ran to the fallen Unfortunate, offering to help her up.

A flame ignited in the Mati's hand, but I lifted the ground around her. Spikes jutted out, snagging her clothes and lifting her in the air. The Mati threw the ball of fire toward the ground, but she didn't aim well. It fell harmlessly to the side. She tried again, but Persy and Kai were already there to blow the flame out like it was merely a candle and douse the woman in water. Any spark fizzled in her palm. She screamed curses our way, and Skylar grimaced.

Amelia whimpered, trying and failing to control her sobs. "Thank you, Miss Fairaway."

"Of course. Go find shelter and don't move until the city is silent. Do you understand me?" I sounded more like my mom than ever, protective and a little hostile, but Amelia was used to that. It might even have comforted her.

She nodded, still whimpering, and ran into the nearest

building. Using the trees along the sidewalk, I extended their reach until they became a bramble of wood and vine around the entrance. No one would enter without excessive effort. *She would be safe*, I reminded myself over and over. *She would not be the only one.*

I smiled, the action unusual in this environment, and sped off toward the castle before we had another moment to lose.

We fell into a familiar formation when we first escaped this city with Persephone and Kai at the front, Leo, Skylar, and Molly in the middle, and me at the back.

We passed Galdor Square, desolate and abandoned. We zigzagged past wandering squads and markers. We reached the commercial district. Skyscrapers towered all around us, glistening in the faint moonlight. The world was silent, and then it was ablaze.

A bomb rippled behind us. We turned, expecting a new onslaught of enemies. Instead, we watched one skyscraper sway and then tilt in our direction. At first, we stayed motionless in a daze, the glass shimmering in its descent. And then a cascade of denotations rumbled in all directions. Smoke filled the air. Our options dwindled.

"Run!"

I couldn't process who shouted. Maybe we all did.

We sprinted forward, taking tremendous effort to look *away* from the building about to flatten us. He would not stop me. This would not stop me.

I trained on the building in front of me—a business center. We ran inside, taking note of the grand lobby for its emergency exit. My eyes found the stairwell, and I charged for it in a panic. The others did too, all of us using our Gifts to advance us upward.

Another explosion. This time below us.

"Go! Go! Go!" I pushed everyone forward despite having no idea what to do next. If this was a Simulation Lab—

Skylar and Persephone swung open one of the doors when everything tilted on its axis. My body flung backward; I reached for the railing but missed. I hit the base of the stairs with a hard thud.

Looking up, I saw that Skylar managed to catch Leo, though he dangled in her hold. Kai and Molly caught the railing on either side, and Persy pulled Molly to safety.

The building groaned and snapped. Gravity pressed me against the wall as I tried standing. Everything began to shift and teeter to the right. Skylar was almost directly above me now. Unseen objects screeched across the floor and crashed into each other from behind the door.

"Almost there," Skylar struggled to pull Leo up, colliding into his sister. They worked together, falling back from the momentum as he reached safety, and the door clamped shut.

"No!" My scream lost its sound, barely audible as the light fixtures shattered from the increasing pressure. I raised my hands, smoothing out the glass as it fell.

Kai observed his vantage point and dropped to my side. At least I wasn't alone.

"What should we do?" Time was running out. In a few breaths, the skyscraper would completely fall backward and take us with it. The flight in front of us was impossible to climb at this unnatural angle.

Before he could answer, I grabbed Kai's hand, and we began half-falling, half-rolling down the stairs. We found a different door, almost on its side. Together, we used our shoulders to ram it open, and our bodies dropped from a sudden weightlessness. Wrong door.

One hand held the knob with a ferocity while the other

wrapped around Kai. His fingers turned cold, making just enough ice to connect us at the wrist.

The skyscraper fell. All the furniture—desks and chairs and rolling boards plummeted around us. Small, usually insignificant objects like markers, lamps, and books stung our skin as they dropped. We swayed but did not falter. Wires snapped from hanging equipment, and picture frames jumped off walls.

I looked down, preparing my Gift for the exact moment the windows smashed into concrete. I didn't have any free hands to use; my feet dangled carelessly. My power didn't come from those movements, but they were often more focused that way. *Focus*, I urged my panicked brain instead. *Focus.*

Glass fractured, and I forced myself to stare at every last shard that came our way.

Minutes stretched in agony. Everything settled in its new place. Our eyes adjusted to the darkness. We still hung by the door on its last hinges.

Kai adjusted his breathing. "Do you think you can get us back into the stairwell?"

His voice was an incredible comfort, breaking the silence that rang in my ears. I looked around aimlessly. "I think...there was a potted plant somewhere."

I concentrated for several breaths. Vines crawled along the wall, inching in our direction. I sighed, relieved, as greenery wrapped around our waists and adjusted us upright. Nausea flooded to the front of my face, but I choked it down. Kai melted the ice connecting our hands and brought the water to the satchel at his side.

I brought us to the stairwell. Part of the ceiling dipped down over our heads.

"Time to follow *your* lead." I gestured to Kai.

He tried to laugh, but it came out dry. "Come on."

Strenuously, we traversed the new terrain. I wielded glass when we needed to push ahead while Kai froze unstable beams into place so we could walk across. We stopped a lot as he observed and decided our best course of action. None of our other teammates were in sight.

A single door with the label EXIT taunted us. A sliver of a window revealed the outside world, but a build up of rubble blocked us from pushing through. I pushed anyway, using my body and then beckoning the grass just out of reach on the other side, but the door nor the rubble budged.

I raised my fist to crash through the window and use the glass for a better purpose when the grate to our left fell onto the floor, rattling so loudly I jumped back.

Kai readied himself, wielding water around his form.

Leo poked his head out, weary but alive. "Need some help?"

My shoulders relaxed. I collapsed to my knees and embraced him with all the energy I could muster.

"Woah." He threw his hands up. "Save that mush for Nora."

Kai lowered his guard and crouched to be by our side but not to be a part of the hug. "You and your ventilation systems, I swear."

"That's because they *work*."

Kai shrugged but didn't argue. We crawled into the vent, guided by a trusty fire light.

Emerging out into what I assumed used to be a back alley, the rest of our team was waiting for us. Their shoulders visibly relaxed. Bruises and scratches blossomed over their bodies, and I wondered how I faired in their sight. The most concerning injury went to Skylar, who was leaning heavily on her left side. My arms shook from holding our weight for so long, and a headache began at the base of my forehead.

The city was in worse disrepair. Every building around us, tall brilliant structures, now lay on their side or were on top of each other. I wouldn't expect backup anymore. We were effectively cut off from the rest of our forces, but so was he.

We were so close now. Even at night and among this ash, the castle towers illuminated in their white brilliance. I craned my neck to the point where I saw Nora last. The window only reflected darkness now, but I pictured her nonetheless, watching us go and waiting for our return.

Nora. I stopped myself from reaching out. We were in the heart of the king's stronghold. If I accidentally connected with the wrong person or if Cassius caught my thoughts so close to the castle, our position would be compromised.

Galdor Academy's wall came into view. The northern watchtower shone beams of light across the street and within the Grounds on the other side. There wasn't an entrance on the northern side. If we moved westward, we could see how the gated entrance faired. Time mocked me. No. I promised to be careless, not cautious.

"How can we tear down this wall?" I asked.

Our team contemplated their ideas. Leo shot Skylar an impish look. "We could strike it with lightning."

She returned his comment with a serious expression. "Do you think we can? It's not raining."

"Doesn't need to." Leo glanced at Kai. "What's the likelihood?"

"I'm not a meteorologist," Kai deadpanned and then glared. "The conditions are perfect."

Leo rubbed his hands together. "Then let's go."

Skylar yelped as their hands touched. "You shocked me!"

"Just a preview." He winked.

"I'll take over the watchtower," Molly stepped forward. "In case they call for any backup in the Grounds."

"I'll go with you." Persy strode beside her, and they exchanged a smile.

That left me and Kai again.

Kai spoke up, "We'll hang back until the wall breaches or you need backup."

"Speak for yourself!" I blurted. "You want me to watch?"

"Yes. We're counting on you to bring Nora back, especially if she's..." He stopped himself, but I knew what he meant. We all knew what he meant.

If I can't kill you, then I'll just make Nora forget you altogether.

I crossed my arms, frustratingly silent. The others fanned out to their appointed positions.

"I'm sorry, Fern," Kai whispered.

"No," I waved him off, huffing. "You're right."

"Are you ready?" he prompted. "Do you know what you're going to tell her?"

I rested against the wall and sat down next to him. "No."

Such a short answer because in all honesty, I had too many things I wanted to tell her.

Kai considered me. "We don't know a lot about his Gift, but the brain can be a fickle thing. As much against his favor as it is in his favor. Try to jog her memory of things he hasn't thought of or was careless with. Specific things only you would know or powerful moments between the two of you."

"You've given this a lot of thought."

"I'm starting to feel left out of all the romance," Kai joked.

"What about Persy and Molly?"

Kai stared at me for a breath too long. *Oh.* Maybe.

A flash of lightning struck the sky. An explosion and an array of sparks snapped our attention to the castle. Though we couldn't see Skylar and Leo, their mark landed true. The northern wall now had a fracture and a line of scorch marks. Lightning struck again and again, carving deeper into the wall like an ax finding the tree stump.

The watchtower caught fire as the fissure became large enough for us to squeeze through. I could see a sliver of the Grounds and the castle beyond.

I sprinted out of the alleyway, Kai quick on my heels.

Skylar volleyed herself to the top of the wall while Leo moved through the opening.

Kai grabbed me before we could follow. "Find Nora," he commanded. "We'll cover you."

I nodded before I could fully comprehend his words. Finding Nora could mean I had to run away—trust that no one would die in my absence. But we were already through the breach and found ourselves in direct opposition to an organized fleet of Anti-Gifted soldiers. At least fifty soldiers stood in five rows. Cassius stood at the central back of their formation, the last defense and symbol to the throne. Isaac Winters stood at the front of the formation with another soldier next to him.

Seeing Isaac again brought fresh pain and worry. The last two times we encountered each other, he tried to kill us. Leo must have blinded him in Doverly because he now wore a red bandana over his eyes. Cassius did something to his brain—made him believe that we were enemies instead of allies. I couldn't help but think what he might make Nora believe if he truly fulfilled his threat. She and Poppy were nowhere in sight. My heart sank.

The watchtower door closed with a hard shove, and Molly and Persephone joined our side.

We stared at each other: a legion of fifty-three versus six. It would have almost been laughable if the prospect wasn't so scary. Tension thickened the air. The more they didn't move, the more my limbs twitched with anticipation.

Cassius stared at us the same way he had in Caliel. *Testing if he can mind-control us*, I guessed. But no. He couldn't. Not when Prince Henry was so close to shield us. Cassius must have figured this out because the slightest hint of irritation crossed his confident features.

"Kill them," he ordered, and the AGM attacked.

Against my instinct, I ran toward the castle and away from the battle. Our team followed my lead, veering right. Skylar landed like an arrow, a powerful wind snapping the air in her wake. A line of soldiers halted in surprise, allowing me past. The twins ignited flames; Molly kept her back to Persy as she attacked those in front of her one-by-one, disarming them and using their weapons against the next.

Kai ran for Isaac. The soldier right next to the Ice Mare stared directly at me. "150 degrees, left!"

My eyebrows furrowed, my pace slowing in the confusion. Before I could understand his meaning, a thin sheet of ice cut through the Grounds and hit true. I screamed as the tips of my index and middle finger separated from my hand and my cheek split open. Tears stung my face as blood poured from my wounds, hot and stinging.

"145 degrees, left!" The soldier barked.

I gasped, using the earth to shift my position back. Another shard of ice sang through the air where I was, and I didn't want to imagine where he would have sliced me next. Isaac was blind, but he was not helpless.

"Here!" Kai tossed me a roll of bandage. Prepared as ever. He would make a great ERS doctor when this was all over.

With quick work, I wrapped my left hand as Kai beelined for the assistant.

"120, left!" the soldier shouted.

Kai heard and registered the order. He pivoted off course just as Isaac sent another sheet of ice, thin and sharp. The ice shattered on impact with the standing wall.

Bandaged as best I could, I charged the assisting soldier too. I closed in and leaned down, grabbing a fistful of leaves with my good hand, and stuffing them in the soldier's mouth. His eyes widened in surprise, jaw opening wider in disbelief.

Kai deviated to attack Isaac again, successfully kneeing him in the face and throwing him to the ground in a kneeling position. Their arms interlocked. Frost began to crawl up Kai's arm; both Mares bared their teeth at each other, fighting for control.

My feet turned to help him, but more soldiers closed in. I remembered what Kai demanded of me. *Find Nora.* Even if that meant I had to trust him to defeat Isaac Winters alone.

The assistant spat out the leaves, withdrawing a knife from a hidden sheath at his ankle.

I pivoted and ran toward the castle before he could attack.

AGM soldiers stormed me, but I barely registered them. I was too hyper focused, my heart full of terrible emotions like fear and sadness and rage. They attacked in sync with the spiral of my feet, and I encouraged the earth to trip, ensnare, or drag anyone who tried to stop me.

"She's not there."

Cassius's dreadful voice found my ears. I made it past all other defenses. We were practically side by side, thirty paces away from each other. I paused, unsure if he was lying or toying with me.

"Where then?" I yelled.

He didn't smile. He *grinned.* "Come find out."

His hideous joy was enough for me to race toward him instead of the castle. I was *done* with his games. I was going to wipe that smirk off his face and make him spill every last secret he had to the Divine. Nora was *so* close, and that blossomed in me something protective and dangerous. I would find her. He *would* tell me.

He cocked his head but made no attempt to prepare himself. I closed in, my head dizzy with effort and need. The earth shaped around my hand a plethora of vines. More than I needed. More strands than I conjured before. Chunks of earth lifted off the ground as I ran, rumbling under my feet.

He still didn't move, watching me with those cold eyes.

I pulled my arm back, ready to punch him with everything my Gift had to offer when a glint of silver flashed in the corner of my vision.

I gasped, adjusting my body as a blade reached for my torso and cut through the greenery instead. I half-fell from the momentum, using the earth to propel me back to my full height. Cassius was in front of me now and—my breath caught in my throat at the sight of her.

Her. My heart swelled with a delightful new emotion, overwhelming everything else I felt.

"Nora!" I yelled, my body gravitating toward her as it burned to for so long.

But she didn't return the same affection. She remained still and held her weapon offensively in front of her.

Cassius's words rang true. Nora did not know me, and she stood *protecting* him by his side. I looked into her eyes, noticing the focused look she had when she searched for a connection. An understanding. Maybe there was hope for me yet. I just needed to jog her memory. Use her mind against him as Kai suggested.

But before I could decide on anything, she attacked again.

Remember Me

FERN

———

Nora swung at my chest.

I jumped back and lifted an upheaval of earth between us. Her blade struck and cleaned straight through, the unexpected release sending her to the ground. I could have wrapped her in the grass or closed the earth around her form, but I breathed unsteadily instead, my fingers twitching with indecision.

"Nora." I tried to speak her name with all the tenderness

I could give.

I reached forward and then hesitated as she regained her footing, observing me through a squint. She was right here in front of me, but we were as good as strangers.

"Kill her, Nora." Cassius spoke as smooth as poison.

She snapped out of her hesitation, darting to my right side. I jumped, shifting the barrier with one hand to block her again. "Nora, it's me! Fern!"

She didn't listen, jumping over the blockade like it was nothing more than a gate, and this time I screamed.

The blade sliced upward along the front of my shirt, ripping away the leather patting my chest. I stumbled back, checking for a wound but nothing came up on my hand. She charged again, faster and more determined than she was in our usual training.

I gasped, backing away as greenery wrapped around my arms and grew at my fingertips. "Nora, you have to believe me!"

I sounded so pathetic, giving her vague inclinations of trust. But what time was there for poetics? For all the details fractured somewhere in her mind?

She roared as she missed, releasing more energy with her offensive. Gaining speed, she struck at my knees, but I prepared for that move and used the foliage to hoist me into the air. Nora didn't back away. She craned her neck upward, calculating her next move. I would not waste these precious seconds.

"Nora, I know that you were a servant at the Montgomerys!"

She sliced through one stalk holding me up. My body sank to the left; I called onto the grass to repair, to reconnect, but my Gift was beginning to wane. *No. Not now!*

"Be more personal!" Kai called out from below.

Isaac dueled him with an ice sickle; Kai stumbled to block another blow.

More personal. I bit my lip. "You lost someone!" I yelled.

Nora cut through the stalk holding my right-side. Kai grunted; I glimpsed Isaac's weapon lodge in his back as I toppled.

Using the remaining vines to soften my fall, I yelled his name.

Kai pressed against his wound with one hand and started melting the sickle away with the other. "I'm…okay."

Nora ran toward me with furious speed.

Isaac reached down, but Leo and Persephone were already there, fire blazing.

I tore myself away, sickly trusting, and stood my ground. My voice wavered. "A servant named Valerie! You made a promise to her!"

Nora closed the distance, aimed to strike. If I died here, would a part of her mourn me?

A ringing sound fizzled at the back of my mind, the Avlis Gift within myself begging for rest. All I could manage to defend myself was a small shield of earth no bigger than the size of a doily. "You imagine living in a cottage far away from here!"

She was so close I could feel her panted breath. The tip of her blade halted and rested on my shoulder.

I kept going, pulling from our collective dreams and conversations outside of everyone else. "The cottage gleams like it's made of amber, and chocolate chip cookies are always baking inside. There's no one for miles, and you pictured that with her, didn't you? When you two would escape together?"

I knew the answer but asking flickered something behind

Nora's dark eyes. Recognition, I hoped, that she hadn't shared her fantasy with anyone else.

I pushed the sword off. She almost didn't catch it as the weight shifted and dropped to the ground.

I lowered my last defense and dared to step closer. "We made cookies together, you know. Enough for the servants, and Amelia actually liked them the way you—"

"How do you know that?" A shake betrayed her demand.

Nora squinted, scrutinizing, as though that would help her see me better. Heat flushed my face as she examined my freckles. With her free hand, she reached up and began tracing them with her thumb. Connecting the dots until she recognized what she was doing and stepped back with a jolt.

It took every fiber in my being not to grab her shoulder, to make sure she didn't turn away and run. She stayed to my immense relief; her eyes drifted to the two flowers still tangled in my braided crown. The white peony and red poppy that marked the unity flower.

I pulled them into my palm so she could see them without getting too close to my face again. She flinched but stopped herself from reacting any further.

Please, I thought desperately. *Please remember.*

The battle raged on around us. We were further away now so Cassius wasn't directly in our line of sight, but that didn't mean we were safe. Poppy was still somewhere at the king's command, and our friends couldn't possibly keep everyone at bay. And Kai–

I forced myself to keep a steady gaze on Nora.

"It's a unity flower," I urged. "We—"

"It's your favorite." She muttered, so low as though to herself.

I nodded, "Yes. *Yes*, that's right. We danced in a field of them together. At Emerald Park."

She stared at the flowers, unblinking. "Who are you?"

"I am your friend."

Then I dared to add, "I am your confidante, and I am your constant."

She lifted her head to meet my eyes.

I continued. "I am the one you made a promise with. To protect Gifteds and Unfortunates. Right up there—" I pointed to the castle windows behind her, repaired now.

"I am the one who orchestrated all of this to fulfill that promise for you." I gestured around us.

As she looked around, I released the flowers and watched them rest at our feet.

My hand reached out and brushed her cheek. She caught it and held me there, her expression both horrified and elated by the touch.

Tears wet my lashes. "And I am in love with you, Nora."

She inhaled, frozen in place. *Love.* That frightening word she didn't think she deserved.

We stared at each other for several breaths, unmoving except for her eyes that throbbed violently, holding back the waterworks.

"Who am I?" Her voice came out as a whisper, a plea.

"Enough people have defined you, Nora."

"Then who am I...to you?"

I smiled. "You're my best friend. You're who I think about, and you're who I want to be around all the time. You're tenacious and brave and a little worry flurry."

A soft laugh broke through her terror. An odd, sweet sound among the chaos. She started to ask a question when someone cut in.

"Nora." Cassius stood a chasm away, but his words rang

strong as his army fought on either side, parted in such an unnatural way that it had to be his influence. Our team fell back and held a defensive stance around Kai's form.

Nora turned around, blanching in surprise. My hands rested on her shoulders protectively; Cassius watched with his jaw set in clear disgust. Her sword still held loosely along her fingertips.

"She killed your friends and comrades," he continued. "Kill her and set things right."

Her grip tightened around the hilt, but seconds passed by.

"Don't let her destroy everything we built."

Nora bristled and lowered her attention to the ground. I bit my tongue. If I started shouting against him now, that would be a losing battle. *Please, Nora. Remember me.*

After several shaky breaths, she struck the earth with an incredible force, the blade shattering to pieces on impact. One piece flew back up and sliced her along her collarbone and shoulder, barely avoiding her neck. She gasped and dropped the hilt, stumbling back with a hand over the wound.

"Nora!" I caught her before she could tumble, her eyes locking on me. I pushed her hair away the best I could; alarm twitched at my fingertips. "Are you okay?"

"Fern," she breathed, blood spilling over her fingers. *My name.* She said my name.

"You stupid girl!" Cassius interrupted our moment, seething. Any relief vanished from Nora's face as pain overwhelmed her and she screamed and thrashed in my arms.

"No!" I knew her pain all too well, his Gift needling her brain. She tried to push closer into me, and I tried to hold her steady for relief that didn't come.

Shield her, I thought desperately to Prince Henry, but she continued to writhe. If only we were connected as we had been whenever we focused on each other. Then–then she would be shielded.

"Nora, focus on me! Focus on my voice!" I tried to jostle her, but she pressed her eyelids closed even tighter.

A connection. We needed a connection.

Divine this better work, or I don't know what I'm going to do.

I tilted her in my arms, leaned down, and kissed her.

CHAPTER FORTY-TWO

To Become God

NORA

Everything—absolutely everything dissipated. Only Fern and I remained.

My body relaxed in her embrace, molding with hers. The awful connection with him severed, replaced with her. Familiar and secure. Like coming home.

She pulled away but hovered just above me, her expression unsure if the kiss worked or if I was still under his control.

"Was that...?"

I reached for her, and our lips met again, like something crashing and careening down a cliff. She kept my head steady, drawing me closer still. If we were to fall, we would fall together.

Desire and comfort stirred inside me. I whispered her name between kisses, and something light and delicate brushed my ankle. Opening my eyes, a patch of unity flowers laid around us. Blooming in the dead of winter. Fern's eyes fluttered open too, her eyelashes tickling my cheek. She smiled, whispering my name in return. Our kisses quickened and slowed in tandem until we caught our breaths, dizzy from shock and longing and exhaustion and bliss.

We sat up, still entangled with each other as she helped me to my feet. I pressed closer to her form, the sweet scent of pine and eucalyptus overtaking my senses. One hand still clamped over the cut on my left side, I used the other to roll my thumb over her hand.

"You're really here," I whispered, worried that once I declared the sentiment she would vanish in the next instant. "You did this."

"I'm really here," Fern's voice caressed my ear. "*We* did this."

We. I adjusted to look up at her again, slowly in case she thought I was drawing away. Taking in her features, my heart bloomed something fierce. I recalled what she confessed and how close we were. My eyes drifted to her lips, partially chapped from fighting and now glossy from...from. Heat washed over my cheeks, and I imagined both of our faces darkened to the same shade as her hair.

Sharp, unnatural lights erupted all at once, blinding and all consuming.

We immediately turned to its epicenter, interlocking our arms.

Cassius glared at us with all his wrath, crushing the entire bracelet into his palm. He cast the world in a deep red, a pale orange, then dark brown.

Gifts absorbed into his body, sometimes so quickly the colors ran together, even as I refused to blink. The veins along his wrists, arms, and neck protruded in a yellowish glow, whitening as more Gifts flashed and then ran through his limbs.

He screamed through clenched teeth, the burn so intense, clothes that clung to skin began to melt under its touch. I recalled how his body reacted to three Gifts fighting for space within him. Then, it was enough for Cassius to stumble back and wipe the Lux Gift out of his system. But now he was more prepared, more determined, more desperate.

The sudden light and his subsequent screams managed to stall the fighting within Galdor Academy. The world watched him struggle with bated breath.

What remained of the bracelet fell from the king's hand. Shards of glass and a broken string dropped to the ground.

He stood straight again, his chest puffing and his fingers twitching with unchecked power.

Clouds swirled above our heads and suffocated the stars. Galdor plunged into near complete darkness. The wind strengthened; thunder rumbled.

His eyes glinted in our direction.

I pushed Fern with my body as he threw his hands to the sky. Thunder rumbled, and lightning struck the earth across the entire Grounds, including the exact spot we were a heartbeat before.

The wind's howl deafened my ears, but I could see running silhouettes, his and our soldiers alike—all running away from their king. My friends were swept up in the exodus, but I hoped they were helping those they were just fighting to safety.

Thunder continued overhead in warning. I grabbed Fern's hand and changed positions as more lightning cast judgment; its fiery explosions brushed dangerously close.

"Nora!" Fern rotated me to her other side and patted me

down before I caught fire.

Rubble from the wall's breach flew through the air, appearing weightless and tearing through the castle on impact. We moved further away, scrunched together and as insignificant as ants. Surely, he couldn't contain this form for long, but the damage he was inflicting would be irreversible.

"We have to stop him!" I shouted over the storm.

"*How?*"

The doubt and fear in her voice exemplified my own. I reached for my sword and grabbed at nothing. I cursed, fumbling through my pockets for any weapon. The action was futile. I would find nothing there, too.

A round, cool object brushed my fingers.

Bewildered, I pulled the object from my lieutenant's jacket and discovered a marble emanating a light grey hue. A Makan Gift. A Gift that ruled over all; could remove all. But how—?

Poppy. When we fought in my room, she stuck her hands in my jacket. I thought she was looking for hidden blades as I was now, but she planted something instead.

You have the power to finish this. She pointed straight at my heart. She called me the brightest Unfortunate. Only once. Only right now.

My free hand rested over my heart. It pumped viciously against my rib cage. Where a Gift was supposed to reside.

Fern watched me, shock and fear etching her features. "Nora, no," she said but made no move to stop me.

I examined both palms. One held a Gift and the other was painted in blood. "How bad is my cut?"

"That's a Kai question." Fern pulled at my collar to examine me better. "But it doesn't *look* bad. And I don't see or feel any lodged metal."

I took my jacket off and wrapped it across my torso. Hopefully that would be enough to staunch the wound for now. "I need you to find your sister and bring her here when I'm done."

She overlaid our hands over my heart. "I'm not leaving you."

I bit my lip. I wanted to tell her that I would be safe, careful. I wanted to promise. But I couldn't. I was separating us again. Maybe even forever. I wished the Divine created a Gift that stretched milliseconds into minutes. I wished He created me with such a Gift breathing life into my soul. He created a bright Unfortunate instead, and that was enough for what needed to happen.

"I love you," I said before forcing my body to turn and run toward Cassius, hoping the stun of my words would be enough to stop Fern from following.

She tried anyway—reaching again for my hand—but lightning ignited right in front of her, splitting us apart in a flash of terrible light. She stumbled back, and I continued running forward, my sight on the king.

He narrowed his eyes. Pointing straight at me, he mouthed something unheard.

Nothing happened for several heartbeats.

I gained ground and then abruptly stopped as a black, shapeless form morphed in the air behind him. Confusion and alarm crossed my face, studying the floating anomaly as it drew closer. A small black circle struggled to stay in formation, and I realized with horror that bees were swarming at me as a unified front. His Fera Gift.

I tightened my hand into a fist, deciding this was a better time than any.

A pale grey light shone through my knuckles; the Gift

rushed through my veins. I instantly collapsed as a heaviness overtook my chest and a tightness swelled my throat. My mouth opened, and I screamed despite my best efforts.

My hands fell in front of me, and I watched a thin layer of my flesh rip away, my cells reprogramming. My gash ached with a terrible burn. My entire body ran hot, headache and nausea threatening to shut me down completely. I craved the winter air; I extended my face to the wind in desperation.

I needed to be the brightest Unfortunate. I needed to be hopeful. Determined. Resolved. I inhaled as deeply as I could, closing my eyes and imagining when I was exactly that.

Fern came to mind first. How the sight of her was enough to change my entire trajectory. How she tasted. How she laughed as we reunited. How she encouraged me for all the time I've known her.

Kai came to mind next. How he defended me when I first arrived at Galdor. How our trio was born out of an understanding.

Persephone and Leo. How they took me to their secret hideout for post-training snacks. How Persy always kept her brother in check while matching his energy. How Leo always had something funny to add.

Molly. How she fueled my determination when we were enemies. How we sat side by side in the training room, and I was thankful she was alive.

Skylar. How she pleaded for her father. How she looked at Leo when we stumbled upon them during a private conversation.

Mr. Harris. How he saw potential in me as a student instead of a servant. How his relaxed posture and casual words ignited my core. A feeling of complete certainty and autonomy.

Valerie. My first love before I knew what love was. Our promise. I escaped servitude. I fought to keep my freedom.

Now I would defeat the king who granted no freedom to his citizens. No matter what happened. Whatever the cost.

Bees buzzed, hovering around my frame. I opened my eyes and vanished with a snap of my fingers. The insects plunged; I rolled out of the way. Some caught on my dress, and one stung my thigh. I cursed, plucking the one out of my body and brushing the others off my clothes. I fell onto one knee, but I shot up quickly and avoided the bees as they hummed, absent of a target.

Cassius bared his teeth, still able to see me through his own Makan Gift, and tried to redirect the insects in my direction. His orders must have been too vague because the bees advanced forward and missed me as I ducked toward the dirt.

He cursed something before changing stances. Opening his arms out wide to both sides, water fell from above. *Rain.* His Mare Gift.

The bees frantically flew away to avoid drowning from the cascade of droplets. I looked up, memories of Valerie dead and alive again flashing through my mind. *No.* Remember something else. I stalled as I did that day. Something else!

"The rain?" Fern inquired. We were at the Flower Festival, weaving reeds into baskets. The sun shone through the canopy. She put me in a purple butterfly dress representing change. She wore clothes denoting an oak tree for strength.

I needed both change and strength now.

I rose to my feet and stepped forward; Cassius tensed and the downpour turned into a monsoon. His Auran Gift. I covered my eyes as the winter wind drilled half-frozen droplets onto my skin. I took a few more cautious steps as the dirt turned into mud and then suddenly, snow and sludge replaced a flood.

A light sprinkling of snowflakes gently decorated my hair. Dazed from the sudden peace, I turned my focus to the sky for several moments before landing on Cassius again. He held his stomach with a firm hand, struggled breaths flaring from his nostrils.

Remember that Gifts are not visible by natural eyes. His advice to Delilah returned to my mind.

Focusing myself within the invisible plan, I studied him. I was invisible. I was seeing the world in another existence. *See him in the same place*, I thought. Squinting, I imagined his body turned invisible too. See-through. His silhouette and what laid behind flesh and bone.

Slowly, slowly, as if against resistance, Cassius disappeared and became a form bound by a human-shaped line. My eyes widened at the discovery of ten lights—Gifts—swirling within his chest and emanating a glow throughout his silhouette. So bright it stung my eyes. I watched them bounce and clash with each other in a brilliant chaos, making no sound but causing Cassius to tighten his grip on himself, wince, and choke.

I couldn't see my own Makan Gift when I looked down, but I could feel it resting close to my heart and emanating an unnatural power to my limbs.

He vomited. I blinked back into the natural plane to see a mixture of bile and blood pooled below him. To become God was killing him, but he made no effort to expel any Gifts from his body.

He wiped his mouth with the sleeve of his billowing coat.

I sprinted toward him, fixating on the invisible plane—the Gifts inside him.

He read my thoughts. Bringing his hands together, he pulled them apart through strained arms. The earth ripped apart in response, his Avlis Gift, but I've trained with Fern long enough to know how to navigate through. The snow helped me spot where the earth fell and rose. I skipped and hopped over loose rock and weaved through rising dirt before it enclosed around me.

I reached for him, an arm's length away.

He dodged. His nails filed sharp like claws.

He lunged and caught my shoulder, slashing through my jacket and grazing my open wound. I shrieked and held the tear as fresh blood spilled down my arm, wobbling away from another swipe.

He bared his teeth again, licking over distinct fangs. His Imitation Gift. A *Wolf* Imitation. Oh, Divine, help me.

He lunged again, this time for my throat; I dodged out of reach, my fear spiking as his coat brushed against my calf. I scanned the ground for anything I could use. A half-buried shield resided next to a fallen AGM soldier in the snow.

His eyes followed my gaze. Sprinting, I could feel him at my heels. Sliding close to the ground, I ripped the shield from the corpse and covered my face as Cassius pounced again, jaws open wide. He collided with the plate, and I screamed as my skin severed further apart along my shoulder, oozing blood from the sudden pressure. In my haste, I used my left arm to hook through the shield's strap.

He clawed at the sides; I jumped backward in a crouched position to create distance.

He growled, his appearance a cross between a man and a beast. My limbs jittered in the anticipated stillness, probably flickering in and out of the visible plane as fearful Makans tended to do.

Cassius watched me. He crept another step before straightening his back. His nails filed down and rounded. His canines became less pronounced but remained pointed as a reminder of what he could turn into. He didn't need to be an Imitation for me to know that he was a monster.

"Enough of this," he snarled.

He clenched his hand into a fist, and the icy feeling crawled up my spine like a spider. I tried to yell to shake the invasion away before it reached my mind, but it was too late. A numbness overtook my struggle. His Animus Gift.

"Fall."

His voice absolute, I obeyed. My legs buckled out from under me. The shield laid limb to my side.

He strode over and lifted my chin so our eyes met. If he held any remorse, he didn't show it. My throat tightened with the effort to move away, but I remained limp, obedient.

"I'll remember you," he said, the only hint of grace left.

His thumb touched my temple. I imagined biting his hand, but I remained still.

He opened his mouth to begin the ritual when the words caught in his throat, and he choked. He fell onto one hand, holding himself with the other like he had before. His power over me released as the plethora of Gifts wrestled inside him.

I focused on his heart. The Animus Gift eclipsed the others in a royal purple hue, violently shaking. Unstable and ready to explode from the inside.

He flailed, eyes bulging and body convulsing.

I dove, hovering above his crumpled form and pressing my entire palm against his forehead. He fought me, but I held on. I could recite the words he used to take and take and take. I memorized them from all the wait stations he forced me to endure.

"If you can see it with the mind of your heart—"

He grabbed the fold of my elbow, sinking his nails into the soft flesh, but I closed my arms tightly around his head and withstood the blooming agony. My hands pressed harder against his temple, my fingers digging into his hair. The storm raged above us.

My voice trembled but continued, "And feel it in the depths of your soul—"

He switched tactics, thrashing his entire body until I flung to the ground sideways. I didn't break contact despite the awkward position and despite the growing warmth of blood soaking my clothes.

His hands found my waist and pulled me close; his head strained to reach my neck, mouth open with razor-sharp teeth ready to rip out my throat and silence me forever.

I resisted him with everything I had left and shouted now as if to the Divine Himself,

"*—then you will hold it in your hands!*"

An explosion of color erupted as it had before and tore us apart.

CHAPTER FORTY-THREE

Promises Fulfilled

NORA

—

My hand moved first, reaching out into the open air and landing back onto the grass. Warm. Catching on my fingers. My arm followed, bending at the elbow, pressing down as my torso lifted and fell again. A tightening in my ribs. Catching a wince. The other hand, the other arm, the other bending elbow. I stared downward at my shadow in a slumped sitting position. Fractured glass littered the ground around me, drained of all color and power.

My panting shallowed. My head turned to my side, in his direction.

The explosion spat us out opposing each other. The remaining dust and smoke swirled across a deserted battlefield.

I stood awkwardly, as if for the very first time. My legs wobbled as one leg stepped forward, but I took another step and another and another. My arms laid limp at my sides, lathered in red and smelling of iron.

He lay flat on his back. Smudges of blood and soot covered his face and clothes. Signs of life grasped at his searching, wide eyes and clenched in his throat with each desperate breath.

Reaching him, I collapsed to my knees. My right hand hovered over his chest where I had seen all the Gifts of Iridion, all the lights of this world. A dark grey color a few shades darker than his Makan Gift denoted the emptiness where I imagined his heart was, beating vacantly to a drum slowing down.

It was a strange sight to see him downcast, an Unfortunate. To understand what he meant all that time ago. *Unfortunates are hollow*, he said. *Void of any light.*

But seeing through my eyes, I had to disagree. Perhaps when he saw how brightly Gifts illuminated, anything else appeared lackluster. There was an emptiness sure, but we weren't hollow and certainly not incapable of our own light.

His eyes, so blue and overflowing with water, caught my closeness. His hand connected with mine so quickly I jolted. His torso lifted with the last ounces of his energy.

"Nora," he rasped. A clear strain in his voice. Clinging onto hope. Refusing defeat. "Do you believe in the Divine?"

I allowed the question to sink into my skin, to process through every memory and every experience that led us here. How Minister Gabriel twisted the Great Book to separate entire groups of people. How Cassius used those same words for his own gain. Showing us a freedom so bright we couldn't see the cracks in his logic against Gifteds and downcastment and his rise to power. How Poppy and her battalion learned what was actually written instead of what was decreed and how most died for that understanding. How even I, wrapped up in debates, began to understand too.

"Yes," I replied. A smile softened his face as his eyes fluttered close and mine swelled open, "but I don't believe you're Him."

His body tilted back; his fingers relaxed.

I inhaled a deep breath and released his hand onto his chest.

As I motioned to stand again, a sharp pain stung my chest and I collapsed. My hand pressed along my skin, burning as the torment rose up my neck and clenched my throat. I coughed and heaved, my breaths short and quick. My limbs began to throb just as Cassius's did, and I realized that the Makan Gift inside me was unstable.

The explosion. Taking that many Gifts must have compromised my own.

I tried to picture Fern, my team, moments of triumph— but my lungs continued to contract sharply and my body spasmed. Hope was not enough to sustain me anymore.

I fell onto my back again, looking up at the sky. The clouds had dissipated, removed from their caster, and the stars shone brightly instead.

The grass cradled me, and Fern came into view a few heartbeats later. Her mouth shaped into my name, but I didn't hear her. Two more forms peered overhead, but my eyes struggled to stay open. They closed.

And opened again.

I was standing in front of a stove. Looking around, I saw a rustic kitchen. Copper pots and pans hung below cabinet shelves filled with matching porcelain plates, bowls, and cups. Greenery filled the empty spaces between kitchenware, and a vase full of baby's breath sat next to the sink. A kettle hummed on the stove's front eye. Sunlight poured from a small window high up on the left wall and revealed the bright blue sky.

"Do you love it?"

I spun around, and you stood in the kitchen with me.

"Val?" My hands rounded over the oven handle to make sure this was real, but all my pain had vanished like smoke and my hands were free of any blemish.

A red checkered apron wrapped over your puff-sleeve white dress. Your hands intertwined behind your back. "Welcome home."

A heartbeat of silence and then the kettle began to screech. I jumped away as you rushed forward, turning off the stove and moving the kettle to another eye. I watched as you navigated the kitchen with ease; a handful of tea leaves fell into the boiled water and two empty mugs rested on the counter.

"We'll give it time to steep." Your hand pulled on my wrist, and I followed. "Let me show you around."

A pit rose in my throat, but I swallowed it down. We entered a cozy living room where two white antique couches resided, embroidered with flecks of purple, orange, and yellow. Two plants in large pots arched over the seating. Bookshelves filled the rest of the space, climbing all the way to the ceiling. The wood paneling remained silent under our feet.

"Do we read any?" I asked.

"Plenty," you laughed. "Way more than cookbooks."

You led me past the front door and up the stairs. At the top was one large loft with an attached bathroom. Heat flushed my face and then receded. I stepped inward, taking in the lumpy queen-sized bed with thick blankets and stuffed pillows. A half-open closet displayed more dresses and a cubby of pants, scarves, and belts. Two wooden desks resided on the other side of the room and against the window, their chairs facing each other. I strode over to the right-most desk, knowing it was mine without any words exchanged.

A photo of me and Valerie in front of a cobblestone cottage—this very home. Pen and paper and a leather journal. I thumbed along its edge, brushing the paper but not opening its contents.

Looking out the window, I fixated on the sight. Red poppies and white peonies intertwined at their stems in a great expanse. Swaying gently in the breeze, they beckoned me outside. Fern was in a dream similar to this one, just outside this cottage. I ran to her, in truth believing she was Valerie, but when I saw her instead, I wasn't disappointed.

Is it okay that it's me? Her question seemed to float along the wind that brushed each petal.

"What's wrong?" Your voice drifted behind me.

I forced myself to turn back to you. "It's nothing."

You walked over, and our fingers interlocked. "You want to go back, don't you?"

"No," I said quickly, my voice rising and then falling. "It wouldn't be fair."

You smiled, glancing from our hands to my eyes. "Go, Nora."

I shook my head, gripping you tighter, trying to will away my desires. "I can't. I can't leave you."

"Nora." Your voice drew out my name, and your hands drew away too, cupping along my jawline instead.

It took all of my strength to look at you in earnest, to not showcase how I imagined Fern's hands there instead. Hers were uncalloused from manual labor, and her fingernails would have grazed the tips of my ears. I failed to hide my confliction.

Light twinkled in your eyes as your smile deepened. "You fulfilled your promise to me. Go fulfill your promise to her."

You leaned in and kissed my forehead. Trembling.

I withdrew, and you released me. My legs wobbled to the beat of my fear and certainty.

Running down the stairs, I reached for the front door and swung it open.

My eyes closed in the sun's presence, and when I opened them again, I returned to Galdor, to the twinkling stars, to Fern.

She adjusted so her arm wrapped securely behind my back. Delilah and Poppy leaned on the other side of me, panting and relieved.

I blinked several times, my body still aching but numbed in comparison to what I felt before. Fern cried out, tears reddening her face as she stared down at me and held me closer.

"What happened?" I murmured.

"We removed the Makan Gift from your body," Delilah answered first. She offered a weak high-five, and Poppy took it.

Fern blubbered, trying and failing to speak. I smiled, stroking through her red hair. "Hey, hey, I'm here."

Our foreheads pressed together, and I grinned despite the wince of pain.

"You need a hospital," Poppy noted, looking down at my crumpled form.

I glanced over to her and then at my limited surroundings. "Did we win?"

Poppy scoffed at the mention of "we" but didn't argue.

Fern nodded, joyful. "We did, we *really* did. He's gone,

and the AGM has called a ceasefire thanks to *this* one's effort."

"You're welcome," Poppy managed, still catching her breath.

I nodded, vague and sloppy.

Craning my neck to the sky, I let out a deep exhale before snuggling back into Fern's chest. "Then take me to a hospital."

CHAPTER FORTY-FOUR

First Unfortunate Reign
NORA

Winter shifted to spring and spring blossomed into a new summer. Six months swept by; the days running into one another as we recovered and rebuilt.

The hospital claimed me first, swaddling me in sterilized blankets, a mirage of nurses, and friendly visitors. Fern brought me enough flowers to supply a florist, and Poppy came by with Mr. Harris to deliver news of the aftermath. They worked tirelessly to subdue flares of Anti-Gifted unrest as some members refused defeat.

The Senior Circle pushed me to my limits after I was released from the hospital. The round table included Mr. Harris, Ms. Fairaway, our team, Poppy, and the remaining five regional ministers. We fought daily as we tried to determine our next steps, and I imagined we would chip away at each other forever, slowly perfecting into a united statue.

After losing my voice and all of my sleep, we came to a consensus, a start. We could fully agree on supporting and sustaining Prince Henry. There was no doubting his Animus Gift. His right to the throne was based on our existing laws. Laws that we, I aspired, would dismantle and tweak and change for the rest of our lives.

Now, I adjusted my collar. Looking in the mirror, I could see myself fully dressed in the peacetime Senior Royal Crest Knight uniform. A black blazer hugged my arms and matched my black tie. My white collared shirt tucked into my dark dress pants, and I remembered how Mr. Harris wore this exact outfit when he first arrived at the Montgomery House three years ago.

My hair trimmed to my chin, Fern pushed a few fly-away strands behind my ear. Her touch gently rolled down the back of my neck, and I smiled at her through the reflection. She wore the same peacetime Senior RCK uniform, and the outfit suited her long limbs better.

She plaited her red hair carefully, still learning how to do so with two of her fingers missing. Severed by Isaac Winters, who regained himself after Cassius died. He apologized once and steered clear of us as much as he could ever since. I helped her tie the ends, the braid resting close to her hips and filled with white peonies. Her freckles stood out more; one day we would lay down and count them.

"Let's add some color," she mused, smiling as she caught me staring. I looked away quickly, my cheeks flushed.

Fern began rummaging through her bag while Skylar finished an intricate knot for Leo's tie. She pulled at his blazer to admire her work fully.

"How does that feel?" she asked.

"I thought you'd take your chance to choke me," he

grinned.

She gave him a disapproving face. "Ha, ha," she said dryly, roping their arms together. "Look at how handsome you look."

"I trust you."

"That's so sweet." She playfully rolled her eyes, "I still want you to look."

They stepped in front of me and leered at their reflections. They both wore the peacetime RCK uniform, which was identical to the senior one except for the cream collared shirt under their blazers instead of pure white. Leo pulled Skylar into a half-hug and kissed her cheek. "We look ready to steer an empire."

Skylar looked at him, startled. "So, you've decided?"

"Oh, I have a *lot* of ideas."

"Oh no."

"*Oh yes.*"

While I was in the hospital, everyone spared time to bring me up to speed. Skylar confronted her father and put him in prison for treason, where he still resided as a lot of Gifteds were now on trial for treason. The Stanton House was effectively in her hands, and she asked Leo to run it with her. Business partners as much as romantic ones. She had a lot of old money, and he had a lot of new ideas on how to use it.

"Write it down, and I'll add it to the spreadsheet," she said as he spouted random ideas like creating schools, buying homes then selling them for one mila, and simply more crime.

Kai sat on the bench along the wall, adjusting the bronze cufflinks that denoted him as an Emergency Response Service doctor. An anchor gleamed on his left cuff and an infinity symbol on his right; one denoted his Mare Gift and the other denoted his oath to protecting life.

We spent the most time together, since our hospital beds were crammed right next to each other for lack of space. It wasn't all that different from the dorm rooms, so we didn't mind. I swallowed hard, remembering how he looked when they first wheeled him in. If Isaac struck a few centimeters deeper, an empty seat would replace him at the ceremony. His spot would be filled with blue and white flowers and his namesake—but not him.

He wore a navy-blue suit denoting his chosen path with a cream collared shirt and no tie. A robe of ocean blue and vibrant fish overlaid his outfit like a cape. For special occasions, as he and everyone else explained to me. His hair appeared inky black, styled with gel and combed back to make him appear sharper than usual.

"I like your first two ideas," Kai chimed in. "I'll give you one mila right now for my mom to have her own house." He held out an imaginary coin.

"We could be neighbors," Leo smiled, devious.

"What about the one we went to—where we first met your mom?" Skylar asked, surprisingly gentle. I had to get used to her gentler voice. She still had her wit and general aura of superiority, but she completely transformed too since the last time we crossed paths. Now she showed her concern more openly, and I had to remind myself that there wasn't a hint of malice in her question.

"Oh, that one's rented." Kai spoke quickly, dismissive, but Skylar sat down next to him and they discussed in whispered voices.

Ever since I gained my memories back, they flooded me constantly. So thinking over Kai's comment, I remembered how his mission since day one was to work hard at Galdor

Academy so his mom never had to work again. But Kai was also a strategist. Becoming an ERS would secure his mission without Skylar's help. It was still nice though to see her actively try and help others with what she had.

"I'll be happy to see what you choose." Persephone addressed her brother.

She and Molly were sitting on the couch to our left. They were already ready, wearing what they wanted rather than a uniform. Persephone wore a flowy yellow dress draped over her form and supported by spaghetti straps. Her hair waved down her back with the top layer pushed up into a bun, and bronzer highlighted her dark features.

Molly wore a maroon velvet gown that hugged her frame and rested at her crossed ankles. It was a bold choice, and not just because the dress greatly contrasted against her pale white skin. She wanted to tell the world that she was a proud Unfortunate, now and forever. Copper curls framed her face and rested on her shoulders as she leaned her head against her wrist.

"Have you thought about what you're going to do?" Leo asked his sister in return.

Resting back in her chair, Persephone crossed her arms. "Not really," she admitted, "I'm still looking at my options."

Molly's eyes lit up, "Well, if you ever decide to join the Unity Core, you are welcome."

I titled my gaze to Molly. The Unity Alliance disbanded once the Lady Lilacs realized they wouldn't receive the official two-year clemency we supposedly promised them and returned to their homestead. They left with little bitterness. They had no reason to fear another wipeout from the next Iridion ruler.

The Unity Core quickly filled its absence, a collective of

Gifteds and Unfortunates who went town to town and provided services while showcasing how the two groups could work together. Molly joined them as a downcast Unfortunate and was leaving for Cherryville soon to work there and be close to her sister.

"You could always reform Norburn," I noted. "It'll be a lot of effort, but they could use a Mati who stops fires."

She mulled the thought over. "The Lady Lilacs already approached me. I might take their offer."

Fern found what she was looking for and returned to my side with a cheer. "Here!"

She offered me a headband, one she definitely made herself. Green stems intertwined in the shape of a crescent moon, and a cluster of red poppies and a few leaves sprouted at the top.

Adding the accessory, I looked at myself in the floor-length mirror. The red flowers arched over the shape of my head almost like a crown and contrasted well with my dark hair. Alongside my suit, the poppies restored a child-like quality in my face. A quality I didn't know I missed until this moment.

Then, I remembered a long time ago when I told Maya to dawn me in red so I looked like the Anti-Gifteds soldier Minister Gabriel expected me to be. Both were dead now, and I shouldn't have remembered.

"Won't this send the wrong message?" I hesitated.

"What?" Fern shouted in alarm. "No, no, look." She turned around and interlocked our arms. "*We* are the unity flower."

White peonies interwove in her hair and red poppies adorned mine. Connected at our sides.

She was right.

I wrapped my arms around her waist and rose to my tiptoes. She leaned down, and our lips met. We kissed for several heartbeats, faltering as Leo teased us, and slowly retracted, still staring at each other.

"Is that okay?" she asked.

I nodded and pulled her down again by her tie for another kiss.

The door burst open, and all of our attention deviated. Poppy used her foot, bringing it back to the rest of her body before marching in.

"Your pins came in!" she declared, thumbing through the bundle in her palm.

We crowded her.

She handed the Senior RCK pin to me and Fern. The Iridion flag's symbol was half purple and half gold—the same pin Mr. Harris wore when we first met too. Everyone else earned Royal Crest Knight pins (fully gold in color) as an honorable title, even if they weren't going to be active members. After everything we endured, we earned our graduation.

Poppy already wore a Senior RCK pin on the lapel of her peacetime uniform. Her hair was down and relaxed. She elbowed me and played with the poppies in my hair, "Look at *you*. Love the color."

"We're a unity flower," I said, wrapping around Fern for emphasis.

"Adorable. But this—" she gestured between me and Fern—"won't deter me. You and me—" she gestured between us—"are debating for life in the Senior Circle."

A low chuckle resonated in my throat. "I look forward to it."

She turned to the group, "Are you ready?"

We nodded, but Skylar shouted, "Wait!"

She grabbed blue earrings, a mark of her House colors, and placed them in her ears as we walked down the hall.

***

The Determination Arena was demolished. In its place, some Avlis created a circular plaza with tiles individually filled with the name of a person lost in the conflict. Gifteds and Unfortunates. Unity Alliance and Anti-Gifted. Royalty, servants, guards, and students. Civilians and their families. The judged.

Chairs formed in a circular pattern, their legs meticulously placed on section lines so as to not rest on the names. Most of the seats were already filled. Hundreds of Anti-Gifted affiliated, Unity Alliance affiliated, and previously appointed Iridion officials took their places together, all looking forward.

At the center of the circle was a platform with an altar, empty at that moment.

I kept my hand intertwined with Fern's as we walked through, passing all the trailing eyes and flashing cameras. My head cast downward, I looked at all the engraved names in search of those I knew and lost.

Later, I would come back after the ceremony was finished and the memorial cleared of decoration. I would slowly walk in a circle from the outside in, pulling toward the center until I read each and every name.

I would find *Bree*, *Ellie*, and *Holly* side by side together in the seventh row without a House name given because they died free and hadn't yet chosen their own last names. I would find *Sylvia Douglas* soon after, the first Anti-Gifted soldier I met and who had claimed her own last name. I would find *Ebony Nique* and *Minister Gabriel Parvus* muddled in the thick of other names. And I would pause when I found *Cassius Iridion* beside *Maya Iridion* and the rest of the royal family killed at the Determination, their titles in smaller, almost indiscernible script below.

I met these people. I loathed and loved and defended these people. I would sit down—looking down at the royal family didn't feel right—and I would trace the lines of each letter in the stone and ask the Divine for whatever he could offer. Forgiveness or mercy or peace.

Right now, Poppy led us right to the front row and gestured to seats reserved for us. We took our places together, looking forward with the rest of the congregation.

Time passed quickly as more figures arrived. A crowd formed around the plaza's edge: thousands of standing civilians flocked to Galdor for the ceremony. We didn't implement security because it would appear like a threat. I prayed everyone was here for the same goal.

Two people passed us and stood side by side on the center platform. One was Poppy and the other was an elderly woman holding the Great Book.

"That's one of the Gifteds we rescued," Fern whispered. "She's a Lux."

"Is she anything like Minister Gabriel?" I couldn't help but make the connection.

"She was," replied Fern, "but she often comes to meet with me and my mom to discuss it."

I could trust that response, knowing Ms. Fairaway's peculiar kindness to Unfortunates.

Finally, there was a brief silence and then Poppy's voice rang through hidden speakers. "Please stand for the arrival of our new king."

The plaza rumbled as we rose and turned around. Soft triumphant music thumped in our hearts as Mr. Harris stepped out of a carriage and walked down the aisle, slanted at an angle so Prince Henry, two and a half years old now, could walk hand in hand with him.

Mr. Harris wore an all-white military jacket with gold buttons and trimming. Ms. Fairaway fashioned a prosthetic hand out of metal that hid behind white gloves. A deep purple sash and a second dark grey sash securely wrapped over his left shoulder and crossed over his right side in a flash of color. A large pink rose blossomed over his left breast pocket. Purple for his Animus Gift. Dark grey for his Unfortunate status. Pink for the joining of red and white: a unity flower in its own right.

Prince Henry wore an all-white outfit and fiddled with his purple sash denoting him as an Animus.

The two reached the center; the world followed, and the triumphant music faded out.

Poppy spoke again, "We are gathered here today to witness the crowning of our country's first Unfortunate king who will act as regent until Prince Henry Iridion, Third Born of the Third Auran Reign, is of sound body and mind to assume leadership. Please be seated."

We sat.

The Lux woman adjusted the Great Book in her hands so Mr. Harris could lay his left hand down on its cover and lift his right palm to his side. With her free hand, she began to anoint Mr. Harris with oil, starting at his temple.

Poppy continued, "Do you swear to lead Iridion with all your heart, with all your strength, and with all your faith?"

His voice resounded for all to hear. "I do."

"Do you swear to protect your citizens, both Gifteds and Unfortunates, with all your heart, with all your strength, and with all your faith?"

"I do."

"Will you honor the title bestowed to you this day, and will you guide Prince Henry as he learns more about his Gift, his people, and his duties?"

"I do."

Poppy smiled, "Then it is my great honor to announce you, King Peter Iridion, First Unfortunate Reign, to your people."

The two women stepped back, and the world thundered with applause.

Right now, we are unified, I thought as the collective sound roared through my ears. *Right now, we're moving forward and we're doing so together.*

Tomorrow, we may fray like ribbon or scatter like stars, but we are capable of returning to the knot, to the sky, to each other. We are capable.

Epilogue
NORA

———

I watched the purple and gold wax dry on the parchment paper, the Iridion Crest embossed in its royal colors. The regional ministers grumbled to themselves, three disputing with the other two. The Senior Circle had since dwindled down to seven active advisors, and two were enough alongside my and Poppy's vote for the repeal to pass into law.

The wax set.

Poppy exhaled, a croak in her voice from fresh tears as they spilled down her face. I latched onto her hand, joy flourishing inside me with an astonished smile. We turned toward the king, still sitting at the head of the table with a pleased expression on his face.

"Congratulations." King Peter stood, lifting the document in his steady hand. "I will make the announcement this evening. Enjoy the Flower Festival, Nora."

Poppy exhaled again, and I lifted my free hand to cover my mouth. I couldn't stop smiling. *This evening,* I thought. The lead up to change always took so long. This evening was faster than I could ever expect.

We practically skipped out of the Senior Circle meeting room where Fern was waiting for me. Two duffel bags laid at her feet, and a cheerful smile brightened her face when she saw mine.

"Did you—?"

"It passed." I couldn't spill the words fast enough, a childlike giggle overcoming my relative composure.

Fern squealed and wrapped her arms around my frame. Poppy let go of my hand so Fern could lift me off the ground in a deep hug. Delight soared with my rapidly beating heart. My feet found marble again as she put me down, but we stayed encased in each other.

"How does it feel to abolish the Unfortunate Laws of Servitude?" she asked.

My voice elevated with my hope. "It feels *fantastic.*"

***

The train to Northbrook was packed with people—more than I expected so soon after the war's end. Unfortunates disguised themselves among Gifteds wearing their Sunday best or Flower Festival costume. The only indication of status was the branded U resting on a person's lap, but I knew something they didn't. In a few short hours, all branding would cease and these Unfortunates would have a fearsome freedom unseen in our lifetime. Their future sisters and daughters would never have to know a single Choosing Ceremony. Their fathers and mothers could register for a last name; anyone, despite their status, could seek employment outside their chosen Houses without retribution. There would be vengeful Gifteds, threatened by the prospect, but the Unity Core would be vigilant and the Iridion military would be held accountable.

Before departing for Northbrook, Fern and I changed into our outfits sent up ahead of time. Our bodies almost overlaid with how dense the train packed, slouched to the left and closest to the window. I leaned against her for comfort, feeling more exposed wearing a short purple dress instead of my usual training gear. A butterfly shaded in the security of an oak tree.

Instead of vinery consuming the train at its arrival, Avlis Gifteds constructed an archway with blossoming buds of bright purples, whites, and yellows. Royal colors. We walked through, the scent of sunflowers, asters, and peonies filling the air.

Stalls formed a central bazaar where vendors offered bouquets, sold gardening tools, and served floral desserts. More booths and entertainers clustered around the scorched earth, still ashen from their queen's poisonous touch. In place of the wait station that downcasted Gifteds, foxgloves grew into tall vibrant pink stalks and created a hedge maze in the left-most corner of the festival.

It was all here, just as it had been last year. Made even more splendid with celebration. The king's coronation, the newfound peace, the upcoming changes—it was all worth an expression of glee.

Music played all around us. Looking up, I noticed Gifteds residing in balcony-shaped ledges within the tree line. Mostly Avlis by the look of their green and brown ensemble. They played string instruments, the sound wafting through the air and enchanting in its slow, swaying melody.

"What would you like to do first?" Fern scanned the festival, easily seeing further than I could in this crowd.

I managed to twirl so I could create space and turn toward her with my palm out. "I'd like to dance with you."

"Dance?" For once she looked unsure as people passed around us, but the music hummed through my body.

"I believe it's how we show our joy."

She beamed, taking my hand and leading me through the mass. We came to the tree line where a few families ate their fill on tree trunks or picnic blankets. One group of musicians resided right above us, their tune louder but still delicate.

Our hands connected; I swayed us to the left. On our return to center, I extended my right foot behind my left and then back into a sway.

Fern tried to mimic me, kicking her leg back in a reflection that had me burst out laughing.

"What are you laughing at?" she coaxed.

"I just love you."

As I extended my leg back again, Fern took the lead and pushed us into a more formal dance I didn't recognize. She twirled me, shifting our positions from side to side.

Her hand at my waist, she bent closer and lifted me off the ground. My arm draped over her shoulder, and my legs scrunched closer to my chest in an effort to be smaller, more compact.

She spun us around and around, the orchestra swelling as though perfectly made for us. I laughed in a way I hadn't in all my life, holding her closer as the world blurred and unfocused. We slowed, both of my arms now wrapped around her neck. The music calmed. Our eyes met; our noses brushed.

"Say it again," she breathed.

"I love you." I kissed her and then remembered all she did for us to be here right now. The promises we kept to each other.

I kissed her again, more urgently. "I love you. I love you. I love you."

She touched my chin, just enough to stop me from saying or doing more so we could see each other fully. Her eyes sparkled in the summer sunlight, like warm rays that warded off the rain.

I would promise to her for all my days.

Acknowledgments

In 2016, I spent countless hours typing away at what would become this trilogy. I still remember pacing between my bedroom and the shared bathroom, talking out loud to my reflection in both mirrors, and trying to figure out who the Diviner was. I remember every iteration—at one point the world was laid out *Game of Thrones* style with each Gift type represented by a House name. The first *first* draft was a portal fantasy, the prologue a kidnapping. The only consistency throughout it all was Nora's name and her status as a servant. It's been a marvel to see her grow, to witness her story unfold, to take each step in tandem. It's amazing to daydream for so long and then one day that dream is not only a reality but a complete one. Bless my God for granting all the passion, time, and energy I could ever need, especially when I did not know Him.

Thank you for pulling me into Joel Seymour's orbit like a comet. At the time of publication, we will still be engaged so let it always be known that I'm excited to marry him. Our love story is truly one for the books. Maybe we'll write it together someday.

Thank you for my grandparents. I'll always cherish

nanny's reaction to holding *Unfortunate* for the first time, accent thick with tears. I'll never stop telling skeptic readers that my grandfather, resident skeptic, enjoyed my work. Thank you for my mom and how she will literally not stop until every person she knows has purchased a signed copy. Thank you for my sister who tolerated me coming into her room at eight in the morning every Saturday to write on the family computer. Thank you for my church community and the women who taught me about unity.

Thank you for my gracious editors, Claerie Kavanaugh and Whitney McGruder. I cannot imagine writing this trilogy without them, and I don't want to imagine. They saw potential in rough drafts and inspired me when I was stuck. Thank you for Catherine Downen and her willingness to layout this book. Thank you for my impeccable cover artist, Milan Krstevski, and my amazing illustrator, Bojana Gigovska. Their patience with me knows no bounds, and I am always gleeful to see my imagination come alive. Thank you for Darian Ray, my dear friend and sticker designer. She, too, is patient with my shenanigans, especially in this latest release.

Thank you for everyone who preordered my third and final book in this series! It's always, always a joy to hear your excitement and reactions. I hope you smiled; I hope you gasped; I hope you had to cover part of the page with your hand so you didn't accidentally spoil yourself.

Joel Seymour	Amanda Mills
Emily Craig	Billy Wilder
Lexi Sterling	Brenda Wilder
Isaac Cook	Lauren Krechel
Joyce Cavignac	Shelley Shealy

Kimberly Cumbie
Katelyn Cumbie
Carrie Irick
Morgan Ferqueron
Michel Way
Hanan Taylor
Mackenzie Blumberg
Whitney McGruder
Megan Scot
Arielle Wilder

Lauren Talley
Katelynn Schmidt
Catie McKee
Maryann Sterling
Rita Rose
Mark Seymour
Deborah Seymour
Johnna Internicola
Anna Connelly
Aimee Robinson

Thank you for Alyson McNamara, Pvris, Hozier, Of Monsters and Men, and The Head and The Heart—all artists whose music pairs well with the scenes I write. Thank you for Jonathan Morali specifically composing Lone Wolf/Blood Brothers from *Life is Strange 2*. I replayed that track for hours at a time when writing felt impossible.

And thank you for Marissa Meyer. I'm irreversibly changed by her storytelling. *Unity* wouldn't be half as exciting if I hadn't catapulted into her fantasy retellings. Go pick up the *Lunar Chronicles*, *Heartless*, and *Gilded* when you're ready to be destroyed again.

Appendix

GIFTS

Animus: Ability to manipulate objects, read minds, and influence human actions. Only granted within the royal bloodline.

Examples: King Cassius Iridion, Prince Henry Iridion

Aura: Ability to manipulate and control air.

Examples: ~~King Daltus Iridion~~, Mr. Stanton, ~~Mrs. Stanton~~, Skylar Stanton, ~~Cal Hilfrey~~, King Cassius Iridion

Avlis (Ah-v-ILL-ss): Ability to manipulate and control nature.

Examples: Fern Fairaway, Ms. Daphne Fairaway, King Cassius Iridion

Fera (F-AIR-a): Ability to call upon a specific animal.

Examples: ~~Mr. Peter Harris~~, Lady Saleema, King Cassius Iridion

Imitation: Ability to gain features, behaviors, and attributes of a specific animal.

Examples: Mr. Malcolm Montgomery, ~~Molly Montgomery~~, ~~Lady Sanchiko~~, King Cassius Iridion

Lux: Ability to see in the dark. Night vision.

Examples: ~~Minister Gabriel~~, Mrs. Martha Montgomery,

Melanie Montgomery, King Cassius Iridion

Makan (M-ah-kin): Ability to transition between the visible and invisible plane.

Examples: King Cassius (Ka-see-uhs) Iridion, Delilah Fairaway

Mare: Ability to manipulate and control water.

Examples: Isaac Winters, Kai Lancer, King Cassius Iridion

Mati (M-ah-t-ee): Ability to manipulate and control fire.

Examples: Leo, Persephone, King Cassius Iridion

Mute: Ability to shape-shift into any seen humanoid.

Examples: Ebony Nique, King Cassius Iridion

Nox: Poisonous to the touch.

Examples: ~~Princess Maya Iridion~~, King Cassius Iridion

Unfortunates: The Giftless.

Examples: Nora, Poppy, Bree, Ellie, Holly, ~~Valerie~~, ~~Sylvia Douglas~~